For Roberta

From Peter & Ling

Diamond Deception

A Novel by
Skinner

ACTIVUS PUBLISHING

Library of Congress Cataloging-in-Publication Data

Skinner, 1951-
    Diamond deception : a novel / by Skinner.
    p. cm.
    ISBN 0-9774386-3-5

    1. Fraud—Fiction. 2. Murder—Fiction. 3. Diamonds
—South Africa—Fiction. 4. South Africa—Fiction.
5. Namibia—Fiction. 6. Suspense fiction.   I. Title.

    PS3619.K558D53 2006   813'.6
                          QBI05-600216

Library of congress control number 2006900055

Book design by Abacus Graphics, Oceanside, California

Edited by:
    1. William Greenleaf
    2. Frances Bond Literary Agents

10 9 8 7 6 5 4 3 2 1
Printed in the United States

To Pluto

PROLOGUE

$\mathscr{H}$ugh Barlow arrived at the Johannesburg Mining Institute just after 9:00 PM. He dismissed his chauffeur for the night and strolled into the entrance of the building. The doorman took his coat and asked if he wanted some refreshments. Hugh ignored him and headed towards the auditorium where his father, Victor, was delivering the 1981 annual report on the financial results of his southern African corporations.

Hugh expected that it would be a full house, with all Victor's senior directors and their spouses in attendance, so he had decided to arrive near the end of the monologue, knowing that his absence would not be noticed. Just as Hugh slipped into the back of the auditorium the audience burst into applause. Hundreds of enthusiastic employees jumped out of their seats and cheered Victor.

Hugh watched impassively as dozens of the guests engulfed Victor to offer congratulations. When Victor became completely obscured by all the commotion, Hugh hurried along the center aisle towards the podium, clapping and cheering along with everyone else. When the crowd around Victor diminished, Hugh made his dutiful appearance and greeted his father.

"Well done, Father," he said, rolling his eyes when his father wasn't looking. "Another inspiring speech."

"Thanks, Hugh," Victor replied. "Not bad for a seventy year old, eh?"

Hugh watched as Victor struggled to pull a large briefcase from behind the podium, noticing the veins on his father's temples bulge as he grasped the briefcase and held it under his arm.

"That looks heavy," Hugh said, as he reached out to take it. "Let me help you. I'll find somewhere safe to put it."

"No problem, I'll keep hold of it," Victor snapped, as he picked up a drink with his other hand.

Hugh shrugged. "I thought I'd meet you at the house earlier today and drive over here with you, but your secretary said you went to a government office in Pretoria."

"Yes, it was urgent so I came straight here from Pretoria."

As Victor raised his glass of whisky to take a drink, Hugh stretched his arm out and knocked Victor's hand, sending the glass flying.

"Sorry, Father, that was clumsy of me," Hugh said in a deliberately concerned tone. "Let me get you another." He turned and shouted to a waiter. "You! Come here and clean this mess up."

Hugh hurried in the direction of the bar brushing aside the greetings of several of Victor's senior people and pushed his way through the crowd.

"Two large scotches and make it snappy," he barked out. "Make sure it's Glenfiddich."

The barman stopped serving champagne to a group of women and poured Hugh's drinks. His hands shook as he placed the drinks on a small tray and handed it to Hugh.

"I'll carry it for you, sir," the barman said.

"Don't bother, just give it to me." Hugh grabbed the tray. As he turned away he heard someone call.

"Unusual for you to carry trays, Hugh."

Hugh recognized the voice but ignored the sarcastic comment of his half-brother Jack.

Hugh didn't return directly to his father. Making sure that no one noticed him walk behind a curtain that separated the main auditorium from a display area, Hugh put the tray on a table, reached into his pocket, took out a small bottle, and tipped half the contents into each glass. He swiftly reappeared from behind the curtain and pushed his way back through the crowd to his father.

Victor was talking to one of his managing directors when Hugh approached. With an upward and sideways flick of his head, Hugh signaled him to get lost.

"Here's your drink, Father."

"You took your time," Victor said.

"The place is busy."

Hugh watched him gulp the scotch down.

"That's better," Victor said. "I think I'll have another."

"Have mine, Father. I had a few earlier."

Victor nodded, took the drink, and walked away without saying anything else to Hugh. Hugh's eyes followed Victor intently as he made a beeline towards his latest girlfriend. She was an ex-model, tall, curvaceous, and in her late twenties, who had hooked up with Victor six months earlier.

Hugh milled around the hall for a while, occasionally stopping to issue orders and threats to members of Victor's staff, before finally sitting down at the end of the bar and ordering another drink. He swirled it around his glass, gulped it back, and stared nervously at his watch, deliberately breathing slowly and deeply to calm himself.

Ten minutes passed and he was about to order another drink when a scream from the center of the hall diverted his attention.

"Call an ambulance! Quick, get a doctor!"

Hugh pretended to be as surprised as everyone else and hurried over to join the crowd that had gathered around the podium.

"Hugh, it's your father," someone in the crowd shouted.

Hugh saw his father lying motionless on the floor with a man kneeling next to him.

"Must be his heart again," Hugh said, as he handed his empty glass to an onlooker. Hugh bent down and loosened Victor's tie. "Father, it's me . . . Hugh. Don't worry the ambulance is on its way."

"It might be too late for that I'm afraid, Mr. Barlow," the man trying to revive Victor said. "I'm a doctor. Looks like a massive heart attack."

Hugh told everyone to stand back as he placed one hand firmly on Victor's briefcase and called for his personal secretary. "Announce that the meeting is over. I'll issue a statement on his status later in the evening."

The paramedics rushed into the hall carrying a stretcher. No one moved nor spoke. They all watched the doctor take an oxygen mask from the paramedics and place it over Victor's face. The silence continued for almost a minute until one of the paramedics spoke. "He's breathing."

They lifted Victor onto a stretcher and hurried to the exit. Hugh grabbed Victor's briefcase and followed. He snapped the lock and rifled through the contents while the paramedics loaded Victor into the ambulance. *It's a copy of the Turnhalle file. Just what I wanted. I knew that's why the old bastard went to the government offices in Pretoria.*

Although Hugh only visited his father a few times during the next three months, he phoned the hospital each week and spoke to the doctor, but the news rarely changed. Victor drifted in and out of a coma until Hugh finally received the news that he had died of a massive stroke. Hugh knew Victor's death would usher in a period of uncertainty for his business empire and outright war between his family members.

Hugh had contacted the family attorney long before Victor's death in an attempt to obtain a preview of his will, but the attorney avoided Hugh's demands on every occasion. He also insisted that the reading of the will should take place the day after Victor's death, but after much argument among the family members it was set for five days after the funeral.

When the day finally came, Hugh's limousine pulled up outside the attorney's office an hour early. He leaped up the two flights of stairs to the attorney's conference room and barged through the double doors.

"Let's get this formality over with," Hugh announced.

He was surprised to find the room full. His brother, Jack, was seated at the far end of a long conference table. Hugh stared at him without blinking and almost immediately noticed an unusually comfortable look on his face—the look of a contestant in a quiz who knows the answer to the next question. Hugh felt a hard mental jolt and his stomach lurched. Something wasn't right but he couldn't rationalize it. He quickly suppressed any overt reaction and scanned the silent room for other familiar faces.

His mind turned to memories of his father—married four times and nothing but trouble to show for it. Hugh knew full well that two of the ex-wives, including his own mother, died in unusual circumstances, but due to Victor's wealth and influence the police did not investigate the deaths too thoroughly.

Hugh spotted the two surviving avaricious ex-wives who had seated themselves along the back wall of the room. Hugh pictured them like vultures waiting for their prey; their prey being his inheritance. Several aunts, uncles, and distant relations were scattered around the room, not speaking, just waiting for their spoils. Hugh knew every one of them hated both him and Victor.

Hugh's attention switched from the greedy faces of the relatives to a stunning young woman as she entered the room. He recognized her as Victor's last girlfriend. Her long blonde hair and perfectly matched clothes stood out from the other drably dressed women seated around the table. She beamed like a Cheshire cat as she slipped into a seat and crossed her legs. Everyone in the room stared at her and Hugh smiled when he noticed the outraged expressions of the female relatives. The embarrassing scene ended when the senior attorney walked into the room and nudged one of his assistants to distract him from his lecherous gaze.

"Close the door," the senior attorney said to his assistant. He tapped the large conference table with his pen to get the proceedings underway.

Hugh stared at the lips of the smartly dressed attorney and almost tried to lip-read as he spoke.

"Thank you all for coming. Victor left instructions for me to read his will in your presence. As you know he was a very wealthy man. When he died his total estate was valued at 10,000,000 US dollars. I valued the estate in dollars since many of his holdings are in overseas companies and funds. At today's exchange rate that's equivalent to 7,000,000 South African rand."

The attorney went down the list of recipients, announcing the trivial and insulting amounts for the ex-wives and distant relatives —over 100,000 for Victor's girlfriend. Hugh sniggered as each item was read.

Five minutes passed before the attorney uttered the crucial words. "And to my son, Hugh, I leave 50,000 rand. The balance of my estate I leave to my younger son, Jack."

Hugh froze with disbelief. Seconds later the whole room seemed to explode into anarchy. When Hugh recovered he saw the hateful looks on the faces of the two ex-wives as they hurled abuse at the attorney and Victor's girlfriend. One of them ran to the conference table and spouted a diatribe of meaningless obscenities. She picked up a coffee tray and threw it at Victor's girlfriend. Hugh watched in amazement as the other ex-wife grabbed the attorney's hair and hit him across the back with her handbag. He noticed Jack attempting a quick exit, so he leaped across the table and grabbed Jack around the neck. He wrestled him to the floor and pinned his head against a wall.

Hugh was over six feet tall and strongly built. Jack was physically similar but rarely showed his strength. Hugh remembered however, that when Jack finally lost control nothing could stop him. He tried to gouge Jack's eyes but felt a pair of strong arms pull him up and away from the conflict. Several young clerks had burst into the conference room and separated the combatants. This ended the pandemonium.

PART ONE

The Best Laid Plans

ONE

A year had passed since Victor's death and the inevitable fight for his fortune was coming to a conclusion. Hugh was at home one sunny afternoon in his fashionable estate in Sandton, Johannesburg, awaiting some important news from his attorney while his live-in girlfriend, Susan Smith-Peterson, basked in the sun next to the swimming pool, reading a newspaper. He paced around the grounds, circled the swimming pool, and walked between the conservatory and the patio for the tenth time that afternoon.

Hugh always tried to portray the phlegmatic side of his personality because he hated revealing even a flicker of emotion. Today he found this impossible. He deliberately slowed his walk to a crawl, whistled to feign calmness, and adjusted the position of several perfectly aligned potted plants alongside the stone pathway. As he fussed with the patio furniture, he noticed the worried look on Susan's face and realized she was just pretending to read the newspaper. The servants caught his eye. They mumbled amongst themselves, cleaned the same area of the patio over and over again, and avoided looking directly at Hugh. Their erratic behavior reminded Hugh of wild animals sensing the onset of a tropical storm. Susan finally broke the tension.

"You're very restless, Hugh."

"Think so. Well I'm waiting for my attorney to call."

"I hope it's good news," Susan added. "You haven't had your nose out of that government file for the last six months."

"Watch what you say. It's the only alternative if I don't get the old man's money. I intend to continue living in luxury."

Ten minutes later the telephone rang. Susan answered it, exchanged a few words with the caller, and handed the phone to Hugh. "It's him."

"Barlow speaking. So what happened?"

"The appeal was thrown out of court. The will remains valid. Jack keeps the lot."

"Damn it, you incompetent clown," Hugh screamed. He smashed the phone down on a table and felt his face tighten with the outburst of rage. He turned abruptly towards Susan.

"Useless," he shouted. "Jack keeps everything."

"Surely there's something else you can do?" Susan asked.

"According to my highly paid legal council there is no recourse. The legal method has failed me."

"Try speaking to Jack again," Susan said, "after all he is your brother."

"Half-brother . . . and I wouldn't lower myself. I've got enough money to keep this lifestyle going for about two years. After that I'm in trouble. Or should I say . . . we are in trouble."

Hugh took several deep breaths and called for one of the servants to bring a scotch on ice. He sipped the drink and looked into the distance, his mind focusing on the plan he'd been developing for almost a year. He checked his watch and then hurried into the house. The study door was open, and as always his original oil paintings acted like magnets, momentarily distracting him, but he quickly regained focus. He slid his hand along the polished teak desk and fell back into his leather armchair.

His mind flashed back almost a year to the scene in the attorney's office and the strained atmosphere in the meeting room. Hugh's last memory of the scene was of Jack's triumphant eyes looking straight into his own.

Hugh was jolted back to the present when his glass slipped from his hand and shattered on the floor. He kicked it aside and turned to look at himself in a mirror. The hatred in his eyes said it all. *Forty-two years old, lived in luxury all my life, and now I'm almost broke,* he thought, as he ran his hands through his dark brown hair. He fingered aside some of the gray hairs on his temples and stretched the slight creases in his tanned forehead.

Hugh was still a physically strong, athletic man, and most women he met were initially attracted to him. He was mentally very sharp and cunning, but he could never apply himself to a job or profession for long. After a one-year stint in the army his father found various jobs for him in securities trading, bank finance, and advertising. At one point he put Hugh in charge of the family business during one of his celebrated divorces. Nothing lasted for long.

He opened the safe behind the mirror and pulled a file of handwritten notes that he had prepared from information in the stolen government file. The dog-eared paper opened at section six—"the diamond industry." He flicked through the pages, and as each heading and piece of underlined text passed he formed a mental image of the words being put into action.

Hugh closed his eyes, waited a few seconds, and then shouted. "Susan. I'm going through with it."

Susan popped her head around the study door. "There's a big distance between planning something and turning it into reality."

Hugh ignored her. *It's my only chance of keeping up this lifestyle; and I'll bankrupt that bastard Jack to boot,* he thought.

Hugh grabbed the telephone, dialed the long distance operator, and asked to be connected to the Steinkop Diamond Mining Corporation in the Northern Cape province of South Africa.

"Put me through to the General Manager, Chris Conway, straight away," Hugh said to the Steinkop operator.

Chris Conway's secretary answered. "I'm afraid Mr. Conway is out on the mine at the moment, sir. He's not expected back until later this evening. Shall I ask him to return your call?"

"No, I'll call back." He replaced the receiver and left his study. In the hallway he smelled the rich aroma of meat cooking on the barbecue. He followed the enticing smell along the hall and back into the conservatory where he found Susan, adjusting the food on the grill.

"Get me another drink," he shouted to a nearby servant. "You know," he said to Susan, "I'm almost glad the appeal failed. Now at least the waiting is over and I can get on with things. I know it's dangerous but I don't see an alternative."

Susan took his arm and said, "I don't know, Hugh. People could get hurt. If it goes wrong you'll be ruined. So will I."

"It won't go wrong."

Susan kissed his cheek. "Did you speak with Chris Conway?"

Hugh shook his head. "I'll try later."

"Does he know about the file?"

"No! Absolutely not. Just you and I know. I doubt the government even realizes a copy's missing. I'm lucky I lifted it when Father had the heart attack. You wouldn't believe what's in it."

"It's better I don't know."

"That's right. Don't breathe a word to anyone," Hugh replied, as he threw a rolled-up paper napkin at one of the servants and signaled for him to move the food into the house.

He walked into the dining room holding Susan's hand. When the food was brought into the room Hugh placed a few pieces of meat and some vegetables on his plate and sipped his drink. He unenthusiastically picked at the food and made trivial conversation while his mind focused on the plot that he knew would consume his life for the next few years, the outcome of which would set the course for the rest of his days.

A thousand miles away at the Steinkop mine, Chris Conway finally returned to his office late in the day. He sat at his desk sipping coffee and flicking through the pages of the previous day's production report. Several times he lost concentration and had to re-read some pages. He finally forced himself to put aside the many distractions and frustrations of the day and concentrate on its contents.

His office window was slightly ajar, allowing a pleasant breeze to enter, which further calmed his overloaded mind and body. For several minutes he sat progressively becoming more content and able to absorb the information in the report.

A thunderous roar of voices jolted him to his feet. Chris dropped his coffee mug, threw aside the papers, and rushed to the window. Two groups of black workers were facing each other at the entrance of the processing plant with a handful of men standing at the front of each group. They screamed and charged at each other, almost coming into contact, but falling back at the last moment.

The rest were in a mass behind their leaders, brandishing pieces of metal piping and clubs, jumping up and down and chanting in unison with each jump. Chris grabbed the telephone and called the Security Department.

"Quick, mine fight!" he bellowed down the phone. "Just outside the north entrance of the processing plant. Looks like about twenty Zulus and thirty or forty Xhosa."

"We're already on our way, sir," was the reply.

Chris ran outside the office building and across the parking area towards the entrance of the plant, but he stopped dead in his tracks as the two groups surged forward. The fifty or so bodies merged into a single mass as they clubbed, screamed, and stabbed at each other.

A security officer ran up to Chris and shouted, "Better let them fight it out, Mr. Conway, you'll never stop them."

Chris nodded his agreement with the security officer and they stood, mesmerized as the fighting intensified, unable to affect its outcome. Chris had seen these tribal fights before but had never seen such savagery.

About thirty men were already on the floor, some unconscious, others bleeding and screaming. Although the Zulus were fewer than their opponents they were physically larger and much more savage. Chris watched as the remnants of the Xhosa gang ran off, chased by a half-dozen Zulus. He saw an exhausted fighter, prob-ably a Zulu, stagger over the bodies to reach another badly injured man. Sweat and blood splashed from his body as he gulped air into his lungs, desperately trying to regain his strength. The man on the floor begged for mercy as he struggled to stand. The Zulu lifted an iron bar above his head and positioned it ready to deliver a fatal blow, but his strength gave out, and he staggered backwards and dropped the weapon.

Chris ran over to him as he attempted to pick up the iron bar again. He snatched it, pushed the Zulu onto his back, and hurled it over a fence. To avoid being caught in the melee he ran back across the road as fast as he could. Chris held his protruding stomach as he fought to regain his breath. Although very fit in his younger days he was now overweight and completely out of condition.

Chris spat out dust and wiped at the splashes of blood on his safari suit. He expelled a mouthful of vomit as he gazed around at the bleeding and broken bodies stretched out in front of him and walked away, unable to stomach the carnage any longer.

Several police and mine security vehicles skidded to a halt in front of Chris. The officers rushed over to the aftermath of the fight and separated the remnants of the combatants. They forced the walking wounded into their Land Rovers and the first-aid team began removing the more seriously injured in open-back trucks. Chris stood in disbelief as the corpses of fifteen men were laid out.

"We'll collect the bodies later," one of the policemen said to Chris.

"Have you caught all of 'em?" Chris asked.

The policeman replied, "Maybe one or two still scattered around the mine."

A police sergeant approached Chris. "That was a bad one, Mr. Conway, not the worst I've seen though."

"Yes," Chris replied, "any idea why it started?"

"Trouble in the township over the weekend after a lot of beer drinking and fighting—must have carried over here," the burly Afrikaans sergeant replied indifferently.

"Revenge I suppose," Chris said.

"Mind you," the sergeant eagerly continued, "up in the Transvaal I've seen hundreds go at it. Once I saw three Zulus chase one poor bastard for almost a mile before they caught him. They took turns raping him."

"Please, that's enough," Chris said, as he gulped to avoid vomiting again.

The Sergeant seemed pleased with himself as he continued, oblivious of Chris's revulsion. "They told the Judge it wasn't done for sex. It was a sort of victory ceremony. The judge didn't buy that; he gave them an extra ten years."

Chris interrupted hastily, "Better get this lot cleaned up. I'll close the shift for today."

The sun was setting on a typical, bright winter's day in the Northern Cape Province. The trouble ended almost as abruptly as it had started, and it was now quiet apart from the sound of the wind slowly throwing up dust and sand into the air. Chris entered the rather old, but solid building, and walked along the long drab corridor that led to his office. It had been a disastrous day that began with production problems and complaints from head office and ended with savage tribal fighting.

Chris kicked open his office door, slumped into his old leather chair, put his feet up on the steel desk, and threw his head back. He closed his eyes for a few seconds, rubbed his temples, yawned, and looked up at the wall clock to check the time. A newly delivered pile of documents and papers caught his eye. "Another day like this one and I'll just give up," he said under his breath. He remained still for a few minutes before picking up the production report from the floor. After finding his place he continued to scan through the dozens of pages of detailed information.

As the Mine Manager, his last duty of the day was to read and approve the report and then send the information to head office. He cleared his mind and focused on the first section of the document, but the telephone interrupted him. *Ignore it,* he thought.

However, it was quite late and his secretary had left, so he reluctantly answered the call. He grabbed the receiver and shouted, "Conway."

"Chris, old friend, how are you this fine day?" the voice on the other end of the line slowly and deliberately replied. "Answering your own phone these days?"

Chris felt uneasy when he realized it was Hugh Barlow, and from past experience he knew it wasn't a social call.

"Hugh, good to hear from you," Chris replied, as he raised his eyebrows. "Sorry for the sharp tone. I've had more labor problems —strikes and tribal fights. The government wants us to take a hard line with them, but the owners want their profits. The Steinkop board is an unforgiving bunch of . . . "

"No problem," Hugh responded sharply. "Listen, I'm holding a party on the tenth of June in Johannesburg and I would like you and your charming wife Cherrie to come along. I assume you still have use of the company aircraft?"

"Oh yes," Chris said enthusiastically, "I use it quite a bit. What's the party for?"

"For Susan, my girlfriend. But I've got some ideas I want to run by you."

Chris felt suspicious because Hugh had never asked his opinion before. He said nothing and waited for Hugh to continue.

"It's government related in an unofficial sort of way, so I don't want to say too much on the phone."

"Give me some idea."

"My contacts in the Department of Mines are concerned about the upcoming independence of South West Africa . . . well technically I should say Namibia. They want to make sure the mining industry in South Africa isn't affected in a negative way. Anyway I'll tell you more on the tenth."

"I'm intrigued," Chris said, forgetting his apprehensiveness. His voice increased in pitch. "How do I fit in?"

"We're looking for people we can rely on. People that have the best interests of the mining industry and the country at heart. Of course no pain without gain for those involved—so to speak."

Chris felt himself being pulled in but couldn't resist asking more questions. "Where will it be held?"

"The rowing club. You know the place. I'll send you an invite in the mail." Hugh rang off abruptly.

Chris had known Hugh since their school days but had only kept up a distant relationship. He knew that Hugh thought very little of people who were easily manipulated and that he fell into this category. Although wary of characters like Hugh, Chris couldn't resist keeping in contact with them if it profited his career in some way.

Chris's mind turned to what Hugh had said, and it wasn't long before he conjured up all manner of images of his elevation into high level positions in government and business, which deep down he knew could never be connected with reality. He desperately wanted to get back to civilization and into a cushy head office job but could find no realistic way to bring it about. Chris knew he was only an adequate manager, dumped in an out of the way mine that made a steady profit and could provide no hope of promotion. Cherrie was causing problems. She kept pushing him to resign and move to Cape Town or Johannesburg where she could mix with her affluent, snobbish friends. The problem for Chris was that he had no means of earning enough money to keep Cherrie and the kids in the luxurious lifestyle they demanded. He also knew his career had already peaked and there was nowhere, outside of a few remote mining towns, where he could find work. He stopped depressing himself with these thoughts and turned his mind to the daily report again.

The report contained several sections in a dry, standard format. The first section was of the highest interest as it contained the total carats of gem and industrial diamonds produced that day. Chris checked the figures with the overall mine plan to see if the monthly target had been met. He viewed the summary paragraphs of the other sections that contained statistics on things such as the amount of earth mined and processed, equipment outages, personnel injuries, and total manpower employed. Not very interesting stuff, but for the bean counters at head office it was their daily bread. Chris signed the original and threw it into his out-tray ready for his secretary to telex the information the next morning.

His thoughts returned to the upcoming party and whether he should tell Cherrie straight away or wait until the last moment, because it was certain that she would want to fly to Cape Town before the party and buy an outfit or two for the occasion. Then would come the body waxing, the facials, and the Chanel cosmetics. That would mean two long trips and money he could not, and did not want to spend. The mining town of Steinkop was 400 miles from Cape Town and over 1,000 from Johannesburg, and there was very little opportunity to buy high fashion clothes outside of these cities.

His mind drifted back to his past experiences with Hugh. They had been close friends during their school days but only kept up an intermittent relationship after Hugh went on to business school in Cape Town and Chris went to Witswaterand to study engineering and mining. They kept in contact mainly through school reunions and at events organized by mutual friends.

Chris knew Hugh's obsession with being number-one at everything and in control of events, and how he would go to extraordinary lengths to come out on top. He recalled the time Hugh broke into the headmaster's study, stole the history examination papers, and left behind another pupil's notebook. The pupil in question was expelled and Hugh passed the examination with flying colors. The irony was that Hugh didn't need to cheat because he was already the best history student in the class.

Chris also remembered a number of occasions when he bore the brunt of Hugh's malice, but they were minor compared to most of his antics. Through all of this, deep down, Chris admired someone as duplicitous and dishonest as Hugh. It was part fear and part admiration for someone he would like to have emulated but didn't have the ability or the motivation to do so.

While Hugh had it easy working for his father, Chris worked for some of the larger mining concerns as an engineer, and after twenty years, became an assistant general manager of mining operations. When he transferred to the Steinkop Corporation he was promoted to General Manager of Mining.

Chris rose out of his chair ready to leave for home. The elation caused by Hugh's phone call more than offset the other events of the day.

As he left the building the janitor said softly, "G'night, baas."

Chris nodded and raised his right hand in acknowledgement, still deep in thought.

The Steinkop Township was only twenty minutes drive from the mine, via the back route. He drove slowly along the rough road, glancing at the red sky on the horizon, still thinking of his conversation with Hugh. There was no sign of human activity for ten minutes until he passed the black township on his right.

He was careful to watch for rock throwers by the side of the road, especially as he left the township area, because several nasty incidents had recently occurred. Township youths would aim missiles at fast moving vehicles in the hope of forcing the driver to stop. If a driver didn't put up any resistance the youths would steal as much as possible and abscond into the bush, but heavily armed drivers plus the desperation of the attackers made for a lethal combination.

Chris drove slowly to give the impression of not being afraid and to lessen the impact should a rock hit the windshield. Fortunately he passed through untroubled and soon came to the outskirts of the white neighborhood. It was completely dark by the time he reached home. He parked the Land Rover, picked up his briefcase from the backseat, and let out a sigh of relief as he greeted his teenage son and daughter.

"Cherrie, I've got some good news," he said, as if he'd just had a premonition. "Do you remember Hugh Barlow? You met him at the school reunion a few years ago."

Cherrie put her hands on her hips and said, "The one that insulted me."

"Well, he didn't mean it; everyone had too much to drink. Things got out of hand."

"Don't make excuses. What about him?"

"He's invited us to a party in Johannesburg in June and says he's got something important to discuss with me."

"Really."

"It about South West Africa's independence and what the mining companies are doing up there. All very hush-hush but he thinks there's something in it for me."

Cherrie sniggered. "Yeah, what exactly?" she asked in a disbelieving tone.

"He didn't say, but it could be something big in the Department of Mines in Johannesburg. If I play my cards right it could get us out of here."

"Okay," Cherrie said, "Pray to god it works out. What sort of party is it? Is it Formal? And where in Johannesburg?"

"He's sending the details."

TWO

*H*ugh's party was set to begin at the Swartkop Rowing
Club in fashionable Sandton. It was a private club with about
150 members who jointly owned the club, and membership was
restricted to influential leaders of industry and business. It boasted
a fine restaurant and bar, and senior members like Hugh were
allowed to hold private parties and conferences on the premises.

Hugh used Susan's return as the superficial reason for the party,
but it was really to keep up his standing among the club's membership and to further his manipulation of Chris and others.

Susan had recently returned from America where she put
the finishing touches on her post-graduate degree in psychology.
Susan was socially very adept but a little naïve in her relationship with Hugh. She was in her early thirties, always perfectly
dressed, with styled shoulder-length, blond hair. Hugh was particularly attracted to her large, blue eyes and her ability to conduct
herself with grace and charm in awkward social situations. He first
noticed her when she won a beauty contest sponsored by one of his
father's companies ten years prior, but their intimate relationship
had only been going on for the past three years. Although they
were quite close in many ways, Hugh never revealed much of his

inner feelings and true self. Susan however, shared everything with Hugh.

Hugh's wife had left him four years earlier and taken the children. This was after ten years of "treatment" as she put it, and they had not spoken or seen each other since then. Hugh had never seen eye to eye with his only brother, Jack, which was exacerbated after their father's death and the subsequent skewed distribution of his great wealth. Because of this Hugh was now financially pressed. He had enough money to keep up his expensive lifestyle for a couple of years, but after this he would have to rely on his wits and his connections. Apart from his crafty, ruthless mind he had no way of making an honest living, so he knew he would have to take chances and use information in the secret Turnhalle file to further his cause. Hugh was not only determined to get his hands on a fortune but he also yearned to get even with Jack.

The party started at 8:00 PM, and Hugh and Susan greeted the guests as they arrived. As always, Susan's appearance stunned everyone, especially the magnificent diamond and emerald necklace that Hugh had given her. She wore a long, straight-cut, décolleté, black dress, which had been hand-sewn in Paris. Hugh wore an equally expensive tuxedo, which accentuated his athletic physique. Everyone commented on how well they both looked together.

Hugh's greetings oscillated between pleasantness for those guests whom he needed for some reason and outright rudeness, intimidation and scorn for those whom he controlled. He didn't invite Jack out of any motive other than wanting to keep watch on someone he viewed as a mortal enemy and target of his revenge.

"Jack, pleased you could make it. You remember Susan. She's just back from the States."

Jack didn't respond, but Hugh noticed that Jack couldn't take his eyes away from Susan. Hugh knew Jack had a strong attraction to her and although it was not reciprocated, it was cause for more animosity between the brothers.

"She must be like a lot of women you've never managed to attract —even with all that money," Hugh said, as Jack walked into the hall. Jack went to the bar, ordered a drink, and took up position in the elevated seating area just above and behind the stage.

"I told you he'd sit there," Hugh whispered to Susan. "He likes to observe but hates being observed. He always preferred to watch a group of people interacting far more than actually taking part."

"Callous, unfeeling people are often like that," Susan replied.

The club quickly filled and the guests' initial reservations soon evaporated after a few cocktails.

Hugh was surprised when a rather overweight, gray-haired man made a beeline for him. It was Bill Murdoch, a vice president from the Provincial Bank. Hugh couldn't remember inviting him—he'd sent the invitation to the President of the bank.

"It's the first time I've been here, Hugh," Bill blundered out.

Hugh gave him a disapproving look but decided to be reasonably polite because he had a large overdue loan with the Provincial Bank.

"Did you rent the hall?"

"No, actually it's owned by the members of the club. That way we allow in only the right class of person."

"Who does all the rowing then?" Bill asked.

"I don't think anyone's seen a rowing boat for years let alone actually rowed one. Legally we had to create the club for a specific purpose to bypass the arcane drinking laws."

"Plenty of whores but not many oars, eh!" Bill responded coarsely.

Hugh gave him a disdainful look, adjusted his silk tie, and turned his back. He always became annoyed when someone was crude in front of Susan or made a pass at her. He took this sort of thing as a personal slur, not because of jealousy or the maintenance of social graces, but to keep his ego where he felt it belonged.

Hugh noticed Chris and his wife, Cherrie, standing a few yards away. While Bill jabbered on, he beckoned them over with a flick of his index finger. He turned back, stared at Susan, and waited for her to speak.

Susan sipped her drink and said, "I hear the government will concede independence to the blacks in South West Africa quite soon. We'd better get used to calling the place Namibia."

Chris jumped right into the conversation. "Yes, I suppose we better had. They say five years at the most for independence. Let's hope it doesn't turn into another terrorist haven."

"I doubt it," said Hugh, "the border area is only lightly populated and it's mostly open countryside—not good for insurgents. They'd need a massive army to make an impact. A handful of SWAPO terrorists would only be a nuisance."

"What about all the mineral wealth in the mines?" Bill interjected. "What if the South West, or I should say the Namibian Government, nationalizes the lot?"

"That's a possibility," Hugh replied, "but more likely they'll just raise the taxes on the mines. If they nationalize, the mining corporations might withdraw their engineers and metallurgists. The place would collapse economically. Not a good start for a fledgling nation."

Everyone agreed.

"In any case I think our government has the financial situation under control," Hugh said after a pause, looking pointedly at Chris.

"Susan, how long have you been overseas?" Bill inquired, leering at her.

"Three months."

"What were you studying?"

Hugh noticed that Susan became nervous as Bill openly ogled her, so he winked and smiled at her, making it clear that he was only tolerating Bill's behavior because it suited him. He felt pleased that she was wary of him. *If I wasn't overdrawn at his bank I'd have security throw him out,* Hugh thought.

"Psychology," Susan responded after a pause. "A PhD. I spent the last three months in America finishing an assignment."

"Must be interesting reading someone's mind," Chris said.

"Well it's not that easy."

"What do you make of Jack?" Bill blurted out. "He's an odd one if you don't mind me saying so, Hugh."

"Not at all," Hugh responded, suppressing a smile.

"Inadequacy sums him up, physically and mentally," Susan said. Everyone laughed heartily.

"He's always tried to get the better of Hugh. The only time he did was when he inherited his father's money, and that was actually none of his doing. I guess that's where the insecurity comes from. He lacks confidence in himself."

"He'd be the same broke," snapped Hugh.

"Where is he?" Chris asked.

Bill looked around and said, "I think he's left. He was next to the stage but I don't see him now."

"No, I think he came back," Susan said. "Oh well, no loss one way or the other."

The group dispersed as Hugh's uncle, Ralph, joined Hugh. Ralph was shaky on his feet but had a firm, deep voice and a strong handshake.

Ralph put his arm around Hugh. "Oh, it's you, Hugh. I thought for a moment it was Jack."

Hugh suppressed his annoyance. He knew they looked alike but didn't like to admit it. His hair was a shade darker than Jack's but he deliberately let it grow longer and combed it to the back of his head to differentiate himself as much as possible from Jack.

"How have you been since Victor died, son? You're looking well, nice suntan and everything."

"Well, Ralph, it's been difficult, especially with the trouble with the will. It's forced an even wider gap between the family members. Especially Jack and me."

"Your father was an old bastard and he probably went to his grave knowing the trouble he'd caused. I shouldn't say that about my brother, but it was the same with him all his life. I hope you and Jack don't turn out like him. Life's too short."

"I don't think I will," Hugh replied in a convincing tone.

Hugh ended the conversation and watched as Ralph hobbled over to speak with Jack whom he now saw had moved to another vantage point. *I wonder what they're talking about,* Hugh thought.

Casually he circled around to their rear and listened to their conversation as best he could. Hugh noticed Jack looked a little disheveled.

"Hey, Jack, don't you talk to your old uncle anymore?" Ralph said to Jack.

Hugh made sure he was out of sight, behind a column at the edge of the dance floor, but well within hearing distance.

Jack looked down when he replied.

"What have you been doing with yourself?" Ralph said. "Getting rid of all that money I suspect."

"No, I live a very quiet life."

"You should make up with Hugh. It's a bad thing when two brothers fall out. Why don't you take the first step?"

Hugh sniggered when he heard this.

Jack shrugged and said, "Maybe."

"You should get yourself a good woman. You're not getting any younger."

"If I find a decent one."

"What about that young thing over there," Ralph said, pointing to a young woman enjoying herself dancing. "If I were younger . . . well."

Hugh saw it was Susan's friend, Elaine Franklin.

"She's probably a slut," Jack mumbled.

Hugh realized that Ralph had difficulty understanding Jack, plus he was struggling to keep the conversation going.

"Oh well, I'd better mingle. Bear in mind what I said."

Hugh darted away to avoid either of them noticing him.

Jack scurried off towards the toilets, giving a few furtive looks to some women on the dance floor before he darted inside. He slammed the lavatory door, pressed his back against it, and looked at the ceiling. *Thank god I'm away from all those people.* Sweat ran down his brow as he clenched his fists.

He began to relax after a few minutes and pulled some photographs from his inside pocket; and one by one he examined them, running his fingers around the edge of each before proceeding to the next. The last photo was of his mother just after she married Victor. He turned the photo over and stared at the plain white surface until he saw an image of his mother appear. She was lying on her back, naked and still. Jack threw the photos down, closed his eyes, and banged his head on the lavatory door several times.

"You okay in there?" A voice rang out.

Jack instantly flipped back into reality and the image of his mother evaporated.

"Just fell against the door," Jack responded.

"What have you been eating?"

Jack opened the lavatory door, lowered his head, apologized to the men waiting outside, and walked over to the basin. He washed his face and hands in cold water and hurried back to the party.

The party was now in full swing. The musicians played without a break and the caterers charged around filling empty glasses and offering platters of food.

Hugh finished greeting the guests and took the opportunity to pull Chris aside. They went to the large sliding doors leading to the garden and stood just outside. The biting mid-winter night air in Johannesburg, exacerbated by the high altitude, caused Chris to shudder and cross his arms over his chest.

Hugh noticed Chris's discomfort, and he suspected it was not only due to the environment but also to the upcoming conversation. Hugh stared into Chris's eyes, without blinking, to make him feel even more uncomfortable.

"Chris, my sources inside the government expect South West to become independent in about five years—at most. They've seen Rhodesia give up white rule. The Portuguese territories in Angola and Mozambique are gone, and now the pressure is on South West Africa. They don't mind giving up the territory because it buys the Afrikaners in South Africa some more time. What they really object to is losing control of their investments in the mines. Many of them see this as an opportunity to get rich personally, not just to perpetuate the white government in South Africa. There are a lot of schemes in the pipeline which I can't tell you about, but one of the most important ones involves you and the mine you manage."

"Go on," Chris said, moving closer to Hugh.

"Let me give it to you hypothetically first of all. Let's say your diamond production at Steinkop is at 100,000 carats per month. What would happen if that figure rose by 20,000 without increasing running costs? The profits would increase in proportion. The share price would fly up and everyone involved would make out handsomely—especially if you owned a great deal of the shares and senior management's bonuses were linked to profitability."

"Yes, but the obvious question is where will the extra 20,000 come from?"

Hugh sipped his drink and replied, "There's no need for you to know at the moment. However, all your counterparts in the South West African mines are South African and very pro-government. Get the picture? Let's just say that we are robbing Peter to pay Paul, but Peter and Paul will soon be separated. Different countries, different governments and legal systems, and perhaps they'll even become enemies or uncooperative neighbors."

Hugh realized by Chris's face that he did not follow the logic completely but could see that he was intrigued. He continued the conversation emphasizing the personal benefits that would be available to everyone involved in the scheme.

"Apart from money," Chris asked, "what will I, or should I say this hypothetical manager, get from the government? You mentioned it over the phone."

"Johannes Krieger is the Director of Mines. He's retiring in a couple of years and he reports directly to a cabinet minister. Who do you think he'll nominate assuming he's involved in the scheme?"

Chris's face lit up. He had the satisfied look of someone in possession of classified information.

"I see," Chris said, nodding, "just what I was thinking."

Hugh smiled and finished the conversation by inviting himself to Steinkop the following week with the promise of more details of the scheme.

They returned to the party, which was now getting a little wild. Chris's wife, Cherrie, had consumed a few too many cocktails and was attempting her version of the "Dance of the Seven Veils", much to the amusement of the onlookers. Cherrie was somewhat eccentric and extremely pretentious, but when drunk she was an outright embarrassment.

Hugh, in a moment of unusual compassion ordered the musicians to play some fast dance music and encouraged everyone to dance. This gave Chris a chance to extricate his wife and save some of his own pride. He bundled her into his rental car with Hugh's help and made off for their hotel.

Hugh stayed outside and got some more fresh air while he thought about his next move. He walked around the partially lit grounds of the club for fifteen minutes before returning to the party.

Harold Budd, the Barlow family's long-standing financial advisor, was talking to Susan. Hugh jostled his way over, pulled Harold aside, and winked at Susan to indicate he wanted to be alone with Harold.

Harold puffed on a cigar and adjusted the jacket of his loud suit. "I haven't seen much of you or your money recently, Hugh. I hope you're not avoiding me."

"Not at all," Hugh replied laughing. "I haven't been very active on the investment front recently, but don't worry, I'm not using anyone else."

"Glad to count it! I mean hear it, Hugh."

"I'll contact you soon with some . . . very confidential investments."

"You've got my number."

Hugh and his father had involved Harold in several shady financial deals over the years and Hugh knew he would need Harold's services for his latest scheme. The term "very confidential" was used as a euphemism for their various illegal financial dealings.

Hugh saw Gavin Brown at the bar, so he walked Harold back over to Susan and left them to resume their conversation.

Gavin was in Johannesburg on business for a week. Once Hugh had discovered this he made sure that Gavin attended the party. Gavin was a senior metallurgist at a mine in Namibia owned by the Allied Diamond Corporation of Johannesburg. He held a senior position and was responsible for running two large processing plants. Hugh could not contact him by phone at his home number because Gavin had already started his business trip, so he sent a telex to him via his office at Allied, and fortunately his secretary replied, providing Gavin's contact number in Johannesburg. Hugh went to great lengths to reach him to make sure he would attend the party.

"Gavin, You've lost a lot of weight since I last saw you." Hugh gulped when he saw the deterioration in Gavin. His face looked drawn and yellow, and his suit appeared two sizes too big. Gavin was as tall as Hugh, over six feet, but now he stooped so much that Hugh looked down at him.

"I've been under pressure. There's a lot going on at Allied."

"We were just talking about the political situation up there."

Gavin looked into the distance and said. "Not just that. On the production front we've radically changed our approach."

"How so?" Hugh asked, knowing that Gavin loved to discuss technical details.

"Instead of aiming for a fixed target of carats each month and holding up production when we reach it, we've started to extract as much as possible and let head office store the excess for future years."

Gavin continued talking and became increasingly excited as he went into excruciating detail about the new approach; so much so that Hugh had to move a glass in front of Gavin's face to distract him. *At least his mind's still sharp,* Hugh thought.

"I read about it in one of Allied's internal papers," Hugh said cockily.

"How did you get your hands on that?"

Hugh smiled. "I have contacts at your head office."

The conversation alternated between Gavin plunging into minute technical details and Hugh pulling him back into more general topics. When the conversation dried up Hugh took a large gulp of his drink, looked into Gavin's face, and said, "How's Harry Van Rensberg these days?"

Hugh watched with delight as Gavin went white and almost choked on his drink.

Gavin recovered. "Harry Van who?"

Hugh smiled and paused but continued to look directly at Gavin. "I'll drop by next week."

"Well . . . okay . . . if you want," Gavin stammered. "But you'll need an invitation to get in. It's a high security area."

"You'll manage." He started to walk away, but suddenly stopped and turned back. "I'll telex my arrival date. Say hello to Harry for me."

Hugh's government file had identified Gavin a possible blackmail victim due to his involvement in some low-level pilfering at Allied, and Gavin's wife and a miner called Harry Van Rensberg were also involved.

Nice little lever I have on old Gavin, Hugh thought, as he looked around for Susan. *Father was right—if possible, only deal with people if you have something on them.*

Hugh joined Susan and stood silently by her side while she chatted to Jenny Adams and Elaine Franklin, two of her best friends from her school days. They hadn't seen each other since Susan left for America so there was much to catch up on.

"Okay, who's the man in your life these days, Elaine?" Susan asked.

Elaine replied, "John Bradford, you remember him, the sports fanatic. He's at the party tonight; he's hooked up with some rugby fans over at the bar. He used to work for your father, Hugh. He left just before I joined your father's Aegis outfit in Pretoria."

"That's correct," Hugh replied. "He's a complete bore."

The conversation continued until Hugh saw John Bradford stagger over to Susan and place his hand on her rump. Hugh pulled him aside and whispered in his ear. "Make yourself scarce you drunken oaf otherwise I'll make sure you never work in a decent company anywhere in South Africa."

John disappeared quickly.

"I'm glad Hugh got rid of him," Jenny said to Susan, making sure everyone could hear.

Elaine changed the subject. "Hugh, why did your father close down Aegis so abruptly? It was a great job."

"No idea, Elaine. I didn't even know you worked for him. What was the company called?"

"Aegis Investigations. There's another girl here tonight who used to work there too. She's the catering manager for the party tonight —got divorced after she left Aegis."

Hugh shrugged and left the group after Jenny told everyone that she intended to move to Cape Town in a few months time to take up a new job.

Hugh noticed Roger Hamilton in the crowd, near the buffet. A rather sinister looking character flanked Roger, dressed in black and wearing dark sunglasses.

Roger owned and ran a personal security and protection business, called Action Services, which catered to corporations and executives. He employed a large number of ex-military types to protect traveling executives and perform certain private investigations. He also had a semi-secret unit that assisted the government in unofficial activities relating to terrorism, both in South Africa and abroad. Hugh had heard about this side of Roger's operation from his father, who had used Action Services on several occasions.

Roger was a short, solid looking man in his early sixties, with naturally dark hair and a round friendly face. Although he was a millionaire and could retire at any time, he was a workaholic who loved the covert side of his profession.

Hugh's father once told him that he thought Roger continued to work in order to make sure his past dealings were never uncovered, especially those concerning the government.

"Roger, how's business these days?"

Roger shook Hugh's hand heavily and replied, "Business is booming in this political climate, but I can't get enough good people."

"Who's the big fellow behind you?" Hugh asked, scowling at the sinister-looking man.

"Don't worry, he's friendly. My bodyguard actually. Peter Fourie. Can't be too careful in my trade."

"Exactly. There's probably a whole army of people trying to get their own back on you. I hope you're behaving yourself, Roger? I know what a so and so you can be. Remember that job you did for my father five years ago? Absolutely brilliant."

"Mums the word on that one, Hugh," replied Roger. "I'm surprised you know about it."

Hugh could see the look of concern and surprise on Roger's face and decided to follow through on the veiled threat. "Yes, Father told me a lot about his business associates before he died—all neatly filed away."

Roger quickly changed the subject. "If you ever need my services you know where to come. Your family has been good to me, especially Victor. Sorry to hear about his death. It must have been a shock."

"Yes, but we've all got to go some day," Hugh replied in a deliberately serious manner.

"One more thing, Hugh. Did Victor go to Pretoria the day he fell ill?"

"No idea."

"We were supposed to meet lunchtime but he didn't show."

"Was it important?"

Roger nodded. "Government stuff."

"He never said anything."

The guests finished their drinks and said their farewells to Hugh and Susan. By 1:30 AM the rowing club was empty, save for the janitorial staff, and Hugh and Susan were on their way home.

"Is Chris on board?"

"Most certainly—hook, line and sinker," Hugh replied smugly.

Hugh had confided in Susan the salient details of his plan but told her not get too close, just cooperate, keep silent, and they would be made for life.

"Do you have everyone you need lined up?" asked Susan.

"Not yet. I'll approach the right resources when I need them, then I'll tell them their part in the plan. They'll only know what they need to know. As long as they see an advantage in it, I don't really have any problems."

"Nothing like the team approach," Susan said, with a twist of irony.

"Quite," Hugh said, smiling. "My philosophy on these things is simple. There could be any number of events happening at one time, each one independent from the others and meaningless to each other. It's only when they all meet at one point in time and for one reason that it all makes sense. If you control where and when this happens you have a tremendous advantage. In any case enough theory. Let's get some sleep.

"Oh, by the way, I'm going to Steinkop next week to see Chris Conway. Then I'll contact an old acquaintance of mine who works for the Allied Mines in Namibia."

"How will you get there?"

"I'll fly to Steinkop and then drive up to Allied mine just across the Orange River in Namibia. It's a massive open-cast mine."

Susan pouted a little. "You can't arrange things over the phone then?"

"Too risky, especially at Allied. They monitor the phones. In any case, I need to apply a little pressure to my acquaintance there. That's always done better in person."

"Security is pretty tight there, eh?"

"You can pick the diamonds off the sand in some places."

"Isn't Steinkop the same?"

"Well Steinkop is a diamond-pipe mine. They mine down in the ground in a circle about a half-mile in diameter. So the area to protect is much smaller. Allied is an open-cast mine. The diamond bearing rock and sand covers hundreds of miles. I'll explain it all to you some time, but I'm exhausted. Let's get some sleep."

THREE

$\mathcal{H}$ugh and Susan were enjoying a late breakfast in the conservatory when Johnny, their Zulu butler-come-jack-of-all-trades, interrupted them. "Boss, there's two police people want you. A boss and a madam."

"Two what?" asked Susan.

"Police people, madam."

Hugh looked up. "Johnny, are they wearing police uniforms?"

"No, boss."

Hugh went into the dining room and glanced out of the window that overlooked the main entrance to the house and saw a rough-looking man about fifty years old in a gray suit, and a plain-looking woman in her late twenties, dressed quite smartly.

"Johnny, bring them into the reception."

Hugh finished his breakfast before introducing himself.

"I'm Captain Muller of the South African Police, Chief Detective in the homicide unit, and this is my assistant, Detective Karen Van Der Berg."

Hugh declined to shake hands and just stared at the captain. "Homicide! How can I help?"

Captain Muller continued. "We're investigating the murder of Catherine De Jong. Her body was found dumped in the woods about a mile from here. She was reported missing four days ago, on the eleventh, and her remains were found yesterday."

"So," Hugh said indifferently, as he watched a frown of irritation form on Captain Muller's face.

Karen interjected. She spoke rapidly. "She was last seen on the night of the tenth at the Swartkop Rowing club. She was the catering manager. Did you know her?"

"No," Hugh replied stiffly. "I don't get involved in that sort of thing."

Susan walked into the room and introduced herself.

"Were you at the club that night, Miss Smith-Peterson?" Karen asked.

"Yes, all night. Hugh arranged the party for me. I think I remember her—a very tall woman—about five feet eleven. She did all the catering and floral arrangements. Very efficient and pleasant."

"Well I'm afraid she is rather efficiently but unpleasantly dead now," Captain Muller said abruptly. "She's the fourth girl to be killed in this manner over the past year."

"How unfortunate," Hugh said. "Probably blacks."

"No, can't blame them for this one," snapped Karen. "It's a serial killer we're looking for—blacks don't fit the profile."

Captain Muller cut in. He pulled a sheet of paper from his pocket and showed it to Hugh. "Is this guest list complete? We want to speak to everyone at the party to make sure that we know her every movement."

Hugh casually flicked through the list as he listened to Karen and Susan exchange a few niceties.

"You don't think it was someone at the party do you, Captain Muller?" Susan asked.

"Well, we know she left at 10 PM. Her car was still parked at the back of the club and she didn't make it home. She was murdered somewhere and then dumped about a mile from here. No blood found outside the club or in her car, and no sign of a struggle. Forensic hasn't finished yet but they think she's been dead for three days. That would indicate she disappeared on the tenth and was murdered the next day. The body was moved sometime after that and dumped in the woods."

Karen interrupted. "It's possible someone abducted her when she left the club. The partygoers might have seen something."

"How do you know it's a serial killer, Detective?" Susan asked Karen.

"Certain damage to her body. It's the same in all the other cases."

Hugh finished checking the guest list. He added a few names of people invited at the last minute and passed the paper back to Captain Muller.

"I think that's it, Captain," he said.

"What about servants?" Karen Asked.

"Ask the club's administrative and financial manager, Rupert Davies, he'll be able to give you that information," Hugh replied dryly, as if such information was far beneath him.

After they left Hugh began to get concerned. He didn't like the idea of the police getting anywhere near his plans or business. He turned to Susan. "I hope this nonsense doesn't get in my way. Some stupid girl gets herself murdered and the police are all over the place looking for clues. I don't like it."

Hugh felt a tug on his arm as Susan pulled him back away from the door. "I'm sure they won't pry too much."

"You never know what they'll uncover. That captain has a sixth sense about him and the woman seems too smart by half."

Captain Muller and Karen walked along the pathway leading from the house to the street.

"What do you think?" Muller said, as he reviewed the updated guest list.

"He's a bit of an arrogant bastard."

"But no serial killer," Muller said. "Split the list up and start our team on the detailed questioning of the guests and the servants. Tell them to tread easy with Barlow's guests. Most of them are high-fliers. They don't need to use truncheons and army boots —they're not dealing with riffraff."

"Okay, Cap," Karen replied, using Captain Muller's universal nickname.

Back at police headquarters Cap and Karen assembled the team and began the briefing. Karen gave a summary of the known facts in the De Jong murder with the aid of a flip chart and then allocated tasks to each team member. As usual, she rattled off the facts at lightning speed.

"Her sister reported her missing on the evening of the eleventh, but no other action was taken. The sister, Joann, called every friend and relation she knew to see if Catherine could be located but no one had seen her. She even contacted Catherine's ex-husband, a fellow called Cushing, to see if he knew anything; but again nothing. Apparently it was a pretty nasty divorce.

"Her body was found on the thirteenth at 1:00 PM by some blacks walking through the woods at Kleinpark gardens."

Karen sipped from a glass of water and continued. "The forensic report is just in. The MO is the same as the other four murders. She was slowly strangled, hands and feet missing, sexually assaulted with sexual organs mutilated. The body was dumped some time after the actual murder."

She turned to George Nortier, the oldest officer in the team and most experienced assistant detective in the station. "George, get that black officer Phillipus and interview all the servants at the club, the blacks working in Catherine's apartment block, and the ones that found the body."

Cap sat back and watched while Karen organized the investigation. When the team dispersed he sternly told Karen not to miss any detail in the inquiry in a way that was as good as a pat on the back from a proud mentor.

Cap (Stefanus) Muller was fifty-two and had been in the police for most of his career save for the two years he spent serving in the British South African Police in Rhodesia. Cap was fit for his age, still slim around the waist and wide-shouldered. He looked a little older than fifty-two and his weathered face did not match with his short, thick, dark hair. He was happily married with two children in their early twenties.

Cap was a strategic thinker, deliberately not quick to jump to conclusions. This had earned him the dubious honor of being assigned to the most difficult cases that were mostly political and capital offenses relating to whites. This necessitated dealing with the feared and brutal Bureau of State Security (BOSS) when political issues arose. He would always try to temper their heavy-handed tactics by showing them that more could be gained through slyness and methodical data collection than by the fist or the size-twelve boot. He wasn't always successful; especially when BOSS decided their candidate was a leftist sympathizer or a black-lover. Their view of human nature was essentially bifocal. Whites were either true patriots who loved rugby and cricket, or they were leftist black-lovers; whereas blacks they saw either as "Uncle Toms" or terrorists.

Cap passed a part-time degree in sociology and criminology with honors when he was forty, and he was often invited back to the university to lecture on specialized subjects due to his enormous practical experience and the scientific way he could synthesize ambiguous information.

The serial murder case had so far stumped him and even his patient, logical mind had failed to draw any firm conclusions. However, he knew just one small mistake by the killer would be enough to open up the whole case.

Karen was Cap's star pupil and his confidence in her had grown ever since he had noticed her energetic and discerning mind after she was transferred to his section two years earlier. For a woman to be promoted to this position in the SAP was unusual. Karen was a tall, plain-looking woman in her late twenties with short, jet-black hair. Although she was unmarried, she was popular and had a lively personality, especially outside work. Cap often worried about her because she would work herself almost to collapse when she led a case.

A week after the party in Johannesburg, Hugh began his trip to Steinkop and Allied mines. Chris Conway had arranged for Hugh to fly on one of Steinkop's cargo planes. A last minute change in itinerary meant the plane had to land in the town of Springbok to pick up supplies before going on to the private airfield at Steinkop. Hugh decided it would suit his purpose to take the first leg to Springbok and then rent a car for the rest of the journey.

Hugh boarded a rather well used and overloaded DC2 plane early on the seventeenth of June, at Jan Smuts airport. He sat just behind the pilot, facing the back of the plane in a comfortable if not glamorous seat, preparing for the four-hour flight. All he could see were crates, boxes of equipment and supplies, and what windows existed were boarded up.

Captain Schmidt, the pilot, told Hugh he had been flying in the area for years and could navigate without a compass if the need arose. His confident charisma did not alleviate Hugh's feeling of apprehension. The cabin wasn't pressurized so Schmidt did not fly more than 11,000 feet above sea level for the whole flight. The altitude at Jan Smuts airport was 5,000 feet, so for the first few hours of the flight they would only be about 6,000 feet above the ground.

Hugh braced himself as the engines revved and the whole plane and its contents shook violently. He clutched a metal strut next to his seat as the plane struggled to reach its takeoff speed. When it finally got into the air the vibrations eased a little. At 200 feet it dipped into an air pocket and plunged down to ground level in just a few seconds.

Hugh's stomach wrenched as the plane went back up again almost as quickly. He closed his eyes and he clasped the metal strut even harder. His arms ached, and the pain in his ears intensified, partly due to the noise of the engines and partly due to the fluctuating air pressure. Hugh was soaked with sweat and on the verge of vomiting as the plane was bounced around in the turbulent air.

"This is damned uncomfortable, Schmidt. Who trained you to be a pilot? Can't you fly in a straight line?"

Schmidt didn't reply.

The turbulence subsided after an hour when they flew over a barren part of the Northern Cape, just below the border of Namibia. Hugh recovered his composure and asked Schmidt if he had ever landed a plane in this type of landscape, especially as it seemed to be fairly flat in many places.

"I've landed in an emergency a couple of times, but never taken off again. When I flew in Namibia for the mines there, a few idiots tried to land, even in one-seater planes. They didn't last long. Most of them had romantic notions of stealing a stash of diamonds and going home with them on the quick. Forget it. You need a proper airstrip. Even if it's just dust and gravel it needs to be maintained. The sand blows across the strip and forms small piles that'll tip a plane easily. You can't even see them from close up."

"Any radar up this way?" Hugh inquired in a deliberately casual manner.

"Yes, but it's very crude. Mind you there are so few planes about even a simple system can spot them. It's mainly used by the South African Air force."

Hugh probed some more. "Can it pick up small, low-flying craft?"

"Anyone that flies that low out here is mad. The sand and dust can ruin an engine pretty quickly and it's difficult to notice hills in this landscape. You'll see when we land. I'll keep it at 11,000 feet until the last minute and then I'll spiral down as tightly as possible to avoid the low level stuff and any SWAPO shoulder launched missiles. Unlikely this far down south but you never know."

"How will that avoid missiles?" a surprised Hugh asked.

"They're Russian jobs. They don't go above 10,000 feet, and to hit a spiraling plane they have to be near the center of the spiral, within a few miles in fact. The South African defense force guards the perimeter of all the airfields to minimize the threat."

True to his word, Schmidt, near the end of the journey, put the plane into a sharp, spiraling dive. Hugh tried to release the pressure in his ears but nothing worked. He almost threw up as his stomach reacted to the sharp drop in altitude.

Schmidt and his co-pilot were unperturbed by the battering, even with the sounds of the groaning engines and the creaking and shaking of the plane. After what seemed endless spiraling, the plane leveled off, and bounced onto the runway to come to an unceremonious halt. Hugh was reeling from the experience. He clambered out of the plane onto the runway and without thanking Schmidt, made his way to the small airport control building and then smartly into the prefabricated toilet where he emptied the contents of his stomach.

After Hugh recovered in the toilet he could hear quite clearly a conversation between Schmidt and another person outside.

Schmidt and the co-pilot were laughing as the other person spoke. "What did you land like a Stuka for? You know you don't have to do that this far south."

Schmidt replied, "Just practising."

The co-pilot added, "We like to give all these spoiled, stuck up bastards a joy ride now and again. Anyway, he said we were lousy pilots."

Hugh was fuming at first and decided to phone a high-level contact at Steinkop to get the pilots fired, but since he had pumped them for some very useful information, he just let it go.

Hugh hitched a ride from the airport into the sleepy town of Springbok and went to the Springbok Hotel, where he had arranged to pick up a rental car. He was soon on his way north, towards the Allied mining town of Steinkop and his meeting with Chris Conway.

The road was all but empty of traffic, just a few delivery trucks coming back and forth from the many mining concerns in the area. The landscape was monotonous, with large, open areas of parched land broken only by barren granite hills and small mountains that had been polished smooth over millions of years.

He left the paved road after fifty miles and turned west on a rough, dirt road leading to the mine. Apart from some small Bantu encampments situated a few hundred yards from the roadside, there was no sign of human existence. A far cry from the Johannesburg metropolis that Hugh had just left.

Chris Conway had given him directions to his home once he reached the township, to avoid a meeting at the mine. Hugh soon found the house and because he did not want to meet with Cherrie alone, he waited across the street until he saw Chris's Land Rover enter the driveway. He drove over and stopped next to Chris, just as Chris jumped out of his vehicle.

"Chris, thanks for arranging things."

"Come in and have a drink. You look beat."

"Yes, it was a tiresome journey."

"Cherrie won't be back until after eight. She's gone to some school play or something, so let's get down to business."

Hugh was relieved. *The last thing I want is that pretentious, loud-mouthed bitch asking stupid questions,* he thought. He suppressed the desire to make a nasty comment. "What a shame."

Hugh paused for a while to collect his thoughts before speaking. "There are two main issues to be discussed. If I provide a large cache of diamonds, between 200,000 and 300,000 carats, how could you introduce them into the production stream? And how can you fiddle the returns to make it look kosher?"

They exchanged ideas for over two hours, probing and criticizing each other's arguments, before agreeing on a realistic plan. Chris would introduce the diamonds into the final extraction process over a period of six to eight months. Any quicker would raise too many alarm bells. Since the assay of the area had proven to be very accurate Chris was concerned that the head office would notice something was amiss and launch an investigation.

"We'll be producing more carats with the same amount of earth mined." Chris said. "It'll set off alarm bells."

Hugh stretched out on the sofa and thought for a few minutes before replying. "Okay, I'll put out a rumor that some of the old assay reports underestimated the yield when the mining is done at a certain depth below the ground – pretty much where you're mining at the moment. I'll get a reference placed in one of the mining journals and feed a few people on the Johannesburg stock exchange with the information. When your management team hears the good news they won't be too suspicious."

"I'll request new assay reports and doctor the results a bit," Chris added eagerly, "and make it look a little rosier."

"Now you're thinking."

Although Chris had edged around the question of his financial rewards, Hugh had remained deliberately vague, trying to determine the minimum amount Chris would accept.

Chris poured two drinks, toasted to their success and said, "I know you mentioned the position with the Department of Mines, but I have a couple of questions."

"Fire away."

"The government folks are definitely behind this aren't they?"

"One-hundred percent, Chris. Take my word for it."

"What about the . . . er . . . financial side? I'm running short you know."

Hugh jumped up from the sofa. "Here's what I propose. I'll buy shares in Allied and put 1000 in your name on my offshore company's books. They're at ten rand each at the moment – about fifteen US dollars. When the share price goes up because of the extra dividend returns and future speculation, they'll be worth about 100 rand each. An uncut carat of diamond sells for 105 rand at the moment, so without adding to their costs at all, Allied will make 30,000,000 in pure profit before we're finished. We'll sell our shares gradually to avoid suspicion. Your 1000 shares should net you about 100,000 rand. I'll even send it overseas in a dollar account for you."

Hugh saw Chris's face light up.

"Sounds good to me, Hugh. When do we start?"

"About ten months. Don't do anything silly like get promoted or fired, will you?" Hugh said only half-joking.

"Try not to," Chris sighed.

"Oh, and keep this to yourself, don't even tell Cherrie."

Hugh finished the conversation and in order to avoid Cherrie again he feigned tiredness. "I think I'll turn in now, Chris. It's been a long day. I'm driving to Namibia tomorrow so I need an early start. What time do you leave for work?"

"I get up at six and get breakfast on the way to the mine."

"Ok, I'll join you for breakfast."

Chris and Hugh ate breakfast together the next morning and finalized a few more details before parting company. Chris loaned Hugh a handgun for the journey because he was traveling alone in a remote area and several incidents had recently occurred on the Steinkop road. It was only a .32 Beretta, but it was reasonable insurance.

It was rough going from Steinkop to a small fishing village on the coast called Port Nolloth. Rocks and potholes littered the unpaved road, but fortunately there was little traffic, and although the road snaked through some dangerous passes and wild terrain, Hugh made reasonably good time. He drove due east for fifty miles until he was just outside Port Nolloth.

After checking that no one was around, he drove off the road behind an outcrop of rocks, parked the car, and pulled a military map from his briefcase. The map showed a narrow track leading from the Steinkop/Port Nolloth road, which circled around the fishing village, finally ending up at the coast about ten miles south. There were no signs to identify the beginning of the track, but it appeared to start just after a double "S" bend, five miles from Port Nolloth.

Hugh doubled back and found the track after several attempts. It was reasonably flat, a little sandy, but a regular saloon car could just manage to traverse it. He drove the length of the track, stopping at several of the narrower parts. At each stop he measured the width of the road, taking into account the boulders and rocks that jutted out from the small hills and craggy outcrops through which the road passed. The narrowest part of the road measured twelve feet.

He inspected the coastline where the road terminated and checked the type of sand and stones on the beach. He measured the distance to the sea from the nearest place that could afford cover. Finally he took several photographs of the beach area, both from the nearest point of cover facing the sea, and facing inland from the edge of the sea. When he finished, he turned the car round and drove back to the main road.

After carefully checking that no other vehicles were nearby, he opened the trunk, pulled out the wheel wrench, and walked over to a large limestone rock at the roadside. He chiseled out a circle and a cross on the rock, about four feet in diameter, which could be seen easily from a slow moving car—if the occupants were actively looking for it.

Hugh continued on the next leg of his journey, which took him fifty miles north to the Orange River and the border between South Africa and Namibia.

FOUR

*N*amibia was still South African sovereign territory so there were no customs or immigration details for Hugh to worry about, only the suspicious security guards at Allied. Hugh stopped at the security post on the South African side of the river.

"What business do you have here," the guard asked.

"I've come to visit the Chief Metallurgist, Gavin Brown, on personal business,"

"Show me your identification and Mr. Brown's invitation."

Hugh scratched around and produced the documents. The guard took the letter, went back into his hut, and picked up the phone. Hugh listened to him while he exchanged a few words in Afrikaans over the phone. The guard returned and told Hugh to complete a form, which he snatched back after Hugh scribbled in the information.

"Park your car over there and wait for the company bus to take you into town."

The bus left after five minutes with a half-dozen other people and made its way across the bridge towards the township. Hugh noticed the landscape change dramatically once over the Orange River. There was much more loose sand and many more small dunes on the Namibian side, and not as much desert vegetation.

The residential area of the town began about seven miles beyond the river crossing. The landscape changed again. Hugh saw deep, green lawns, trees and flowerbeds everywhere, with in-ground water systems pumping away to keep them alive. The houses were large and neat, each one with a nicely manicured garden.

The bus dropped Hugh at the recreation club, where Gavin was actually waiting for him in the outdoor bar area. Hugh assumed that the guard had called Gavin and told him of his arrival.

"You got here quickly," Hugh said, holding out his hand to greet him. He noticed a strong smell of alcohol from Gavin's breath and his face was red and bloated.

"Yes, security noticed you after you left Port Nolloth."

"I'm impressed," Hugh replied sarcastically. "When do they start monitoring people then?"

"Port Nolloth onwards, actually. There's no other way into the mine other than by that road unless you've got a tracked vehicle or a helicopter."

Gavin finished drinking a beer and said, "Let's go for a walk."

They went along the main street next to the post office and the shopping center. Hugh deliberately kept silent, knowing that it would make Gavin nervous.

Gavin broke the silence. "Look, Hugh, what exactly did you mean at the party when you mentioned Van Rensberg? I've been worried ever since."

"Gavin, I know what you've been up to. A little birdie told me that you've been pilfering small amounts of rough diamonds and our Mr. Van Rensberg has been polishing them on the sly, inside the township."

Hugh smiled when he saw Gavin's face lose its red glow. "Each time you leave the diamond area your wife puts them in her rather large jewelry collection, which of course has been previously declared and recorded by Mine Security. Then you bring it all back after exchanging the real diamonds with paste copies."

Gavin dropped his head as Hugh continued. "Security are obviously only interested in what goes out of the mine so they don't check June's personal items to make sure they are genuine when she re-enters.

"One thing I can't work out is how Van Rensberg got the diamond cutting and polishing equipment into the mine. It's illegal to have it and I know they check every piece of machinery that comes in. In any case this is small stuff, only about five carats each month, but a good cut stone sells for 1000 rand per carat. That's a big mark up on the hundred or so Allied gets for the rough stuff."

Gavin raised his head and looked at Hugh. "You've got me by the balls, but what the hell do you want, Hugh? You're rich. What's a few thousand to you? And how did you find out about Van Rensberg?"

"Well," Hugh replied smugly, "I'll tell you about old Van Rensberg later, but I've got much bigger fish to fry. Tell me more about the new production goals—the ones we mentioned at my party."

Gavin gradually regained his composure as he became engrossed in technical detail. The current practice was to work to the cartel's target of 180,000 carats each month. If they fell short they would mine areas where the yield was known to be above average. If they reached the goal earlier in the month then they would mark time, do maintenance work and special projects. The entire mine's resources were geared around this approach.

After a high-level seminar at head office, and due to the political situation and some very sound business reasons, it was decided to ignore the artificial targets and put more men and equipment into the operation. They would go for the maximum at all times; hitting the richer deposits first rather than conserving supplies for the long haul.

Any excess diamonds would be stored at head office and released on the market if and when needed. The mine planners were discussing estimates of 250,000 carats each month.

Hugh felt extremely smug as he nodded and said, "That's where we come in. Where there's change there's always confusion. I want you to divert some of the new production."

"How can I do that?" Gavin spluttered, obviously frightened by the thought. "How will I get the stuff out of the mine? How much are you talking about? How can we dispose of it?"

A phlegmatic Hugh responded, "Break the problem down. Your

only goal is to divert 20,000 carats each month and hide them somewhere on the mine. Leave the rest to me."

"20,000, that's impossible, Hugh," Gavin shouted.

"Keep quiet," Hugh snapped. "You said yourself production could go up 70,000 carats each month, and no one really knows how high or what impact it will have on costs and resources. What I'm saying is think big—Allied is and so should you."

"I don't know, Hugh. This is big stuff. I just can't do it."

"Look, Gavin, I'll be blunt. Come up with a plan for this or I'll make sure everyone knows about your 'Van Rensberg' caper. You'll be ruined and I'll make sure you spend the next twenty years in prison."

Gavin put his head in his hands.

"Let's go fishing tomorrow," Hugh suggested. "Take the day off work. We'll come up with something, don't worry."

Gavin arranged for Hugh to stay in one of the company's guesthouses during his visit to avoid any contact between Hugh and his wife and children. He knew trouble was brewing after Hugh's unwanted invitation and he wanted to keep Hugh under control as much as possible. Gavin walked with Hugh to the guesthouse and reluctantly agreed to meet him the next morning. He bade him a frosty goodnight and walked back to the clubhouse for a drink, where he proceeded to get paralytic drunk.

The next morning Gavin awoke in the front passenger seat of his car, feeling pretty bad and not remembering much about the previous night. He looked around and realized he was in his garage. *June must have brought me home,* he thought. After a few minutes the gravity of the situation Hugh had created hit him like a brick. He put his head in his hands and began speaking to himself. "Maybe it was a bad dream." But as his senses returned the illusion wore off. "I'll kill him and that'll be an end to it. No. He's probably told someone else. I can't be sure. Maybe I'll get rid of Van Rensberg and Barlow, the pair of them. That should do it."

As he pulled himself together the idea of actually carrying out Hugh's plan seemed to be the course of least resistance and even quite appealing in some aspects.

"I'm in it too deep to get out now."

A voice from behind him bellowed, "Yes, Gavin, far too deep." It was Hugh.

A stunned Gavin turned sharply but pretended nothing was said.

"Hugh, you're up early. I had forgotten all about our conversation. I had a little too much to drink last night."

"Yes, a little too much. I went to the bar at about ten, just as the barmen were carrying you to your car.

"I was upset."

"You'll have to cut that out for the next year or so, otherwise this little scheme is going nowhere, and you know where you'll be headed. Clean yourself up and let's get out of here."

"Have you seen June around?" Gavin asked.

"She left over an hour ago."

They drove to a remote point where the Orange River met the sea and made themselves comfortable on the riverbank. They set up their fishing equipment and sat on two foldout seats, with a wind breaker screen behind them to stave off the wind. Gavin explained to Hugh that regardless of the season, the prevailing wind was from the west and the sea and the tide in that part of the world, called the Benguela current, was extremely powerful. It flowed up from the Antarctic, which made the sea temperature unusually cold for that latitude. Although the weather was hot and dry in the summer, the coastline up to twenty miles inland was cooled dramatically by the prevailing winds. Sea fogs and mists that stretched inland for miles were quite common.

Hugh realized that Gavin was still suffering from a hangover, so he pulled out a flask of coffee and some sandwiches from a rucksack. Gavin reluctantly sipped the coffee and took a few small bites at a sandwich.

Hugh cast his fishing line in the river. "How many people live in the township, Gavin?"

Gavin was slow to answer. "About 3,000 whites in the town including their dependents . . . and just over 5,000 black miners live in hostels outside town . . . and up north in the mining area. The blacks are mainly from the Ovambo tribe from the border between Namibia and Angola. Quite a few belong to SWAPO, the terrorist group, and some to that MPLA crowd. They're communist fighters in Angola. The border is porous, so they go back and forth whenever."

"Ever get any trouble from them?" quizzed Hugh.

"Hardly ever," responded Gavin. "There's a company of the South West African Territorial Army billeted quite close by.

"Oh, what are they there for?"

Gavin threw his line out into the water. "They're called 'Koevoet'. Roughly translated from Afrikaans it means 'Iron Bar', and that's a good indication of their activities."

"What about security patrols on the mine? How many security men are there?"

"About 200. Some patrol the outskirts of the mine and others are posted around the processing plants. Oh, and a few work undercover as normal mineworkers to pick up gossip. They have helicopters and a couple of light aircraft, but the land is bare and waterless, so it would need a pretty determined bunch to get in and out unseen. There's the Orange River to the south, over 300 miles of semi-desert to the north, and the Kalahari Desert to the east. And don't forget a very inhospitable coastline to the west with a wicked current."

"Interesting," Hugh said. "Let's go back to our little problem we spoke about last night. You're already taking a small amount of the stuff at the moment, right? What's stopping you from adding to it?"

"Well, Van Rensberg works on the final diamond sorting team. He puts aside a small amount each week; that's all. No one notices because it's so small and he takes just a few from each sorter. That way, when the statistics are calculated, no one sorter stands out from the rest. I pick them up each week, take them into town, and give them back to Van Rensberg, who cuts and polishes them in a shed at the back of his house. There's much less chance of me getting searched you see. Anyway, he fits them into June's jewelry settings and . . . you know the rest. Van Rensberg and I split the profits."

Hugh thought for a moment and said, "Okay, two things stick out. One is the statistics and the other is a question. How many sorters are there?"

"Six, but there's room for twelve. Two shifts a day. There's a long funnel-like tube that contains diamonds and other small debris that can't be distinguished from the real thing. The tube comes in from the last automatic processing step into the sorting rooms. The sorters pick out by eye the real diamonds and put them into special containers."

Hugh probed some more, "Good. Now when your production increases you'll no doubt employ more sorters. Right?"

"Yes, definitely."

"Who controls that?"

Gavin perked up a little. "I do."

"You said the sorters are monitored by checking their figures each day, but does anyone apart from you know that on any one day eleven sorters are on duty instead of ten?"

Gavin shook his head and slowly replied. "No, I don't think so."

"When the production increase occurs no one will really know how many sorters will be needed, will they?" Hugh asked, getting unusually excited.

"Correct."

"Okay, promote that stooge you have thieving for you now. Give him a new title say . . . 'Sorter Scheduler' or something. His job is to organize who sorts where and when in the new scheme, and to perform quality control . . . or some other bullshit role. What he really does is to work as an unrecorded sorter. All of his output is unrecorded and put aside for us. The others are checked statistically as normal, so nothing will be noticed."

"That sounds okay, but how can my man walk out with his stuff each day and avoid giving the security guard his diamonds. And don't forget the paper work for the weight and number of diamonds collected."

Hugh asked another question, "Is it normally the same security guard on each shift?"

"Normally yes, but they change shifts twice a month."

Hugh began to fire questions at Gavin. "But you know in advance who will be working each shift?"

"Yes, correct."

Hugh stood up and faced Gavin. "Do you know them personally?"

"Some of them."

"Any of them susceptible to corruption or blackmail?"

Gavin looked down. "I don't know. The ones I know are married with young kids I think."

"Okay," Hugh said, "give me the name of the first one to leave the mine for any reason. Get me as much detail as possible – wife's name, how many kids, where the relations live, and any other personal information. Also when and where they plan to go. Leave the rest to me."

"What will you do?" asked a puzzled Gavin.

"Leave it to me," Hugh said confidently. "If the candidate does cooperate, which I am sure he definitely will, how would you manipulate things to get the diamonds out of the plant?"

Gavin replied quickly this time, "That would be a pushover. I mean if there's collaboration, it's fairly easy."

"Get a name to me and I'll let you know when to approach that person."

"There's a young fellow, Ivan Richards, he's due to leave for vacation next week. I'll get all the details for you."

"Good, Chris, now in the meantime assume you have collaboration and work out a detailed plan. Go over it time and time again until it's foolproof. Once you stash all the diamonds we need, I'll worry about getting them out of the mine."

"By the way, Hugh, what can I expect from this, apart from the threats going away?"

"I'll give you 50,000 cash when it's all done. You can pay off the others however you please." Hugh flicked his hand in a dismissive manner. "Oh, and by the way, can you get me a detailed plan of the whole mine?"

"I've got a couple in the office. They're confidential so I'll drop one in the mail. They x-ray all the mail looking for diamonds but rarely open it. You don't want to get caught with a map while you go through the security checkpoint. They might hand search you."

They finished their discussion and after couple of hours of actually trying to fish they packed up the equipment and left. Neither of them said much during the drive back. Gavin lost concentration several times before they reached the town, and after he swerved violently to avoid a collision, Hugh made him stop and he drove the rest of the way.

When they reached the guesthouse Hugh jumped out of the car and simply said, "I'll be in touch."

The next morning Hugh took the bus to the security checkpoint at the Orange River crossing. He was surprised to find that the bus stopped at an office on the edge of town and he was told to wait. After a few minutes a security officer guided him through a room containing an x-ray machine. He was quickly processed and given clearance to proceed through to another waiting area at the back of the building, where he boarded another bus that took him to the original checkpoint. He retrieved his identification documents and drove south towards Port Nolloth.

There was a heavy mist during the first hour of the journey, but as Hugh turned east towards Steinkop the mist cleared and he increased his speed. He couldn't help but glance back at the sign scratched on the rocks just outside of Port Nolloth.

Twenty minutes later Hugh noticed a Volkswagen about 300 yards up ahead pointing towards the side of the road with a mob of animated figures around it. He stopped the car about 100 yards away from the Volkswagen.

The mob hadn't noticed him as far as he could tell. They smashed the windows of the Volkswagen with clubs and began throwing rocks at the occupants. Hugh panicked at first and thought about turning the car round and leaving, but he stopped himself. There was only one road leading from the mine to Springbok, so he would have to come past this point later, and it would be dark by then. Plus he would miss the next scheduled flight from Springbok to Johannesburg.

He reached over to the back seat and grabbed Chris's Beretta. After clumsily loading the eight-shot magazine into the butt of the gun, he jerked the barrel back ready to fire the first bullet, but the Beretta slipped from his hand and landed under his seat. He recoiled, half-expecting the gun to discharge, but nothing happened. *Oh Christ, pull yourself together,* he thought. He fumbled around for the gun, and when he found it he checked that the safety catch wasn't on and wound the window down.

The mob pulled a screaming victim from the Volkswagen and held him on the ground. Seconds later one of the attackers turned and pointed towards Hugh. Another turned round and stared, but the others were too busy ripping out the contents of the car to notice Hugh. They pulled someone else out of the car. It seemed to be a woman but Hugh couldn't be sure.

Hugh reversed the car off the road ready to make a U-turn. He fired one shot into the air hoping it would frighten them off, and then put the car into first gear and revved, ready to accelerate away in case the mob came towards him. As he was about to flee a police Land Rover roared past heading towards the Volkswagen. The mob dispersed as the Land Rover came to a halt and four policemen jumped out. They opened fire with shotguns and hit at least four of the attackers. Two of them crumpled to the ground and the other two were clearly wounded. The policemen spread out and continued to fire on the attackers, who were now mostly out of Hugh's sight.

Hugh thought it safer to get nearer the police vehicles so he began to drive his car towards them. Out of nowhere a man, with blood pouring from his neck and face, raced towards him from the side of the road. He screamed at Hugh, who froze, petrified with fear and shock. The man punched the side window out and screamed again. Hugh closed his eyes and squeezed the trigger twice at point blank range. When he opened them he saw the man spin around ninety degrees and collapse on the ground.

Hugh was amazed at the power of the pistol. It was only a .32.

He stared at the lifeless body for a minute, his own body still numb with shock, until a police officer ran up to his car. Hugh recovered his composure quickly.

The officer looked at the body and said, "Well, my friend, you took care of this one all right."

Hugh inspected the body. His legs were a little shaky so he leaned on the side of the car to conceal his weakness from the officer. Two large holes had been punched out of the dead man's back. He looked at the spare ammunition clip and noticed the bullets were flat nosed and had probably exploded on contact with the victim. *Maybe I've underestimated Chris,* he thought.

The policeman asked him to stay near the victims with one of the other officers while he went to his Land Rover and used a radio to contact his station. Hugh heard him ask for helicopter support to trace the other attackers.

The officer pushed and kicked the three wounded attackers into the back of the Land Rover, ordering them to stay still otherwise he would shoot them. He then pulled three dead bodies off the road by their feet and dumped them on the roadside.

The male victim was coming to his senses, cut and bruised, but not critically hurt. The young woman was badly shaken, having narrowly avoided being raped. She was sobbing hysterically as the officer asked her which one had tried to rape her.

She pointed to one of the wounded attackers and just managed to splutter out, "Him."

The officer pointed the gun at his face and without hesitation discharged his nine-millimeter Luger. He unemotionally commented, "They're a bunch of Cape Coloreds up here on contract work. They got paid this morning and went on a drinking binge. It's the second car they've attacked. We'll round up the rest and charge them with assault, rape and murder."

"Murder," Hugh said.

"Yes, they killed the poor bugger in the other car this morning."

An ambulance arrived later with another police vehicle and the two victims were treated on the spot and then taken in the ambulance towards Springbok. Hugh asked the officer if they needed his name and address or if they needed him to fill out a police report. The officer took Hugh's business card and said he would be contacted if needed.

Hugh continued his journey to Springbok where he boarded a scheduled flight to Johannesburg. As the plane was taxiing on the runway he went over the events of the past few days. *Just one mistake back there on the road and everything would have been for nothing. It's the last time I'm going to take any chances. I'd hate to go to my grave knowing that Jack could live out his life in luxury with my inheritance. I'll make a fortune out of this caper and get even with that bastard—and get my inheritance back. Oh well, things are underway now. There's no going back. The two main players are suitably duped. That clown, Chris, thinks it's all government sponsored and he actually thinks he is getting money and promotion out of it. Gavin is suitably blackmailed. I'll have to watch his drinking. That'll ruin everything if he goes on the bottle. I don't know about Susan. I'm not sure how far she's willing to go. I'll keep her in the dark as much as possible—just in case. I wonder if the old man told anyone else about the Turnhalle file. I doubt it, knowing that sly old dog. It was an original manuscript, not a copy, so maybe someone in the government will miss it. No one has asked any questions. So far so good. I need to get back to Johannesburg right away and contact Roger Hamilton for the next piece of the puzzle. At the party he seemed very interested in Father's movements the day he collapsed—strange. I know he does work for the government . . . no, I'm just being paranoid.*

The plane took off and Hugh fell into a deep sleep, happy that things were going his way and keen to get on with the next stage of his plan.

FIVE

$\mathcal{I}$n Johannesburg, Cap Muller finished reviewing the results of the investigation of Catherine De Jong's murder and called Karen into his office to summarize his thoughts.

He was sure the murderer was a male who chose white woman in their late twenties. The victims were probably unknown to him. They were abducted in fashionable areas, normally late in the evening, assaulted and murdered in one place, and then dumped in random locations.

Forensic reports indicated that a soil type found on all of the victims came from a hard brick that was frequently used in house foundations in the Johannesburg area. Cap surmised that the murderer had some sort of den where he committed the murders. The police psychiatrist told Cap that the murderer probably lived alone and kept the body parts of his victims as trophies.

A bloodied imprint of a fist with a large ring on the forefinger was found on the remnants of Catherine De Jong's white blouse. Although the pattern left by the ring imprint was too vague to determine what it was or what it represented, Cap was convinced that it was a key clue in the case.

"That's all we have," Cap said.

"So you're saying we have to catch him in the act next time because we are really clueless."

Cap rolled his eyes and raised his hands in surrender. "That's a subtle way of putting it! Well, it's not quite that bad. Let's concentrate on this ring mark. It's a long shot but maybe it'll lead somewhere."

"How so?"

Cap responded thoughtfully. "Go to all the jewelry manufacturers in the area and ask them who makes this type of ring. Check the stores that sell the stuff and get names or descriptions of people buying them. Who makes the special designs? Are there groups or sects that have special designs?"

"That'll take months, Cap."

"What else can we do?"

"What about planting policewomen to trap him?"

"I thought about the 'plant' idea before, but I'm not sure. We'd have to provide a large team of support officers every time they go out."

"Let's try it for a while."

"Okay, try it on Friday and Saturday night for a month. Begin in six weeks time because I don't think he'll strike immediately after the De Jong murder. Go through the department's personnel files and find some suitable policewomen."

Back at Allied, Gavin had reduced his drinking considerably. The shock of his precarious situation had brought about a sobering reality. Although abstinent for most of the time, there was an air of nervousness about him, and whenever anyone mentioned it he just shrugged and blamed his workload. June told him that she was pleasantly surprised at the change, but Gavin knew she was not so naïve to believe that there was nothing else behind it. She constantly asked him about Hugh Barlow and his recent trip to Allied, but Gavin deliberately remained a closed door.

During slack times at work he reviewed the various scenarios involved in Hugh's plan and took his advice about repeating and practising his movements and responses to unusual situations.

Gavin received a registered mail slip and decided to collect the item from the post office before going to work. He opened the thick brown envelope, flicked through its contents, and then shoved the package into his briefcase. He shook his head and thought, *that poor bastard. How can I do it to him?*

He drove to work, completely forgetting to stop and eat breakfast on the way. When he reached the office he answered several urgent messages, cleared his in-tray, and examined the security officer's shift assignments for the diamond sorting rooms. He called to his secretary. "Ask Ivan Richards to come in. Make sure we're not interrupted."

Ivan bounced happily into Gavin's office. "What's up chief?" he asked enthusiastically.

"Shut the door and have a seat," Gavin said quietly, avoiding Ivan's eyes. "Ivan, this is not something I want to do. But I'm in a bad position."

Ivan stood up. "What? You're not firing me are you?"

"I wish it were that easy. Sit down."

Gavin threw the brown envelope over to Ivan. "Take a look at those photos." He sat back in his chair and covered his eyes with his hands. Moments later he looked up and saw the puzzled look on Ivan's face change to shock. It was as if he had been punched. He was speechless.

"What's this?" Ivan stammered out. "Where . . . did you get these? Why?"

Gavin stood at Ivan's side and put his hand on his shoulder. "Some very unpleasant people have us by the throat, Ivan. I'm in the same boat for different reasons. You know that girl in the photos is a Cape colored don't you?"

"No, she can't be. I don't . . . "

"She is. It wasn't just a suntan. Well, not only are they threatening to tell your wife and ruin your marriage, they'll also inform the police and Allied's personnel people."

"Why?" Ivan cut in angrily.

"Keep calm, Ivan, let me explain," Gavin said trying to keep Ivan quiet. "If you're reported to the police you'll be charged under the Immoral Activities Act. It's still illegal to have sex with blacks or coloreds. Apartheid isn't dead yet. That means you'll get the boot from Allied and forget about getting another decent job."

"But why, Gavin? Who's doing this and what the hell do they want?"

"Some very nasty people. Basically the deal is simple. If you don't cooperate you'll be turned in and ruined."

"Cooperate? How?" Ivan choked out.

Gavin saw tears roll down Ivan's cheeks. "We have to remove some of our illustrious mining company's raw materials. Quite a few of them actually. If you cooperate then the photos are turned over to you along with a decent amount of cash."

"How did you get involved, Gavin?"

"I was an idiot. They've got me in the same position as you. There's nothing we can do. Cooperate or get ruined for life."

"What if we tell the police?" Ivan said, after a period of silence. "I'm sure they'll be lenient if we turn these bastards in."

"And what about your family? Sleeping with non-whites . . . I don't think so, Ivan."

"How did I get myself into this?" Ivan said holding his head in his hands. He repeated himself several times before breaking down in tears. When he finally managed to pull himself together, Gavin explained in detail what they had to do, how they would do it, and when it would start. He didn't wait for Ivan to agree. It was a foregone conclusion.

"Take the rest of the day off," Gavin said as he ushered Ivan to the door. "I'll put you down as sick. We'll talk tomorrow."

Gavin waited for his secretary to take her lunch break before calling Hugh. He used the name "John Martins" as a cover, just in case the conversation was monitored.

"Mr. Martins, it's me, Gavin."

"Did the insurance policy suit your needs?"

"Yes it was just what I needed. All systems go."

"Give me a call in a couple of weeks with any questions."

As soon as the call finished Hugh dialed Roger Hamilton's number at Action Services.

"Roger, thanks for arranging the setup with that security officer, Ivan Richards, from Allied. It went perfectly."

"I thought it would. I put my best people on it."

"What's the damage?"

"10,000 I'm afraid. It's not cheap with all those people involved, plus the background work needed and the protection."

"Okay, I know. I'll send a check in tomorrow's mail."

"Thanks. Any other work coming up? Don't drop things on me at such short notice next time. I can't always pull staff from other engagements you know."

"I do have something else but not for another six months. I'll contact you well before it's needed."

Hugh then called Harold Budd's private number.

"Harold, it's Hugh. Can you talk? It's very confidential."

"Just a minute, I'll close the door."

Hugh heard voices diminish in the background and then the noise of a door slamming.

"Listen, I need to buy some shares."

"Okay, what's hot?"

"It's a mining company—100,000 rand's worth should do it."

"What! Are you sure, Hugh? Mining stock is stable but it's not going anywhere. What's the outfit called?"

"I'll tell you the name later. However, you'll see a rocket attached to those shares within a year."

Harold's tone changed immediately. "You know something?"

"Absolutely," Hugh responded confidently.

"How will you pay for them?"

"Twenty in cash and the rest I need to borrow."

"Well these days it's difficult raising money like that and your house is already mortgaged."

"Harold, buy some of those shares yourself. You won't be disappointed. I'll even tell you when to sell."

"I'll have to charge you fifteen percent interest on the eighty and I'll hold the share certificates as security against the loan."

"Okay, but make it ten percent."

"Sorry, Hugh, I can't."

"Okay then, I'll make a deal with you. Buy some of the shares for yourself and if they go up more than 100 percent . . . then I don't owe you any interest. Any lower and I'll give you twenty percent interest."

"Interesting."

"Look, you said yourself mining shares are stable. If anything goes wrong you just sell them and get your money back."

There was a short pause. Hugh could almost hear Harold's brain working overtime. "Okay, Hugh. You seem certain about this. Reminds me of old Vic. What's the name of the company then?"

"You draw up the agreement first and then I'll tell you."

"I'll get right on it."

"Oh, make sure you buy the shares through my offshore company. Don't put them in our names directly. If you see what I mean."

Harold chuckled greedily. "Never crossed my mind to do anything else, Hugh."

Just as Hugh was finishing the call with a few personal niceties, Harold cut in and asked, "By the way, Hugh, who's handling your brother Jack's new found wealth?"

Hugh was annoyed at the request but stopped himself from showing his true feelings when he realized that some advantage could be gained if Harold discovered where Jack had invested his father's inheritance. "Well, Harold, I'm not really sure. Have you contacted him?"

"Yes, but he never returns my calls."

"He lives in Father's house now."

"Yes I heard about that after Vic's will was read. I'll go around there on the weekend."

"Let me know how it goes. You probably know I'm going to sue to get some of the money back, so if you find out where it's invested, let me know."

"Will do, Hugh."

"Anyway whether Jack invests the money with you or I do, doesn't make much difference."

"True."

"Finish the paperwork and I'll sign the contract."

SIX

*G*avin Brown sat outside the General Manager's office waiting for the weekly senior staff meeting to begin. He was reviewing his progress report when his secretary came running along the corridor and told him John Martins was on the line from Johannesburg and the call was urgent. Gavin took the call in the GM's spare office.

"This is the GM's line, Hugh, so it's okay to talk openly," Gavin whispered. "What is it? I'm just going into the weekly meeting."

"Have you kicked things off yet?"

"Not yet."

"Why not? It's been weeks now. I don't understand the delay."

Gavin peeked outside the door to make sure no one was listening before answering. "Hugh, all the reorganizations that we need in place are being discussed at this meeting. If it's accepted we can begin in two weeks."

"I hope so, Gavin. I'm getting impatient. It'll take almost a year to build up enough stock."

"I know, but these reorganizations take time in the corporate world. There are hundreds of people involved."

"Call me after the meeting and let me know what happened."

Gavin went into the conference room. In order to make it easier to misappropriate the diamonds, he had carefully crafted his department's organizational and procedural changes so that they would be in total alignment with Allied's new operating model. He planned to use this particular weekly meeting to get final approval.

Mike McCarthy, the General Manager, opened the meeting by summarizing the plans for the upcoming year. After the Chief Engineer and the Personnel Manager explained their plans to support the increased production of 300,000 carats, McCarthy asked Gavin how the processing plants would cope.

"I've reorganized several of the sections to take the additional tonnage of earth arriving at the plants and recruited another shift of diamond sorters. One new position has been created to manage and optimize the sorting process and another to oversee security in the sorting and auditing sections. That needs to be done because of the increased numbers of workers in the plants and the extra diamonds that we expect to recover."

"Who will that be?" Mike McCarthy asked. "They're important jobs."

"Ivan Richards for the security role. He's a young guy but shows a lot of promise, and the Chief of Security has approved the promotion. The manager of the sorting process will be an old hand, Harry Van Rensberg."

"Okay, good," Mike McCarthy said. "What about plant capacity? Any need for capital improvements?"

McCarthy closed the meeting after Gavin spent thirty minutes answering the question. Gavin left the meeting and immediately announced the reorganization of his department and the date when it would be implemented. He called Harry Van Rensberg and Ivan Richards into his office for a private discussion. Although he had spoken to each of them separately about his plan he had never done so collectively and neither of them knew the other was involved.

"I've spoken to you both separately about my little scheme, but now it's time to put it into operation." Gavin noticed Ivan and Harry exchange apprehensive looks as he continued. "We're all involved in this scheme against our wishes. If we fail our reputations and private lives will be ruined—possibly even a stretch in prison. So basically we have to go along with it and cover ourselves as best we can. That means sticking together and working out a foolproof plan. In a year's time we'll be off the hook, and who knows, maybe we'll make some money as well."

"I agree," Harry said. "We don't have a choice, but if we get caught I'd like to know that the bastard who forced us into this also gets his share of the shit. So far you haven't said who's behind it."

"He's right, Gavin," Ivan added.

Gavin reluctantly replied, "Well . . . okay . . . his name is Hugh Barlow, and he comes from a rich family in Johannesburg. I'll give you his address later. Keep this secret because this guy and his whole family are very influential and very dangerous. Don't underestimate them. You've experienced it first hand, Ivan."

"And how!"

Harry interjected, "Why don't we write down what we've been forced to do and lodge it with an attorney? Only to be opened if we all consent, or we're killed, or die in unusual circumstances."

"We'd be admitting our own guilt in that case," Ivan said.

"True," Harry responded, "but who cares if we're all dead?"

Gavin added, "If one of us dies then the other two can decide what to do. Make the letter public or take action on their own volition."

"Do you know a trustworthy attorney, Gavin?" Ivan asked.

"Yes, my cousin Richard Brown. We've been very close since childhood and he's been a good friend since then . . . and he's not a money-grabbing scumbag."

"Okay," Harry said, "Let's write our reasons for getting into this and let you handle the rest, Gavin,"

"That's fine with me," Ivan added.

"Now that's settled, let's move on," Gavin said.

"Starting Monday; Harry, you supervise the sorters and put time aside for your own surreptitious sorting."

"I've given that a lot of thought," Harry said. "The best way is to let the sorters do their normal jobs, albeit two more teams of them, and randomly choose one set of returns not to record. Since Ivan is on security it won't be a problem."

"Good idea," Ivan said. "The forms the sorters use are numbered sequentially on a daily basis. The form contains the sorter's name, date, total number of diamonds, and the total number of carats. So I'll have to make sure that the highest numbered form is the one we hide. That way there's no break in sequence.

"When my security team re-weighs and counts the diamonds at the end of each shift they take one copy of the form and put it in a sealed bag with the diamonds. The bag is stored in the safe. The second copy is sent to head office and the third is given to a security supervisor. That's me from now on. I'll total the whole take for the day and send the numbers to the accounting people."

"I'll handle the monthly reporting," Gavin said.

"Now comes the difficult part," Ivan continued. "How to get those small bags out of the safe before a completely separate security team shows up randomly and clears the lot out."

"Or don't put the bag in there in the first place," Harry suggested.

"How so?" Gavin quizzed

"The bags are small and it would be easy for me to pocket the lot after the last sorter hands in his returns. There'll be twelve separate sorters each day, and on average each one will hand in about 1000 carats. That's more than just a pocketful but not too difficult to hide. I'll wear a loose safari suit so I can just spread them out lengthwise and slip them in a pouch inside my pants. I'll sew the bottom of the pouch to my pants and sew a zipper on the top of it. With my protruding stomach the bottom of my safari suit jacket will cover them nicely!"

"One thing," Gavin said to Harry, "be careful when a sorter notices a particularly large diamond or one with an unusual color. They always bullshit about that sort of thing and everyone gets to hear it. If it goes missing someone might get suspicious."

"If that happens," Harry replied, "I'll tell Ivan to hand the batch in as usual."

"Now we have the diamonds in our hands, actually getting them out of the processing plant is easy," Ivan said, "but how will you get them out of the mine? That's when your problems begin."

"Our friend, Mr. Barlow, tells me he has it all sorted out—excuse the pun," Gavin said, as he shook his head in disbelief.

"Can't wait to hear about that," Harry added.

"Okay, let's try it out next Wednesday," Gavin said, "but if anything unusual happens just stop, and merely go through the motions of pocketing the diamonds and fiddling the returns to see what happens. If things look good we'll put it into operation every day, starting in two weeks, when the production increases really take off."

A week later at exactly 4:00 PM, when the afternoon shift ended, Harry Van Rensberg issued instructions for his teams to finish their sorting activities and commence the classification and counting of the daily diamond output.

Thirty minutes later several of the sorters handed in their diamonds and paperwork at the security checkpoint. Harry stood and watched as Ivan checked the first batch. Ivan weighed the batch and then carefully passed them through a counting machine. He then checked his results against those already written on the form by the sorter, signed the form, and stapled it to the bag, which he then placed on a table immediately in front of the security safe.

One by one each sorter passed through the security checkpoint. Ivan repeated the process until he saw sequence number thirteen written on the top of a form, the highest number of the day. Ivan signaled to Harry by scratching his left ear several times. Harry moved between Ivan and the sorter, who was by now passing through the checkpoint, and quickly took the bag from Ivan and slipped it into a pouch underneath the front of his safari suit.

Harry could see Ivan was nervous, so he casually turned and greeted the next sorter as if nothing had happened. When all the sorters had been processed, Ivan tore off one copy of the forms from each of the twelve bags. Harry then helped Ivan put the bags into the safe.

Ivan went to the computer terminal, logged into the accounting system, and entered the information written on each of the forms.

He batched the forms together, put them in a sealed envelope, and told a messenger to deliver them to the accounting department.

Harry filed his normal end-of-shift report and calmly proceeded to leave the plant with a jubilant Ivan on his tail.

"As easy as taking a piss," Harry said to Ivan as they left the plant.

Ivan, Harry and Gavin met the next evening in Gavin's office to discuss the events of the previous day. Most of the other staff had left by this time.

"Where did you hide the stuff?" Gavin asked Harry.

"Underneath the floorboards in my room. That should be okay for a few weeks, but after that we need to find somewhere safer and with more room."

"What about that abandoned building a mile up the road from B-Plant?" Ivan suggested. "Plenty of places to hide things and nobody goes there anymore."

"That'll do," Gavin replied. "Oh, the month-end audit is due next week and if anyone notices anything out of the ordinary with the paperwork or checks and balances, we'll soon get to hear about it. If not, we can begin removing one bag each day from then on."

"Gavin, how long do we have to do this?" Ivan asked.

"Barlow wants about 250,000 carats over the next year."

"He's not greedy by any chance," Harry muttered.

"After that we can get on with our lives," Ivan said.

"What makes me think we'll never be off the hook?" Harry said despondently.

"I'll call Barlow and give him his good news, and then Ivan and I should drive out to B-Plant."

Gavin called Hugh and in guarded language gave him an update. Hugh was ecstatic and his final statement was definitive. "If anyone gets in your way just call and I'll deal with him – or her for that matter. And remember any mistakes or backtracking from you or any of the gang and I won't hesitate to turn the lot of you over to the police. My hands are still clean don't forget."

Ivan drove Gavin to B-Plant to determine if it was suitable for their purposes. It was situated part way between the two largest processing plants on the mine, A and B, about a mile inland from the coastline and about the same distance from the main dirt road connecting the plants. It was previously used as a field repair station for heavy trucks and earth moving equipment, but as the mining activities moved further north it was abandoned in favor of more convenient locations.

It was dark when they entered the building, but Gavin had a powerful flashlight that he used to search the large floor space. Ivan suggested a spot in the corner of the main area. It was covered with heavy, rusted metal and would not be casually discovered. It had large wooden floorboards, and had probably been used as an office adjacent to the workshop. Ivan lifted two of the floorboards with a crowbar and cleared a space below them. Gavin placed the first bag of diamonds in the hole and replaced the floorboards.

"Let's get going," Gavin said, "we don't want to be caught hanging around here."

"I'll drive you back to A-Plant."

"Remember the next time we come out here we'll have ten times that amount of diamonds, so you had better find a good place to store them in your jeep."

"I'll get my hands on some stronger bags, something that will hold about ten pounds. I worked out that if we eventually get 250,000 carats the total weight would be about 110 pounds. So ten or eleven ten-pound bags should suffice, and they'll be fairly easy to carry."

"Good idea," Gavin said as they drove into the parking area at A-Plant. "I'll speak to you tomorrow."

SEVEN

Almost a year had passed since Hugh set the plan in motion. Gavin was dutifully stashing Allied's diamonds away while Chris was still an accomplice in waiting. Hugh decided it was time to move to the next and most difficult part of the plot—actually moving the diamonds from Allied over the Namibian border into Chris's eager hands.

He arranged to have lunch with Roger Hamilton at the Rowing Club in order assemble a suitable team for the task. After his experiences during his last trip to Allied and Steinkop he decided not to be part of the team executing the plan; he would just control things remotely. Although he personally knew several likely candidates, he felt comfortable allowing Roger to perform the actual recruiting. Hugh knew that Roger had carried out several similar projects for his father, so he was confident it was the best course of action.

They exchanged greetings at the club and got straight down to business. Roger told his ever-present bodyguard, Peter Fourie, to wait for him outside the club.

"Roger, I know I can count on you keeping this completely confidential. I need a team to cross over the South African border into Namibia and retrieve a very valuable package, and then get it back to me."

Roger interrupted. "Namibia . . . I see. Where exactly?"

"The diamond area along the coast," replied Hugh.

"Let me stop you right there, Hugh. I'm under orders from high up to keep my mitts off that stuff. I have trusted clients who have legitimate interests in that field so I can't in all honesty work against them. It's a matter of professional ethics. If any of them thought I was double dealing I'd be out of business inside a week."

"I wish I hadn't mentioned it now. I've put you on the spot, haven't I?"

"Look as far as I'm concerned it was never mentioned, but a word of advice. Keep out of it, Hugh. Many people have tried this sort of stunt and failed miserably. The ones that succeeded initially almost always got caught when they tried to sell the stuff. There're a lot of informants out there you know."

"Okay, I got that from the top," Hugh replied, finishing the serious side of the conversation.

They chatted for about thirty minutes, mainly about Roger's shady interactions with Hugh's father. Hugh deliberately pushed this line of conversation as a veiled threat should Roger mention the reason for their meeting.

Hugh returned home disappointed and somewhat worried that he'd revealed critical information to Roger. However, he trusted Roger's discretion, especially after the innuendoes thrown around at the meeting. Hugh would use this as a counterweight if things got nasty.

Susan was at home when Hugh arrived.

"I've got to leave for Port Elizabeth tomorrow. Things didn't go according to plan with Roger."

"What happened?"

"He couldn't help. Conflict of interest he said. Something about the government telling him to keep out of the Namibian debacle."

"Do you believe him?"

"I think so. He's normally honest with our family. Can you get Johnny to pack some clothes for me? Three day's worth should be enough. Tell him to put in some older casual clothes as well. I'll see if I can find Karl Emberg when I get to Port Elizabeth."

"Will do," Susan replied.

Hugh left by plane the next morning and arrived in Port Elizabeth just after lunchtime and booked into the Elizabeth Hotel. Later in the evening he dressed in an old leather coat and blue jeans and went down to the hotel's taxi stand. He told the driver he would need him all night.

"Take me to that club down by the docks, the one near Front Street."

"You sure you want to go there, sir?" the taxi driver replied. "It's a rough old place."

Hugh just nodded.

At the Seafront Club Hugh told the driver to park across the street from the entrance. "I shouldn't be too long." Hugh stopped just inside the doors while the two bouncers looked him up and down. One of them crudely signaled for him to enter.

"No fighting," the other one said, "and no beating up the tarts."

Hugh didn't answer. He walked along a dimly lit corridor that led into the main section of the club. There were only about twenty customers, mainly men, shouting above the deafening music. The club was like a large, dimly lit barn with uninviting thin metal tables and chairs spread unevenly around. The bar was stuck in a corner, leading to what appeared to be a storage room, and was only large enough to seat about four people.

A few groggy-looking prostitutes were hanging around the men's toilets trying to make themselves noticed. The smell of their cheap perfume barely concealed the stench of stale urine. Hugh went over to the bar.

"Castle lager in a clean glass," he shouted over the din.

One of the barmen grumbled as he dumped the bottle and glass on the bar. Hugh threw a ten-rand note on the counter and said to the two barmen, "I'm looking for an old friend of mine, Karl Emberg. Either of you know him?"

Hugh just managed to suppress laughter when the barmen, one very tall and the other short, shook their heads in unison. The taller barman noticed the note and began muttering to his co-worker in Afrikaans. He eventually replied in English with a heavy Afrikaans accent. "He doesn't come much now. If he's not here by ten you might see him in the Algoa Hotel."

Hugh found a small table in an inconspicuous part of the club and waited. Several small groups wandered into the club during the next thirty minutes, most of them drunk, but no sign of Karl. The DJ turned up the volume of the music as the crowd increased and became rowdier, making it even more uncomfortable for Hugh.

Finally as he was about to leave he caught sight of Karl and walked over to the bar. Karl was showing his age but he still looked fit. It had been ten years since he'd last seen him and ten again before that when he was a sergeant in the South African Army.

Hugh was an officer but had only served for eighteen months. Karl had served over twelve years and a further six as a privateer and mercenary. He was just under six-feet tall and solidly built with a hard, worn, confident-looking face.

"Let me buy this one for you, Sergeant Emberg," Hugh said.

Karl jolted his head back, obviously surprised. "Mr. Barlow, what the hell are you doing in this shit hole?"

"Good description of the place," Hugh replied, holding out his hand. "How have you been? It must be ten years."

"Let me get you a drink, sir. Oh, by the way this is one of my pals, Lordy Everton. He's a dethroned lord from England."

"How do you do, sir," Lordy said. "Giles Everton at your service."

Hugh shook hands with Lordy while looking him up and down. Lordy was very tall, slim and wiry, with long aquiline features.

"A lord eh? What are you doing here?"

"It's a long story," Lordy replied, looking at Karl. "I'll tell you all about it if you have a couple of weeks to waste. Led on by bad company you might say."

They all laughed, toasted each other, and finished their drinks. The threesome continued to exchange amusing stories for ten minutes until Hugh turned the conversation to more serious matters.

"Karl, I've got something important to discuss with you."

Lordy took the hint and made an excuse to leave.

"Listen, Karl, I've got a little bit of business underway. It's risky, but there's a big payoff attached. Interested?"

"How big, sir?"

"Twenty thousand for you. Ten regardless of what happens and the rest after a successful mission. You'll need three or four others on the team, but you can pick them. Ten thousand each for them."

"Let's go somewhere quieter than this place, sir. I can hardly hear myself think. Oh by the way, Lordy's done a lot of missions with me. He's pretty good you know and he knows how to keep his mouth shut."

"Can I talk openly in front of him?" Hugh asked.

"Absolutely, no problem there."

They finished their drinks, signaled to Lordy to leave with them, and walked out of the club. Hugh's taxi was still waiting across the road.

"Make for the Algoa Hotel," Karl shouted at the taxi driver.

The Algoa was full and a little noisy, but no music to shout above. They found a place at the end of the bar and ordered drinks.

"Tell me, Karl, are you working at the moment?"

"No, sir. We finished a small job in Angola last year supporting an outfit called the FNLA. It was run by a fellow called Daniel Chipenda in Southern Angola. We were fighting the Marxist MPLA."

"And several other unfortunate outfits I might add," Lordy added.

Karl continued, "The pay was lousy and there was no real organization. So the majority of the men were robbing churches, UN storerooms, and anything else they could find. Not that there was much to take. We, Lordy and me, left after a few months and came back to Port Elizabeth."

"What about you, Lordy? What were you doing before you met Karl?"

"In a nut shell. I was kicked out of Eton, kicked out of university, swindled my father out of a fortune, lost it all in Monte Carlo, joined the British army as an officer, and got kicked out of there after four years for behavior unbecoming an officer."

"Caught on top of his commanding officer's wife," Karl interjected.

They all belly-laughed.

"Then I came to South Africa and for the last ten years I've been a soldier of very little fortune I'm afraid to say."

Hugh got down to business. "I take it you're both interested in a job, so let me elaborate. I need a team to help me plan and carry out a complicated mission. If we're careful there'll be no shooting or anything like that, but if necessary I will expect you to go the full distance. It's in South Africa and Namibia so if you get caught it's a prison sentence or even the rope if you kill anyone. Still interested?"

"What's the remuneration?" Lordy asked.

"Ten thousand for you," Hugh replied, not mentioning Karl's cut.

"I'm interested," Lordy replied.

"And me," Karl added.

"Okay, let's meet again tomorrow somewhere more private and I'll go into more details. Once in on this there's no getting out. You both realize that?"

Karl and Lordy said they understood and were 100 percent behind him. They went back to their drinks and talked about old times again. Hugh pretended to listen and made sure he laughed at the right times but his mind was elsewhere. He was trying to focus on the next phase of his plan, but the rowdiness of the patrons crowding around the bar was too much of a distraction. He finally gave up and just observed the bedlam.

A small, insignificant man was perched at the bar reciting poetry and his friend next to him was too drunk even to speak. An Afrikaner, wearing a safari suit, had placed himself against the bar a few feet from Lordy. He was quite short but extremely broad, with massive arms and hands, and no neck to speak of.

Hugh listened as the large Afrikaner snapped at the barmen, "You, barman, give me a drink! Quick!"

The barmen, who apparently knew him replied, "Jan, calm down, I'll get you a drink."

"Make it quick," Jan replied.

Jan gripped the edge of the bar with his hands, pushed his backside out and broke wind.

"I hate the Brits," Jan shouted, as he hammered on the bar. "I hate the kaffirs and I don't like barmen who keep me waiting."

Hugh said to Karl and Lordy, "Looks like he's spoiling for trouble."

Lordy replied, "Yes, he does seem to be." He moved a few feet away and fanned the air in the direction of Jan.

"I'd keep away from that one," Karl warned, "he's impossible to hurt. He's a farmer's son—throws 300 pound bags of grain around like cotton wool."

"I say old chap, if you're going to be so flatulent kindly transport yourself elsewhere," Lordy said in his upper class accent.

Jan didn't understand the sarcasm and continued insulting everyone around him. "I can't stand coolies or coloreds and the pork-and-cheese sea-kaffirs you get here now. Let them get back to Portugal and Mozambique, or wherever they came from."

Hugh noticed Jan had knocked back six cane spirit doubles and a couple of beers in the last thirty minutes and he was becoming more obnoxious with each drink. He could see that the barman had given up trying to pacify him, but stood in amazement as Lordy continued to goad him.

"What was the name of that Afrikaans chap in the Boer War? Jan Smuts wasn't it? I always thought he was bit of a colored you know, like most of these Afrikaners."

Jan went red with rage. He hammered on the bar again and crushed a metal ashtray with one blow. He turned towards Lordy, growled, lurched backwards, and then sideways into the drunken thin man, crushing him against the bar and causing a sickening crunching sound. Hugh thought the collision must have broken the thin man's ribs but Jan hardly seemed to notice it. Jan careered forward into Lordy throwing punches into the air with his short, powerful arms. He stopped for a moment to hurl a barstool across the room, which landed on a nearby table soaking the occupants with beer and covering them with glass.

Jan tripped and fell to his knees before reaching Lordy. Karl jumped forward and delivered a hard kick flush in Jan's face. Jan's head jerked back and then forward again as blood poured from his nose and eyes.

"Who kicked me in the face?" Jan shouted.

He staggered to his feet as Lordy and Karl delivered several savage punches and kicks to Jan's head and body. Jan was like an ocean liner being hit by a large wave. He shuddered at first and then resumed momentum. With blood covering his eyes, Jan was unable to see. He lurched into groups of fellow drunks knocking them flying and throwing punches at random.

"Quick, Jan's gone kaffir," the barman shouted, "get out of his way."

Hugh, Lordy and Karl took this opportunity to exit the Algoa along with everyone else still sober enough to do so. They piled into Hugh's taxi. "Get moving," Hugh said to the driver, "before that animal gets out."

The next morning they met in Hugh's hotel and after a quick breakfast got down to business.

"I didn't want to say too much last night. I wanted to make sure you both still want to get involved. Basically the team has to cross over the South African border into Namibia, pick up a very valuable package, and return it to me at a location in the Northern Cape."

"That seems remarkably easy," Lordy remarked.

"Well it's the diamond area you're going into and nobody must know that you've done it."

"Oh, not so easy then," Karl said.

"Exactly. However, you don't have to steal them. Someone has already done that, and unnoticed to boot."

"Intriguing," Lordy added.

Hugh laid out his conclusions. The main problem was getting the team in and out of the mine unnoticed. There were three possible routes—overland after crossing the Orange River, by helicopter or light plane, or by boat landing on an isolated beach.

He quickly ruled out the second option. Lordy and Karl agreed completely. It was doubtful whether they could get a helicopter, let alone find a pilot that would be willing to fly one. The noise would be heard for miles, and at night it would be difficult to find the pickup location. A small fixed wing plane would also be problematic. Hugh knew from his uncomfortable flight to Steinkop that the South African Air force employed radar in the area and there was no means of landing at night without giving away their position. If they landed far enough away from the pickup point to avoid being detected by radar, or being heard by the security people, then it would be too far to walk. Again they all agreed with Hugh about using aircraft.

The overland route was a possibility but they would need to get a tracked vehicle. A four-wheeled drive Land Rover might be adequate in good weather, but it would either have to cross the Orange River at night from the South African side, or be brought down from the north of the country and then dumped when they returned to the river. Fording the river would not be easy, but it was possible; and a truck would be somewhat noisy, especially at night in the desert.

Lordy suggested using cross-country motorbikes, but Hugh said it had been tried before and failed badly. Lordy ended the discussion on the first two options. "So it looks like the default is a sea journey."

"Exactly, Lordy," Hugh said. "A smallish boat could leave from fifty or so miles south of the border on the South African side. Go out to sea ten miles and then north along the coastline for about sixty. When the boat reaches the pickup point it turns east towards the shore. The noise of the sea and the processing plants would drown out the sound of the boat's engine, and at nighttime it would not be seen."

"How will you recognize the pickup point in the dead of night?" Lordy enquired.

"Well, there are four big processing plants along the coastline, which can't be missed. They're lit up like Christmas trees. I've seen it myself. The boat could line up roughly in the middle of any two of the plants and then watch for a flashing light shining from the shore. That would be our signal to come in."

"The sea is very rough in that part of the world," Lordy added, "that's why it's called the skeleton coast. Hundreds of wrecked ships all the way up the coastline."

"True," Hugh continued, "but of the three approaches it's the one that provides the best chance of success."

"The boat will have to be powerful and have a range of over 120 miles, and carry at least three of us," Karl added. "One to steer, one to act as a guard, and one to go ashore and pick the stuff up."

"Probably two men needed to pick the stuff up, especially if the boat can't go onto the beach," Hugh added.

"Who will be on the other side dropping it off?" Lordy asked.

"Two men," Hugh replied.

"So we need two more men on the boat," Karl said, "and how will we launch the boat sixty miles from the target?"

They began examining the problem. Hugh had already developed a plan, but he wanted to explain it to the group piecemeal, so he wouldn't feel embarrassed if holes were found in his thinking. Eventually a consensus was reached. They would acquire a boat in Cape Town, put it in on a trailer pulled by a Land Rover, and drive it into the back of a large furniture removal truck. Concealed in this fashion the boat wouldn't be noticed during the trip up north. The Land Rover could also be driven straight out of the truck on a ramp, pulling the boat with it.

Hugh told them that he had already identified a place where the boat could be launched. Karl convinced Hugh that at least three more men should join the team because someone would need to drive the truck and look after the Land Rover while the rest of the team were out at sea. Karl then turned to the subject of finding three more recruits.

"I know a young fellow who would be perfect. He was in the Rhodesian Army. Fit as a fiddle, and if I recall he's an excellent swimmer. Might come in handy if the boat can't get onto the beach."

"Excellent," Hugh said.

"I'll contact him."

"Yes, but don't say too much until he's definitely committed," Hugh warned.

"Don't laugh at what I'm going to say next, just listen," Lordy said. "I know a woman who planned and took part in some of the government's covert missions in that BOSS outfit. She's well trained and has a grudge against them. They kicked her out on some trumped up charge. Apparently the males there were jealous of her."

"What makes you think she'll want to join us?" Karl asked.

"She's done a few hush-hush things over the last year or so, since she was kicked out of BOSS. I know because I had a brief fling with her. I actually know her quite well."

"What's her name?"

"Virginia Wilson."

"Okay, Lordy, but be careful. If she doesn't join us after you've told her about the project then we'll have to kill her. Same goes for your Rhodesian friend."

Karl and Lordy nodded in agreement.

"What about someone to look after the truck and sort things out on land?" Lordy said.

"What about Ron Farmer?" Karl interjected. "He doesn't have any military experience, but he's a half-decent crook and I know he can drive large trucks."

"Yes, he'll do," Lordy replied.

"Okay, I'll leave it to you then," Hugh said.

They finished discussing the plan after about four hours and all agreed to meet in two weeks with the new recruits.

EIGHT

*H*ugh had just finished breakfast in his room in the Elizabeth Hotel when he heard a heavy knock on the door.

Must be Karl and the team, he thought.

He opened the door and to his surprise it was Chris Conway.

"Chris, what the hell are you doing here?"

"I'm in town for a conference and I thought I saw you checking into the hotel yesterday. The receptionist gave me your room number."

Hugh had to think quickly because the last thing he wanted was for Chris to meet his co-conspirators.

"Chris, it's a bad time." He winked at Chris, tossed his head back, and moved his eyes to the side. He made an hourglass figure in the shape of a woman's body with his hands, implying that there was actually a woman in the bedroom.

"I'll call you tonight and we can talk," He whispered to Chris.

Chris smiled, gave Hugh the thumbs-up sign and walked back along the corridor.

That was close, Hugh thought as he breathed a sigh of relief.

Less than a minute later another loud knock on the door revealed Karl.

"I told the others to come up one by one," Karl said without greeting Hugh.

"Probably the best thing—can't be too careful."

Lordy came next followed by Henny De Wit.

"Hugh, this is Henny De Wit," Karl said.

"Has Karl explained things to you?"

"Yes, sir," Henny replied, standing upright as if he was on parade. Hugh looked Henny up and down and realized he was extremely fit. He was short and broad, and his blonde hair highlighted a deep suntan.

A few minutes of small talk was interrupted by another tap on the door. "Must be Virginia."

Hugh was surprised to see such a fine looking woman. She was tall and athletic looking, in a feminine way, with long auburn hair tied at the back. She had large grayish eyes and well fitting facial features—not at all what Hugh had expected. Hugh stood back to get a better look at her. *Not as beautiful as Susan,* he thought, *but something about her is very attractive. She must be in her early thirties I would think.*

"Hello, Mr. Barlow, I'm Virginia Wilson," she said, holding out her hand to greet Hugh. "Lordy has told me a lot about you."

Hugh replied, "Oh, good. It's nice of you to join our merry little group. I hear you've had a lot of experience in the covert arena —planning and such things."

"Yes, in the field as well," she replied cockily.

Hugh could tell immediately that she was intelligent but he wasn't fooled by her pleasantness. He could see a ruthless streak in her.

After Ron Farmer joined them, they all went over the plan outlined at their last meeting. Hugh noticed that Virginia just listened to the conversation and he was concerned that she was not interested in the proceedings, but when everyone had finished speaking she reeled off all the preliminary activities required to put the plan into motion. She then wrote down each person's tasks right up to and including D-Day. Next she worked out the approximate costs for Hugh to consider. Hugh was very impressed but neither expressed his feelings nor questioned any of the details.

"By the way, has anyone worked out the weight of 250,000 carats of the stuff?" she asked.

"Yes," Hugh said confidently, "It's about 110 pounds and about two cubic feet. My contact on the other side will put them into metal cases."

"Tell them to wrap the cases in life jackets attached to rope," Virginia added. "That way if they go into the sea we'll be able to extricate them fairly easily."

"Good idea," Hugh replied and gave up trying to compete.

Hugh went over the payment details and made arrangements for them to meet in Cape Town one more time before D-Day.

Hugh went up to Chris's room later that evening to see if had noticed any of the team members and to find out if he was really attending a conference.

"Chris, I didn't expect to see you in town. What's going on?"

"It's the Steinkop manager's annual get-together. It's an excuse for a booze-up really but everyone looks forward to it. How's your little plan going? I've been practising my little part every week."

"Everything's ready. As of last week it was 250,000 carats. Pretty good eh?"

"Excellent, roughly when will you deliver?" Chris asked.

"In about four weeks. I'll give you the exact day and time and whereabouts one week prior. Is that okay?"

"That's fine. I've got everything ready."

"Okay, I'd better be going," Hugh said. He walked to the door.

"Back to that curvy female I suspect."

"Something like that," Hugh replied coyly.

Virginia wasted no time. She went to the meteorological office and obtained detailed historical data about the winds and tides in the pick-up area, along with several physical maps of the region. She gave Karl the minimum specifications for a vessel that would be required to make the sea journey and a list of tools and equipment needed for the whole project. Since Hugh had given her the responsibility of accounting for all the cash spent on the project, she decided to go along with each team member to acquire the equipment.

Lordy's job was to obtain weapons. They all agreed that having powerful ones would be of little use. All they needed were some handguns with silencers and a couple of R1 automatic rifles. If it came to gunfire then most likely their plot would be discovered and the whole area would be swamped with security patrols and police. A firefight in these circumstances would be suicidal. Just enough weaponry to be comfortable was all that was needed.

Lordy immediately went to see one of his old friends in the small city of East London, 200 miles along the coast from Port Elizabeth. Virginia went with him. His name was Eric Strausser, an Austrian immigrant, who was a known small arms dealer and low-life. He had a strong German accent and always pronounced "w" with a strong VEE sound.

"Eric, how's your little firearms business going?"

Eric rubbed his hands on his protruding stomach. "Well I'll be a son of a gun. Lordy bloody Everton. What do you want? And who's this piece of crackling?"

Virginia just listened to the proceedings because she realized Eric thought she was just a bit of fluff that Lordy had picked up.

"Don't be like that, Eric. I don't owe you any money do I?"

"No, but something tells me trouble's brewing. I still suspect you of telling that black guerilla in Angola that my guns were always misfiring. He cancelled a second order after that."

"The guns were blowing up in their faces, Eric, and you know the MPLA were using small kids to fight for them."

"So what do I care about kids? The fewer blacks around the better for everyone I say. I don't care if the idiots blind themselves as long as they cough up the money for the weapons. In any case I sold the same crowd medical supplies at a discounted price. So that makes it even, don't you think?"

Virginia listened in amazement.

"You haven't changed much, Eric. All heart, just like I remember."

"Anyway, what can I do for you? You English pig."

"I need to buy a few good quality weapons, nothing fancy just basic stuff. A couple of military rifles and a few handguns with ammo."

"Okay, come around the back. I've got a couple of spares you can buy. I'm doing you a favor; normally I only sell in bulk."

Virginia stood in the background as Eric showed Lordy several used weapons and allowed him to test fire them in his underground firing range. Lordy chose the best of the batch and after haggling for twenty minutes with Eric over the price, Virginia handed over a wad of cash to Lordy, who in turn placed it in Eric's greedy palms. They left with the weapons and ammunition.

When Virginia returned she gave Henny the money to buy a second-hand Land Rover that he had identified, along with a strong pulley rig, rope, life jackets, camping equipment, and canned food. Ron Farmer bought a scrambling motorcycle and some electrical equipment. The biggest problem was obtaining a large covered truck that would hold a Land Rover and a boat. It was too expensive to buy so they were looking to lease or steal one.

Karl tried for two days to locate a suitable boat without success, so Virginia offered to help. They visited several small boat yards in the area but found nothing suitable. Finally she looked through a newspaper and found an advertisement for an older thirty-foot seagoing vessel with an inboard 30 horsepower diesel engine.

They examined it thoroughly. The engine was working but it was underpowered for the strong currents of the skeleton coast. It had a small upright cabin nine feet wide, about the width of the boat, and six feet long. The electrical system was crude but in working order and the wooden hull had been recently painted.

The owner took them out in the ocean for a trial. It struggled in the choppy sea, mainly due to the underpowered engine, but it remained reasonably stable. When they got back to shore Karl and Virginia weighed up the pros and cons of buying it.

"That engine will never hold the current up there," Karl said.

"I know. What if we buy two outboard engines and bolt them to the back? Two engines each about 100 horsepower would do it. We'd need to make a few alterations to make them fit and maybe install an additional fuel tank, but I think that would do the job. What do you think?"

"Okay. It won't take us long to fix it up."

They bought the boat on the spot and arranged to pick it up in a week's time. Much to their delight the owner threw in, at no charge, the stocky trailer he used for hauling the boat.

"Maybe he knows something we don't," Virginia said sarcastically as they left.

They all met the next day at Henny's house in Uitenhage, inland from Port Elizabeth. The house had a huge garage-cum-workshop that Henny's father had used for his plumbing business before he retired to Rhodesia.

They sat around the garage on makeshift seats while Virginia asked each of them how the procurement was going.

"Henny, did you get everything?" She asked.

"Yes," Henny replied pointing to the vehicle. "All the equipment and supplies are here in the house and I bought this second-hand Land Rover."

"Excellent. Lordy, you might want to tell everyone what happened with your humanitarian friend in East London."

"Glad you asked."

He produced a large angler's rucksack and emptied its contents on the floor. Four nine millimeter Lugers, a Beretta, an Uzi, and two South African R1 standard issue rifles, one with a grenade launching attachment and the other with a telescopic sight. He then hauled over two large ammunition boxes and revealed the contents. Apart from the ammunition there were a dozen hand-grenades, phosphorous grenades and even two small anti-personnel mines.

"Bit of overkill," Karl commented.

"Better safe than sorry," he replied. "Never know who you might meet on a cruise."

Virginia noticed how the presence of firearms made everyone tense and Lordy's amusing remarks seemed to relax the atmosphere. She looked on as Karl briefly explained the overall specifications of the boat and then brought in two outboard engines from his truck. "They are 50 horsepower each," he said, "so that should be more than enough power."

"Henny, when the boat arrives can you fix them up?" Virginia asked.

"No sweat. Is the back of the boat metal or wood?"

"Wood, I think."

"I'll help, Henny," Ron added. "I've got the scrambling bike and all the electrical stuff we'll need."

"That's excellent, Ron," Virginia said. "Did you get the flashlights and the timers?"

"Absolutely! Everything's ready."

Lordy went down Virginia's checklist reading each item out loud. There were only a few things missing.

"We'll need an extra fuel tank for the boat," Karl noted.

"How much room is there at the back of it?" Henny asked.

Karl explained the overall shape of the boat again and this time drew a diagram to make sure everyone was absolutely clear.

"I'll bolt a steel plate to the deck at the stern and weld the tank to that. A forty-gallon tank should be more than okay for our journey. How large is the diesel tank for the inboard engine?"

"Not sure," Karl replied.

"Me neither," Virginia said, disappointed that she'd missed a detail.

"We can probably make do with a few large jerry cans for that," Henny added. "I'll see when the boat arrives."

Two days later they all met again after Lordy reported that he had stolen a truck and had paid some of his underworld contacts to re-paint it. They also painted logos on its sides depicting a non-existent removal company.

"How did you manage to get it, Lordy?" Virginia asked.

"Well, I called one of the large removal companies and arranged for them to pick up some pre-packed furniture that I told them I wanted delivered to an address in Durban. I gave them a false address of course. It was a warehouse down by the docks. When the driver showed up I said the packages wouldn't be ready for about an hour and offered to buy him a couple of drinks. We went to a bar and I proceeded to get him absolutely paralytic drunk. A friend of mine, of dubious character and background, stole the keys from his pocket and drove the truck to a paint shop on the other side of town. I left the bar when the driver staggered off to the toilet. By the time I got to the paint shop our newly painted removal truck was waiting for us, new license plate included. Not bad service for 200 rand I thought."

"I'll have to remember that one," Virginia said, absolutely disgusted with Lordy.

A week later everything and everyone was loaded on Lordy's borrowed truck ready for the 500-mile journey to Cape Town, where they planned to meet Hugh in a hotel north of the city, and finalize D-Day.

The Land Rover, the boat and trailer plus all the equipment fitted nicely into the truck. It had metal runners ready to pull out so that the Land Rover could be driven out of the back of the truck pulling the boat and trailer with it. Karl, Virginia and Lordy had plenty of room in the cabin while Henny and Ron sat inside the cargo hold on a couple of comfortable camp beds.

At the hotel Karl, who was driving, let the others check-in while he went to find a safe place to park the truck overnight. One person was to stay inside the truck at all times just in case of unwanted visitors. Karl took the first watch, from 6:00 PM until midnight and then Lordy from midnight onwards.

Hugh appeared at 7:00 AM to find everyone drinking coffee in the hotel lobby. He marched into the hotel and without exchanging niceties asked, "Where's Lordy?"

"In the truck, it's his turn to be night watchman," Virginia replied.

"Good idea. Where's the truck? I can drive over and get him."

"Let's all go," Karl said. "We can talk privately in your car, Mr. Barlow. It's only five minutes away."

Lordy was walking around the truck checking the tires when they arrived and happily gave them the thumbs-up sign when he saw them. They walked over to a small café just across the road from the truck, ordered breakfast, and seated themselves out of earshot of the staff and other patrons.

"Okay," Hugh began, "let's get down to business. The pickup is planned for Saturday night. It's a three-quarter moon then, but it should be cloudy, so it'll be fairly dark at sea, and the tide is perfectly timed to help you get up the coastline. You can thank Virginia for that piece of intelligence.

"Your contacts will be waiting for you from 11:00 PM. They will intermittently flash an orange and a green light out to sea every fifteen minutes. A half-dozen orange flashes will be followed by a half-dozen green ones, repeated for two minutes. This will continue for two hours, just in case you're late getting to the rendezvous point. Remember, watch for the first two processing plants. They can't be missed with all their lights shining at night.

"If there's a heavy fog you'll have to abandon the mission. If this happens just go back to the launching point below Port Nolloth and wait until Sunday. Your contact will know what's happened in this event. If Sunday is the same, then the plan is postponed for a week—same time and place only one week later, using the same drill. If you have to wait a week then load everything back on the truck and drive back to Cape Town.

"Take your time and it'll look like you've made a delivery and you're returning to Cape Town. Change your hotel after each night to make it look good. I thought about leaving the boat behind, hidden in the rocks, but I think it's too risky. Sometimes you get fishermen up that way and if they see an abandoned boat it'll be sold to someone within two hours. I've already explained the route you need to take once you get to the outskirts of Port Nolloth. Any questions on that?"

No one commented.

Hugh continued, "Once you get back to the embarkation point, sink the boat, drive the Land Rover to the main road at noon, and wait for Ron to come with the truck. If all is well just wave him on and drive to Steinkop in the Land Rover, where I'll be waiting for you. If not, Ron will stop and you can reload the Land Rover and the boat and start the whole process over again.

"Ron, you go straight to Cape Town if you get the thumbs-up sign and dump the truck. Stay in Port Nolloth overnight on Saturday with the truck and if you have to return on Sunday because the team doesn't meet you, make some excuse at the hotel that the truck has a small engine problem. Virginia, did you work out how long the boat journey should take?"

"Yes, three to four hours going and five coming back. If we leave at 7:00 PM it'll already be pitch black and we'll have a few hours contingency just in case we're delayed. Coming back will be rough because the sea won't be with us, but I've allowed five hours, which means we should get back to the original embarkation point at about 5:00 AM. It's dark at that time but we'll still have to be careful."

"How will we spot our original starting point?" Karl asked. "It all looks the same along that coastline, and as you said—it'll be dark."

Virginia interrupted, "Ron will leave his hotel at about 4:00 AM and jump on the scrambler and ride to the beach. He'll assemble a flashlight with the automatic timer set to flash orange every ten seconds. He'll then return to the hotel and wait until later in the morning before leaving in the truck. The place is deserted anyway so I doubt anyone will see him or us. We're just being overcautious really."

"Quite," Hugh said. "Now you know what to do and when to do it. What are your biggest concerns with the plan?"

"The sea journey and picking up the cargo are the two things we can't practise," Karl said.

Lordy jumped in. "Getting the boat off the beach and into the sea. It's a heavy boat, if it tips on the beach we're sunk, so to speak. I know we've got the right equipment but it might take longer than we think. If we have to abandon the first attempt, then getting the boat out of the sea and back to the truck will be even harder."

"Virginia, what about you?" Hugh asked.

"Something stupid happening, like the police stopping the truck for some reason and checking the contents."

"Ron, any worries?"

"Similar to Lordy. Reloading the Land Rover and the boat if we miss the first night's rendezvous. The road is near deserted, but you never know who will be passing by at that time. It looks suspicious."

"Henny?"

"Nothing in particular."

Hugh thought for a moment and tried to rationalize their worries. "We can't do anything about the pickup at sea, but you've all practiced a little in the boat. So I don't think there's much more we can do. As for the police stopping you on your way to Port Nolloth . . . just don't exceed the speed limit, and if you are stopped just say that you're going all the way to Windhoek and Swakopmund to drop off the Land Rover and the boat. Virginia and Lordy, you can say that you paid Henny and Ron to ship the stuff on the quiet. The owners don't know about it. Anyway, I'm sure you can think of something.

"Now as far as unloading and reloading the Land Rover is concerned. It only takes two minutes to unload, so I doubt that will be a problem on a deserted road. Reloading takes longer so don't try to reverse it in. Just drive the Land Rover in front first. You can always reverse it in later in a more private spot."

"We're all set then," Karl exclaimed.

"Yes, let's get on with it," Virginia added.

"Oh, one more thing," Hugh added. "Make sure you don't reveal your identities to our shore contacts. They've been told the same. It's better this way, just in case someone gets caught."

Apart from Hugh, everyone spontaneously rose, shook hands, and patted each other. He walked behind the group, avoiding the display of unanimity.

PART TWO

Action Speaks Louder

NINE

Virginia and the team set out in the truck at 3:00 AM, heading north from Cape Town. She expected they would reach the outskirts of Port Nolloth late in the afternoon. Despite the discomfort, all five of them were crammed into the cabin at the beginning of the journey. Virginia looked at their faces and realized that not one of them would consider missing out on any part of the mission. Whether it was talking about the details of the plan, or even exchanging stupid stories from past lives, she knew it was impossible to stifle the energy and enthusiasm of the team.

During a quiet moment Virginia considered her involvement and why Hugh started the mission in the first place. She was lost in her thoughts. *A typical Friday for most people I suppose—wintertime, 1982—but not for the five of us. Why are we doing it? Is it financial gain, revenge, or just for the thrill of participating? I don't think anyone cares anymore. The plan's in motion now and we couldn't stop it even if we wanted to. Hugh triggered the chain of events for his own benefit and he's trying to control everyone involved in the escapade. Hundreds of others will be unwittingly involved in its outcome. I wonder about Hugh sometimes. He thinks all this will happen just as he planned—just like throwing a dice after convincing himself that he's covered the six possible outcomes. If only real life was so simple. There must be a million things that could upset our mission.*

Lordy interrupted her thoughts. "I think I'll buy into a business with my cut."

"Maybe I'll come in with you," Karl added. "What do you have in mind?"

"A small bar or hotel on the coast somewhere. Maybe Durban or somewhere with a large tourist trade. Nothing low-end, mind you. I've had enough of that sort of thing. Maybe a place for married couples with a swimming pool for the kids and a couple of dozen decent suites. It'll have to have a decent restaurant also, so I'll need to find a good chef."

"I'll come in with you, Lordy," Henny said. "I can do all the maintenance and stuff like that. That's no problem for me. If I sell my house and with the money for this job, I could put up 20,000."

"I'll run the bar," Karl added.

"What about you, Virginia?" Lordy said. "You could do all the books and deal with the bankers and the advertising."

"I need to do something with my life. It could be a good start. Maybe we could get a small place up and running quickly and then expand into bigger things. I'm interested and I've still got some money my parents left me. It's just sitting in the bank doing nothing at the moment."

Ron was generally quiet in company but even he became hooked in the general excitement of the idea. "I was a cook for a few years. Nowhere near the level of a chef though, but okay for breakfasts and snacks. I think I could handle the catering if we could get a real chef for the evenings."

"Let's all pledge to make a go of it," Virginia said.

After they made commitments Lordy asked, "What shall we call the place?"

"Don't call it the 'Diamond Motel' for Christ's sake," Karl said.

At 4:00 PM Virginia saw a road sign—Port Nolloth was ten miles away. The road was empty so she told Ron to take over the wheel and drive dead slow. The others went into the back of the truck and prepared for a quick exit. Virginia eagerly scanned for Hugh's marker that had been carved on a rock at the side of the road a year earlier.

They passed through a double "S" bend just as Hugh had told them. There it was, just as she had imagined, the cross and circle scratched on the rock. Ron sounded the horn twice and stopped the truck. Henny ran out and opened the rear cargo doors. Virginia followed and got into the driver's seat of the Land Rover. She waited for Karl and Lordy to pull out the two heavy steel runners and position them on the road. They secured the top section of the runners to the floor of the cargo hold and signaled to Virginia, who edged the Land Rover down the steel runners, pulling the boat and trailer with it. The boat swayed from side to side as the trailer rolled down and met the road. Within four minutes the truck doors were closed and Ron was on his way to Port Nolloth.

Karl joined Virginia in the Land Rover, while Henny and Lordy stood on the deck of the boat, as they started along the track.

After four miles they approached a winding uphill section of the road that passed through a long narrow gorge. Virginia thought that the gorge was probably cut out of the rock when the dirt road was originally built. In places its walls were over thirty feet high.

The Land Rover inched through the first section safely, but the boat was badly scratched and dented by several outcrops of jagged rock. They snaked their way through this piece of the road at two miles per hour.

On a particularly steep, downhill section of the road, Virginia turned her head to check on Lordy and Henny in the rear.

"Stop," she heard Karl scream.

She turned her head back and saw a large boulder ahead directly in the path of the right-side wheels. The Land Rover skidded to a halt just inches from it.

"Lucky we weren't going too fast; that rock would have finished us," she said.

Karl shouted to Henny and Lordy, "Get those sledge hammers down here quick."

They smashed the rock into small pieces, cleared the remnants away, and told Virginia to drive forward slowly.

The next mile passed without problems, but shortly afterwards the wheels of the Land Rover began to lose traction in a patch of loose sand. They spun at high speed, spewing out blue smoke caused by the friction of the hot tires on the sand. The Land Rover and the trailer slipped sideways off the track and stopped, pressed hard against a rock wall.

"Get the shovels out," Karl shouted.

"We'll need the aluminum tracking," Henny shouted back. "I'll get the short pieces."

Karl and Lordy dug out the sand under the Land Rover and wedged a jack under the chassis. Henny pushed a metal plate under the jack to prevent it from digging deeper into the sand. Slowly but surely the wheels rose. They filled in the holes in the sand made by the spinning wheels and placed flexible aluminum runners under them. Karl lowered the jack until the wheels took the weight of the vehicle. "Okay, Virginia, move ahead dead slow."

The Land Rover edged its way forward onto the track. Lordy and Karl ran ahead and laid out the aluminum runners. The whole rig moved ahead another twenty feet across the sand. They repeated this six times until the patch of loose sand was behind them.

"We've used up most of our slack time," Virginia said to the others, "but there's still a little left. And the ground looks firmer up ahead."

Five minutes later Virginia felt a cold sea breeze blowing against her face and she knew they had finally reached the end of the track. One final sharp turn and the sea opened up in front of her eyes.

"There it is," she shouted out of the window, "that's the first hurdle behind us." She heard Lordy and Henny cheer. "The sun's setting so let's just launch the boat. No need to wait for complete darkness."

Virginia uncoupled the Land Rover from the trailer and drove it along the beach about twenty yards to the right where it would be hidden from the seaward direction as well as from anyone inad-vertently using the dirt road. She covered it with a sand-colored tarpaulin and rejoined the others, who were busily laying flexible aluminum treads across the beach to hold the weight of the trailer and boat.

They hammered a steel stake deep into the loose stones on the beach, fitted another four-foot stake on top of it, and hammered that down until it hit bedrock. Karl set up the pulley and ropes and Henny fixed one end of the rope around the stake in the bedrock and Lordy tied the other to the trailer. Karl pulled the ropes through the pulley and the trailer began inching its way over the aluminum treads.

The trailer moved the first twenty feet down the beach. Lordy and Henny repositioned the treads, and Karl hauled it another twenty feet. They repeated this five times before the trailer reached the sea. Karl fell to his knees panting as the others jumped in the sea, attempting to push the boat out.

Virginia struggled to stay upright when the first waves slammed into her legs, but Henny grabbed her under the arms and held her steady. They tried again and again to push the boat the last few feet into the sea, but the waves brushed it back to shore. The fourth attempt failed, leaving the boat parallel to the shoreline. Luckily it tipped towards the shore. In the other direction it would have flooded when the next wave rolled in, and almost certainly sunk.

Karl regained his breath and joined them as Virginia shouted, "Wait for the next big wave to hit and everyone push together. Wait for my signal." A few waves came in but Virginia said nothing.

She saw a large wave approaching, the third one out. The first wave broke, but hardly moved the boat. The second came in, which shifted the boat a few feet and knocked Karl and Lordy into the sea. They quickly recovered after Virginia shouted, "Ready everyone. Let the next one break and wait for my command to push. One . . . two . . . three . . . everyone push."

They screamed and pushed like crazy just as the water gushed back out to sea. The boat righted itself and floated with the outgoing water, but still parallel to the beach.

Henny jumped aboard and started the main engine. The waves pushed the boat towards the shore but it didn't beach. The engine grumbled and spluttered a few times before revving high and gaining enough power to allow Henny to point the bow out to sea.

Virginia put on a wet suit, and with the aid of a guide rope, hauled herself out to the boat. Lordy and Karl tried to pull the trailer out of the sand, in case they needed it for a second attempt, but it was stuck so firmly that after a few minutes of pushing and pulling they gave up.

"Leave it, Lordy, you'll never shift it," Virginia shouted. "Just get the rest of the stuff out the way."

Lordy and Karl gathered up all the other equipment on the beach, ran back to the Land Rover, and shoved it under the tarpaulin. Virginia watched them from the stern of the boat as they carried the petrol cans from the Land Rover to the edge of the beach. Lordy threw out a rope to Virginia and told her to pull the petrol cans onboard. She hauled each can across the surf and hoisted them onto the deck, stowing them safely behind the cabin with the aid of ropes and some preset wooden forms nailed to the deck.

When all the cans were aboard, Karl and Lordy pulled themselves from the beach onto the boat using the guide rope and started the outboard engines. When both outboards and the main engine were purring away Henny filled the additional fuel tank with petrol from the cans and lashed four spare cans of diesel fuel to the deck, ready to refill the main engine's tank later in the journey.

Virginia set the compass due west and kept that course for forty-five minutes before turning due north. The sea was much rougher than she had expected, and the bone chilling combination of a roaring westerly wind biting into wet clothes made conditions unbearable. Even wetsuits over their normal clothes didn't keep the cold at bay. Henny and Karl vomited uncontrollably and could do nothing but hold onto the safety bars around the outside of the cabin.

Virginia steered the boat according to the compass as best she could, with Lordy doing his best to help by shining a flashlight on the controls. The heater inside the cabin shorted out and the overhead light was too dim to be of use. Seawater washed around their feet as the boat was tossed in the six-foot swell. The boat listed forty-five degrees in the merciless westerly wind, and after she realized that they were being blown towards the shore she adjusted the rudder to compensate, but it was at the expense of speed in the northerly direction. She struggled to keep control of the vessel as the spray thrown up by the wind and the breaking waves cut her visibility almost to zero.

"We're taking on too much water—it's flooding the engine," Lordy shouted to Virginia. "The electric pump's fucked."

"Try to bail it," she shouted back.

"Okay, I'll bail it from the engine compartment."

"Give Lordy a hand," Virginia shouted at Karl and Henny, as Lordy braved the deck. But they were still retching constantly and were useless.

A huge wave washed across the boat and hurled everyone to the deck. Virginia punched and kicked to free herself from the tangle of arms and legs, but the boat tipped to the port side and the three intermeshed bodies slid back across the deck. She watched helplessly as the cabin wall rushed towards her. The top of her head rammed into a wooden strut and every-thing went quiet. The cabin spun violently. She felt liquid pour over her head, and then stupefying numbness. *My head's split open*, she thought. *Blood everywhere.* She gasped, freed her hands and felt her head. *It's water not blood, my skull's not cracked—thank god.*

The freezing water, enveloping her body and filling her mouth, soon brought her round. She pulled herself up, spat out the water, and grabbed the wheel. "Come on. Get up and take the wheel. I need to help Lordy."

To her surprise both Henny and Karl dragged themselves up from the deck. Henny took the wheel and Karl staggered out of the cabin. Virginia followed him.

"Where's Lordy?" Karl screamed.

"He must have gone overboard," Virginia shouted back.

Karl screamed, "Lordy, Lordy, where are you? Virginia, stop the boat! We have to find Lordy."

He rushed to the stern and looked overboard for signs of Lordy. "He's gone, he's gone." Karl struggled to the port side, desper-ately searching for Lordy. Another huge wave hurled the boat into the air. It threw Karl across the deck, straight into the fuel tank. Virginia tried to grab him, but he was too heavy, and he slid back across the heaving deck.

She looked up and saw Lordy's head appear above another wave just as it hit the boat. A surge of water crossed the deck carrying

Lordy with it. He grabbed hold of Karl's leg and the two of them held on for dear life.

"Where did you come from you fucking English idiot?" Virginia heard Karl shout.

"Got washed over with that first wave and back again with the second," Lordy screamed. "The boat went in a circle. I couldn't swim; I just grabbed the side."

Virginia helped pull Karl and Lordy back into the cabin. "Stay inside. It's pointless trying to bail water out."

Wave after wave heaved the hapless vessel over ten feet in the air and then down again into the next waiting trough. Water was everywhere. It smashed out the windows in the cabin and sent shattered glass across the deck. All Virginia could do was keep the boat pointing in the right direction.

"It can't get much worse than this can it?" Lordy screamed.

"Who knows?" Virginia shouted back.

"Turn the boat into the wind and the waves for a while," Henny shouted, "maybe we'll take on less water."

Virginia steered the boat to port to face the wind and current. They all gasped as an enormous wall of water came towards them. Everyone clutched a piece of the cabin and waited for the inevitable. The sea heaved the boat upwards; then down into what looked like a bottomless pit created by the trough of the wave; up again as the next wave hit, and then down again. They were dashed against the walls of the cabin like puppets, awaiting whatever fate the elements would bring.

Karl began to sing at the top of his voice to distract himself from what he thought was certain oblivion. One by one they joined in until all four of them were screaming at the tops of their voices like maniacs in Bedlam.

They endured another twenty minutes of hell before the swell reduced to about four feet and the wind dropped off. Virginia took this relative improvement in their plight to turn the boat back to its original course. Lordy bailed out the bulk of the water from the engine compartment, but the main engine had lost much of its power. However, the two outboards were purring away, unworried by the elements.

"What's that light bobbing up and down over there?" Karl shouted.

Virginia and Lordy stretched to see. As they did, a light beam from a searchlight passed over the boat.

"Cut the engines, quick."

Henny charged to the stern and set the outboards to idle.

"What is it?"

"Patrol boat, must be."

"Lordy get the grenade launcher ready," Karl ordered.

"Go see what it is Lordy," Virginia shouted.

Lordy climbed on the cabin roof to try to identify the source of the light. He popped his head down into the cabin a few seconds later. "Virginia, Karl, arm yourselves. Another boat coming straight for us."

Lordy climbed back on the cabin roof while Karl and Henny waited inside. No one spoke. The low booming sound of a diesel engine filled the cabin. Lordy's head popped down from the cabin roof again.

"It's a fishing boat."

"Have they seen us?"

"Must have."

"Okay, when they come alongside let 'em have the grenades," Karl said.

Virginia saw two men on the port side of the approaching vessel. They threw ropes over to the boat and someone up above them shone the searchlights directly into the cabin. Virginia shielded her eyes from the light. She heard shouts but could not understand what was being said. She felt a bump as the fishing vessel touched them, side on side. Then came the noise of the first explosion; and the second; and the third. Lordy had hurled the grenades from the cabin roof. Karl and Henny took turns throwing their grenades out of the cabin's side window.

"Follow them, Virginia, we have to sink them," Karl shouted.

The fishing vessel's engine cut out suddenly. Karl and Henny threw the last grenades and ran to the stern to start the outboards.

Virginia hovered around the fishing vessel, but the loss of engine power and the strong current made it difficult. Karl threw one of the spare cans of fuel onto the deck of the fishing boat. It punctured as it hit the rigging but did not ignite.

"Did you see what happened to them?" Lordy shouted, as he dashed into the cabin.

"Take the wheel," Virginia said to Lordy. She pulled her handgun and went outside onto the deck. When the fishing boat was no more than a yard away she leaped across. She grabbed a handrail, pulled herself alongside the boat, and went into the main cabin.

It was filled with smoke and impossible for her to see anything. She was about to give up the search, but the boat suddenly turned about and the smoke inside the cabin cleared. A small light on the wall was enough for her to find her way around. She stepped past two bodies in the cabin and began checking the other compartments. An open door at the end of the cabin banged against the wall with the movement of the boat. Virginia saw that it led down a flight of stairs to the engine compartment. She looked down and saw a man's legs at the bottom jerking uncontrollably, as if their owner was in shock. A flashlight rolled backwards and forwards next to the legs, illuminating the stairway. She jumped to the bottom of the steps, picked up the flashlight, and shone the light into the man's face. He was a colored fisherman, barely alive.

"We try to help you," he muttered. "Why?"

Virginia held the fisherman's head in her hands. "Sorry." She wiped her eyes and looked away.

She could see that one of the grenades had not only damaged his legs but also had also torn open his stomach. The smell of his flesh, the smoke, and dead fish made her feel sick. When she regained her composure, she noticed water flowing into the engine room. A couple of scans with the flashlight revealed a large hole below the waterline. It was only a matter of time before the vessel went under.

She began to climb back up the stairs but stopped when she heard the fisherman groan. Virginia turned around and looked at him. *I can't just leave the poor bastard,* she thought. Two short, loud cracks from the handgun and it was all over.

She went on deck and waited for Lordy to bring the boat alongside.

"Anyone left alive?" Lordy asked, as Virginia jumped on board.

"No—all killed by the grenades. Their boat's holed under the waterline. It'll sink soon."

For the next four hours they made good progress in a much friendlier sea. Visibility had improved enough for Virginia to notice the distant lights from the township of Alexander Bay on the starboard side.

"We've come about sixty miles," she shouted. "See those lights over there."

Everyone cheered and continued bailing water. They were at last beginning to control their environment.

"How far offshore are we?" Karl asked Virginia.

"About five miles. We've drifted towards the shore quite a bit."

"About an hour to go then," Henny said.

"Just about," Virginia replied. "Everyone keep your eyes open for the next cluster of lights. That'll be the first processing plant."

As she finished speaking the main engine grumbled and cut out. It was impossible to even attempt to fix the problem because of the lack of light and the pitching of the boat. Henny staggered over to the two outboard engines and turned the throttle controls on each one to the maximum position. A week earlier he had attempted to run cables from the outboards to the cabin, so that the throttle settings could be controlled centrally, but he gave up due to lack of time.

Although the outboards were working at the highest speed possible for this type of engine, they still did not compensate fully for the loss of power in the main engine.

"I hope those outboards don't overheat," Henny shouted. "They're going at full revs."

"There's the first processing plant," Virginia shouted, pointing to the distant lights. "Ten minutes to go before the pickup. Get the ropes and the life jackets ready."

Lordy and Henny untied the equipment stowed on top of the cabin, ready for the pickup.

Five minutes passed and the lights of the second plant were clear and unmistakable. Judging when they about halfway between the first and second cluster of lights, Virginia turned the boat towards the shore.

Lordy and Henny climbed halfway up the sides of the cabin hoping to catch sight of the flashing signal lights they were expecting. It was difficult for Lordy and Henny to remain in those positions, so Virginia told Karl to relieve them.

"There it is," Karl shouted down.

Everyone yelled with excitement. Virginia zeroed-in on the flashing lights and made a slight adjustment to their course. When they were about fifty yards from the shore she turned the boat so it was pointing out to sea. Henny put the two outboard engines in reverse and they slowly backed into the shore. It was a difficult maneuver because Virginia had no control over the throttle setting of the engines. Henny took control of one, while Karl took the other, as they tried to synchronize the speed and position of the boat with Virginia. This left Lordy to handle the loading of the cases of diamonds single-handed.

On the beach, tucked behind a small outcrop of rocks, Gavin and Ivan lay hidden from view. Only the flashing light could reveal their position from the seaward direction.

Hours earlier, Gavin had left home for an unnecessary night shift. He picked up Ivan in the town and drove out to B-Plant. They headed straight to the main storage warehouse where Gavin emptied a small bottle of gasoline over one of the wooden pallets. He ignited it and quickly left with Ivan. Fifteen minutes later the alarms sounded.

"Fire emergency!" one of the other security guards said to Gavin.

"What's the problem then?" Gavin asked, feigning surprise.

"A fire in the store room. The fire safety people are there now. The whole place has gone up."

Gavin and Ivan rushed out of the office. "Let's drive over and get the stuff," Gavin said to Ivan.

They drove to the road connecting A and B plants and stopped at the abandoned buildings. It was pitch black. Gavin didn't see any headlights behind or in front of them, so he turned off the road, cut the headlights, and steered towards the buildings.

They parked the jeep out of sight and went into the buildings. Ivan used a crowbar, which he had hidden a week before along with a flashlight, to pull up the wooden floorboards covering the hiding place. They dragged out a dozen small sacks and carried them out to the jeep. Gavin picked up the flashlight on the way out and double-checked the batteries. He placed everything under the back seat of the jeep and set off over the sandy ground between the abandoned buildings and the shoreline. Gavin checked his watch. It was 10:30 PM.

They hid the jeep behind a small hill about 200 yards from the shoreline and walked to the beach, each carrying half of the sacks of diamonds in backpacks. When they were about halfway Ivan stopped dead in his tracks. "Stop, listen. Do you hear that noise?"

"No, what is it?" Gavin asked.

They both dropped to the ground. Even above the monotonous drone of the processing plants they could hear voices nearby. Gavin focused on the voices, attempting to negate the effects of the constant drone.

"Sounds like Ovambos," Ivan said in an excited whisper.

"Yes, you're right and they sound drunk," Gavin replied in the same tone.

"What the hell are they doing here?"

"They're probably mine laborers, Ovambo bedrock sweepers I would guess, skiving off from their shift for the night."

"What'll we do?"

"Let's take a closer look. Leave the sacks here."

They crept nearer to where the voices appeared to come from and listened. A few seconds passed and the shifting clouds allowed the moon to illuminate the source of the mysterious voices.

"Ovambo workers, definitely, Ivan."

"They're blind drunk by the looks of them."

"Let's just ignore them. I don't think they'll be conscious for long. Did you see all those empties?"

"Okay, let's go."

They hurried back to collect the diamonds and then made for

the shoreline, where Gavin located a rocky outcrop about four feet above sea level. They waited for 11:00 PM, lying flat on their stomachs with the diamonds and the flashlight at their sides. Gavin checked his watch constantly and at exactly 11:00 PM he began to signal using the pre-arranged sequence.

The boat backed slowly towards the shoreline. When it was twenty yards out Lordy threw a rope to the two anonymous figures waiting on the beach.

"Put the stuff inside the steel case and throw the rope back."

The case had three compartments, two were airtight and the third was large enough to take around twenty pounds of diamonds. It was tied to a life preserver to give it more buoyancy.

Lordy watched the two animated figures grab the steel case and stuff bags inside.

"Catch the rope," a voice shouted from the beach.

Lordy caught the rope, hauled it back to the boat, opened the case, and placed the bags in a larger container inside the cabin. He repeated the whole maneuver three times, while Karl and Henny constantly alternated the outboard motor controls from forward to reverse, to keep the boat in position.

Lordy caught the rope for the fifth and last time. As he began to pull it, a large wave lifted the boat upwards and to the left. Lordy was thrown on his side and the rope slipped from his grip. He jumped up and grabbed at the end, but again it slipped from his grasp and the metal case and life preserver floated away in the surf. He stood flabbergasted as almost 5,000,000 rand's worth of diamonds bobbed up and down in the sea, just out of his reach.

Henny didn't wait to be told. Lordy watched as he dived straight into the sea and swam towards the life preserver and the case of diamonds. Lordy followed his movements in the sea with a flashlight. Henny's strong arms plowed through the surf at first, but they were no match for this sea. He grabbed the rope but the surf tossed him over and over. Lordy was about to dive into the sea when the boat suddenly turned sideways, knocking him to the deck. Karl's outboard had cut out, and now the boat pointed in the wrong direction to help Henny.

In a final, desperate act, Henny thrashed towards the shore with the rope between his teeth. With only ten yards to go he suddenly disappeared from Lordy's view. Several seconds later he reappeared, coughing and expelling seawater, but still holding the rope, which he had coiled in several loops.

"Here it is," Henny screamed as he hurled the coiled rope towards the shore.

"Swim, swim," Lordy screamed at Henny. But nothing could save him. Lordy stood helpless as the undercurrent sucked Henny beneath the surface. He charged around the deck frantically searching for the slightest sign of Henny's presence.

One of the men on the shore shouted at Lordy, splashed into the sea up to his waist, clutched the rope, and pulled the case of diamonds back to the beach.

Lordy heard Karl scream, "I've restarted the outboard."

Virginia shouted back, "I'll circle around and look for him."

Lordy saw the two men running along the beach with a flashlight, obviously trying to find Henny, but after a few minutes they gave up searching and stood motionless on the beach.

Lordy knew it was hopeless but he urged Virginia to keep looking. She circled the area three more times before Lordy finally accepted Henny was gone for good.

"Back the boat into the shore," he shouted to her.

Lordy caught the rope and hauled in the last batch of diamonds.

The two groups never exchanged a word of greeting or farewell. They just left to return to their own domains, accepting that the elements had won a partial victory.

One of the outboard engines overheated and stalled again. Now with only one outboard working, albeit at full power, the boat just chugged back out to sea, fighting the relentless current and gusting wind.

"We'll never make it back against this current," Virginia yelled. "We can hardly move now, and we're running in parallel with it, let alone when we turn south."

Karl and Lordy agreed.

"We're taking on more water too," Lordy said in desperation. "It's hopeless."

"Let's turn northwest and follow the coast line as best we can —the tide and the wind will help us," Karl said. "Try to pass the diamond area and maybe we can struggle into Luderitz."

"I don't think we'll make it that far," Virginia said, "and there's nothing in between—no towns, no fishing villages or people. So it's give up or take a long shot to the north."

Lordy grabbed the wheel. "I'm not giving up. Twenty years behind bars is not for me."

They all agreed to go northwest and hope that the long shot would pay off. After the discussion, Virginia carefully sealed the diamonds in two long watertight containers, tied polystyrene around them, and placed them into sturdy backpacks. They weighed about sixty-five pounds each, and to be sure they would float she attached them to two spare life preservers.

She took over the controls from Lordy and turned the boat due west, to get as far from the shore as possible. It took almost two hours for the boat to push five miles through the sea. Karl turned the outboard down to half power and Virginia pointed the boat northwest.

The sea calmed considerably and they were at last able to eat some damp sandwiches and drink a little tepid coffee. After Henny's demise, seasickness and discomfort were too embarrassing even to contemplate.

Dawn was upon them before they realized it. None of them could sleep, especially Karl, whose intermittent bouts of sickness added to his misery. They drank the last dregs of coffee from the thermos and awaited their fate.

"We've got enough fuel for about three hours," Virginia said, "then the tide will drive us into the shore."

"Any idea where we are?" Karl asked.

"Well," Virginia replied, "it's six-o-clock now, and we started from the pickup point at about midnight. So based on what I remember . . . the rate the tide runs, plus five miles an hour this engine can manage . . . comes to sixty miles. With fuel for another two hours I think we'll hit land in the middle of nowhere. It's seventy-five miles from Luderitz and about double that to get back to our starting point. With the water and food we have I doubt we'll last two days."

"Thank god it's wintertime otherwise the heat would finish us off even quicker," Lordy added with a fatalistic twist.

"I wonder where Henny is?" Karl asked. "I mean where his body is?"

"Doesn't pay to dwell, Karl," Lordy replied.

"I know, but we all made plans, almost a pact, and now it wouldn't be the same."

"Do you remember that dog I had a few years ago? That Labrador, the black one?" Lordy asked Karl.

"Yes, the one that kept following you around."

"When he died I actually cried. It was the first time I'd done that since I was at Eton. I felt worse than that when Henny went overboard, but I couldn't bring myself to weep. It was the same feeling in my stomach though."

Virginia stepped in and said, "Hey, come on you two. Any more of that and I'll get my fucking violin out and play the funeral march."

They pulled themselves together and began focusing on their plight again.

It was 8:00 AM and the sea had calmed to a gentle roll, with the sun's rays warming their bodies for the first time in twelve hours.

Lordy jumped up. "Look over there. I can see land. It can't be more than a few miles."

"We might as well steer towards the shore while we still have some fuel and try to land gracefully," Virginia said.

After Karl and Lordy agreed she turned the boat eastward and hoped for the best. An hour later they found themselves less than fifty yards from the shore. It was an ominous looking welcome.

The coastline was riddled with low-lying, evil-looking rocks that had been constantly punished by the large breaking waves. They looked at each other with foreboding as they fastened their life jackets and stuffed the leftover supplies in the backpacks.

Virginia and Lordy stood at the bow waiting to jump, while Karl was at the rear of the boat, revving the engine as high as he could.

An enormous crunching sound reverberated in the air when the bow hit rock below the waterline, followed by a jolt from the rear caused by a breaking wave. They were thrown forward violently by the first blow. Lordy and Virginia were hurled onto the slippery rocks. Virginia was washed back into the sea, but fortunately another wave threw her onto a flat piece of rock, and she escaped more serious punishment. She stood and watched helplessly as the force of the next wave knocked Karl to the stern. He tried to get up but the water washing back over the deck threw him down again. Lordy scrambled over the rocks unhurt, still grasping the ropes attached to the diamonds.

Virginia saw that Karl was stunned and was not making any attempt reach the shore. When the deck started to crumble she screamed at Karl to jump. He moved to the side of the boat but then suddenly froze.

Lordy began shouting at him. "Karl! Throw that rope over to me. Karl! Throw that rope over quickly."

"He's knocked senseless," Virginia shouted to Lordy.

The cold water seemed to bring Karl back to his senses. He grabbed the rope tied to one of the backpacks and threw it to Lordy.

"Jump in, Karl, now! Jump in. I'll pull you ashore."

Virginia held her breath as Karl took the plunge and swam wildly towards the rocks. Luck had it that he clambered ashore, unharmed by the breaking waves.

They all lay prostrate on the barren soil, with the rocks transformed from an enemy into a friendly barrier keeping the violent sea at bay. Virginia looked inland over the flat semi-desert landscape but could see no signs of life or any landmarks to give them even a clue to their whereabouts. The sea crashing on the rocks was the only noise and movement. Everything else was deadly still and desolate.

"Okay, let's see what supplies we have left," she said, breaking into their despair.

"Two handguns with ammunition, a compass, four quarts of water, six cans of meatballs, five-hundred rand in cash, and a wet blanket," Lordy announced.

Virginia reeled off her possessions. "I've got some maps, powdered milk, a spare wet suit, a box of matches, and some packets of porridge. Oh, and a transistor radio that still seems to work."

"Not much to live on," Karl lamented.

"We've no idea how far the boat drifted up the coastline so we can only guess which direction to go."

Lordy piped up, "I've just remembered. There's an old ghost town along this coast somewhere. The miners abandoned it in the twenties. It's called Elizabeth Bay. I read about it a few years ago."

"So!" Virginia snapped.

"Apparently a travel company brings tourists overland to visit the place. They camp out and pretend they're roughing it."

"Oh, I see."

"Maybe, just maybe, if we find the place, they'll be some leftover food and water for us to scavenge. Failing that, we got a seventy-five mile walk to Luderitz on a couple pints of water each."

"Trouble is we don't know which direction it's in," Karl added.

"I think it was nearer Luderitz than the diamond mine, so I think we should head north along the coast," Lordy said.

"We have to try something," Karl said. "We can't even give ourselves up. There's nobody to surrender to."

They spread the load out evenly and began the trek north. The ground was dusty but firm, so walking was not too difficult, and they managed a decent three miles per hour. Cool winds from the sea made the temperature pleasant even though the sun, still strong in the wintertime, beat down on them constantly. The landscape remained flat and boring with only distant visions of mountains, twenty to thirty miles inland, to break the monotony. A few shipwrecked hulks along the coast reminded Virginia of a fate that could easily have been her own, if luck had not smiled upon them.

Four hours passed before they took a brief break to drink some water and share a can of meatballs. Virginia noticed that Karl was suffering badly. She assumed he'd lost a lot of fluid during his bouts of seasickness, so without mentioning anything she allowed him extra water to compensate.

The sun began to drop and still no sign of Elizabeth Bay, only merciless flat and dry land. Virginia knew that eight hours of walking in these circumstances would exhaust the fittest of humans, but they had to keep going. There was no other choice.

"Let's camp here," Karl suggested, pointing to a convenient ridge in the otherwise flat ground, "That should shield us from the cold wind during the night."

Lordy found a chocolate bar in his backpack, which he proceeded to share with Virginia and Karl, and apart from tasting a little of the sea, they all found it refreshing.

Virginia mixed some of the powdered milk with water and handed it out, to each in turn, in the only cup they had. Five minutes passed and they were all unconscious, huddled together in a deep sleep with a blanket wrapped around them, Virginia flanked by Lordy and Karl.

TEN

*R*on returned with the truck to the pre-arranged meeting place at precisely the agreed time on Sunday morning. Since the team was not there he decided to return to Port Nolloth and wait, as planned.

However, he had a gut feeling that something was wrong, so later in the day he returned to the beach area on his scrambling bike. His signal light still flashed away, but there was no evidence of anyone else having been there. He checked the Land Rover, and again, no sign of anything disturbed. He reasoned that they had obviously started the mission, and since there was no fog in the past twenty-four hours, they must either have landed in the wrong place on their return, or they had been captured, or possibly had an accident at sea.

He drove along the beach, first to the north and then to the south, to look for any signs of the missing party. Using powerful binoculars he scanned the coastline for miles in either direction but did not find a single trace of the team's presence. After three hours he returned to the hotel in Port Nolloth and left a message for Hugh, via a special telephone answering service that was only to be used in dire emergencies.

Five minutes later Ron's phone rang.

"What's the problem?" Hugh asked.

"No sign of the boat or the team. They left but didn't return. I checked earlier."

"The stuff was handed over last night around midnight. They must have landed somewhere else. Maybe there's been an accident."

"What shall I do now?"

"Return to the embarkation point later tonight and again tomorrow. If you don't see anything dump the truck, pick up the Land Rover, and proceed to Springbok. Stay in the hotel there until I contact you. If they didn't go down at sea then they're probably washed up along the shore somewhere."

Ron could not locate the team so he drove back to Springbok and checked in to the hotel.

Hugh was actually in Steinkop staying at a small guesthouse, waiting for one of the action team to contact him. He had become very edgy and angry because he'd heard nothing. Since Gavin had told him that the pickup had been successful, one of the team member's fate aside, he assumed that everything had gone well and the team would contact him on Sunday. He was totally untroubled about the one that had drowned as he considered it one less person on the payroll.

Hugh at first suspected treachery, assuming that the team had absconded with the diamonds. Was Ron lying? Did the team exclude Ron? He made contingency plans, thought about what revenge he would exact on them, and worried himself sick about his financial problems.

After four hours he calmed down and came to the conclusion that he was being paranoid. He decided to wait for a day and if nothing more was known he would travel to the embarkation point and see if Ron's story was true.

Hugh called Susan to see if anyone had contacted her. She told him that Chris Conway had made several attempts to reach him on Sunday to find out why he had not been contacted and to see if he should still meet Hugh on Sunday evening as arranged. Susan told Hugh that she pretended to know nothing about what was in progress when she spoke to Chris.

Hugh finally called Chris at his home on Monday at 6:00 AM. He didn't want to sound alarmist or appear incompetent, so he merely said that there had been a small delay and he would let him know the new date and time in about a week. Chris seemed to accept this without question.

At about the same time Karl, Lordy, and Virginia were awakened by the morning sun shining in their faces. They had slept heavily and without interruption throughout the night. They drank some more of their precious water and demolished another can of meatballs.

Virginia walked to a high point fifty yards away and looked into the distance. She could see the mountains to the east quite clearly and to her right, monotonous, barren land stretching to the horizon. She looked north and saw a large bay about ten miles distant with a number of dots neatly aligned in rows and columns situated near the coastline.

"Hey, Karl, Lordy, quick! Come and see what I've found."

They rushed up to Virginia and danced around like idiots when they realized it was Elizabeth Bay.

"Can't be more than ten miles away," Karl shouted.

"Let's get going then."

"Be careful in case any tourists are about," Lordy added with caution.

"How often do you think they show up then, Lordy?" Virginia asked. "Do you remember?"

"I think the travel outfit brings a party from Luderitz every two weeks. They use the old ghost town as a base to go on sight-seeing trips."

"Not much to see," Karl added dryly.

"There's the shipwrecks along the coast and some wildlife if you know where to look; even whale watching in some of the bays —things like that. You can sometimes spot groups of Bushmen too. I don't know how they live in a place like this."

"Look at this map," Virginia said. "One thing's for sure, we must have drifted a lot further than I thought if that's Elizabeth Bay. It must have been almost 100 miles. The outboard was a lot more effective than we thought."

"True, but it wouldn't have got us back to Port Nolloth in that wicked current," Lordy said.

They set out eagerly for Elizabeth Bay and after three hours reached the outskirts of the town. Virginia thought it was eerie to see hundreds of dilapidated houses lined up neatly with piles of sand encroaching on their walls, and not a soul in sight.

They broke out a boarded-up window in one of the houses and looked inside. Everything was dry. It even smelled dry and what paint there had been on the walls was long gone, fallen to the floor and mixed with sand that had blown inside over the years. A lone wooden table stood in the middle of the room. It seemed hardly able to keep itself upright let alone support the weight of even a dinner plate.

"I wonder who lived here," Lordy said as he pulled his head away from the window. "We're probably the first people to look in here for sixty or seventy years."

"Must have been a hard life back then," Virginia said. "How did they mine the diamonds? I don't see any signs of old processing plants or rusted equipment."

Lordy was waiting to be asked. "Basically they got hundreds of black workers to lie face down in the sand in the mornings and evenings and look directly into the sun. When they saw a sparkle in the sand caused by sunlight reflecting from a diamond they would pick it up, put it in a bag, and continue crawling forward. Most of them went blind after a while. Terrible when you think of it now.

"Some of the miners used seawater to wash the sand and earth away leaving the diamonds and other dense materials behind. All very good for the high yielding areas, but when that ran out it wasn't economical to mine like that anymore. Oh well, so much for the mining history lesson. Let's go to that big building over there. It looks less shabby than these houses."

They walked along what was obviously once a main street when the town was inhabited. Virginia was amazed that the buildings were still in place after such a long time, and thought the strangest thing was that all the houses were in a similar state of disrepair, as if everyone left at the same time.

Their walk ended when they reached a large barn-like building at the end of the main street. Karl noticed a side door that had a new lock fitted to it, so he went to investigate. Lordy opened the main door at the front and walked inside with Virginia. Apart from the fact that the building had been cleaned thoroughly, the first thing that caught Virginia's eye was a neatly placed row of about forty suitcases along the wall, positioned next to a locked door. As they began to investigate, Karl came running in the front door, out of breath.

"Fresh tire marks in the sand at the back of the building. Two or three trucks probably. They can't be more than a few hours old. I saw two tents as well. Those big bell-shaped things."

"Anyone around?" Virginia asked.

"No, seems to be deserted."

"Must be one of those tourist groups," Karl said. "I suppose they've dumped their gear here and gone off sightseeing."

"What's in that locked room?" Virginia asked. "Force the door open."

Lordy picked the lock and opened the door to reveal a small office with a desk in the corner. There was a cabinet next to the desk, with a few papers and tourist brochures strewn over it, and a briefcase wedged between it and the desk stuffed full of files and correspondence.

Virginia read through the files and concluded that a tour guide by the name of Julie Wood was the owner and she was escorting about twenty people on an adventure vacation. They planned to stay in Elizabeth Bay for one night before returning to Luderitz.

"They must have food and drink with them if they're staying overnight," Virginia said, "Check those tents and the rest of this building."

Lordy ran off while Virginia kept on reading through the litera-
ture in the office. They reassembled in the office and took stock of
their situation.

Lordy piped up first. "There's plenty of canned food and water in
plastic containers in the tents; cooking equipment to. They must
have just left it, assuming no one else would be crazy enough to
show up here."

"Yes, but the problem is, if we take it they'll report it to the police
when they get back to Luderitz," Virginia said. "Or maybe they
have a short wave radio, which would be even worse for us."

They all thought for a few minutes until Virginia broke the
silence. "I've got an idea. It looks like there are two ways out of
this mess. Number one—take them all hostage when they return
and then drive off with one of the trucks. That would work but we
would have broken Hugh's golden rule for this mission, which is
to get out unnoticed. Plus, someone might come looking if they're
not back in Luderitz tomorrow.

"The second idea is much more subtle. Hear me out before
you cast judgement. I noticed that our Miss Wood does all her
paperwork and correspondence while she's on tour. It's all over
her briefcase; you can see for yourselves. Now, we need to contact
Hugh to tell him the diamonds are safe but he needs to come and
rescue us. So what I propose is to write a letter to Hugh's address
telling him where and when to get us, and just put it in with her
letters and the tourists' postcards. She must be planning to post
them in Luderitz while the tourists move on to the Etosha Game
Park. I've checked the itinerary. That's what she appears to be
doing next.

"If she posts them tomorrow night, Hugh will get the letter on
Saturday. That gives him seven days to reach us, because according
to Miss Wood's upcoming plans, the next group will arrive here
one week from Sunday."

"What if she doesn't post them or Hugh doesn't get the letter?"
Lordy asked.

"If the next tourist group arrives one week from Sunday and
there's no sign of Hugh, then we opt for the first plan and take one
of their trucks."

"What about food?" Lordy asked. "We don't have any. If we steal their food they'll be suspicious and inform the police."

"What about Bushmen?" Karl added. "If we make it look like a band of Bushmen stole the food and water they might just forget the whole thing and put it down to bad luck. The police would never try to chase after them."

"Good idea," Lordy interjected. "We'll mess up the tent a bit, throw some of the food around, and pretend they just had a feast and left. Make it look like a dog's dinner. Leave all the fancy stuff and any equipment because the Bushmen would never know what to do with it.

"Virginia, you write the letter. Better put it into some sort of code just in case someone gets suspicious and reads it."

"Okay, I'll get going," she said, "but what about the postage stamps?"

"Take a stamp from one of the other letters and put it on ours," Lordy suggested. "I'm a half-decent forger."

"Wait a minute," Karl interjected. "Why don't we tamper with one of their vehicles tonight, while they're asleep. So they'll have to leave it behind. I mean, keep on with this plan, but if it doesn't work we can use it to get out."

"Makes sense to me," Virginia said, "but make sure you're not noticed. They might post a guard after all their food has been swiped."

They ran off to collect the food and mess up the tents. Virginia deliberately opened some of the cans with a screwdriver she found in the tent and threw the food around to make it look good. Karl emptied the other cans into plastic bags for their own consumption later in the week.

Virginia wrote the letter to Hugh.

> *Dear H.*
>
> *Having a great time in Elizabeth Bay. The people with Advent Tours are really great guides and very knowledgeable. I hope you can join the next tour group, which leaves Luderitz on Sunday 21st. The earlier sea journey was a bit difficult but all of our baggage is safe. Sleeping is a bit*

rough here but enough food to go around. Hope to see you
before Sunday.
Love V.
   P.S. I hope you managed to get the advertisement for your
new business on Radio Southwest. I'll listen every evening
after six in the hope of hearing it.

Lordy removed a postage stamp from one of the tourist's letters
and stuck it on the letter to Hugh. He did this with remarkable
ease and passed the finished article to Virginia, who placed it in
the middle of the pile of letters. She then proceeded to replace
everything in the office back to its original state.

"I've just thought of something," Karl said suddenly.

"What?" Virginia asked.

"Footprints. They'll notice our footprints in the loose sand inside
the tents. Bushmen are tiny; our feet are huge. The tour guides or
drivers might notice."

"Okay, we need to smooth over the ground and make small footprints, hundreds of them, so it looks like a feeding frenzy," Lordy
said.

"Break off some of that rotten wood over there and use the screwdriver to gouge out a small foot with toes – better make a left and
a right foot," Virginia said laughing.

Karl went to work and quickly made two crude foot shapes, and
with some practice in the sand he produced a passable footprint.

"Okay," Karl said, "let's find a hiding place for tonight. When it
gets dark we'll pick a vehicle to doctor."

The trio checked everything once again and then began looking
for a suitable hiding place. They chose a house on an elevated
part of the town about 100 yards from the main building, which
provided a good view of the town and the tourists' tents, plus did
not stand out from any of the other houses. They stored their food
and belongings and waited for the return of the visitors.

Virginia and Lordy looked around the one-storey house and

familiarized themselves with the various views provided by the decaying windows. In one of the rooms a wooden frame that resembled the leftovers of a bed sat awkwardly in the corner. Lordy kicked it aside and examined the contents of a closet blocked by the bed-frame.

"Shit!" Lordy screamed as he fell back into Virginia. The door fell from its hinges, revealing a human skeleton.

"Quick, come and look at this," Virginia shouted to Karl.

Karl ran into the room. "My God, it must have been here for decades."

"Look at this," Virginia said, pointing to a knife tangled in the ribs of the skeleton. "Whoever it was met a sticky end."

"Hard to say," Lordy added. "I think insects feasted on the flesh a long time ago—or maybe rats. Strange—no remnants of clothing around. Do you think clothing would disintegrate completely like this?"

"Unlikely," Virginia replied, "looks like someone took the clothes after he was killed."

"The knife wouldn't be in that position if someone stripped the clothes off," Karl said.

"True," Lordy replied. "I'll look over the rest of the place to see what other mysteries this old house holds."

Virginia picked the knife out of the skeleton's ribs and put in her pocket. "I'll take this for a keepsake," she said. "You never know when things like this come in handy. I'm surprised it's still in such good condition."

Lordy added, "It reminds me of my old Uncle Wainwright. His wife murdered him thirty years ago. She stuffed his body inside a huge grandfather clock and dumped it in the attic of their mansion. No one could workout how she dragged the old lush up there."

"Did the police catch her?" Karl asked.

"No. She died ten years later. When the staff cleared out the mansion they found his decomposed body."

"How did they know she killed him?" Virginia asked.

"She left one pound sterling in her will to 'The miserable old bastard in the clock'. The police in their lightning fast way put two and two together."

"Funny family you come from Lordy," Karl added, "every time something unusual happens you come out with one of these stories about your relatives."

"That's the upper classes, you see. They like to be eccentric."

Lordy finished searching the house but found nothing else of interest. Karl checked the attic space and uncovered a wooden chest filled with books, personal effects, and papers. He began pulling the box across the attic, but the box fell through the ceiling, spilling the contents across the floor.

"Leave it for later, Karl, it looks like junk," Lordy said to Karl when he saw the mess strewn across the sand-covered floorboards.

Virginia climbed into the attic and then on to the shaky roof. "I'll keep a lookout for a while, just in case they return," she shouted down.

About an hour before sundown Virginia saw dust rising in the distance and shortly afterwards heard the sound of motor engines gradually coming closer. Four vehicles approached in procession —a twelve-seat Land Rover followed by three Volkswagen vans.

There must be a gravel track that leads back to the main road to Luderitz, otherwise those Volkswagens would never make it across this landscape, she thought.

The four vehicles stopped in front of the tents and discharged their smiling tourists. Virginia saw the drivers unloading the vans after most of the tourists had paraded into the main building. A few minutes passed and two men ran out of the tents.

She climbed down from the roof and back into the house. "Looks like they're giving Miss Wood the bad news," she said. "Hope they haven't got big appetites."

At midnight, Karl and Virginia crept towards the parked vehicles, with Lordy twenty yards behind covering them with his handgun. Karl had a Swiss army knife, a small reading light left over from the wreck of the boat, and a bottle taken from the tents. It was pitch black and deathly quiet; even the sea couldn't be heard. Karl's heart was thumping as he crept over to the Volkswagen, parked furthest away from the tents.

"Nobody on guard," he whispered to Virginia.

Karl slipped under the front of the van and fumbled around with his right hand until he found the release catch for the hood. His heart jumped in unison with the click of the hood as it flipped open. He froze momentarily while he waited to see if anyone had heard the noise. Virginia's tap on the shoulder was a sign to continue.

She opened the hood while Karl got out from under the van. He held the small reading lamp over the engine and began searching for the power steering fluid line. When he found it he worked his hand down to the lowest point until he detected the drainage cap. After unscrewing it, he allowed the fluid to drain into the bottle he had brought along. It took a few minutes and it was difficult to accomplish, but most of the fluid made it into the bottle. He screwed the cap on and signaled to Virginia that he was finished. She pressed on the hood to close it.

Karl and Virginia searched the other vehicles to make sure that none had any replacement fluid in the repair kits. After satisfying themselves that all was clear they crept back to their temporary home.

Morning came. Virginia, who was on watch, noticed the tourists milling around outside the tents with their belongings. When they finished loading the vehicles they sped off in a cloud of dust along the dirt road. Virginia carefully climbed on the rickety roof of the house and looked through a small telescope to watch their departure. Just as Karl had estimated, about a half mile out of town the doctored van stopped.

They crowded around the van, and after what seemed to be a heated discussion, the tourists and drivers stopped delving into the engine and loaded all the luggage onto the other vehicles.

Karl and Lordy were awakened by Virginia when she jumped down from the roof.

"Who's ready for breakfast then?" she exclaimed.

"Have they gone?" Karl asked.

"Yup, minus one van. It's less than a mile out of town."

"I'll walk over there later," Karl said, "and make sure it's not completely ruined."

Lordy ripped up some floorboards and made a small fire to cook their first hot breakfast in days.

"It's all canned I'm afraid, but at least it's hot," he said.

Karl finished breakfast and then examined the abandoned van, while Lordy went off to explore the other buildings in town. Virginia contented herself by looking through the personal effects of the long since deceased owner of the house. After about an hour she found a large scribbled note stuck to one of the books. She began to read it but Lordy interrupted her.

"Virginia, come with me. I've found something interesting."

She followed Lordy to another large building in the center of the town. As she entered she saw Karl returning from his inspection of the disabled van and shouted for him to come over.

"What's so important, Lordy?" Virginia asked, as they walked into the building.

"Come and look at this."

"What?" Virginia replied.

"Looks like this building was some sort of saloon and casino. It's got an old roulette wheel in the center of the floor. It's full of sand and falling to bits but it looks like it'll work. If we get bored we can gamble with our pay!"

Virginia was annoyed with Lordy's stupid comment and sat down and finished reading the scribbled note, while Lordy and Karl fiddled with the roulette wheel.

"Hey!" Virginia shouted. "That skeleton isn't that old. Look at this letter. I found it among the others in the house."

Lordy scanned the letter and without commenting, grabbed the table holding the roulette wheel, and turned it on its side. A corroded metal door covered the space below the table. Karl stepped forward, pulled it from its hinges, and threw it aside.

"Pull that sack up," Virginia said to Karl.

Karl just nudged the sack and the material disintegrated. They stared, spellbound, as the contents spilled into the sand.

"Are they real?" Karl asked.

"According to this letter they are," Virginia replied. "The skeleton belongs to a security guard from the diamond mines . . . Hinrich Van Der Walt. He hid the diamonds in here but appears to have been double-crossed by his partner. He ran out of food and water waiting for this partner of his to collect him. Must have killed himself with this knife. Ten years ago according to the suicide note. No water or food left so he had no choice I suppose."

Karl cupped the diamonds out of the hole with his hand and put them into Lordy's hat.

"Must be 200 carats here," Lordy said. "And look at the incredible colors."

"What should we do with them?" Karl asked.

"Well I'm not giving them to Hugh that's for sure," Lordy said.

They stood fondling the diamonds until Virginia tossed one in the air and said, "Notice anything unusual about these?"

Karl and Lordy shook their heads.

"They're all cut and polished."

"Good god," Lordy ejaculated. "They must be worth a fortune."

"About twenty times more than our rough ones," Virginia said.

"I vote we hide them away for a rainy day and get them back when our little adventure is over," Lordy suggested.

They all agreed. After an hour's discussion they disposed of the skeleton, the letters, and hid the diamonds under the foundation of their temporary home.

"Who double-crossed him?" Karl asked. "And why didn't he come back?"

"He probably did come back, but our skeleton friend had already hid them and killed himself. Probably left the note so that some day his partner might be caught."

Virginia looked at the note again. "Someone by the name of Harry Van Rensberg."

ELEVEN

$\mathcal{I}$t was Tuesday afternoon when Hugh and Ron arrived at the team's embarkation point south of Port Nolloth. Hugh convinced himself that the team had not returned and that at least Ron was not double-crossing him. Hugh decided to find a fishing vessel in Port Nolloth to take him along the coast and look for the boat.

They drove into Port Nolloth and walked around the small harbor. A dozen or so indifferent fisherman, cleaning boats and arranging nets, ignored Hugh's offer of money for a few hours fishing. He was about to give up when a waiter from the hotel ran up and said that the Hotel Manager would lend them his small powerboat for the afternoon. Hugh accepted the offer and after changing into warmer clothes set off with Ron.

They sped north along the coastline for twenty miles searching for the team, but without luck. They returned, refueled the boat, and went south for ten miles before giving up the search.

Hugh felt thoroughly defeated. He said to Ron, "They must have sunk, or maybe landed further north in the diamond area. In either case we're out of luck I'm afraid. Let's go back to Johannesburg. There's nothing else to be done."

They stayed the night in Port Nolloth and began the two-day drive back to Johannesburg on Wednesday morning.

Hugh arrived home on Thursday evening. He dropped Ron off at a cheap hotel and told him to collect his cash on Monday, as part of the agreed deal.

Susan had been on tenderhooks since Hugh had left, but realizing he was depressed, she didn't bombard him with questions about future plans. They spent the next three days at home, avoiding serious conversation, and generally wasting time.

On Monday morning Susan got the surprise of her life. She checked Hugh's post office box and after discarding the junk mail saw a letter posted from Luderitz.

"Anything in the mail worth looking at, Susan?" Hugh asked, calling from the bathroom.

"Not really, mainly bills and advertising . . . and one letter."

"Who from?"

Susan opened the letter and almost fainted. She darted up to the bathroom and burst in on Hugh, who was still sitting on the toilet.

"Have I got a surprise for you," she said, putting on a serious tone and placing her hands on her hips.

"What's wrong?" Hugh asked.

Susan tightened her face. "Do you know a woman who signs her letters 'Love V'?"

"No," Hugh replied defensively.

"Well she knows you!"

"How so?"

Susan thrust the letter in his face. "Your little scheme isn't finished yet."

Hugh read the note and forgetting his pants were still around his ankles, grabbed Susan and shouted, "They did it after all." He tripped, pulling Susan down with him.

Johnny ran into the bathroom. "What's wrong boss? What's wrong?"

Hugh helped Susan up and said to Johnny, "Don't worry, Johnny, we've just had some good news."

Susan laughed as she watched Johnny walk off shaking his head as confused as ever.

Hugh quickly got down to business. He told Susan to dream up an advertisement for the Southwest Radio station and make sure it was broadcast immediately. Hugh had to reach them before the following Sunday, and Susan had to make sure that Virginia would understand from the advertisement that they would be rescued either Friday or Saturday.

Susan listened in amazement as Hugh began thinking aloud. She had never known someone to dream up so many schemes in such a short time. He analyzed several different approaches on how to access the diamond area overland. With Susan acting as a devil's advocate he articulated and then dismissed several plans before settling on one.

"I'll collect Ron and drive towards Luderitz."

"But you said the overland route was more difficult than going by sea?"

"Yes, but remember they're 120 miles north of the plants, and nobody is mining there anymore. It's still a restricted area and patrolled by police, but it's such a massive expanse of land that it must be impossible to control all of it. The most difficult part of the plan was getting the diamonds away from the processing plants and I chose the sea route for that. Mind you, don't think this will be easy."

Just then the doorbell rang. It was Ron. Susan let him in.

"Ron," Hugh snapped. "We have to leave for Luderitz immediately."

"What? Why?"

"The team's holed up about thirty miles south of there in a place called Elizabeth Bay. Ever heard of it?"

"Yes. I used to drive for a haulage company between Windhoek and Johannesburg. I often picked up cargo from Port Luderitz. That's near Elizabeth Bay."

"Can we drive from Luderitz to Elizabeth Bay?"

"No. There's no road connecting the two places and the terrain is impassable. You have drive east from Luderitz for fifty miles and then south on the main road for about forty, and then back towards the west, across open country. A four-wheeled vehicle will do it."

"What about security?"

"The roads are fenced off but you can get around them. Mind you, you might run into a few police checkpoints along the way. So you have to be careful."

Hugh thought for a moment and said to Ron, "We don't have time to plan this properly. We have to get to them before Sunday."

"Why?"

"I'll explain on the way."

Ron and Hugh quickly put a list of useful items together. They divided the list equally between each other and hurried off to acquire them, leaving Susan to arrange the advertisement.

It was 10:00 PM by the time they finished loading the Land Rover so Hugh decided to get a good night's sleep and leave early on Tuesday morning.

It was another long drive, clear across the country, along empty roads stretching for hundreds of miles, with only a few towns breaking the monotony. Hugh didn't speak much and when he did it was about the rescue attempt, never asking nor offering any type of personal information or encouragement to Ron.

At last they came to within 100 miles of Luderitz. It was 5:00 PM on Wednesday and the sun was low on the horizon, shining straight into their faces out of a cloudless sky. The road passed through a long, wide valley with patchy grassland at either side. To the north and south were silent hills and mountains, completely uninhabited.

The nearer they got to Luderitz the more barren and uninviting the landscape became. Hugh was scratching around with a map, trying to determine the best place to leave the road, when Ron spotted an opening in the fence that was wide enough for the Land Rover to pass.

"Let's go off here," Ron said. "I saw a rough track through the hills. And there's no one else on the road."

"Okay," Hugh replied. "According to the map if we go southwest about now we should be able to follow that long valley between those mountains over there. After that we cross a high plateau and then we get to the tricky part."

"That's when we'll have to cross stretches of loose sand," Ron added, "and we'll need to get our directions by compass."

"This has four-wheeled drive," Hugh said, as he tapped the dashboard, "so it should be okay."

They bumped off the road, turned the vehicle around and back-tracked until they came across the dirt path Ron had noticed. The path took them about twenty miles before disappearing into nothing. After that it was rough going, with loose sand in some places and uneven, rocky ground in others.

Hugh accelerated at the foot of a steep incline, hoping to get enough speed to reach the summit, but the Land Rover skidded sideways and stopped with the rear wheels suspended over the edge of a sheer drop. He revved, but the front wheels could not get enough traction to move the Land Rover. Ron threw the supplies out and jumped up and down on the hood while Hugh revved the engine again. The Land Rover inched forward until the rear wheels made contact with the ground; then it jerked forward, turned anti-clockwise and stalled, pointing downhill. Ron reloaded the supplies and took the wheel from Hugh. He slowly reversed the Land Rover to the top of the hill and parked.

Hugh decided it was too dark and dangerous to continue so they camped for the night. Ron filled the petrol tank ready for the morning and checked the oil and radiator fluid. Hugh threw a can of baked beans and a loaf of bread to Ron. "Better get stuck into that. We have a long day tomorrow."

Hugh contented himself with two sandwiches and some luke-warm coffee before telling Ron to sleep on the roof of the Land Rover. He set an alarm clock for 4:00 AM, climbed into the Land Rover, wrapped himself in a blanket, and drifted off to sleep.

In Elizabeth Bay, Virginia tuned the small transistor radio to Radio Southwest's frequency and listened eagerly for any sign that her message had reached Hugh.

A representative for the South African Government said in an official announcement today that they would not yield to threats by any terrorist groups regardless whether they were acting alone or sponsored by another country. He went on to say that the current increase in township violence was directly due to communist agitators seeking to capitalize on differences between the various ethnic groups in South Africa.

Turning to sports, the Springboks are scheduled to play the Australian national team in Cape Town tomorrow. The team is confident that they will put up a good showing even though they have been absent from international competition for some time.

There will now be a short commercial break before our nightly classical music hour.

Visit your local Barclays Bank for the latest information on our special savings accounts and low interest mortgages. There is a Barclays' branch near you.

Foscini stores are giving away high fashion dresses at ridiculous prices. Go to one of our stores in Johannesburg, Windoek, and Cape Town today, before stocks run out. Remember Foscini the best in fashion.

A Virginia Hughes cosmetics consultant will be in a shopping center near you every night for a week. Get a free facial with every purchase of our new Virginia Hughes perfume. Offer starts in all locations in South West Africa this Thursday and all other locations on Saturday. Don't miss it.

Virginia ran over to Karl and said, "It's the signal from Hugh. He's coming tomorrow."

"How do you know?"

She repeated what the advert said and added, "There's no cosmetic company called Virginia Hughes, and the use of both our first names makes it certain."

"We'll get everything packed for first light tomorrow," Lordy said, "and make sure we're prepared to ship out if Hugh does show up. Do you think he'll come by boat or overland?"

"I don't think he'll risk another boat trip and he knows he'll never be able to land a plane anywhere around here," Karl replied.

Apart from the mystery of the skeleton and the unexpected diamond find, they were utterly bored. For over a week they had nothing to read, scant rations, and were confined to the house because of the risk of being seen by police aircraft. They became so energized with this news that even in the limited light, they quickly collected everything they might need for the journey and stacked it at the back of the house. Lordy and Karl paced up and down and eventually walked outside in the dark to burn off some of their excitement.

At 4:00 AM the alarm clock woke Hugh. He jumped out of the Land Rover and tapped Ron, who was still sleeping on the roof. They drank some water and ate a couple of sandwiches before starting out on the next and most difficult leg of the journey. Hugh estimated that they had another thirty miles to cover before reaching Elizabeth Bay. It was downhill most of the way but the loose sand would be treacherous.

"Better keep our speed low until full light," Hugh said, pointing to an eighteen-inch ridge in the ground. "We don't want to crack the axle on these bumps."

"Okay," Ron replied. "If it gets any worse I'll walk ahead and check for bad patches. Once we get back down to sea level it should be easier."

For two hours the Land Rover's wheels slipped and spun on the loose ground. It threw up sand and smoke in its wake and jerked up and down as it traversed uneven ground. When the ground leveled out they saw a rough track, which appeared to lead in the direction of Elizabeth Bay. Hugh walked away from the Land Rover and took a compass reading. "Looks like this track goes straight into Elizabeth Bay. I wonder where the other direction leads?"

"Look at those tire tracks over there," Ron said. "Three or four vehicles must have passed by. I'm guessing the track must wind through the hills and come out on the main road somewhere. Otherwise where would they be going?"

"It's probably that tour group Virginia mentioned in the letter," Hugh surmised. "We'll go back that way."

After driving another hour Ron spotted the sea in the distance and the rows of abandoned houses of Elizabeth Bay.

"There it is." Ron shouted.

Hugh noticed someone on the roof of one of the houses so he told Ron to check with the binoculars.

"Woman with dark red hair, Mr. Barlow."

"Excellent," Hugh shouted.

As he drove into the main street Karl and Lordy ran towards the Land Rover waving their arms, with Virginia following a few yards behind.

"Welcome to our ghost town," Lordy said.

Hugh jumped out of the Land Rover and shook hands with Lordy and Karl, while Ron hugged and kissed Virginia.

"The letter was a long shot," Virginia said to Hugh.

"I still can't figure out how you did that," Hugh replied.

"We had a little visit from some tourists and they rather kindly let us steal their food and use their mail facilities."

"They didn't know you were here then?"

Lordy interjected, "No, we made it look as if Bushmen raided their supplies, and Virginia put the letter in with the tour guide's other letters. They very kindly mailed it for us from Luderitz."

"You sly bastards," Hugh responded.

They all laughed except Hugh, who began carefully examining the cases of diamonds.

"Load this stuff and let's get going," Hugh ordered.

"Mr. Barlow, we'd better wait for sunset, a police patrol might spot us," Ron added.

Hugh thought for a second and replied, "You're right, let's not be too hasty."

"We'd better keep enough food and water for another day just in case we run into more problems," Virginia said. "And let's have a hot meal before we leave."

They ate an improvised meal late in the afternoon and then packed all their possessions on the Land Rover. An hour later, with Hugh driving, they set off along the dirt track for the second time.

Things went well for the first twenty miles due to the good condition of the track. Hugh took advantage of this, and coupled with his impatience to reach the main road, he gradually increased speed. However, the track dipped sharply just beyond a tight bend, and the Land Rover plowed into a boulder. Hugh jammed on the brakes, but it was too late. The boulder disappeared under the Land Rover, hit one of the wheels, and thumped and scraped against the chassis. Everything shook violently.

"Shit!" Hugh screamed. "I think we've blown a tire. I hope it's not the axle."

Ron and Karl jumped out to look.

"Driver's side front tire," Ron shouted to the others. "Completely blown. We can't go any further. Let's get the spare ready while it's still light."

"Damn! Damn!" Hugh shouted. "Okay, everyone out and get this fixed."

Karl unbolted the spare wheel, while Ron loosened the front wheel and Lordy jacked-up the Land Rover. By the time they changed the wheel the sun had set but since the moon was very bright, Hugh decided to keep going.

Ron and Karl walked ahead of the Land Rover checking the track for unexpected obstacles and potholes, but after ninety minutes they all agreed to give up because of the excruciatingly slow pace. Hugh drove 100 yards off the road and parked behind a small hill. They could not risk revealing themselves with any type of light, so they couldn't start a fire, which meant another cold meal in the dark and chilly air.

"At least it's food," Karl said as he munched on an improvised sandwich.

"Look on the bright side," Virginia added. "Only another day of driving before we reach the main road."

They finished eating and found themselves places to sleep. No one spoke much, and when they did it was in whispers.

An hour later Lordy broke the silence. "What's that noise?"

"What noise?"

"Listen."

"I can hear it now."

"And me."

"Spread out and see what it is," Hugh ordered.

They spread out in a circle around the camp and watched for signs of movement under the bright rays of the moon. Lordy jumped on top of the Land Rover to get a better view of the land-scape. He returned after a few minutes and whispered to Hugh, "I saw the silhouettes of several figures moving in a line about 100 yards away."

They gathered together near the Land Rover and discussed what to do next.

"Keep everything very quiet, sound travels a long way out here," Karl whispered exaggerating his consonants.

"Maybe it's Bushmen," Virginia suggested.

"Could be a South African army patrol," Lordy said.

"No, they would be in jeeps or trucks," Karl said.

"Any SWAPO guerrillas in the region?" Hugh asked.

"Unlikely this far south," Karl answered.

"I wonder if it's a group like us," Virginia said.

"No, too many of them," Lordy added. "I think I saw about thirty of them."

"Can't be Bushmen then," Karl said. "Too many, and they would never walk in line like that."

"I'll go and check them out," Karl said.

"Okay," Hugh said, "but be careful. Take this rifle with you."

"I'll follow twenty yards behind and cover your back," Lordy said.

Karl crept out from the camp and went in the direction that Lordy last saw the group of figures. He moved ahead, crouching and feeling the ground with his hands. Using the low murmurs of the intruder's voices as a direction finder, he inched forward until he came within thirty yards of their camp. He lay flat on the ground and lifted his head to catch a glimpse of the mysterious group. The voices were much clearer at this distance and Karl immediately noticed they were speaking in the Ovambo language.

Must be SWAPO, he thought.

Fearful that they might have posted a lookout, he considered turning back but changed his mind and worked his way around to the back of the group. He could only hear a few voices so he surmised that most of them were probably sleeping, or at least trying to sleep.

Karl moved into an elevated area looking straight down into their camp, about thirty yards away. He could smell cigarette smoke and could hear a couple of voices exchanging comments. He couldn't discern from the dark lumps strewn around the camp just how many there were, but Karl counted at least twenty.

If only I had a grenade, he thought.

He waited a few minutes and then stepped back, trying not to make any noise. Just when he felt safe, his heel hit something hard and he fell backwards onto the ground. He felt the form of a human body underneath him. It just stirred at first and groaned, but then punched and kicked wildly in an attempt to throw Karl off. Karl hit down on the body with the butt of his rifle three times before rolling sideways and jumping to his feet.

His opponent did the same, yelling at the top of his voice. An awful silence followed as the two faced each other, both completely startled. It seemed an eternity to Karl. The crack of a gunshot broke the silence, its echo a reminder of what had happened. The Ovambo's head jolted back and he collapsed.

Karl felt Lordy pull him by the arm. "Quick!" Lordy shouted. "Let's get moving."

"No, I'll hold them off. Go back and tell the others to get moving."

Lordy ignored him. A few seconds passed and they both instinctively began firing into the camp. With Lordy's handgun and Karl's rifle, they fired off about twelve shots before the inevitable return fire began.

Hugh ran towards Karl and Lordy and stood behind them as the return fire came in. After a few seconds of silence Hugh heard two more gunshots, then a groan and Karl's body crumpled to the ground. Lordy crouched, discharged all his rounds, and then turned to check on Karl. Hugh grabbed Karl's rifle and ran back towards the Land Rover.

"Virginia, get in," Hugh shouted, as he jumped into the back seat. "Ron, you drive. We don't want to get trapped here."

"Hugh, we have to wait for Karl and Lordy; they might have been injured," Virginia replied.

"Forget them, let's save ourselves," Hugh ordered.

Ron shouted to Hugh, "Mr. Barlow, I just can't leave them. Give me that rifle and I'll go back for them. You can drive out if you want."

"That's right, Hugh, we're not leaving them," Virginia shouted.

"Okay, we'll wait then. Just get the Land Rover ready to go."

Ron drove the Land Rover nearer to Karl and Lordy and waited.

Hugh expected the Ovambos to come on, but they stayed within the confines of their camp, obviously assuming they were being attacked by a South African army unit. Just as Hugh ordered Ron to drive away again, Lordy's lanky frame appeared in front of the Land Rover.

"Quick, get in. Where's Karl?"

"He's dead," Lordy said, as he jumped into the back of the Land Rover. "Get moving before they realize there's only a handful of us. There must be at least thirty of them—SWAPO guerrillas."

Ron accelerated as fast as the rough ground allowed, intermittently turning the headlights on for a few seconds and then off, trying to locate the track. Once he found it he kept the headlights on and raced dangerously for about a mile before slowing down and dimming the lights.

The gunshots stopped but Hugh still felt nervous, especially being bounced around inside the Land Rover in the darkness. He could feel the tension of the others as he wiped sweat from his brow.

"They probably don't have any transport," Virginia said to Hugh.

Hugh told Ron to slow down to make sure no more unnecessary damage was inflicted on the Land Rover.

"What should we do now?" Ron asked.

"Keep going until we reach the main road," Hugh replied. "With all that gunfire who knows who heard it. I'm sure the army will be on their trail, if they're not already."

"What happened to Karl?" Virginia asked.

"Shot twice. Two right in the body—dead before he hit the ground. You should know, Barlow. You made off with his rifle."

Lordy put his head in his hands and began to choke up.

Virginia patted him. "Don't blame yourself, it could have been any of us," she said.

No one spoke for a while.

Just when they were feeling confident of reaching the road Ron shouted, "Mr. Barlow, look at the temperature gauge. It's way in the red. We'll have to stop and check it out."

Hugh swore.

Ron stopped the Land Rover and jumped out to examine the engine.

"All the oil's gone," Ron shouted. "That rock must have hit something underneath. It's too dark to see where the leak is, and anyway, I'm not even sure if we've got enough spare oil."

Hugh said angrily, "Let the engine cool down first, then drive it another mile or so and find a place to hide. Maybe in the morning we can repair it."

Ron drove the Land Rover into a small depression in the ground and shoveled sand around the back and sides. He covered the roof with a light brown tarpaulin and tied it down with rope.

"Let's get some sleep," Hugh said, "and see what tomorrow morning brings."

TWELVE

$\mathcal{T}$he dawn light broke across the wide-open landscape, heralded by the thump of helicopter rotors cutting their way through the air. Lordy and Virginia looked out of their cramped hiding space and saw four helicopters flying overhead, passing by one by one, like migrating birds. They crept out a little further and watched them circle a mile in the distance and then drop down, one after the other.

Virginia quickly focused her telescope on the action and began providing Lordy with a commentary. "South African Paratroopers —about fifty of them. They've jumped and they're moving forward in formation."

They heard a jet fighter scream low overhead, followed by four earsplitting bangs. Seconds later another explosion.

"It's fired rockets about 200 yards to the left of the helicopters. The whole area is alight. There're men running everywhere. They're in flames. Must be that SWAPO group. I thought we left them miles behind. It's either another group or we went in a circle last night."

The noise of automatic gunfire rattled the air.

"The paratroopers are attacking them. There's a heavy machine gun firing from the helicopters. The paratroops are moving in on the right flank. About twenty of the SWAPO troops are still on the ground burning. It looks like the others are being picked off in batches. Two of them are trying to surrender . . . too late . . . they've been cut down. The paratroopers have overrun the encampment. They're bayoneting the survivors. They're fanning out around the camp now. It's over."

"Are they coming towards us, Virginia?"

"Not yet. They're collecting the bodies and looking at the left-over equipment. Looks like they've got two prisoners. One of the helicopters has taken off. It's circling the area, quite low. Must be looking for more guerillas. Better cover up. It's coming this way."

The noise gained intensity as the helicopter approached. The shock waves from the helicopter's blades felt like punches as it passed over them. Virginia tensed, waiting for the inevitable."

"They haven't seen us," Lordy said. "Thank god Ron covered the Land Rover."

Just when Virginia thought they were safe she heard another helicopter in the distance, coming closer. "It's much bigger than the others—must be a transport helicopter. It's landing in the camp. Okay, they're putting the bodies in bags and loading them into the helicopter. Most of the paratroopers are making their way back to the other helicopters now."

Twenty minutes later and all the helicopters were in the air and flying away.

Ron crawled over to Lordy and Virginia. "Did you see that?" Ron said. "If I were a SWAPO guerilla I'd change my occupation."

"Typical of a precise lightning attack," Lordy said, "and if I'm right there would have been an army tracker following that SWAPO band and radioing their location to the helicopters. Did you see anyone being picked up about a mile or so behind the group Virginia?"

"No. Do you think the tracker is still out there?"

"Possibly."

"The helicopter that came over our heads landed a few miles away," Ron added. "I can't be 100 percent sure, but I think so."

"If you're wrong we'll be annihilated as well," Lordy said.

"Where's Hugh?" Virginia asked, raising her arms.

"Still hiding behind those rocks," Ron said in a disgusted voice.

"He's no hero our Hughie," Virginia replied. "Better get him out of his hole and we can decide what to do next."

Virginia crept over to Hugh and without trying to embarrass him too much, told him he could come out of hiding.

"Yes I know," Hugh said, "just being careful. Let's decide what to do next."

Ron slid underneath the engine looking for the oil leak when the discussion began.

"How much spare oil do we have?" Hugh asked.

"About half what we really need," Ron shouted from under the engine.

"Is it enough to get us to the main road?" Virginia asked.

"If we stop when the engine gets too hot, let it cool down, and then restart, we might be able to make it. But it could seize-up at any time."

"What other options do we have?" Hugh asked.

"Walk the thirty miles to the main road and see if we can get a ride, or even highjack a car if we have to," Virginia suggested. "We could bury the diamonds and come back later for them if there's a risk of getting caught."

"Remember it's still in the prohibited diamond area," Hugh replied, "and we could get jailed just for being this side of the main road—even if we don't have any diamonds."

"How are you doing, Ron?"

"I've found the leak. It's a gasket. I can fix it, but we'll need to jack up the Land Rover so I can get to it. Luckily I've got spares, and the tools should be good enough."

"Let's find a place where the ground is hard enough to use the jack," Hugh said.

"Better still, let's dig a trench between the wheels so Ron can get to the engine easier," Virginia suggested.

Lordy and Ron heaved the dirt and sand from under the land Rover and Ron set to work jury-rigging the oil leak, using improvisations only an excellent mechanic would attempt. Lordy helped while Virginia kept watch for any unwanted visitors and Hugh just slept in a shaded spot a few yards away.

Three hours passed before Ron reported success and poured the remaining spare oil into the engine. "Let's give it a shot," he said. "Virginia, start up the engine and let's see if it leaks. I'll keep this pan under the engine and catch the oil if does."

Virginia started the engine, and after letting it idle for a while, she walked around to Ron.

"No signs of leaks," Ron said to her.

She started to help him out from under the Land Rover, but the sand holding the front left wheel suddenly subsided and the vehicle dropped directly on Ron. An awful crunching sound turned her stomach. Ron screamed and banged his head and arms on the ground.

Virginia shouted at Lordy, "Turn the engine off."

She scraped the earth from underneath Ron, but his body and flailing arms prevented her from pulling him clear. His thighs were trapped between the front of the Land Rover and the edge of the trench at the left side. Lordy grabbed Ron around the chest, enclosing his arms, and held him almost upright from the waist so that Virginia could remove enough earth to pull Ron's legs out.

Ron was semi-conscious by the time they pulled him clear. They laid him flat and Virginia examined his wounds. There were two large gashes, both oozing blood profusely, with the broken bone from his left thigh clearly visible.

"Both legs are broken," Virginia said, "and he's lost a lot of blood. Maybe it's an artery."

Virginia got some rope from the Land Rover and tied it around Ron's legs, just above the wounds. Lordy ripped off the arms of his field jacket and used them as improvised bandages. When Ron passed out Hugh and Lordy placed him on an incline allowing his blood to run to his head and away from his legs.

"Let's get the Land Rover out of the trench," Lordy said. He began madly shoveling the earth and sand away from the rear of the vehicle. When he finished he told Virginia to start the engine and put it into reverse. She revved the engine as high as possible and released the clutch. To everyone's surprise it rolled back with ease.

There was no time to waste. They laid Ron on the floor of the Land Rover and sped off in the direction of the road.

"We might be spotted in broad daylight," Hugh said. "Maybe we should wait until dark."

"Ron will be dead by then you callous bastard," Lordy barked.

Virginia reached back, tapped Lordy on the shoulder, and said, "I'll just keep going as fast as possible and hope for the best."

"If the engine overheats we'll all be finished," Hugh snapped, "and there's no water left. We'll have to walk thirty miles if it packs in. Whatever way you look at it, Ron isn't going to make it."

"What are you suggesting, Hugh?" Virginia asked in a threatening tone.

"Let's be logical. Even if we get to the main road, it's seventy-five miles to Luderitz, and the best part of eighty to Karasburg. They're the nearest places with hospitals."

Virginia saw Lordy put his hand on his pistol, "I'm not dumping him."

"Fuck him," Hugh ejaculated. "What about the diamonds? If we wet-nurse Ron we'll lose the lot."

Virginia shook her head at Lordy as he drew his pistol. Hugh kept quiet. A tense minute of silence followed before Hugh said, "Best go to Karasburg then, there'll be too many questions to answer in Luderitz."

After they had driven for ten minutes, Virginia noticed several boulders blocking the track about fifty yards ahead. She jammed on the brakes and skidded to a halt just in front of the obstruction.

Virginia and Lordy jumped out and began to remove the boulders. Suddenly she felt a jolt in her back. She turned to find a black man dressed in fatigues pointing an automatic rifle at her. Virginia glanced over to Lordy, who also had a gun pointing at him.

Virginia called out, "SWAPO! They've got us surrounded."

Two armed men pulled Hugh out of the Land Rover and frisked him. Four others quickly searched Virginia and Lordy and then pushed them all back against the Land Rover. Virginia watched as the leader of the SWAPO group shouted several commands at his men in his native Ovambo tongue. He was a well-proportioned man, with arms like pieces of black iron. His men searched the Land Rover and found Ron lying semi-conscious in the back.

Virginia felt relieved when they left Ron alone, obviously realizing he was no danger to them.

The leader walked over to Hugh and in surprisingly correct but pretentious English, asked, "Where have YOU come from, old boy?"

"We were hunting and sightseeing in the interior but got lost," Hugh replied hastily.

"What happened to the chap in the Land Rover?" the leader asked.

"We had problems with the vehicle and he was trying to fix it when it fell onto his legs."

"Did you hear the gunfire earlier?"

"Was it gunfire? We heard several booms in the distance but had no idea what caused them."

"So your friend was not shot then?"

"No, see for yourself."

"I don't believe you are sightseeing or hunting. Why would you do it here? You are aware it is a restricted area, are you not?"

Virginia piped up. "We were in Elizabeth Bay with a tour group and decided to go out into the desert to look around for ourselves. But as he says, we seem to have got ourselves lost."

"Do you know who we are?" the leader asked Virginia.

"SWAPO, I assume," she replied casually.

"Yes, you are spot on, Madam. I assume you are all South Africans then?"

"Hugh and I are . . . but Lordy over there is from England," Virginia replied, emphasizing Lordy's nationality because of the SWAPO leader's use of an exaggerated, upper-class English accent.

The leader straightened his back and pulled the sleeves of his combat jacket down. "Oh, England, yes. I went to university there you know. Actually in Edinburgh."

"Excellent place, Edinburgh," Lordy interjected.

"Yes, splendid," the leader said. "I loved it there."

"What brings you here?" Virginia impudently asked. "It's a far cry from Scotland."

The leader didn't answer because it seemed to Virginia that he'd noticed the other SWAPO men getting fidgety. He barked a few commands at them and told Hugh, Lordy, and Virginia to sit down by the side of the track.

While the leader issued commands Lordy quickly whispered to Hugh and Virginia, "How many of them are there?"

"Six, including the leader," Virginia replied.

"I'll keep the leader talking. He's got a soft spot for my English accent."

"Okay, but what if they find the diamonds?" Hugh asked.

"They're next to Ron."

"Let's hope they don't move him," Virginia said.

"They all look exhausted?" Hugh said. "I'm guessing they've probably been walking for days. They must be an offshoot from the group we saw get wiped out earlier."

"Let's see if we can find a way out of this," Virginia said. "Their leader seems to be intelligent and he didn't kill at first sight, so I guess he's planning to use us to get away. He must know the South African forces are on his tail, so let's try to prod him and see what we can find out."

Lordy shouted over to the leader, "Do you have any medical supplies, sir? Our friend is in a very bad way."

"You can call me Joshua. The 'sir' seems a bit pretentious don't you think, old man? Especially out here in the wilds."

Joshua barked a few words at one of his men, who produced a rucksack and gave it to Joshua.

"I have some strong pain killers here, some bandages, disinfectant, but nothing to really help the poor fellow," Joshua said. He cut the rope around Virginia's wrists and gave her the medical bag. While she attended to Ron, Joshua asked whether they had any food.

"On the roof," Virginia replied quickly, diverting him away from the two cases of diamonds behind Ron.

"We have water," Joshua added, "but no food left I'm afraid."

"Help yourself," Hugh said.

Joshua distributed the food among his men, who grabbed at the meager offerings and devoured every scrap at amazing speed.

"They've not eaten for days by the look of that," Lordy said to Hugh. "Given the opportunity I think we could overpower them fairly easily."

"Don't try anything silly, Lordy, let's just wait and see what happens," Hugh responded.

Virginia crushed the painkillers, dissolved them with water, and slowly poured the mixture into Ron's mouth. She waited for the medicine to take effect before cleaning his leg wounds and wrapping them with bandages.

Joshua posted his men at various points around the camp, walked back to the Land Rover, and inquired about Ron's condition.

"He's not in pain for the moment," Virginia said to Joshua, "but he needs proper medical attention."

"We can discuss that later," Joshua responded. "Meanwhile let's get a little discussion group underway. The sun is setting and I want to decide what my plans are for tomorrow. Everyone follow me."

Joshua began speaking to them like a schoolteacher addresses a class, standing upright with his hands behind his back and head slightly bowed. Virginia could barely contain her amusement, but she noticed that Hugh looked as if he were in a court being sentenced for murder.

"Look, the way I see things is as follows," Joshua began. "I know you are up to something illegal. I didn't buy that sightseeing explanation. You of course know why I am here; at least in general terms. We both know what happened earlier to the rest of my platoon when your South African countrymen appeared out of nowhere.

"My mission has failed, so we need to get back to the Angolan border without any more trouble. You, I am sure, want to get about your business and of course save the life of your friend. I could easily kill you all and use your vehicle to drive north. However I don't think six blacks looking as we do would get far. I'm sure the police and army are on the lookout for likely terrorists.

"What I propose is to join forces in a temporary alliance. An entente cordiale, so to speak. You drive the vehicle and we will sit in the back and on the roof. If we are stopped for any reason you can spin some yarn about taking us to work for you up north somewhere. At an appropriate juncture we disappear into the bush near the Angolan border, and you can go about your business. And after that, never the twain shall meet, as they say. Of course I will have this revolver pointed at you just in case you decide to terminate our entente a little prematurely."

Joshua smiled broadly and then broke into an extended chuckle.

"Sounds like a plan to me," Hugh said.

"Yes, I think it might work," Lordy added.

"What about Ron?" Virginia asked. "Maybe we could drop him at a hospital on the way?"

Joshua said, "I am not sure about that, Madam. He might say too much under anesthetic. I have to think about the well-being of my men. Allow me to sleep on it."

Joshua untied Hugh's wrists and passed around a bottle of water. They each sipped from the bottle and then sat in a circle, relieved that some sort of temporary arrangement had been reached. Virginia spoke first after a few moments of comfortable silence.

"How did you get into all this Joshua?" she asked. "You're clearly very well educated and a reasonable person."

"It is quite simple really, old girl," he replied. "My ambition is to be the president of a free Namibia. I do not want to be some puppet of the white government in South Africa. The peace talks going on at the moment are a farce. The South Africans only want to give us the impression of independence. They want a quisling government setup in Windhoek while they pull the strings in Pretoria. They offered me a seat at the Turnhalle conference last year as a junior representative for the Ovambo tribe, but I turned it down after I put the whole picture together. Only action, violent action, will force them to give up power, and when real elections are held the people will vote for freedom fighters such as myself."

"How did you get to Edinburgh then?" Lordy asked.

"I won a church scholarship to go to Cape Town to study. After I graduated top of my class I enrolled at the London School of Economics to study philosophy, politics, and economics. I did very well there and went on to Edinburgh to take a Masters degree.

"The English are very good at educating people but they never seem to use it to their advantage. They talk too much, at least the leftists tend to. I went along with all that Marxist rubbish because it was expedient, and it kept me out of trouble with my contemporaries. As you know it is still in vogue in Europe at the moment with the student echelons. I am just using it to rid our country of the white government and then I will make my own bid for power."

"What will you do with the whites once you reach your goals?" Lordy asked.

"They can stay or leave. I don't really care as long as they knuckle down to black rule. I will have to appropriate some of their farms and businesses of course. I can't ask my people to risk their lives and get nothing in return. They would probably turn on me if I did not give them something belonging to the enemy."

Joshua suddenly got up and bade everyone goodnight. He went over to his men and began talking to them in a much softer tone than previously. Virginia became worried when Joshua pulled one of his men by the arm and stood him next to the Land Rover. He lifted the man's rifle and pointed it at them. She breathed a sigh of relief when she realized it was only to keep guard. The others took up position around the camp and began creating makeshift sleeping quarters.

"Do you think the guard speaks any English?" Lordy asked Hugh.

"I doubt it," Hugh responded, "and in any case he looks like he'll drop off to sleep any minute."

"Okay then," Lordy continued, "we can't let these bastards get away. Especially Joshua. He's a psycho if I ever met one."

"What can we do?" Hugh asked.

"I've kept a spare key for the Land Rover," Virginia said. "If we can get that weapon from the guard it'll be easy to kill the lot of them. They're all exhausted, so once they're asleep nothing will wake them."

"What if we kill the guard and just make a run for it in the Land Rover?" Hugh said. "One of us could creep over and be ready to start the engine while the others dispose of the guard. Keep the lights off and they'll never see us driving away, especially after waking from a deep sleep. What do you think?"

Lordy said, "That would work but it still leaves five of them free to go on a killing spree."

"We're not on a crusade to rid the world of black commies and terrorists," Hugh responded. "We're here to get those diamonds out. If you're worried we can call the police anonymously after we get away and give them Joshua's location."

"If we don't do anything Joshua might just use us to get away and then wipe us out when he thinks he's in the clear," Virginia said.

"And what if he notices the diamonds?" Lordy asked.

Hugh responded, "They are both possibilities, but we either trust Joshua or take control of things ourselves."

"I'm not sure," Lordy said. "I think we should wipe them out. That way we get the diamonds and the terrorists."

"It's entirely possible they will get us, Lordy," Virginia added.

Another guard came over and motioned for Hugh and Lordy to turn round. He re-tied their wrists, muttered something, and pushed them onto the ground. Next he pointed his rifle towards Virginia and then towards the Land Rover, signaling her to sleep in the back with Ron.

"That puts an end to those little ideas," Lordy said. "We'd better get some sleep."

They had to sleep on the ground without blankets and with their hands tied behind their backs. To keep a little warmer Hugh burrowed out a small trench with his boots and snuggled into it. He pushed his face inside the lapels of his field jacket and pulled his knees up in a fetal position. This helped to warm him even though the cold wind blew sand over his head and body; and after a while he drifted into sleep.

Hugh awoke at first light, shivering. He shook the sand and dust from his head and nudged Lordy, who struggled to his feet and began running on the spot to warm up. Joshua's men were still fast asleep, apart from the guard, who had perched himself on the hood of the Land Rover wrapped in a blanket. The commotion awakened Joshua and the majority of his men, who huddled around the Land Rover waiting for Joshua to distribute the meager morning rations.

Hugh edged his way over to the Land Rover trying not to be noticed. He saw that Ron was fully awake for the first time since the accident, but he looked ashen. Hugh watched as Virginia helped him take several long swigs at the water canteen. She gave him four painkillers and explained what had happened to the group, and what they had agreed with Joshua.

After everyone had eaten, Joshua shouted some orders at his men. They responded by throwing everything out of the Land Rover that could not be devoured or was not nailed down. One of Joshua's men fumbled about in the back of the Land Rover and found the two cases of diamonds. Hugh went into shock as he pulled up one of the cases, and after failing to open it, looked at Virginia and asked, "Eat? Eat lekker?"

"No," Virginia replied, "Rubbish. Junk. Throw away." She motioned for him to toss the cases away. He didn't question her rather inarticulate advice and just heaved both cases out of the Land Rover. Hugh watched in horror as the whole reason for his escapade was tossed insignificantly in the dirt. *At least he didn't open them,* he thought.

Hugh whispered to Lordy, "We're lucky Joshua didn't see that. I think he would have been a little more inquisitive. When you get a chance kick some sand over them just in case he noses around later."

"Will do. I'll try to get a fix on where we are, in case we get a chance to come back." Lordy walked over to the cases and kicked them out of sight. He indicated to the guard that he wanted to defecate. He also mouthed the word "compass" to Hugh while the guard looked in another direction. Hugh realized what he meant and passed the compass to him. Lordy disappeared behind a small mound and pulled the two cases with him. Hugh followed, but the guard became suspicious and stopped Hugh from going any further. Hugh could just see Lordy around the side of the mound as he dropped his pants and sat on the two cases, one under each cheek. The guard laughed heartily when he saw Lordy's smiling face. He waited for Lordy to finish and walked back to the Land Rover with him.

As they passed Hugh, Lordy slipped the compass back to him and whispered, "Pretend you're having a crap and see if you notice any landmarks. I couldn't turn round with the guard looking on."

Hugh went behind the mound, checked that the guard wasn't looking, and looked into the distance to pick out a couple of suitable landmarks. One large granite mountain to his northwest stood out, but nothing of any distinction could be seen to the east, and the mound cut out his southerly view. He used the center and top of the distant mountain to take a reading. He figured that if the dirt track were followed back from the main road it would only be possible to locate their current position within a mile or two. They had set up the camp about fifty yards to the north of the dirt track, but with the shifting sand and only an approximate compass reading it would be difficult to retrace their steps. Hugh knew full well that if a strong sandstorm blew up, the cases could be buried for years.

He kicked more sand over the diamonds and returned to the Land Rover to find everyone on board. Joshua and his NCO were inside and the other four were on the roof. Joshua signaled to Hugh, using a revolver, to get into the driver's seat. Virginia sat next to him while Ron was left lying on the floor. Joshua sat directly behind Hugh and told Lordy to sit in the rear, opposite his armed NCO. All the other weapons and much of their military clothing were dumped along with the other items from the Land Rover.

"Joshua, we had trouble with an oil leakage," Hugh said.

"Did you indeed?" Joshua replied, with a smug look on his face. "Well fuck me blind!" He looked around for a reaction but everyone remained silent. "I noticed the oil patch in the sand underneath the Land Rover. Just drive slowly and let us hope we have luck of the Irish."

Hugh drove carefully along the dirt track for twenty miles. Then the inevitable occurred. The warning light flashed, indicating that the engine had overheated. He signaled to Joshua to look at the light and asked what to do.

"How far are we from the road?" Joshua asked.

"Can't be more than five miles," Virginia responded.

"Just run the engine until it stalls, we have nothing to lose," Joshua ordered.

"Maybe one of us could walk to the road and get help—flag down a truck."

"I doubt it, old boy," Joshua replied in a dismissive tone, "but let me peruse the map in any case." Joshua pulled a tattered map from his inside pocket.

As he studied it, Hugh noticed Virginia slip her hand into her pocket and slowly turn onto her side in the passenger's seat, towards him. In a flash Virginia moved her leg over to the edge of his seat and jammed her foot on the brake.

The wheels locked and the Land Rover skidded, hurling Joshua forward. Hugh watched in horror as Virginia grabbed his ear with one hand and jammed a knife into his eye. He turned sideways and tried to jump into the rear of the Land Rover but got stuck between Joshua and the steering wheel.

Lordy lifted his lanky leg and thrust the bottom of his foot into the NCO's face. He rammed his head through the side window and held it against the jagged rim of broken glass. The four men on the roof were hurled forward in front of the skidding Land Rover; two landed on the hood and two on the ground. Joshua screamed and convulsed as he tried to pull the knife out of his eye socket.

Virginia jumped into the back of the Land Rover and grabbed the barrel of Joshua's revolver. Lordy snatched the NCO's gun and continued to press his face into the broken glass of the side window.

Hugh froze. Things seemed to happen in slow motion until he felt a blow on the shoulder. He turned and saw that Virginia had kicked him in the back. His mind cleared.

"Run them over," she screamed.

Hugh accelerated hard, crunching over the two men on the ground and hurling the two on the hood into the windshield and then to the ground.

Virginia and Joshua wrestled on the cramped floor, both attempting to get the revolver, but neither of them could pull it away from the other.

Lordy got off a round into Joshua's spine while still pressing the NCO's head against the side window. After the first shot Lordy pulled the trigger several times, but the gun didn't fire, so he kept kicking and punching the NCO until he fell directly on top of Ron. Lordy ignored Ron's screams and beat the NCO on the back of the head with the gun until he shuddered into unconsciousness.

Virginia finally pulled the revolver from Joshua's hand and let off two rounds into his body. He slumped on the floor; his enormous body moribund like a beached whale. She threw the gun back to Lordy, who fired one shot into the NCO and then jumped out of the back of the vehicle. Lordy ran back twenty-five yards to cover the injured men. One of them stood upright with his hands in the air, the other just moaned as he convulsed in the dirt.

"Kill them," Hugh screamed out of the side window.

Two shots rang out and there were instantly two fewer SWAPO fighters in the world. He went back a further ten yards to the other two men, who were both critically injured but still moving. Lordy pointed the revolver and pulled the trigger. Nothing happened.

"Out of ammo," he shouted to Hugh. "Reverse over them."

Hugh crunched the gear stick into reverse, drove over the twisted bodies, slammed it into first gear, and ran over them again. As he tried to reverse a second time, steam belched from under the hood and the Land Rover spluttered to a halt.

Lordy stood bent over in pain with his hands on his thighs, struggling to regain his breath. Virginia pushed the dead NCO away from Ron and readjusted his dressings. Ron briefly regained consciousness, moaned, lifted his head, and passed out again.

Hugh jumped out of the driver's seat and casually walked over to examine the bodies of the SWAPO soldiers. "That'll teach them to mess with us," Hugh shouted as he tapped the bodies with his boot.

"I'll dump them over there," Lordy said, pointing to a small depression in the ground.

One by one Lordy grabbed the dead men by the ankles and dragged them away from the track. Both Hugh and Lordy struggled to pull Joshua's body from the Land Rover and when they finally extracted him they noticed the hideous sight of Virginia's knife protruding from his eye.

"That's the knife we found in the skeleton at Elizabeth Bay isn't it?" Lordy said to Virginia, as he dumped Joshua's body into the depression with his men. "I wonder how many bodies that's been inside. What made you keep it?"

"Don't know," Virginia replied. "I just did. Someone up there must be looking out for me."

Lordy kicked sand and dirt over the bodies and then walked back to the Land Rover to check the oil. "Completely empty."

Virginia sighed and said, "What else can go wrong? We'd better put our thinking caps on and come up with something otherwise Ron isn't going to make it."

"You're right," Hugh said. "By the way what made you start that little fracas?"

"If Joshua had realized that the Land Rover was kaput he wouldn't have hesitated to kill us. We'd have been of no further use. I noticed he lost concentration when he read that map, so I thought I could deal with him and the four on the roof by jamming the brakes on. The knife was in the right place at the right time – pure luck. If you remember they didn't search me very thoroughly, so I just left it in my pocket. The only thing I wasn't sure about was how the NCO in the back would react."

"Quick thinking," Hugh said, handing out a rare compliment.

"The NCO was almost asleep, so that was easy," Lordy added.

"Well, let's stop congratulating ourselves and think how we can get out of here," Hugh said.

"There really is only one thing to do," Lordy interjected. "One of us will have to walk back and get the diamonds while someone else goes to the main road and tries to hitch a ride to the nearest village."

Neither Virginia nor Hugh answered straight away.

"I'll walk to the main road," Hugh said. "It can't be more than five miles."

"Okay, I'll go back to fetch the cases," Lordy said. "It must be twenty miles each way so I won't be back until tomorrow. How much water do we have?"

"About two gallons," Hugh replied.

"I'll take a gallon with me. That should be enough. At least it isn't the middle of summer."

"I won't need any for a five mile walk," Hugh said.

"Ron will need most of the other gallon," Lordy added, "but that doesn't leave a lot for you, Virginia."

"I'll hunt around and collect some moisture overnight and in the morning," she replied. "That should add a couple of pints to our supply."

"We'd better camouflage the Land Rover before we leave," Lordy said.

"We can't," Virginia replied. "Joshua threw all the equipment away this morning. Even the shovels are gone."

"Push it off the track and cover the top with sand," Hugh added, "and hope that'll be good enough."

An hour later Lordy began his long walk back along the track, while Hugh went east towards the main road. Lordy paced himself at three miles per hour to reduce any unnecessary sweating. He would need just over six hours to walk the twenty miles back to the original campsite and an indeterminate amount of time to find the exact location. Since he began the trip at 9:00 AM, and allowing one hour to rest on the way, he calculated he would arrive at the approximate spot with still enough light left in the day to search for the cases.

It was a cloudless day and Lordy strolled casually along under the warm winter sun for the first three hours without any signs of fatigue. He rested for forty-five minutes enjoying the complete silence of the desert environment and drank some water. When he continued he felt his leg muscles cramp. *Not so young any more,* he thought. This triggered memories of his old school days at Charter Hill when he had to take part in a long cross-country run. His thoughts wandered again from events in his youth to his shenanigans with Karl and other mercenaries. He thought about all the people in his past for whom he still held genuine affection and laughed when he could only count two, Karl and Virginia.

His mind flipped back into reality with the noise of distant thunder. He looked at the horizon and saw heavy black cumulonimbus clouds forming. *Unusual in this region at this time of the year,* he thought.

The first raindrops fell, which soon turned into a downpour and then into a cloudburst. Lordy had no cover whatsoever but he continued to press on through the soggy sand and strong winds until he collapsed with exhaustion.

When the rain stopped he sipped water that he had collected in his hat and prepared to continue. "Where's the path?" The contours of the track were no longer recognizable—they had been washed away by the rain and the wind.

He checked his watch and quickly estimated that he had covered about fifteen miles. The only thing he could do from this point was to take a crude compass reading and hope for the best. The large granite landmark, used to take the original compass reading, sat alone on the horizon, but Lordy knew it would be of little use to him unless he could find the track. He could be miles off course and not know it. Lordy strained his memory to try to visualize even the smallest landmark that might lead him in the right direction.

He remembered the track rising in altitude just after they left the original campsite early that morning, so he scanned the horizon and picked out two places in the distance that might be possibilities. He walked for just over an hour until he came to the first of the two inclines, and then circled around the area trying to pick up any remnants of the track. Fortunately just at the start of the incline he noticed a portion of the track relatively untouched by the wind and the rain. At the highest point of the incline he could make out its overall direction. It led away from the other high point, so Lordy concluded that his prize must be nearby. He walked in circles around the high point, each time taking a wider arc, which allowed him to search about ten acres fairly quickly.

He became despondent after hours of fruitless searching until a flapping sound emanating from behind a small hill about twenty yards ahead caught his attention. It was the tarpaulin they had used to camouflage the Land Rover. He rushed over to the small hill and on the ground in front of him, side by side, were the two cases of diamonds, unmoved by the elements and stripped of the sand that he had covered them with. Lordy screamed at the top of his voice and danced around like a man possessed. This burst of enthusiasm soon waned after he realized that he only had two cups of water left and no clear idea of the direction back to the Land Rover.

He scoffed two cans of beans and began the return trek, walking due east and keeping to the remnants of the track. Lordy figured that if he walked until nightfall he would be approximately fifteen miles from Virginia and the others—if all went well.

To reduce the strain on his arms he tied the two cases to a length of wire that had been discarded at the site and looped it around his neck. However the wire began to cut into his neck almost immediately so he scratched around until he found an old blanket that one of the SWAPO soldiers had thrown away. The blanket, still damp from the rainstorm, shielded his neck and shoulders from the sharp wire.

Lordy collapsed after an hour of struggling over the rough terrain. The extra 110 pounds of burden from the two cases of diamonds had taken its toll. He dropped to the ground, wrapped the blanket around his head and body, and fell into a deep sleep.

He had only slept for four hours when the cold night air woke him. He looked at his watch—only 10:00 PM. Another seven hours to wait before daylight and the prospect of a further six hours of walking ahead. Now shivering and hungry, he decided to walk for a while to warm his body. With the help of an almost full moon he managed to see well enough to navigate the rough terrain, but after two more agonizing hours he could no longer continue.

Lordy slept on and off during the rest of the night and continued his journey at first light, now acutely aware that he could be badly off course after walking blind for so long. However he thought if he kept walking due east he would eventually meet the main road. If this happened he would bury the diamonds nearby, mark the spot, and then hitch a ride to the nearest town. After resting he would then try to purloin a vehicle and return to recover the diamonds.

Hugh quickly covered the distance from the Land Rover to the road, where he waved down a large truck heading south. The truck screeched to a halt about twenty yards past him and the truck driver dangled his arm out of the window and waved Hugh aboard. The driver, probably in his early forties, looked overweight, unshaven, and heavily sunburned.

"What the fuck are you doing out here on foot?" the truck driver asked, not bothering to remove a cigarette from his mouth while he spoke.

"Problems with my vehicle. It's parked a few miles back. I'm surprised you didn't see it."

"Jump in for fuck's sake. I can drop you in Karasburg if you like."

"That would be fine. I need to rent another vehicle and go back and fix mine."

Hugh jumped on the truck and the driver took off as fast as its massive engine could manage.

"What are you doing out here?"

"Doing some prospecting for the Government."

"What'ya looking for? More fucking diamonds I suppose?"

"No, uranium actually," Hugh responded and quickly changed the subject. "Who do you work for?"

"Associated Mines of South West Africa. They're stingy bunch of bastards but at least it's a fucking job."

"What's in the back of the truck?" Hugh asked.

"Semi-processed zinc ore—twenty fucking tons of it. I'm taking it to a processing plant in the Northern Cape, near Springbok."

"Are you going to stay in South West after independence?" Hugh asked, trying to keep the conversation in the driver's court.

"As soon as the name changes to Namibia I'm fucking off back to Cape Town to retire. I'm not living under the thumb of a load of ignorant fucking kaffirs—no fucking way. I don't under-fucking-stand why those fucking liberals in Europe and America support them. The place will be in chaos within six months and everyone will be living in fucking mud huts and wiping their backsides on useless fucking bank notes. We'll all be fucked."

"Hmm, interesting analysis and vision of the future you have for Namibia," Hugh said in a sarcastic tone.

"First Kenya and Tanzania, then Rhodesia, then Angola, then Mozambique, and now South West. I tell you those fucking kaffirs will be on the fucking moon in ten years. Dancing around campfires up there and breeding like fucking flies on lumps of fucking shit. My name is Stefanus Kruger by the way. Friends call me Stef."

"Mine's Hugh—nice meeting you," Hugh said holding out his hand to Stef.

Each time Stef changed gear he released a string of abuse and his voice became progressively louder as he went from low to high gear.

"Likewise," Stef responded, as he worked his way through the truck's gears.

"How often do you make this trip?"

"Four times a week. I go out early in the morning and I'm home by four in the afternoon. Mind you, I don't have anything to go home to. My wife fucked off two years ago."

Stef wound the window down and spat.

"Sorry to hear that. What happened?"

"She said I was too crude. Fuck knows why she thought that. She didn't like me drinking neither. I only used to go out with my drinking pals four or five times a week."

"That's a bit too constricting for anyone. Very unreasonable of her I would say."

"That's what I told her and her fucking mother, but they ganged up on me. Made my life fucking hell. The mother's got a fucking tongue like an open razor. One mouthful from that old cunt and you were fucked for a week."

"It's a wonder you didn't beat them both up," Hugh added.

"No, she has two huge fucking brothers, 'hunt and cunt' I call them. Their family name is 'Hunt' you see and one of them is a big fucking queer. They work on their old man's farm. Strong as fucking bulls, both of them."

"Looks like we're coming up to Karasburg," Hugh said.

"Yup, I'll drop you at the post office and you can get help there."

Stef stopped the truck and bade farewell to Hugh. "Nice talking to you, Hughie, old son. If you're in Keetmanshoop at the weekend drop into Kruger's Bar and we can get blind fucking drunk together. My brother owns it, so if you're too fucked to walk home you can camp down at the back of the bar."

"Okay, thanks for the offer, Stef. I'll try and slip it in to my schedule."

"There's a big fat tart works there. We call her the Mattress. She's got tits the size of a fucking cow's udders. Give her half-a-dozen drinks and she goes with anyone. Bangs like a shit house door in a force-nine gale."

"How intriguing," Hugh replied. "Anyway, Stef, thanks for the ride. I hope we meet up again soon."

Hugh jumped down from the truck and shook his head. "What a perfectly appalling fellow," he said under his breath. He walked into the post office and asked the senior clerk where he could get a rental car. After a few phone calls and conversations with other customers the manager recommended asking the local police department for help, as they often patrolled the road up towards Luderitz. Hugh declined and walked over to a hotel just across the road.

He asked the receptionist if she knew of anything in town, and after just one phone call, plus Hugh's offer of fifty rand for a one day loan of a car, an elderly man showed up outside the hotel in a rather beaten up Datsun pickup truck. Hugh talked him out of coming along for the trip and quickly drove away to buy food and drink and eight quarts of oil for the Land Rover.

When he stopped at a gas station to fill the tank, a mechanic noticed that the two front tires were badly worn. He told Hugh that he would be lucky if they lasted ten miles. Hugh became frustrated when the mechanic told him he would have to wait until the next day to get spares. After several attempts to hurry things along, Hugh gave up and stayed in town for the night, leaving the next morning just before eleven, after the tires were replaced.

Hugh bumped off the main road onto the dirt track and drove the five miles across open country towards Virginia and Ron. He sounded the horn several times to announce his arrival.

"Where's Lordy? Is he back yet?"

"Nice to see you too," Virginia replied. "No, I think he must have been held up by the storm yesterday."

"Ron still alive?" Hugh asked indifferently.

"He's taken a turn for the worse—seemed alert a few hours ago but now he's in a coma."

"What time do you think Lordy will be back then?" Hugh asked, ignoring Virginia's comment about Ron.

"No idea, but we might have to take Ron to the hospital if Lordy doesn't show up soon."

"Maybe I should drive inland for a couple of miles and see if I can find him."

"You could try, but the rain might have washed the track away. You could get stuck or lost."

"Here's some food and water and I've got plenty of oil for the Land Rover. You see to that and I'll spend an hour looking for Lordy."

"Okay, but if you don't find him within an hour come back and we'll take Ron into Karasburg."

Hugh drove for thirty minutes but could not find Lordy. When he returned, Ron was fully awake, and since he appeared much better they decided to wait until the next day to resume the search for Lordy, and not take Ron directly to Karasburg.

The next morning Hugh drove inland again, following the remnants of the track. He stopped and stood on the top of the pickup truck to look for Lordy. Having no luck spotting him, he drove west for another ten minutes and repeated the process. This time he saw a figure staggering across the landscape, heading in a northerly direction. *That must be Lordy, but where the hell is he going?*

He sounded the horn but Lordy didn't respond. The ground looked far too treacherous to risk driving, so Hugh ran towards him, shouting as he went. Lordy staggered and fell, got up again, and fell sideways. By the time Hugh reached him he was completely prostrate.

"Lordy, where are you going? You're heading in the wrong direction."

Lordy did not answer at first. Hugh shook him a few times and finally he muttered a few incomprehensible phrases. Hugh wiped sand from Lordy's mouth and realized he wouldn't last much longer without water. He pulled the two cases of diamonds from him and bolted back to the pickup truck. He sat in the driver's seat wondering whether to leave Lordy or take him back. *Virginia might suspect something if I leave him here,* he thought. *I'd better take him back.* Hugh went back to Lordy with a bottle of water and slowly tipped it into his mouth.

Lordy recovered enough to walk back to the pickup truck and although he vomited a couple of times due to drinking too much too quickly, he soon re-hydrated himself.

"We thought you were lost for good."

"I got off track in the night. Dehydration must have played tricks on my mind."

"Oh well, we've got you back . . . and the diamonds. Let's get moving."

Hugh drove back slowly and carefully, retracing the wheel marks left in loose earth on his inward journey and soon reached Virginia and Ron.

"How's Ron?" Lordy asked.

Virginia shook her head. "He keeps going in and out of consciousness."

"We'd better get going fast," Lordy said. "I'll sit with Ron while you drive, Virginia."

"I'll follow," Hugh added.

They drove across the rough terrain without incident and met the main road between Luderitz and Karasburg. Lordy held Ron's head in his hands and tried to keep him awake by constantly speaking to him and encouraging him to hold on.

"Turn east and go straight into Karasburg," he said to Virginia.

"I'll keep to sixty, any faster might cause the engine to blow," she said. "How is he?"

"Not good, Virginia. He's going fast. Barely breathing now. The blood loss has stopped at least. If the engine gives out we'll have to move Ron into the back of that rickety old pickup Hugh's driving. That'll be torture for Ron."

"What's that squeaking sound, Virginia?"

"I think it's the bearings in the front axle."

Virginia and Lordy were willing the engine to hold up as the squeaking intensified.

"Twenty miles to go. Look at the map again. Are you sure there's nothing between here and Karasburg?"

"Nothing that could help Ron," Lordy replied.

They reached the town and drove straight into the main street and followed the signs for the hospital. Virginia ran inside to summon help while Lordy and a reluctant Hugh carried Ron. Two nurses quickly took over and within minutes a doctor appeared.

Lordy said he would explain things to the hospital staff, leaving Virginia and Hugh to find a garage that could fix the Land Rover.

"We were on our way down from Windoek after a hunting expedition. Ron had just finished fixing a problem with the Land Rover when the jack slipped and crushed his legs."

"I'm Doctor Van Zyl," the doctor said, holding out his hand to Lordy. "When did it happen?"

"About an hour ago."

"Why didn't you go to Keetmanshoop? It's much nearer?"

"We panicked and just drove as fast as we could in this direction."

The Doctor walked away without comment and went into a small emergency room to attend to Ron. Lordy spoke to the hospital receptionist and gave her the least amount of Ron's personal details as possible. She only just managed to suppress laughter after looking him up and down—he was way over six feet tall, covered in dust, and with no sleeves on his jacket.

Lordy paced around the reception area until Virginia and Hugh arrived.

"How's he doing?" Virginia asked.

"The nurse said he's critical but the Doctor is confident he'll pull through. They've fixed his wounds and given him a blood transfusion, but they'll have to work on his legs tomorrow. He might lose them. The doctor seemed suspicious when I told him the accident had just happened."

Hugh changed the subject. "The Land Rover will be fixed by tomorrow so I suggest Lordy comes with me to Steinkop, where I'll hand the cargo over to my contact. Virginia, you should probably stay here with Ron."

After Virginia and Lordy agreed, Hugh went away to find a telephone.

"I don't trust him anymore, Lordy," Virginia said. "Especially the way he acted under fire. If Ron and I hadn't been there he would have left you and Karl to the mercy of those SWAPO guerillas. And look what he said after Ron's accident."

"I'll keep an eye on him. Any trouble and I'll eliminate the bastard. If anything happens to me make sure you get even with him. I'll do the same for you."

"Right."

"Where shall I contact you? Are you going back to Port Elizabeth after you hand the cargo over or will you stay in Johannesburg?"

"I'll part company with him in Steinkop and after he leaves double back to see if I can work out who he's handing the diamonds to."

"Wise move."

"I'll call you at the hotel and keep you posted."

"Watch it, he's coming back."

"I'm going back to the hotel to get something to eat and drink," Hugh said. "It's been a taxing day."

The next morning before breakfast, Lordy went along to the hospital to check on Ron and then joined Virginia in the hotel for breakfast.

"How's Ron?"

"Just about awake when I got there. He's looking a lot better. Drugged up to the eyeballs though."

"I hope he doesn't talk in his sleep."

"They'll put it down to the drugs if he does."

"I haven't seen any sign of Hugh this morning."

"The Land Rover is still here so I assume he hasn't done a runner."

"What did you tell them at the hospital yesterday?"

"I wrote it down last night in case they ask you the same questions. Doctor Van Zyl is a bit suspicious but I don't think he'll push the point. The receptionist almost pissed herself laughing at me in these clothes. So I think we're okay."

Hugh didn't join them at breakfast but he met them just after 10:00 AM and held a brief discussion. They agreed on the plan discussed the night before and said their farewells. Lordy and Hugh went to the garage and waited for the Land Rover to be fixed while Virginia went to the hospital to sit with Ron.

Lordy found it difficult to ignore the tense atmosphere in the Land Rover during the drive back to South Africa. They hardly spoke. Lordy had built up a deep animosity against Hugh and he could barely contain himself. However, he knew himself too well. How many times in the past had he been handed wealth and opportunity? Each time a self-destructive element inside him had thrown it away needlessly. If he played along with Hugh and buried his feelings, he would walk away with enough money to start his life over again. Maybe even get back with Virginia. He couldn't make up his mind if this desire to harm Hugh manifested itself out of a need to deliver justice for Karl and Ron, or to please the old demon inside him. In any case he held his temper and the journey passed without incident.

Hugh and Lordy arrived in Steinkop too late in the evening to contact Chris Conway, so they stayed in a small hotel for the night. This suited Hugh's purpose because he had no intention of allowing Lordy to meet anyone else involved in the scheme, least of all Chris.

Hugh put in a call to Chris early the next morning and arranged to meet him at 7:00 PM. He then went to see Lordy in his room just along the corridor. He banged on the door a few times to wake Lordy and told him to take the Land Rover back to Port Elizabeth, where he would contact him in a week.

Lordy became even more suspicious at this change in plan, but he went along with it. He felt obliged to cover Virginia and himself in the event of a double cross. He ate breakfast and drove out of town, waited for an hour, and then returned to Steinkop.

He drove into a small gas station and made an excuse for the mechanic to check the Land Rover. He told the owner that he needed to visit a couple of nearby mines during the day and arranged to borrow a car. He bought some less conspicuous clothing, drove back to Hugh's hotel, and parked across the road to see what would transpire.

He changed his parking space twice, as other cars moved away, in order to see directly into the small reception area. After waiting for an hour he noticed the receptionist walk out of the hotel and cross the street, so he took the opportunity to sneak in and check the register. Hugh had booked for another night.

Just after dark Lordy saw Hugh through the wide glass windows along the front of the hotel. The bright lights inside made it easy for him to see the reception area, the dining room, and a small section of the bar. He saw Hugh speak with the receptionist and then walk into the bar and appear to order a drink.

Ten minutes later a man drove up to the hotel in a jeep. Initially he did not pay much attention, as several men had come and gone in the past few hours. However, after exchanging words with the receptionist, the man walked through to the bar and shook hands with Hugh. Lordy's interest immediately picked up. He had a feeling he had seen the man before but couldn't place him. Lordy continued to watch Hugh and the man chat as they stood at the bar. They touched glasses in a toast and both laughed after the man patted Hugh on the back.

"Chris, let's get down to business," Hugh said. "Are you ready to take the stuff?"

"Absolutely. I've got a good place to hide them and I have someone reliable to help me introduce them to their shiny little brothers."

"Excellent. I'll give them to you when we leave. Come up to my room when we've finished this drink and we can each carry a case over to your jeep. They weigh just over fifty pounds each."

"You mean you've left them in your room?"

"That's right. No one would believe they were diamonds even if you told them so. By the way can you introduce them a bit quicker then we originally planned – say six months?"

"That's pushing it, maybe eight months but no less. It'll raise too many questions and I'll have half of head office down here handing out medals with one hand and digging for the things with the other."

"Okay, I get the message, but do it as quickly as possible."

Lordy saw them leave the hotel, each carrying one of the cases of diamonds, and walk nonchalantly over to the Jeep. *So he's the pick-up man,* Lordy thought. He watched the man drive off into the night after exchanging a few words with Hugh, who returned to the hotel.

Lordy followed the jeep, keeping about fifty yards behind. When the jeep went into a driveway, Lordy passed by, waited a few minutes, and then drove back to make a note of the street number. He overcame the temptation to sneak over to see what the stranger would do with the two cases because of the high risk of being seen. He drove back into the center of the town, bought some coffee and sandwiches, and found a convenient place to park his car. Since Hugh stayed in the only hotel in Steinkop, Lordy had to sleep on the back seat of the car.

The next morning Lordy returned the car and picked up the Land Rover. He went to the town's small post office and flicked through the public copy of the local telephone directory, looking for the name and phone number that matched the address he had discovered the previous evening.

There were only 500 names listed in the directory for Steinkop so it did not take him long to match the address. He called the number under the pretense of being an insurance salesman. Cherrie answered the phone. Lordy told her that Mr. Conway had asked him to follow up on some questions about lower cost insurance. She was fully duped and quickly gave him Chris's telephone number at work.

Lordy soon discovered that Chris held the post of Mine Manager at Allied Diamond Mine, just a few miles down the road. Satisfied that he had placed Chris correctly, and knowing that nothing more could be gained by staying in Steinkop, he drove out of town and headed for Karasburg to see Virginia and to check on Ron's progress.

He arrived there three hours later and went straight to the hospital. The receptionist recognized him and said hello in a rather subdued fashion.

"Sir, would you mind waiting over there and I'll ask the Doctor to speak with you."

"Is there a problem? Is Mr. Farmer all right?"

"The Doctor is just coming. Here he is now."

"I'm afraid Mr. Farmer passed away last night. Gangrene set in to his right leg. We amputated straight away but . . . he died from blood poisoning. I explained everything to Miss, err . . . "

"Virginia."

"Yes, quite. I believe she's still in the hotel."

Lordy left the hospital with tears rolling down his face, and after regaining his composure he went to the hotel, looking for Virginia.

"I've just been to see . . . I mean . . . to the hospital."

"I didn't expect you back here."

"I'll tell you about it later."

"He died last night. I spoke to him yesterday afternoon. He

regained consciousness for about an hour but after that he faded fast."

They embraced each other, both choked up and trying not to cry openly. After a few minutes Virginia said, "That's Karl, Henny and now Ron. Three out of five is not good odds."

"I know."

"That's our little plan for buying into a small hotel kaput . . . unless of course we go back for the diamonds in Elizabeth Bay. I wonder if everyone would have gone through with it?"

"I think so, everyone seemed serious."

"Too late now. By the way, should we contact their relatives and let them know what happened?"

"Karl's daughter and ex-wife are living in Cape Town. Karl was very close to his daughter. Alice, I think her name is, but the ex-wife wouldn't care one way or the other. Henny wasn't married, but I have his parents' address in Rhodesia. I'll send them a letter. I'm not sure about Ron. We can ask around in Port Elizabeth. I'm sure someone will know."

"We can drive back via Cape Town if you like, find Karl's daughter, and then make our way back to Port Elizabeth."

"That's fine. What about Ron's burial?"

"I've made arrangements with the minister of the Dutch Reformed Church in town. All he needs is a death certificate. I'll get that from the hospital in the morning and we can bury him in the afternoon. The police showed up earlier and wanted to get some details on the cause of death, so I told them the same story you told the doctor."

Lordy explained what happened when he followed Chris Conway after meeting Hugh.

"Maybe this guy Conway is selling them for Hugh."

"Maybe. I always wondered how he would do that. It was the only piece of the plan I couldn't explain."

"Where's Hugh now?"

"He's checked out of the hotel. When I spoke to him yesterday he said he would contact us in Port Elizabeth in a few weeks to give us the rest of our pay."

"What about Karl, Ron and Henny. Did he mention their cut?"

"No, but I'm going to ask. I'll give it to their next of kin."

"I'll drop in to see Hugh—unannounced. We'll eliminate the bastard if he double-crosses us."

THIRTEEN

*A*t police headquarters in Johannesburg, Cap Muller was talking on the telephone when Karen burst into his office.

"Cap, we found another one."

"Where? Same MO?" he asked, ignoring his phone conversation.

"Same. The township police found her body in Soweto."

"What's her name?"

"Pretty sure it's Elaine Franklin."

"Strange . . . he hasn't attacked for almost a year. I was beginning to think it was all over."

"Let's put some policewomen back on the street in disguise. Full court press this time. I want at least four out each week, regardless of resources."

"Will do," Karen replied.

"By the way, any luck with tracing that ring imprint from the last murder?"

"We drew a complete blank."

"That's a shame."

Detective Phillipus Matagwe tapped on the door as Karen was about to leave.

"What's on your mind, Phillipus?" Cap asked, knowing that Phillipus would never bother him unless it was something important.

"Sir, my brother visited me from Durban last week and he had with him several books concerning ancient coats-of-arms and flags. He is taking a course in the history of heraldry. As an optional subject you understand . . . "

"Get to the damned point, Phillipus," Cap snapped.

"Well, sir, as I looked through the hundreds of patterns in the book, sir, I saw one which resembled the ring imprint in the De Jong murder . . . "

"What!" Karen shouted.

"Yes, Madam, very similar. It's a marking used by monks from a secret sect from Europe in the fourteenth century."

"What sort of sect?" Karen asked.

"The book never said, so I went to the library to find out more, but I could not get the information."

"Why on earth not?" Cap asked.

"They wouldn't let me into the whites-only library where these books are kept, sir."

"Karen, go with Phillipus and check it out," Cap said as his phone rang.

It was David Foster, Cap's superior, summoning him to a meeting to explain the lack of progress in the serial murder case. He knew unless a major breakthrough occurred in the next few months he would be removed from the case and his reputation and that of his team would be in shreds.

Cap adjusted his tie, buttoned his jacket, and walked into the conference room on the fifth floor to await his fate. The review board members, many of whom knew Cap, greeted him in a friendly tone. After the introductions no one spoke for an uncomfortably long period until David Foster formally opened the review.

The team thanked Cap for all his hard work but warned that unless progress was made in the case he would be removed and another officer assigned. This was especially important since the board members had just heard about Elaine Franklin's murder. One of the board members suggested to Cap that he utilize the security services to help solve the case. Although this was very unusual it was felt that a different perspective might yield some more positive results. After several other recommendations were made Cap was asked to respond.

Cap stood up, rubbed his eyes, and turned towards the board members. He thanked them for their support and explained that it was the most difficult case of his career. Cap went on to explain all the details surrounding the murders and the fact that only a limited number of clues were available. He mentioned the ring imprint and how they tried to find out what it meant, but before he could finish a board member interrupted him.

"Cap, we'll give you six months. After that you're off the case."

Cap left the meeting and later that evening assembled his team and explained what the board had decided. He asked again about the ring-imprint lead that Phillipus had found.

Karen feigned a smile and said, "A dead-end I'm afraid. We looked through all the reference books but we didn't find anything specific. One of the professors at the university thinks it might be related to a French religious cult from the fourteenth or fifteenth century."

Cap's head sprang up as he fired back a response. "Send it to the Vatican? They have an enormous reference library going back well before the fourteenth century. Contact the Department of Foreign Affairs and see if they have a contact in the Vatican."

"Okay, Cap, consider it done."

Back in his home in Johannesburg, Hugh gloated over his success and boasted to Susan about his exploits.

Hugh clenched his fist and punched the palm of his other hand. "Another six months and we'll be made. The hard part is over. Everything's in fast-forward mode from now on."

"What about our expenses, Hugh? You know we're down to our last few thousand."

"Twenty actually. And I have to pay the remnants of the action team 10,000 each."

"How?"

"I'll pay one of them. That's it. Virginia probably. She's the most dangerous. Then I'll have to think about how to deal with the other one. Anyway leave that to me."

They went to the Rowing club for a meal and a few drinks and tried not to appear too pleased with themselves. Hugh dealt with a few business issues while at the club before returning home with Susan.

Hugh walked into the lounge and stopped dead in his tracks when he saw Virginia sitting in an armchair with her arms crossed and her foot on a coffee table.

"Virginia, how nice to see you," Hugh said, quickly recovering from the surprise. "I thought we decided not to meet each other here. Oh, by the way, Susan, this is Virginia."

They shook hands without speaking.

"I really need our share of the takings, Hugh. Karl has a daughter in Cape Town who depends on him, and Henny has parents in Rhodesia. Lordy is looking for Ron's relatives at the moment."

Hugh stretched his arms out and yawned. "Of course I'll pay you and Lordy, but why don't we split the difference with the other's pay? They're dead anyway. Who's to know any better?"

"I will," said Virginia, as she tapped her index finger on the arm of the chair. "And so will Lordy. You made the deal and you'll get an enormous amount out of it. We completed the mission successfully, so we expect you to make good on your promises. And by the way, we know about Mr. Conway in Steinkop."

Hugh shouted to one of the servants to fetch him a drink. "Okay," Hugh said angrily, "I'll give you 20,000 now, but I need a few days to get the rest. Where's Lordy by the way? Does he know you're here?"

Hugh felt Virginia's eyes go straight through him.

"He knows I'm here all right. I'll tell him to pick up the rest of the money next week. Let's say Wednesday night. Is that enough time?"

"There we are then. Wednesday it is."

Hugh got the money from his safe in the basement and returned to find Virginia and Susan glaring at each other.

Hugh threw it at Virginia. "It's all there, count it if you like."

"No need, I trust you," she said sarcastically. She walked out of the house, passing Susan as if she didn't exist.

"She's a nice piece of work," Susan said sharply, "and damned good looking with it."

"Yes, and very dangerous. An ex-BOSS agent apparently."

Virginia returned to her hotel and called Lordy in Port Elizabeth. They had arranged it so that if she didn't call that night Lordy would know something was seriously wrong and he would fly to Johannesburg and exact revenge on Hugh.

She told Lordy what had happened with her meeting with Hugh and they agreed that he should fly to Johannesburg on Wednesday to collect the rest of the team's pay. If Lordy did not contact her by Friday then she would know something was amiss.

Lordy had found Ron's only known relative – his sister who lived just outside Port Elizabeth, and told her that Ron was killed in an accident. Her three children were all very attached to Ron, who supported the family financially after the husband ran off.

"They were all broken hearted," Lordy said, "and I was upset as well."

"Karl's daughter was the same. She's at university in Cape Town. If we don't get his cut from Hugh she'll have to drop out."

"That bastard Hugh has a lot to answer for."

"He'll pay one way or another."

Lordy flew to Johannesburg on Wednesday afternoon, one week later, and prepared himself for the meeting with Hugh. He still harbored a deep resentment for Hugh but was determined to keep his temper and collect the money due to him. He considered taking a firearm but at the last minute decided against it, assuming that Hugh wouldn't be so reckless as to kill someone in his own house. He also worried about getting caught taking a weapon on board an aircraft without a permit.

Lordy stood in line at the airline check-in desk and waited to get a boarding pass. Just as his turn came a man jumped in front of him.

"Am I too late for the Johannesburg flight? My name's Gavin Brown. I'm in business class."

"No, sir, plenty of time," the ticket clerk replied.

"Don't mind me," Lordy said, as he looked the stranger up and down.

Lordy detected a strong smell of alcohol from him, and not wanting to cause a commotion, suppressed his annoyance. He boarded the plane thirty minutes later without incident.

It was dark when Lordy arrived at Hugh's house. Just before he pressed the door bell he felt a deep sense of foreboding, not quite the proverbial "shiver down the spine", but a haunting feeling, similar to what he felt when his father packed him off to boarding school for the first time. Oddly enough Hugh answered the door.

"I suppose you've come about your money?"

"Something like that," Lordy responded, looking deep into Hugh's dark brown eyes and folding his arms.

"Take a seat. Have some wine. It's very good."

"That's very civil of you, but I'm not really a wine man myself."

"Scotch . . . brandy, or beer maybe?"

"Sherry if you have it."

"Of course you upper-class types love your sherry. Come into my study. I keep my best vintages there."

Lordy looked around at the oil paintings and designer furniture before he seated himself immediately opposite Hugh's desk, in a comfortable swivel armchair.

"Reminds me of my father's study."

"Really?" Hugh replied. "Don't get too comfortable."

"I won't. But one never gets over such elegant things, don't you think?"

Hugh handed him a sherry, poured a scotch and soda for himself, and sat down behind his desk.

"Virginia came here last week, as I'm sure you're aware. She seemed very happy with her cut."

"Yes, she was over the moon."

"Hard-earned I must say, but I think we all acted professionally and 'to the victor the spoils' as they say. What will you do with your cut, Lordy? Go back to England or stay here?"

"There's nothing back there for me anymore, just bad memories and a family that has disowned me. No, I think I'll stay here."

Hugh poured Lordy another large sherry.

"Have another drink. It's the best sherry you can get."

Lordy gulped the sherry, smacked his lips, and said, "Yes, it certainly is."

"Well I must say you were very cool during the whole mission. There's nothing worse than someone who panics under pressure. It's a terrible sign of weakness."

"You're right there. It's good to know your weak spots even so. Don't you think?"

"Yes, quite, anyway let's get down to business," Hugh said, as he leaned back to reach a drawer in the cabinet behind him. He pulled out a brown paper package. "Here's your cut, plus Karl's, Ron's, and Henny's. It's all there. You had better count it. I had a lot of trouble getting all that cash in such a short time."

Lordy could see bundles of twenty-rand notes as he tore the package open.

"I see you like cash," Hugh said. "Don't lose count."

Lordy ignored Hugh's comment and focused on counting the bundles of bank notes.

"Some people like cash; some like women; some like power; but it all comes down to the same thing in the end, Lordy. Winner takes all."

Lordy looked up and saw Hugh casually reach into the side drawer of his desk. "Like another drink, Lordy?"

Lordy froze when he saw a large, black handgun pointing straight at his face. Before he could speak a blinding flash filled the room.

Outside in the street, Gavin Brown had just paid a taxi driver and told him not to wait. He had come to Johannesburg for a business meeting and decided to pay an impromptu visit to Hugh to ask about his cut of the proceeds.

His finger just touched the doorbell when he heard the loud crack of a gun. Gavin had been drinking heavily to drum up enough courage to face Hugh, but even in this sodden state he could recognize a gunshot. All the lights in the house appeared to be out, so he went round to the back entrance, where he noticed a light coming from Hugh's study window.

He looked in and saw a tall, thin man lying on the floor, soaked in blood. Hugh was sitting in an armchair a few feet away with his feet on a desk, intermittently sipping from a glass and puffing on a cigar.

Hugh got up and methodically rolled the body into a large canvas sheet, tied each end with thick rope and pulled the body out of the study. When Gavin saw the last piece of canvas disappearing into another room, he jumped back from the window and tripped. He rolled over, vomited several times, and then crawled across the grass on all fours. His mind cleared but he could not decide what to do. After a few minutes of inaction he clambered to his feet and ran off into the night—the effects of the alcohol miraculously gone.

Virginia became concerned when Lordy did not contact her as planned, but she did not want to be alarmist so she waited until Monday before calling Hugh. After four unsuccessful attempts to reach him she decided to go directly to Hugh's house and confront him.

The telephone rang as she was about to leave and she immediately assumed it was Hugh returning her call, or even Lordy. To her surprise it was Colonel Van Starden from BOSS, calling to ask her to rejoin the intelligence agency.

She had thought about it constantly since meeting with Van Starden, and with everything that had happened over the past months, she had decided to rejoin the agency. She was very loyal to Van Starden, especially after he had attempted to protect her when she ran afoul of the establishment within BOSS. She also felt a little sorry for him because he was near retirement age and suffered from arthritis in his right leg and arm, caused by an old injury during a covert assignment. He was somewhat of a father figure to her.

Turning her mind back to the hunt for Lordy again, she drove over to Hugh's house. Hugh and Susan were relaxing in the conservatory when she let herself in.

"How did it go with Lordy then," she asked casually.

Hugh jumped up, clearly startled. "Lordy, oh, he came by on Wednesday night. He seemed pleased with himself."

Virginia slowly nodded her head. "Did he indeed?"

"I gave him the money for the others as well."

"He didn't tell me that."

"Oh! How strange. Maybe he's gone on a bender, or taken another trip to Monte Carlo. You know what he's like with money."

"I don't think so. Listen, Hugh, if I find out that something has happened to him and you're behind it, I'll hold you personally responsible. And you know what I mean by that."

Hugh played it nonchalantly, "Don't be so dramatic. He'll show up sooner or later."

"We'll see."

Virginia left, knowing instinctively that Hugh had harmed Lordy, and she vowed she would find out what happened to him and exact revenge.

FOURTEEN

$\mathcal{I}$t was February 1983—six months after Hugh had passed the diamonds over to Chris at Steinkop. The plan to include them into the production stream at the mine forged ahead undetected. Chris had perfected the art of manipulating the production statistics for head office consumption and almost overnight became the corporation's star performer. Salary increases and bonuses were thrown at him along with promises of board level positions. Chris remained phlegmatic because he really believed the government had sanctioned the whole thing, and if anyone discovered the truth, it would all be hushed up.

Each day he would plant a handful of diamonds into the final stage of the processing cycle prior to the start of the first and second shifts. He went through x-ray screening on several occasions, but only when leaving the mine, so nothing unusual was discovered. Every two weeks he would religiously call Hugh and provide an updated total of the misappropriated diamonds. At the end of February he made his final report.

"Hugh, it's finished. The last of the shipment went out yesterday, the whole lot."

"Excellent, Chris. I'll let you know when your shares can be cashed. How's your position with the Mine?"

"Wonderful, I've been offered a board position with the corporation in Johannesburg. It starts next month. Cherrie is over the moon."

"There you go. I told you things would come right. Great job. And there's a nice tax-free bonus to boot. Plus the Government people will be very pleased with you. I'll call you in two weeks."

Hugh hung up the phone and called Harold Budd and told him to start selling their Steinkop Mining shares. They were worth fourteen times their original value.

"They'll fall quickly," Hugh said to Harold. "I want my proceeds transferred to Switzerland on the quiet."

"Ten percent and it's done," Harold replied. "Send me the bank's details."

Hugh went into the living room to speak to Susan, who was lying on the sofa reading a novel.

"Susan, can I have a word?" Hugh asked meekly.

Susan smiled and patted the sofa, "Yes, of course. Sit here."

"I don't know if you overheard my conversation with Harold but the time has come to sell those Steinkop shares and decide what we're going to do next. I know we spoke about leaving the country permanently . . . so we should really make up our minds pretty quickly."

"I'm up for it. I fancy a nice place by the sea in Monaco."

"First we need to cover our tracks in South Africa, and then disappear. I suggest we tell all our friends we're emigrating to Australia, but fly to Europe instead. Maybe stay in Italy or Spain for a few months before finding a place to live in Monaco.

"I'll have to go to Zurich first to arrange the finances. That's where Harold will send our money. I'll get a safe deposit box there to store all the confidential documents we need.

"There's one thing I haven't told you yet. I'm going to assume someone else's identity to cover our tracks completely. I'll tell you more about that later."

"Is that necessary?"

"Yes, plus it will help me get Father's money back from Jack."

"How?"

"I'll tell you later, don't worry. In the meantime tidy up loose ends, pay off your bills, and sell or dump anything you aren't taking along. And don't forget to tell all your friends we're getting married and going to Australia."

Susan's mouth opened wide. "Hugh, are you proposing?"

"Well, sort of. We can get hitched over in Europe."

Susan screamed, jumped up and hugged Hugh, and then pulled him down on to the sofa. "The last thing I expected was a proposal. What will I tell my sister?"

"You can't tell her what we're really doing but you can keep in contact. We'll get a mail service in Australia and send letters from there. If nobody suspects anything after a couple of years then we're in the clear. No need to hide or anything like that."

"That sounds okay."

They rolled onto sofa, embraced and kissed.

In Pretoria, Virginia sat outside Van Starden's office, waiting for a briefing on a new assignment after successfully completing the previous one—identifying a traitor in the Simonstown naval base. Van Starden explained that the Treasury Department was concerned about the amount of funds being sent abroad without Reserve Bank permission. He reminded her about the severe restrictions on the transfer of South African assets out of the country's monetary zone. Since several leading figures in the business community were involved, the Treasury Department had asked the Security Services to investigate. He emphasized the secrecy surrounding the case. "The results will be reviewed by the Prime Minister and certain cabinet members before any action is taken."

He gave the file notes to Virginia. "There are three contact names in the document representing the Treasury Department and the Reserve Bank. They've been briefed about the sensitivity of this case and will provide you with the necessary background information. Report here in two weeks with an outline of your approach."

Virginia simply nodded and walked out of the conference room.

She returned to her office and read through the file. It contained information on dozens of suspected illegal transfers of funds to overseas banks, with the names of the bankers and brokers in South Africa suspected of initiating them. The file also contained the code name of a paid informant for the South African government who currently worked for Zinnerberg Private Bank, based in Zurich. Several of the transfers were funneled there. She flicked through the names of the suspects—George Smithson, Raymond McCarthy, Uwe Schultz, Barry O'Neal, and Harold Budd. Budd's name appeared several times in the report with references to various police files implicating Budd in fraud, but without enough evidence to prosecute him.

She met the Treasury Department's contact, Frederick Hurley, early the next day. He had a pile of files with him, which he dumped unceremoniously on her desk.

"Hello, Miss Wilson, I'm Freddie Hurley, Under Secretary to the Minister of Finance," he said, as he flicked his hair back. "All these hush-hush affairs make me shiver. What about you?"

"Well it's a job," Virginia said in a surprised tone.

"I've had a tingle down my spine ever since my boss told me to collect all this information and go over it with you intelligence people."

"There's quite a bit there," Virginia said, lifting a pile of the files.

"Yes, I brought the most interesting stuff first."

Virginia watched in amazement as he waved his hands around and rolled his eyes while he spoke. Even the most insignificant phrases were accompanied by these exaggerated gestures.

"I see," Virginia said, as she avoided his waving arms.

Freddie adjusted his cravat, flicked his hair back again and went through his documents. He had a list of transfers over 100,000 rand that were approved in December and January, along with the names of the companies and people that requested the transfers. The sending and receiving banks were also listed. Most of them were for payments for imports into the country and some for the remittance of profits to overseas companies doing business in South Africa. The prices of the imported goods in many cases were twenty percent higher than their suggested sales prices.

Freddie pulled a sheet of paper from a file and thrust it in front of Virginia. It was an example of an inflated sale of Lamborghini sports cars from Italy.

Virginia scratched her head. "So how does the South African importer gain?"

"Let's say you are Mr. Budd and you want to illegally move 20,000 out of the country. You make an arrangement with the Lamborghini buyer in South Africa to pay an extra 20,000 for the cars, which you give to him in rand. The importer buys the cars from the dealer in Italy at 20,000 above the real price. He does this via a foreign currency draft—approved as a valid commercial transaction by the South African Reserve Bank. The car dealer in Italy gets his payment in US Dollars and pays the additional amount to your bank abroad. Of course, the Italian car dealer and the South African dealer get a few percent for their trouble, and you get your funds moved into the legitimate international money system."

"I see," Virginia said. "Does this go on a lot?"

"Not until recently, when severe restrictions were put on remitting money abroad. Plus people don't feel safe leaving all their money in the country, especially if the blacks take over. People like Budd are making millions out of it."

Virginia thought for a while and said, "We can arrest these people now but it's their clients that the government is after. I guess it's the politics behind it. The government wants leverage over their political enemies—the rich, white, liberal English-speakers."

"Exactly."

"Right, let's start with this Budd character. His name appears more than anyone else's does. The next time he tries this little trick we'll trace it back to the originator. If we catch him we'll blackmail him into revealing all his clients. I think he'll be very helpful if faced with bankruptcy and ten years in prison."

Freddie giggled excitedly. "You're absolutely brutal for such a beautiful woman."

"Thanks," Virginia replied, "but I don't know how to take that. So how can we trap him?"

"I can monitor his bank account, but he probably deals in cash."

"You're probably right. He's too smart to leave an audit trail. I'll bug his office and home telephones. That way we'll know when he's up to his shenanigans again."

"I've never been so excited," Freddie exclaimed.

They parted company after Virginia reinforced the need for absolute secrecy.

She went to the Special Operations Section and arranged for a team to bug Budd's home and office. The team loaded a van with eavesdropping equipment, and after nightfall set out for Budd's office. Virginia went along with them to rifle through any useful documents that Budd might have left there.

The building had minimal security so the operations team had no problem getting into Budd's private office. They wired his telephone and placed recording devices in two of the wall lights on either side of his desk. It took about an hour to setup and another thirty minutes to test and tune.

Van Starden made a curt telephone call to the building's owner and commandeered a room one floor above Budd's office, where two officers would record any relevant conversations. Virginia examined all the files in the office and took the liberty of using the office photocopier to record any interesting documents, especially Budd's client list, bank statements, and legal agreements.

The photocopier jammed after five minutes so Virginia asked one of the team, Peter Fourie, to fix it.

"I'm not the best one for this job," Peter replied. "They brought me in at the last minute, in case there's any rough stuff. I'll ask the fellow upstairs who's fixing the phones."

"Most of the action team members are trained in this sort of thing," Virginia replied, looking up at him puzzled.

"I'm not actually with the government. They use us privateers quite a bit these days. I work for a company called Action Services."

When Virginia finished photocopying, the operations team cleaned up the office and left as efficiently as they arrived, even replacing the paper in the photocopier.

Virginia returned to her office and scanned through the purloined documents. It didn't take long before the names "Victor Barlow" and "Hugh Barlow" appeared. She felt elated. *I bet that bastard is involved with this,* she thought. *After the diamond caper I'll need to be careful. I'll expose him but I'll have to stay anonymous. If he goes down he'll take everyone with him.*

It was morning before Virginia finished reading and classifying the documents, and she made sure that no more emphasis was placed on Barlow's transactions than anyone else's. She completed a report of transactions, commissions, bank accounts, intermediaries, and corrupt bank officials used for twelve of Budd's clients. Next she compiled a profile of the clients' names, addresses, and business and political connections.

Step two called for evidence of an incriminating telephone conversation between Budd and one of his clients. Virginia prayed it would be Hugh. The list named several other dealers suspected of illegal currency transactions, but she used the excuse of not having enough resources to justify only concentrating on Budd, hoping this would lead to the incrimination of Hugh.

Hugh and Susan went out for dinner at the rowing club on the following Saturday, primarily from Susan's point of view to celebrate their engagement, but Hugh used it as a vehicle to announce their phony plans for a new life in Australia. Many of their friends and associates attended and Hugh had deliberately invited the worst gossips to ensure the news would spread like smallpox. Just as Hugh had predicted, the phones were ringing long before the party finished.

Hugh and Susan slept late the next morning. While they waited for Johnny to bring them coffee, Hugh explained the next step in his plan, which for the first time involved Susan's direct participation.

"Susan, I need your help with something tomorrow."

"What?"

"I need to get my illustrious brother, Jack, out of his house for a couple of hours so I can have a nose around."

"What on earth are you looking for?"

"Some documents, that's all."

"He's such a weird so and so. What would get him to leave?"

"You know he fancies you. Call him on the pretext of wanting to go to lunch."

"Would he fall for that?"

"Lay it on a bit and he will. You know what I mean. Go somewhere very public so it's safe . . . in case he gets any ideas. Have lunch and suggest that you meet him again in a week or so."

"Why would I need to meet him again?"

"In case I have to go back and search some more."

"Okay, I'll phone him later today."

"Do it now."

Susan called his number several times and on the last attempt Jack answered. Hugh listened to the call.

"Jack, this is Susan. How are you? I haven't spoken to you in ages."

"Susan, what a surprise. You're the last person I thought would call me."

"Really? What makes you say that?"

"Well our last few meetings didn't go very well."

"That's just because Hugh poked his nose in," Susan said, as she tapped Hugh with her foot and covered her mouth to suppress laughter. "Anyway why don't we meet for lunch sometime?"

After a short delay Jack replied. Hugh could almost feel him get excited. "Of course! Where and when? Do you want to come over to my place?"

"Why don't we go out to a nice restaurant, say tomorrow?"

"That's fine. Make the reservations and let me know where to meet you."

Susan rang off and immediately burst into laughter.

"That was easy enough," Hugh said, grinning.

"I'll pick a restaurant outside of the city that'll take him over thirty minutes to get there and the same to get back. Add ninety minutes for the lunch . . . that puts him about two to three hours out of harm's way."

"More than enough time to find what I'm looking for."

The next day Hugh set off forty-five minutes before Susan and drove to Jack's house. Since he had lived there for several years with Jack and the rest of the family when they were younger, he knew the layout perfectly. He decided to park directly across the road from the entrance, where several low hanging trees would conceal his car, but allow him to see anyone leaving or arriving at the house. Jack never allowed anyone in the house unless he was present, so once Hugh saw Jack leave, the coast would be clear.

At 11:30 he watched as Jack drove his Rolls Royce out of the garage and down the long driveway. After five minutes Hugh got out of his car and hurried across the road. Most of the houses in the street were large and set back from the road quite a distance, with lines of trees and bushes separating each one. This enabled Hugh to walk along the edge of the driveway without being detected.

He went to the laundry room and inserted a small screwdriver into the lock of the side door. After a few twists and turns the deadbolt lock flipped back and the door opened. Hugh remembered how easy it was to enter the house via the laundry because in his teens he would often defy his father and go out late at night, returning unnoticed in the early hours. He entered the laundry and quietly shut the door.

Hugh started the search in the study on the first floor. He methodically went through Jack's desk and filing cabinets, making note of anything related to Jack's finances. Luckily for Hugh, Jack had consolidated most of his late father's investments, so it was easy to identify the amounts and whereabouts of the funds. After an exhaustive search he still had not found the main object of his burglary.

Next he went down the wide staircase leading to the basement, but when he reached the bottom a large metal door blocked his entrance. This surprised Hugh. *Must have been added recently,* he thought. *And what's that sickening smell?* He tried to open the door but soon gave up because the smell got the better of him and the door was fitted with a strong deadbolt and combination lock that would be impossible for him to open in such a short time.

He went back up the stairs and into the library. He remembered that his father had installed a small safe behind one of the bookshelves, which he used to store important documents that he wanted to keep on hand. He fumbled around behind and under the books until his fingers touched two keys. Lucky for him, Jack had left the safe keys exactly where his father used to keep them. He opened the safe but found it completely empty. Hugh cursed out loud, returned to the study, and began to think of other hiding places that Jack might have used.

As a last resort he began searching the bedrooms on the upper floor, starting with the bedroom that Jack obviously used as his own. In the bedside cabinet, at the back of the top drawer, was the prize—Jack's passport and identity document, with his birth certificate tucked into the back of the cover. Hugh had brought the cover of an old passport and identity document with him, stuffed with blank pages. He removed the rubber band from Jack's documents and placed it around the fake ones and placed them back into the drawer. Only if Jack opened the documents would he realize they were fakes. Left as they were, they looked just like the originals. Hugh knew that Jack rarely traveled, so he doubted that he would discover the fakes.

Hugh made sure that everything was left exactly as he found it. As he opened the laundry door to leave, he heard voices outside in the garden. He stopped dead in his tracks. The sound of a lawn mower soon drowned out the voices. The noise grew louder and then quieter in succession as the lawn mower moved up and down the garden. Hugh checked his watch and realized that two hours had already passed. "Too close for comfort," he whispered. He considered hiding somewhere in the enormous house until nightfall but worried that a suspicious neighbor might report his car to the police. No, he had to get out soon.

When the noise level of the lawn mower was at its lowest he took a chance and opened the laundry door to see if he could escape unnoticed. "Damn," he said under his breath. One of the gardeners had positioned himself across the driveway, seemingly fast asleep. He looked in the other direction. *Good, no one around,* he thought. As he stepped onto the path the gardener rolled over, grabbed Hugh's leg, muttered something, and then continued snoring. Hugh carefully pulled his leg from the gardener's grip and stepped over him. When he thought he was clear he tiptoed along the edge of the driveway, keeping on the grass. He gasped with relief when he reached his car. *I made it, thank god,* he thought, as he wiped sweat from his face and neck.

Hugh returned home to find Susan flopped in an armchair.

"What's wrong? How did it go with dear Jack?"

"From his point of view, wonderful. He can hear church bells already. From my side it oscillated between fear and boredom. He definitely has a screw loose."

"That bad?"

"Yes. Did you get what you were looking for?"

"Absolutely everything – a few nervous moments but okay in the end. Did you tell Jack you would meet him again?"

"No problem there."

"Good. Oh, by the way I have to go to Zurich on urgent business. Probably tomorrow or the day after."

"Can I come along?"

"Best if I go alone. I need to cover my tracks."

Susan pouted for a while but soon got over her hurt feelings and began packing a suitcase for Hugh, while he booked a flight to Zurich for the following day. As soon as he finalized his travel arrangements he called Harold Budd and asked the name of the private Swiss bank in Zurich.

"Zinnerberg Private Bank. I know the owner very well—Herr Kraus. It's a small outfit but it handles all the services you'll need . . . and it's very confidential—no reporting to the Reserve Bank."

"What's the address?"

"The head office is on Bahnhofstrasse. Any taxi will take you there. I'll telex Kraus tonight and tell him to expect you."

"Good. I want you to transfer my proceeds there."

Two hours later Virginia replayed the conversation between Hugh and Harold in front of Colonel Van Starden. They agreed that with the Treasury's evidence and the incriminating phone call would be enough to convict Budd and Barlow.

"Don't be too hasty," Colonel Van Starden replied, "we want all Budd's clients, especially the high-rollers. The cabinet wants a complete dossier before taking any action."

"They must be after political enemies."

"Exactly, but don't concern yourself with that. Just get all the names and write the report. That's your mission."

"Understood."

"Go to Zurich and meet our little banking spy. Get a list of Zinnerberg's account holders."

"What about the other banks he deals with?"

"All in good time."

"I'll leave tomorrow."

"Remember we're only interested in South African citizens . . . but the Foreign Office will be interested in other nationals."

"Especially if there are blacks and liberals on the list."

Van Starden chuckled and shook his head. "You've got that right."

"Standard procedure I assume—tourist passport, false name, and no help if I get caught."

"And don't forget to contact the embassy in Switzerland before you leave. They'll provide logistical support."

Virginia could hardly restrain herself. She sat in her office going over things in her mind. *I need to find out what happened to Lordy. Only Barlow knows that. At the same time I need to complete the mission, so I mustn't reveal my identity to Barlow. If the government won't prosecute him, I'll take my own revenge. I'll ruin him, and if he did kill Lordy, I'll finish the bastard off.*

FIFTEEN

*H*err Kraus's chauffeur met Hugh at Zurich airport and whisked him into the city for his meeting at Zinnerberg Bank.

Kraus greeted Hugh at the small but elegant entrance of the bank. He towered over Hugh and his arms barely reached past his enormous stomach as he shook hands.

"Follow me, Mr. Barlow." Kraus said jubilantly as he bounced across the lobby and into the main hall.

Hugh couldn't imagine how someone so fat could still manage to walk. Only the exquisite designs on the marble floors and the antique furniture distracted him from Kraus's massive frame traversing the bank.

Kraus squeezed through his office doorway and flopped into a large, solid armchair, which looked as if it had been crushed by a giant press and then reconstructed with metal supports. He attached a napkin to his collar and called to his secretary, "Gretchen, please bring Mr. Barlow coffee and some cake. And a small piece for me if you don't mind."

Gretchen brought in a large pot of coffee and four huge portions of Black Forest cake, three of which Kraus proceeded to devour.

"Well now, let's get down to business, Mr. Barlow," Kraus said, wiping cream from his cheek. "What sort of services can we provide for you?"

"Harold Budd will be transferring 3,000,000 US dollars on my behalf very soon. I trust you hold US dollar accounts?"

"Of course."

"In about three weeks I'll transfer another large sum—about 6,000,000 US."

Hugh watched Kraus go red and almost choke on a piece of cake.

"Naturally we'll classify you as a preferred account holder. That gives you free investment advice."

"I assume the accounts are anonymous."

"We can do that, but there are risks attached. For instance if someone gets access to your account number and pass-code they could swindle you easily and I, that is Zinnerberg, could not be held accountable. Plus there is a one-percent charge on the average annual balance that must be levied."

"I see."

"The other option is to open a regular account in your name. The names are kept strictly secret . . . and we don't report to any tax authorities."

"Okay, I'll open a regular account."

"Fine," Kraus replied and then shouted to his assistant manager. "Obermeier, bring Mr. Barlow the forms for a regular named account immediately."

Hans Obermeier, who had been lurking outside the office the whole time, vaulted forward with a set of application forms. Obermeier looked thin and sickly. He reminded Hugh of a picture of Uriah Heap that he had seen in a Dickens novel years before.

"I have them ready, Herr Kraus," Obermeier said, genuflecting as he displayed them to Hugh and Kraus. "Please come through to my office, Mr. Barlow, and we can go through the formalities."

Kraus shook hands with Hugh and after thanking him for his business ushered him into Obermeier's office. Hugh opened the account in Jack's name and after showing Jack's passport for identification, no other questions were asked. He paid in advance for a three-year rental of a safe deposit box and deposited some personal documents and the South African Government's Turnhalle file.

Just about the same time Hugh opened his account at Zinnerberg, Virginia's flight landed at Zurich airport. She immediately went to the train station and boarded a train to Berne, where she registered her presence with the South African Embassy. John Tobin, one of the officers in the Business Development and Trade section, which Virginia knew to be a cover for the Special Operations Section, briefed her on the various protocols used by the section in Switzerland and gave her keys to a temporary apartment in Zurich.

"Here's an emergency telephone number. It's available twenty-four hours a day, seven days a week, but we can't promise to come to your aid at a moment's notice—staff shortages."

"How can I contact the informant inside Zinnerberg?"

"His name is Hans Obermeier," John said, as he passed a slip of paper to Virginia, "and he can be contacted at this number. Remember he's a paid informant, so don't tell him anymore than you have to. He's loyal to the highest bidder. Use the phrase written next to the telephone number when you call him, then he'll know it's someone from the South African embassy."

"Okay."

"One other thing—these Swiss banks are paranoid about secrecy. If they have even an inkling that someone is trying to invade their privacy they can turn extremely nasty. Both legally and illegally."

"How so?"

"Unknown assailants gave a Yank a severe beating last year. Apparently he represented a family in the United States whose father had an account with a major bank here. They either lost or never had the account details, so the bank refused even to talk to him. The Yank caused a big fuss, and one morning the police found him half-dead in the woods just outside of Zurich—crippled for life."

Virginia was surprised. "I'll be careful."

"Here's a .22 handgun. Give it back when your assignment finishes. If you have to use it, make sure you dump it afterwards."

Virginia left the next morning for Zurich and went straight to the apartment John had allocated to her. She called Obermeier and arranged to meet him at the ferry terminal near the lake later that night.

It was dark when Virginia arrived at the ferry terminal. The strong gusts of wind coming from the lake easily penetrated her heavy winter coat. She huddled up, went to the ticket office, and stared at the schedules printed on large sheets behind a glass window. Someone tapped her on the shoulder. She turned around and saw a tall, skinny, sickly-looking man staring at her.

He said very slowly, "Are you from the institute?"

"Yes. I'm Oscar."

"Good, let's go to a café and talk."

They walked smartly to a small café fifty yards from the ticket office. Even the warm air in the café took a few minutes to stop her from shivering, but Obermeier seemed unconcerned with the sudden change in temperature. They sat at a table at the back of the café and ordered two large coffees.

"What can I do for the South African government today?" Obermeier asked sardonically.

"I need a list of clients that live in South Africa or are South African citizens. And if possible Zinnerberg's major business partners in South Africa?"

"Everything is possible for a small commission," he said chuckling, "and especially if you can wait. The quicker you need things the more expensive they become."

Virginia looked at Obermeier's rat-like features and thought, *I've never met such a saponaceous wretch in my life.*

"Mind you," Obermeier continued, "if you and I spent a little time together in your hotel the price might be reduced fifty percent. We can share the money your people hand over for the information."

"Forget it you scum," Virginia responded. "How much are you asking for?"

"20,000 Swiss francs."

"Forget it you low-life. I'll call you tomorrow night at seven."

"That's fine. What about a parting kiss to seal our little tran-saction?"

"Kiss someone else's backside you pervert." She threw a used napkin at him and strode out of the café. *What an experience,* she thought, as she waved down a taxi.

John Tobin advised Virginia to offer Obermeier 5000 francs for the information, which he later accepted without question. He met Virginia on Saturday morning and handed over a folder containing a complete list of account holder information on computer stationery. To make sure that the information had some credibility she quickly scanned the names on the list looking for "Barlow", knowing that Hugh had just opened an account. Obermeier provided only basic information on the report—Account number, opening date of the account, account holder's family name, citizenship, city of residence, and current balance. She found the "Barlow" entry with an account opening date of March 1983. This gave her a reasonable level of confidence in the validity of the information, so she handed the money into Obermeier's clutching hands. "Here's your money—get lost."

There were over 1,000 client accounts on Zinnerberg's books with an average balance of 1,000,000 US dollars. Barlow's account had a zero balance, which was in line with the information on the voice recording between Budd and Hugh. She plowed through the rest of the file and found over fifty South African residents, several of whom she recognized as being prominent businessmen. One entry contained the same name as a leading member of the opposition Democratic Party—archenemies of the ruling National Party. Virginia surmised that the Government hoped to find this sort of information so they could coerce opposition members not to disagree with their policies.

Virginia caught an early train from Zurich to Berne on Sunday to meet with John Tobin at the embassy. She had the Zinnerberg file with her and a small overnight case. The train was crowded but Virginia had reserved a seat, so she expected a fairly comfortable journey.

Thirty minutes into the journey she went to the restaurant car to get some coffee. The other passengers seemed to be professional types so she had no qualms about leaving her file and overnight bag in the luggage rack above her seat.

In the restaurant car two businessmen struck up a casual conversation with her while she waited to buy coffee. She chatted with them for five minutes before returning to her seat. When the conductor announced that the train would soon arrive in Berne, she reached up to get her overnight bag and the file.

"Oh, no," she whispered, "It's gone." It felt like a blow in the stomach. She panicked for a moment and scratched around the other luggage racks nearby but found nothing.

"Did anyone see my file folder get taken?" she asked the other passengers. They shook their heads initially but then an elderly man spoke up.

"Your husband came and took it," he said.

"What did he look like?" she asked. The English speakers among them laughed, obviously taking her comment as a joke.

"No, I mean I'm not married. I think someone's stolen it."

"Sorry, Miss, he told us he was your husband," the elderly man replied.

"What did he look like?" she asked again.

"Tall and thin with yellow-ish complexion."

"Thanks. Which way did he go?"

The elderly man pointed to the front of the train.

Virginia immediately suspected Obermeier, and rushed along the aisle into the next car searching for him. *He must be trying to resell it to me,* she thought.

The train pulled into Berne station, and the inevitable mass exit from the train blocked her from searching any further. She pushed her way out of the train and onto the platform, and then jumped onto a luggage cart to look above the crowd. About fifty yards ahead she caught sight of a tallish man that looked like Obermeier. She charged ahead weaving in and out of the crowd trying to catch up to him, but when she got within grabbing distance she noticed he didn't have any luggage with him. An instant later she realized it wasn't Obermeier after all. His face was bright red, not at all like the description the elderly man gave her. She cursed herself for making such a stupid mistake.

The crowd dispersed in all directions, so she walked back to the train, picked up her overnight case, and thought about how she would explain the file's absence. She knew there would be consequences.

When she reached the taxi rank she felt a tap on the shoulder and instinctively knew it was Obermeier. She stepped forward quickly and turned to face him.

"Miss Wilson, strange to find you here," Obermeier said, with a sly grin on his face. "Delivered your little package yet?"

"How did you know my name?"

"I looked in your overnight case. You left some of your real identification in there, next to your phony passport. Not very clever of you."

"Okay, you've got the better of me, now hand back the file," she demanded, "otherwise things will get very nasty."

"I don't think you are in any position to threaten me, Miss Wilson. I know what your bosses will think of you for making such a bad mistake. It'll be the end of your career. Only amateurs make such mistakes."

"What do you want and how much?"

"I'm not looking for money, just a little of your time. I find you very attractive, Miss Wilson. My friend has an apartment not far from here. I suggest we go there."

Virginia knew what he wanted, but she had to make sure she could retrieve the file before playing any tricks on him. She assumed Obermeier had given the file to an accomplice, because everything happened so quickly and smoothly.

"How do I know I'll get the file back? I want to see it first."

"Okay, I'll show you the file and you can have it back after we spend some time together. A little friend of mine put it in a left-luggage locker in the train station."

They walked back to the train station and into the left-luggage area. Obermeier indicated to Virginia to follow him into a secluded area behind the rows of lockers.

"Before I show you the file you have to show me something."

"What?" she replied, barely containing her anger.

"Unbutton your coat."

Virginia played along with him and unbuttoned her heavy leather coat.

"Lift up your sweater."

She pulled up her sweater revealing a silk blouse. Obermeier unbuttoned her blouse until her full breasts were clearly visible behind a small bra. He put his hands inside her blouse and released the clip on her bra. Virginia turned her head to the side as Obermeier's face came close.

"Before you go any further show me the key to the locker."

Obermeier chuckled and put his hand in his inside pocket and revealed the key.

"Show me the file and I'll go back to your apartment with you."

Obermeier went to the end of the bank of lockers and opened one. Virginia held her leather coat closed and walked towards him. She saw the file, but being careful not to be cheated again, she flipped through the pages with one hand to check its authenticity.

"Okay, that looks good," she said, and walked back to the secluded area. She turned to face Obermeier, opened her coat and lifted her sweater again, revealing and shaking her breasts. Obermeier, his normally pale complexion now shining with sweat, held his hands out ready to fondle Virginia's breasts.

Just as he touched them she jumped forward and thrust her knee upward between his legs. He collapsed and rolled around on the floor holding his groin with both hands. Virginia quickly buttoned her coat, positioned herself in front of Obermeier, and delivered a hard kick into his right kneecap. She followed through with a kick to the back of his head and then another in the right kidney. He slumped in a heap. She pulled out her handgun and repeatedly whacked him on the back of the head with the butt until he stopped groaning.

She ran back to the locker, which Obermeier, overcome with lust had left open, snatched the file, and walked smartly over to the station exit. Two policemen rushed passed her as she left, heading towards the lockers. Virginia jumped into a taxi and sped off. She changed taxis twice before finally reaching the embassy to avoid leaving a trail for the police to follow.

Just before 11:00 AM she arrived at the Embassy, where John Tobin and another man were waiting for her.

"You're late," John said laughing. "So Swiss trains don't always run on time then."

"My fault, can't blame Swiss railways. I had a small, last-minute problem, nothing to worry about."

"This is Steven Hancock from the foreign office. He has a great interest in the contents of your little file."

Hancock was polite and polished, clearly a senior diplomat. He shook hands with Virginia and thanked her for putting her life in danger for the country.

"Let's get down to business," John said, ending the polite interlude.

Virginia gave an overview of the contents of the file. The names were categorized in alphabetic order by the account holder's country of residence, plus another sort by the value of the account. Some of the accounts were numbered but Obermeier had not included the secret security codes required to access them.

"Only old Kraus has those codes," John said, "he'd never trust anyone else with that. It's probably a code tied to the account holder's first name, that's why Obermeier didn't have it on the report."

Hancock reviewed the list intensely. "I see there are some corporations named here with the country of registration."

"Yes," Virginia replied, "but we can easily find out who the directors are."

"I'll take the foreign list and leave you with the rest, John. We can compromise several of our foes with this little gem."

"I'm sure we can!" Virginia added, the double meaning of the word "gem" having significance only to her.

They wrapped up after two hours and said their farewells. Virginia asked John to send a coded message back to Van Starden in Pretoria saying she was returning immediately. She took the train back to Zurich, packed her things, and went straight to the airport to catch the next flight.

On Tuesday morning she went to Van Starden's office in Pretoria and briefed him on the mission. He had already received her progress report via John Tobin, and was delighted with the results.

"Why did you come back so early? I thought you were going to investigate the other banks."

"I had a run in with our so-called informant. She handed Van Starden the report. "It's all in there."

He read the report, stopping several times to ask questions. "Oh, I see. Did you damage him badly then?"

"Yes, I think so."

"Well it's very honest of you reporting things accurately, especially losing the file on the train. Rewrite the report and omit that part. You don't want someone using it against you in the future, especially after I retire."

"Thanks, sir, I appreciate that," she replied, and turned to leave.

"Just one more thing, Virginia. I have a strange feeling you have a personal involvement in this case. You don't have to respond to that comment but be careful. Many an excellent agent has slipped up because of ulterior motives."

She left the office without comment.

SIXTEEN

*H*ugh arrived back in Johannesburg on Sunday at about the same time Virginia finished examining the Zinnerberg file with John Tobin. Susan ran along the driveway to meet him. "Hugh, glad you're back. I missed you. How did it go?"

"What's all that commotion at Judge McPherson's house?"

"There were police cars and sirens sounding off for a couple of hours earlier today. The police sealed that wooded area at the side of his house."

"I'll call him later. I hope nothing has happened to him. He's a useful contact."

Hugh started to tell Susan about his trip when the doorbell rang. Susan answered it because Johnny had gone out to buy groceries. Hugh stood behind her wondering who it could be.

"Hello. I'm Karen Van Der Berg from the South African Police. Miss Smith-Peterson, isn't it? We met about a year ago."

"Yes that's right. I hope it's not another murder."

"I'm afraid it is. We found a body just along the road and we're asking all the nearby residents if they saw anything or anyone unusual over the past few days."

"No, it's been quiet," Susan replied. "Hugh has been aw..."

She stopped herself from finishing the word "away" and continued speaking. "He's been around the house all day. I'll ask him."

She turned to call Hugh but he was right behind her. "Hugh, Detective Van Der Berg is here. Do you remember her?"

"Vaguely," Hugh replied. "Is that what all the commotion is about?"

Karen nodded and said, "The body was probably dumped here just like the others, but we won't know for sure until the forensic lab performs a post mortem. Did you say you were away, Mr. Barlow?"

"No," Hugh replied sharply, "I didn't say anything. But actually I didn't leave the house for the whole day—in fact for the past three days. I've been in bed with a touch of flu. I didn't see anything unusual."

"Let me know if either of you remember anything."

"Will do," Hugh replied. He opened the door for Karen to leave and slammed it behind her.

Hugh glared at Susan. "You really slipped up there."

"I know. I'm sorry. It just slipped out. I don't think she picked up on it."

"Oh well, just forget it. Listen, Susan, I've got something important to discuss. Come and sit down.

"Is there anything wrong?"

"Susan, you know how much I think of you and how much I'm looking forward to the future with you."

"Yes, go on."

"Well there's something we need to do together and I am afraid it's not very nice. It's to make sure that we can live in luxury and happiness in Monaco."

Susan leaned forward and asked, "What is it then?"

"Are you sure you're committed to our future and there's no going back?"

She squeezed Hugh's arm. "Yes, you know that."

"We'll get quite a bit of money from the diamond deal but it won't last forever. Especially with the lifestyle we both want. And of course we need to cover our tracks and that sometimes costs money. When Father died I expected to get at least half of his inheritance. Jack and I had an unofficial deal that if anything unusual occurred we would share everything fifty-fifty, regardless of the legal issues involved. Of course Jack let me down as you know, and basically I ended up with peanuts. Jack's mental state is worse now than ever I can remember. He's a complete loner and he's doing nothing with Father's inheritance. Basically he is just making the banks richer. I wouldn't be surprised if he commits suicide soon or gets thrown into a mental home. I found out that he's changed his will so that some obscure organization will inherit everything if he dies. I don't think that's fair."

"No, I agree. It's not right."

"There's only one thing to do and I don't see anything wrong with it. It's just bringing forward something that's inevitable. It's like a form of euthanasia really, just doing someone a kindness when their life is a misery and has no point."

"What are you thinking of doing?" Susan exclaimed.

Hugh saw her shocked look, so he held her hands and stared straight into her eyes. "In order to get my rightful inheritance we have to engineer Jack's death. Let's face it—no one will miss him."

"What? Do you know what you're saying?" Susan yelled.

Hugh felt Susan's body tighten as he grabbed her. He hugged her and after a few moments began to kiss her neck and cheeks.

"When I went to Jack's home it wasn't just to get the financial information. I took his passport and identity document and used them to travel to Zurich and open a secret account. With Jack out of the way I can take his identity and transfer all his assets abroad and no one will be any wiser. Remember we are supposed to go to Australia soon, so that means we won't be missed either . . . and no one can associate Jack with the diamond caper."

Susan pushed Hugh away and held her head in her hands. "Hugh, are you crazy? You can't go that far. Murder is murder is murder. It's not just fraud. You're taking someone's life. I'm not sure I want to go ahead with this. Hugh, really, it's too much for me to handle. Besides, he's your brother."

Susan felt a sharp pain in her arm as Hugh grabbed and shook her. "You're implicated in this as well! Don't forget."

Susan began to sob.

"I'm sorry. I didn't mean it that way. Calm yourself. Look, think of it logically. Jack's life is meaningless and it's the only fair way to get my inheritance back—plus you're in this too deep to pull out now. And remember he's only my half-brother. I never really had a close relationship with him. If you don't support me now I'll be exposed and our future is gone. Think of it that way. You say that you love me, so prove it. Prove your loyalty to me."

Susan ran over to the window and held her head against the glass. "If I go along with this, you don't expect me to kill him do you?"

"No, of course not, just lure him to the designated spot and I'll deal with it. After this we are bonded together for the rest of our lives. I love you so much, Susan, please say yes."

"What if we get caught? We could be hanged."

"We can invent a little plan to cover that eventuality. Maybe we can say that he tried to rape you and I intervened, then an altercation began, and I killed him by accident. We were just too embarrassed to tell the police—rich family member and all that."

Susan's mind worked overtime. She was deeply disturbed about the very idea of murder and she began to question Hugh's mental state. She could rationalize the fact that fraud and theft were obviously dishonest but murder elevated things to another level of evil, moving from sociopath to psychopath. The next question for her was whether she really was in too deeply to simply pull out or whether she should try to talk Hugh out of the whole scheme. *Maybe Hugh murdered all those women, after all, the police found a body nearby, and another victim disappeared from the rowing club. And I don't really have any proof that he actually went to Zurich.* She played along with Hugh, not wanting to provoke him, so that she could buy some time to think about what to do next. The whole idea of absconding with him had lost its romantic attraction, now replaced by fear and the nagging burden that her moral code was about to be shattered. She desperately tried to come to terms with the nightmare she was embroiled in.

Hugh was pleased with himself. He thought he'd convinced Susan that disposing of Jack was not only the right thing to do but also positively attractive.

The following morning Hugh woke early. He had slept heavily but only for short periods. Susan had awakened him several times in the night. Hugh watched her toss and turn, get out of bed, and get back again.

At breakfast Hugh deliberately continued to dismantle Susan's moral and ethical misgivings.

"I'm glad you see things my way. I know it's difficult and dangerous . . . but sometimes one just has to do these things to realize an overall benefit. Whenever something positive occurs in the world there is always a negative reaction to counteract it —nothing is free. The main thing is to make sure you are within the positive chain of events and let the losers take the negative hit. Don't worry, when it's all over we'll look back and laugh about this."

Susan merely nodded and remained silent.

"Okay, now you have to lure Jack out into the wilds somewhere. I'll be waiting and we can finish things cleanly. We'll do it outside the country, maybe in Swaziland. No one worries about passports or other identity documents crossing the border, and there are plenty of hotels with nightlife and gambling. You can tell Jack you're having a weekend away from me and you want to spend the time with him. Do you think he'll fall for that?"

Susan looked down and said quietly, "Yes, I'm sure he will."

"You don't have to travel with him, just say you'll meet him in a hotel there."

"If you think so."

"That's all arranged then. Call him tomorrow and set it up for next weekend. I'll make the arrangements. Tell him he can share your room. That'll be enough enticement."

Hugh went to Swaziland and booked into the Sunrise Hotel under a false name. The hotel, which was over a mile away from the nearest town, consisted of a main building with 200 rooms spread over three floors and twenty detached, luxury lodges. Each lodge was enclosed by trees and shrubs and stood on a quarter acre of ground with a small private swimming pool.

Hugh specifically booked Susan into lodge number twelve because it was the farthest from the hotel reception and had access to a large wooded area. He went to the lodge several times and on into the woods to find a place to dump Jack's body.

Hugh waited in his room until 9:00 PM, becoming increasingly concerned because Susan had not contacted him. The plan called for her to get in touch as soon as she checked in, and again after Jack's arrival. The last thing on his agenda was a chance meeting with Jack, so he avoided the reception area and other public places. Also if he called the front desk and asked if Susan had checked in, the receptionist might connect the two of them.

If something went wrong with his plan it could be potentially disastrous, so he decided to wait until later before taking any action. *Maybe the flight had problems. Maybe she decided not to go through with it. Maybe she booked into the wrong hotel or even the wrong room.*

Midnight passed and still no word from Susan, so Hugh decided to go to lodge number twelve to see if she was there. He went into reception and checked that Jack wasn't around before merging with the guests going back and forth from the dining room. He slipped out the rear exit and headed towards the lodges.

A concrete walkway led around the lodges in a semicircle, curving away from reception. Lodge twelve was at the end of the walkway so Hugh walked in between the cultivated bushes and trees aside the walkway to avoid being seen.

He saw that the lights were off in lodge twelve, so he tried the door handle. It was locked. Hugh crept around to the side of the lodge and carefully pulled the handle of the lounge window. *Good, it's not locked.* After checking the back door and finding it locked also, he went back to the lounge window. The window opened outwards, from bottom to top, and allowed just enough room for him to climb through.

He waited for his eyes to adjust for the lack of light and then crept into the first bedroom. It was empty. As he walked out of the bedroom he heard a low, growling sound, almost a snore, coming from the next room. Hugh edged the door of the bedroom open and poked his head just far enough inside to view the room.

Two human figures under the ruffled covers took shape in his eyes. A sickening feeling overcame him at the thought of Susan sleeping with Jack. He shook his head in disbelief. His emotions quickly turned to anger and then to hate and revenge. Hugh refocused his emotions at lightning speed and glared at the two hapless shapes in the bed. He pulled out his Beretta, attached the silencer, and walked to the foot of the bed. Without pausing he fired into the larger human shape three times and then pumped another three shots into the smaller shape.

Just a groan and a twitch before everything fell silent and motionless. Hugh switched on the bedside lamp and whisked the covers back. The two naked bodies were not those of Jack and Susan. He felt instantly relieved and threw the covers back over the two innocent victims. His thoughts turned to Susan and Jack and why they had not appeared. Why didn't Susan contact him and did Jack really take the bait and fly to Swaziland?

Hugh cleared his mind and concentrated on the murders he had just committed. To make the motive look like robbery, not an execution, Hugh quickly riffled through the personal effects of the dead couple. He put their cash and jewelry into his pockets, left a "do not disturb" sign on the door, and returned to the hotel.

He noticed that the bar and dining room were still fairly lively, so when he reached his room he changed his mind and returned to reception in the hope of catching a glimpse at the guest list.

The receptionist was a well-dressed African man. Hugh approached him from the direction of the bar.

"Good night," Hugh said as he walked passed. "It's a very well run hotel you have here. The food and entertainment is excellent."

"Thank you, sir, I'm glad you're enjoying yourself. How long are you staying with us?"

"Only until Monday I'm afraid. I planned to meet an old friend here for a few drinks but I think he must have been delayed."

"Did he book a room with us, sir?"

"Possibly, I'm not sure. His name is Barlow."

"Let me check, just one minute."

As the receptionist flicked through the pages of the register, Hugh looked over the counter and read the names up side down. Although he couldn't be absolutely sure, he saw no sign of the long double-barreled name that Hugh had told Susan to use, so he assumed Susan had not checked into the hotel.

"Yes, here he is, sir, room 65. Do you want me to call him?"

"No thanks. It's too late now. He must have had a bad trip or something. I'll call him in the morning. Thanks again for your help. Good night."

Hugh waited in his room for ten minutes and then walked down the fire exit stairwell and out into the road at the side of the hotel. He waited for a suitable moment and asked the doorman to call a taxi from the rank. Hugh told the driver to take him to the Lakeside Hotel and Casino, about ten miles from the Sunrise Hotel, in the center of the town.

Hugh knew that the murders would be discovered the following morning, and his identity document did not match the name he used to check into the hotel, which the police would surely find suspicious. He decided to stay in the Lakeside Hotel for the night, try to contact Susan in Johannesburg, and finally check out of the Sunrise very early the next morning. The police would certainly interview all the guests, and an inopportune meeting with Jack was a definitely an unwanted possibility.

Hugh called several numbers in Johannesburg in an attempt to find Susan but to no avail. By 2:00 AM he gave up and slept for a few hours. He returned to the Sunrise Hotel just after 6:00 AM, packed his things, and checked out without incident. Any further plans to liquidate Jack were put on hold until he could regain control of the situation.

Back in Johannesburg, Susan also rose early on Sunday morning, along with her sister Julie.

"I have to get away from him, Julie, he's going off the deep end. I thought it would be fun running off with someone like Hugh, but now I know what he's capable of doing I wish I'd never met him. Forget the wealth and high life."

"Where will you go?"

"Run off somewhere, anywhere, fast!"

"I'll have to come. You can't leave on your own in this state. Let's go to Cape Town and stay with Jenny Adams. She's always asking us to come and stay with her. What do you think? Hugh won't remember her. He never took much notice of our friends."

"If you think that's best," Susan said, wiping tears from her cheeks.

"When will he be back?"

"Monday."

"Okay, let's collect your things. Just leave him a note saying that everything's off and you don't want to see him again."

"If you think that's the best thing to do. I just can't think straight."

Susan sat and scribbled a note while Julie rushed through her apartment jamming her things into a suitcase.

"I keep messing up this note, Julie."

"Don't worry. Give it to me. I'll do it."

They charged out of the apartment and drove to Hugh's house. Susan sent Johnny on a fool's errand, and in his absence collected her belongings and packed them into Julie's car. In less than two hours they were on their way to the Cape Province in the south of the country, heading for Jenny Adam's home just outside of Cape Town.

Hugh returned on Monday evening to an empty house. It was Johnny's day off and he could see that Susan had packed up and left. He went to his study and looked through the pile of mail Johnny had placed on his desk. On the top of the pile he saw a white envelope that simply read *"To Hugh from Susan"*.

Hugh, I can't go through with it, sorry. Don't try to find me, it's over. You don't have to worry I have not told anyone about what is going on with Jack and the other issue with the mines, and I won't in the future.

Susan.

Hugh smashed a table lamp over his desk, threw his chair across the room, and screamed abuse at an imaginary Susan. "I'll deal with that deceiving bitch later," Hugh shouted. "Another one letting me down."

Hugh eventually calmed down and allowed logic to take over. He was torn between the high-risk path of removing Jack and taking his fortune, or just being satisfied with the money from the diamond theft. Susan was now a wild card—what would she do next? He felt justified in avenging her perceived treachery. If he merely walked away she would not only have betrayed him personally but also would have prevented him from reclaiming his father's inheritance. No, he had to deal with Jack first and then find Susan and exact revenge.

Using the same tactics as before, Hugh entered Jack's house by the laundry door and waited for his prey in the dark. This time he parked his car at the back of the house behind the three-car garage, where it would not be seen. Having dumped the .22 and silencer in Swaziland he now only had Chris Conway's .32 Beretta, and that would make too much noise in the middle of the night.

As an alternative weapon, Hugh took the poker from the fireplace in the living room and decided only to use the Beretta as a last resort. He doubted that Jack would stay any longer in Swaziland and guessed that he would take the second of the two flights from Swaziland to Johannesburg. It was 9:00 PM and the second flight was due to land one hour later. He estimated approximately two hours to wait before Jack would appear.

Hugh became drowsy sitting in the dark and drifted in and out of sleep until the noise of a toilet flushing on the upper floor jerked him back to full consciousness. *That must be Jack,* he thought. He opened the laundry door. With the aid of a dim light shining from outside the house, he checked the time on his watch. Although annoyed with himself for such a lapse, he was still determined to go through with the murder. He waited for five minutes to ensure that Jack had not come down the stairs and to allow himself time to regain his senses. He crept out of the pantry to the foot of the stairs. Step by step he ascended the staircase making sure not to put too much pressure on any individual step.

A loud creaking rang out when he reached the top of the stairway. He heard a ruffling sound in Jack's bedroom, followed by a ray of light that pierced the darkness through the cracks in the bedroom door.

Damn, he heard it. Hugh thought. He raised the poker and stood next to the door. His muscles tightened and his stomach turned over. He began to pant. The door swung open and Jack appeared, half-dressed in the doorway.

"What the hell!" Jack spluttered. Hugh struck him across the head. Jack hit the floor but quickly got to his feet. The poker had just glanced off his head. Hugh flipped the hall light on to see what damage he'd inflicted. He saw Jack's crazed eyes staring at him and remembered the ferocity of his rages.

Hugh swung the poker wildly. Blood spurted but Jack still did not fall. Jack dodged from side to side to fend off the blows. The poker flew out of Hugh's hand after he attempted one last blow. Jack began to throw punches, missing initially but soon finding his mark.

Hugh fumbled for a weapon. He picked up a small hall table, hurled it at Jack, pulled a picture from the wall, hit Jack with the edge of the frame, and then kicked him in the groin. But still Jack came on.

Hugh ran into the spare bedroom chased by a blood-soaked Jack, groaning like an animal. Hugh was petrified. He grabbed a table lamp, jammed it into Jack's face, and kicked him again and again.

In a last desperate attempt to fell Jack, Hugh threw a bed-cover over him and then picked up a solid wooden chair. He raised it above his head and crashed it down across Jack's back.

Jack lay motionless and Hugh fell to his knees panting heavily. He vomited, almost choked, but pulled himself up. He stared at his brother's motionless body for a few seconds before running back into the passageway to pick up the rope he had brought with him. He recovered his breath and started to bind Jack's arms and legs. Hugh staggered into the next room and pulled up a large Persian carpet.

When he returned he heard Jack groaning. "Still alive I see. Well you're going to meet the same fate as Mr. Lordy Everton," Hugh shouted. He rolled Jack's body into the carpet and fastened the ends with rope. Jack's body convulsed as the precious oxygen inside the carpet was quickly spent. Hugh watched his brother's last throes with satisfaction.

Inside his car Hugh had packed six large, collapsible suitcases. He brought them back into the house and systematically went through each room filling them with Jack's belongings. Hugh spent hours cleaning the blood from the walls and carpets, and when he finished, the house looked as if Jack had calmly packed and left, in preparation for a long absence.

SEVENTEEN

*C*ap Muller sat in his office putting the finishing touches to his crime report for the month of May. Everyone knew not to interrupt him during this task, but this time a mail clerk walked up to his desk and placed a pile of correspondence in Cap's in-tray, pointing to a hand delivered letter on the top. Cap looked up and scowled. The clerk edged back fearing an onslaught of abuse, but Cap noticed that the letter came from the Foreign Office in Pretoria, so he just signaled to the clerk to get lost. This was extremely unusual so he pushed aside his report and read the letter immediately.

"Karen, quick," he shouted. "I've got a response from the Vatican about that ring imprint."

Karen rushed into Cap's office and quickly scanned through the letter. "Well it took them long enough," she replied.

"Maybe our boys sat on it."

"They say it's an early Christian sect founded in Germany. They were banned from the Roman Catholic Church hundreds of years ago. Some of the text is in Latin."

Karen skipped past the Latin and read on. It stated that the sects live in monasteries around the world, including one in Johannesburg, which was established in 1930. The Vatican classified them as devil worshippers and excommunicated all Catholics that belonged to the sect.

Cap wondered if BOSS had a file on the cult, so he called one of his contacts, Colonel Van Starden, and asked for an unofficial favor. After exchanging a half-dozen calls Cap learned that the sect, called the "The Brothers of Salic Law," had been investigated by BOSS four years earlier, and although they were a weird group they were not considered a threat to the state.

The next morning Karen received the complete BOSS file from Van Starden's office and after briefing Cap on its contents, drove out to the monastery with Assistant Detective George Nortier, to dig around for some leads. They decided not to reveal the nature of the investigation and chose the pretext of looking for a missing person to justify their visit.

The monastery stood on ten acres of wooded land surrounded by a high, brick wall, which obscured the view of the monastery building. They drove up to the gatehouse and sounded the car's horn to attract attention. No one appeared, so Karen and George walked to the gatehouse to look for a way of attracting attention. After five minutes of rattling the metal gate and calling out Karen noticed a man dressed in a monk's robe walking along the road leading to the gatehouse on the inside of the perimeter. He looked at them suspiciously and then abruptly turned and hurried back into the undergrowth.

A few minutes later she saw another monk at the gatehouse. "What do you want? This is private property. We don't like strangers here."

Karen looked at the brown-robed man and shouted back. "We're from the Johannesburg Police Department and we want to speak to Bishop John urgently."

He partially hid himself from view and shouted back, "I don't know if Brother John is available."

"Either let me in or I'll get a search warrant and come back and break in."

"Wait a moment, let me check," he replied, and hurried off towards the monastery.

After five minutes two monks appeared at the gatehouse door and told Karen and George to enter. They led them along a winding path to the entrance of the main monastery building. The two monks were absolutely silent during the two-minute walk. Karen gained the distinct impression that she was unwelcome both as a woman and as a police officer.

She looked up at the monastery as they climbed the stone steps leading from the path to the entrance. The steps were inlaid with elaborate designs and there were three separate iron railings, one at the center of the steps and two on the sides, extending the whole length of the fifty-foot stairway. Two carved wooden doors, about sixteen feet high, marked the end of the stairway.

The two-storey building was built with cold, gray stone with only a few windows breaking the symmetric monotony of the stone slabs. As they entered the building Karen noticed a large, circular sign fixed to the wall, about five feet above the ground. Inside the circle was an ornate bronze design that looked like the picture of the ring imprint that Phillipus had uncovered. Around the design was a two-inch Latin text made of a silvery metal.

Inside the hall a strong smell of boiled vegetables permeated the air. It turned Karen's stomach for a few seconds—so much so that she had to breathe through her mouth. George was not so polite and used a handkerchief to mask the smell.

One of the monks stopped outside a room at the end of a corridor and said, "Brother John will be with you shortly."

While he scurried back along the corridor, the other monk stood motionless next to Karen. She peeked into the room and saw several monks busy painting designs on clay pots. None of them spoke.

Brother John, a tall, slim man with mediaeval-looking features, appeared and introduced himself only to George. Karen showed him her identification and realizing small talk would be of no use, went straight to the subject.

"We're investigating a missing person. We had information that the person may have joined a religious sect."

"We haven't had any new members for some time so I doubt we can help," Brother John said, looking disdainfully at Karen, "but go ahead if you must."

"Who said he joined recently," George said.

Brother John did not answer, but as he adjusted his robe Karen noticed he had a ring on his forefinger exactly the same as the large symbol adorning the entrance.

"You all seem to wear the same type of ring," she said. "Is it some form of membership artifact?"

"You could say that."

"What does it stand for?"

"It goes back centuries when the Pope banned our order across Europe. We cast them in bronze and gave them to all the brothers after they were dispersed so that they could recognize each other in secret and avoid persecution."

"Do you have a list of all the brothers that have them?"

"No," Brother John replied sharply.

"Do you keep records on your donors?"

"No, we don't keep any records."

At this point Karen remembered some notes in the file stating that the BOSS operatives searched all the books in the library and found very detailed records on just about every activity and person involved in the brotherhood.

"Would you mind showing me around?" she asked, changing the subject.

"If I must," he curtly replied. "I'll just finish up what I was doing."

When Brother John left, Karen slipped away and circled back to what looked like his study. She rifled through the two cabinets in the study and Brother John's desk looking for anything that resembled a list of names, but could find nothing. She walked into the library, which consisted of about twenty long shelves stacked one on top of the other. There were too many books and documents to go through in the short time available, so she gave up searching and drew a rough map of the rooms in the monastery and the interconnecting corridors.

When Brother John returned he ushered them through to the

prayer hall. Several monks, seated on the wooden benches in the prayer hall, chanted quietly with their heads bowed. Brother John asked the monks to be silent and led George and Karen into a private room next to the hall.

Karen was suspicious and surprised that Brother John had not asked for more details about why the police were so interested in the monastery and the brotherhood, so she decided to goad him a little.

"Brother John, how many monks live here?"

"Twenty seven."

"Could you give me a list of their names?"

"I'll ask Brother William to compile one."

He called for Brother William and whispered in his ear. William hurried off without commenting.

"Have any of your brothers suffered from mental problems?" Karen asked.

"No, certainly not," he replied sharply.

George pushed his face near to Brother John's and asked aggressively, "Any unnatural sexual practices go on here?"

Brother John stepped back and lowered his head slightly. "I'm not answering that. How dare you . . . "

"Hit a raw nerve did I?" George asked provocatively.

Brother John closed his eyes and turned his head away.

Virginia asked if any of the monks ever left the monastery late at night.

Brother John regained his composure. "No, they only go out to buy provisions, and rarely on their own."

"Are any of them married?" Virginia asked sharply.

"No, we are strictly celibate."

"That's not what I asked."

Brother John's face reddened and he clenched his fists. "I believe some of them were married, but we are a male only brotherhood."

He ignored the next few questions and took to tapping his wooden desk. The impasse ended when Brother William returned. Brother John snatched the paper and dismissed him with a wave of his hand.

"Here," he said, and handed it to George.

Karen took it and replied, "We'll check everyone. No doubt we'll have to come back. Oh, by the way, where do you have those rings made?"

"A jeweler in Durban."

"What's his name?"

"Tower Jewelers, the owner's name is Markworth."

Karen and George thanked Brother John and left the monastery.

On the way back to Johannesburg George said that he saw Brother William go behind the altar in the prayer room just before he brought the list of monks. "He fumbled about for a while, but then I lost sight of him. Two minutes later he returned with the list."

"Maybe there's a key to a room or a safe behind the altar. So you didn't see him carry the document away from the altar then?"

"I couldn't see if he did or not."

"If they have another secret list of members or donors it's probably hidden in the same place William retrieved the list of resident monks."

"Maybe so, but can we get it? If we get a search warrant we'll have to reveal what we're really looking for, and that's our only solid clue that the murderer doesn't know we have. He'll disappear if that happens."

"Let's break into the monastery—BOSS did it, according to the file," Karen suggested.

"If we get caught Cap will kill us."

"Let's run it by him tonight."

Later that evening Karen timidly suggested the break-in and to her surprise Cap agreed. She sat in Cap's office as he called Colonel Van Starden to ask for another favor.

"Two of our agents broke in via a disused sewage tunnel that runs from the edge of the property to the back of the monastery. They went in five or six times on successive nights collecting information. It was a bit of a laugh really. We didn't have much going on so the boys treated it like a training exercise."

"Could you help us out tonight, Colonel?" Cap asked.

"We are pretty busy. Several agents took part in the search but they're unavailable at the moment. Hold on . . . if I remember correctly, the agent that developed the plan is in Pretoria. Let me see if she's available—no promises mind you."

Van Starden's assistant called an hour later and told Cap that an agent would meet them before midnight. Karen and George prepared a map based on the BOSS file and their observations from earlier in the day. They assembled a small team to support the effort and all eagerly sat outside Cap's office waiting for the BOSS agent.

At 10:00 PM the duty sergeant brought the BOSS agent to Cap's office.

"Hello my name is Virginia Wilson. Colonel Van Starden told me to help out for the night."

Karen shook hands and said, "We'd better get going, it's late."

"I went over the file to refresh my memory," Virginia said. "It'll be a pushover."

During the drive to the monastery Virginia explained how they previously entered the main building through the disused sewage tunnel and how they got to their financial and legal records stored in a room next to the prayer hall. They quickly worked out a route from the sewage tunnel that would avoid the monk's sleeping quarters and get them to the prayer hall unnoticed.

They easily found the manhole covering the entrance to the sewage tunnel. The bolts used to fasten it to its metal housing had been removed and left at the center of the cover.

George, Karen and Virginia put on breathing apparatus, turned on the flashlights atop of their miner-style helmets, and clambered into the tunnel. It was only four feet in diameter so they had to crouch to make headway. After a slippery and difficult 150 yards they reached the outside wall of the main monastery building.

George cleared the rubbish out of the way, which allowed Virginia to slide through the opening. She was able to stand upright and move aside a square metal cover above her head. This opened the way to the floor of a storeroom. One by one they climbed out of the tunnel and into the monastery. They removed their breathing gear and followed Virginia.

The whole place was dimly lit, but not so dark that they needed to use flashlights. They passed by the monk's sleeping quarters and on into the prayer hall, carefully checking that none of the monks were still about. Virginia went over to the altar, signaled Karen to follow, and moved a wooden tile from the floor. She fumbled around until she found a metal container, which on her last visit had contained a duplicate set of keys.

She whispered to Karen, "They must have moved the keys. Let's check all the rooms."

They checked three doors on the other side of the hall. The first two were open but they were empty. The third room had a sturdy-looking padlock fitted to the door. One by one George tried each of his locksmith's keys to jiggle the padlock open.

The room contained wall-to-wall shelving packed with books and manuscripts of all shapes and sizes. They closed the door, switched on the barely adequate lighting, and searched through the material, item by item. George photographed any documents of interest and then replaced them to look untouched.

Two hours passed. George whispered to Karen and Virginia. "Come and look at this." He showed them a folder containing hundreds of names and addresses with a cross-reference to their brotherhood names.

"This is it," Karen said gleefully.

"Good, photograph the pages and let's get going," Virginia said. "Make sure there's nothing else worth looking at. I don't fancy crawling through that sewer again."

They turned the lights off, re-locked the door, and retraced their steps back to the storeroom. Ten minutes later the van sped back to the center of Johannesburg—mission accomplished.

The next morning Karen retrieved the developed film from the police photo lab. There were fewer than 200 names on the brotherhood's membership list. As she began to sift through the list Cap and George walked into the room.

"I hear you were successful last night."

"Yes," Karen replied, "here's the list."

They were looking at the list of names when Karen noticed something.

"Cap, look, this name's familiar, and look at the address—it's one of those mansions in Stanton."

"Who is it?" Cap asked.

"Barlow, Jack Barlow."

"No. We interviewed Hugh Barlow, not Jack. It's probably just a coincidence. You had better interview everyone. Get as many officers as possible and start with any names that match with known criminals, and any that we've spoken to before. See if we can open this case up at last."

George took a copy of the membership list and compared it against the suspects and witnesses previously interviewed. When he finished he said, "Karen, it's strange you mentioned the name 'Barlow'. Look at the typed list we got from Hugh Barlow's Swartkop rowing club. At the bottom there are several names scribbled in, almost as an afterthought. One of them, the last one, is 'Jack Barlow'. Look!"

"I remember that," Karen said, "he wrote in the guests' names that were not on the original list. I assumed he signed at the bottom of the page."

"No, it definitely reads 'Jack Barlow'. Hugh Barlow wasn't even on the list, because he compiled it."

"You're right, George," Karen said, "let's interview him today. It's too much of a coincidence."

They drove to Jack's house in the afternoon but found it empty. They checked with neighbors but none of them knew where to find Jack. One, an elderly man, told them that Jack had not been seen for some time and the servants who worked for him didn't have access to the house, nor had they been paid for weeks.

Karen noticed that the garage door was unlocked and a Rolls Royce was parked inside with the driver's window down. George tried the handle of a door leading from the garage into the house. It too was unlocked.

"George, this seems fishy. We'd better have a look around. You'd have to be mad to leave an expensive house like this unlocked."

"The furniture looks like it's okay," Karen said, "but there's no clothes or personal items around. And where's that foul smell coming from?"

"Maybe he's on vacation or away on business," George replied.

"I don't think so. Absolutely everything is gone. Winter and summer clothes—everything."

"Since this Hugh Barlow fellow invited him to the party maybe he knows what's happened. Maybe he's a relative of Jack's."

"Possibly. Let's give it a try. He lives near here."

"I'll get an officer to come over and keep an eye on this place until we can give it a good going over," George added.

Karen noticed that Hugh seemed nervous as he welcomed them inside, but his tone soon changed to sarcasm.

"Detective Van Der Berg, nice to see you again. Got anywhere with the serial murder case yet?"

Karen suppressed anger as Hugh grinned smugly. She smiled back at him. "Things are beginning to open up and we're confident that a breakthrough is imminent. Actually we omitted to interview Mr. Jack Barlow. Apparently he hasn't been seen for weeks and his house has been left unlocked. The other unusual thing was that we didn't find any personal effects. By the way, is he a relative of yours?"

"He's my half-brother actually. Jack and I didn't see eye to eye, so we rarely speak to each other. It's common knowledge in the family. In fact the last time I saw him was at the party in the Swartkop Club over a year ago."

"So you don't know his whereabouts?" George asked.

"Absolutely not. I'm afraid I can't help you there."

"Was he married?"

Hugh shook his head.

"Do you know the names of any of his friends?"

Hugh threw his hands in the air. "I don't think he had any—bit of a loner."

"A very rich loner though," George added.

"Yes he was."

"Why do you say 'was'?" Karen interjected, after she noticed Hugh's smug look reappear.

"Just a turn of phrase, Miss Van Der Berg, nothing more."

"Okay, thank you for your time, Mr. Barlow," Karen said. As she reached the door she turned and said, "Have you ever heard of the Brotherhood of Salic Law? I believe Jack is a member."

"No, never heard of it, sorry."

During the drive back to Jack's house Karen said to George, "I'm sure there's something going on between those two brothers. My intuition tells me something is afoot."

"Could be," George replied. "He didn't seem concerned about Jack. I got the feeling he knew Jack was missing."

"Exactly what I thought. Anyway let's give the house a thorough going over."

A police officer met them in the driveway of the house and told them that he was pretty sure that the bad smell came from the basement. George and Karen went into the house, where another officer was trying to open a metal door located at the bottom of a stairway that appeared to lead to the basement. The door was fitted with a combination and a deadbolt lock.

"I've almost got it open," the officer said, as George and Karen approached him.

George and the other officer lent a hand and broke the whole lock housing away from the wall. As the door opened a sickening smell gushed upwards from the basement stairs. One officer retched uncontrollably. George rushed back into the kitchen and out into the garden for some fresh air. Karen pressed a handkerchief in her face and braved the stairs.

She used a small flashlight to help maneuver the dark stairwell and basement. Feeling her way forward, she saw several chains hanging from the ceiling and a number of earthenware jars stacked on shelves around the basement. Her grip on the flashlight tightened as the chains jangled when she brushed past them. She had the impression of an evil force waiting for a victim to be suspended on its iron handcuffs.

The earthenware jars stared at her like fat distorted faces. She froze for a second at the thought of what evil might have occurred in this dank hole. She shuddered and dropped the flashlight. It bounced a few times before rolling under one of the lower shelves. Karen kneeled on the floor and fumbled about in the dark trying to find it. Instead of the flashlight, her hand grabbed something cold and wet. She picked up the flashlight with her other hand and illuminated the object. It was a dismembered hand.

She screamed and instinctively threw it down. The shock jolted her back and she fell into a row of shelves. She heard glass smash and felt liquid pour over her head and face. Her flailing arms hit against a large earthenware jar, which smashed between her legs as she coughed and choked to expel the foul fluid that had spilled into her mouth.

A bright light illuminated the scene. *George must have found the light switch,* she thought. Karen looked at George in horror when she saw what had fallen from the shelves. She screamed and tried frantically to push away the glass and the dismembered human hands and feet. The glass cut her arms and the blood mixed with the red-tipped human remains and the preserving fluid. She froze again when she focused on the dozens of glass jars placed around the basement, some on shelves and others on the floor, each containing pieces of unrecognizable flesh. George grabbed her and pushed her towards the stairs.

She panicked and began yelling when she saw that some of the body parts had fallen inside her blouse. She ripped her jacket and blouse off and charged for the stairs.

No one went back into the basement until the forensic team arrived. Everyone that braved those stairs was warned what to expect. Cap appeared and took over the crime scene, but even he shuddered when he ventured down into Hades. Karen collapsed after her bout of hysteria, and Cap thought her condition so bad that he ordered her removed by ambulance to the hospital for treatment.

The jubilant team gathered in Cap's office that evening, minus

Karen, to plan the next step. At long last the hunt for the serial killer entered its final phase. Cap launched a nation-wide dragnet for Jack Barlow. Within hours he sent Jack's picture and description to every police station in the country and every border crossing—land, sea, and air.

Unknown to Cap, a substituted Jack Barlow in the form of his half-brother Hugh, planned to flee across the border into Botswana, but for very different reasons.

PART THREE

*If at First
You Don't Succeed . . .*

EIGHTEEN

*C*hris Conway sat in his office flicking through the monthly mining statistics that he had just sent to head office in Johannesburg. He could hardly wait to move to Johannesburg and start his new position. His financial problems had finally diminished and Cherrie had become a lot less demanding.

A phone call from head office interrupted him. It was a whole host of people from the accounting and finance section wanting to speak with him urgently.

All Steinkop Corporation's mines submitted their reports regularly to the central accounting group who reviewed the results and produced a combined report for Steinkop's Chairman. Once accepted, the results were sent to the Government's Department of Mines, for inclusion in overall national statistics.

The Chief Accountant thought Chris's latest report was a bad mistake or some sort of prank because the current yield of carats had fallen twenty percent from the previous month's figure, but the amount of earth mined, machine usage, power usage, and employees paid remained constant.

Chris said nervously, "Let me double check everything and get back to you."

The accountants were not having any of Chris's excuses. They refused to send the report to the Chairman unless the differences could be explained. They pushed Chris further. They went over the statistics of the other mines in the area, none of which followed this pattern. The percentage of gem diamonds verses industrial grade had reverted back to the previous year's level—completely anathema to the new assay report.

Chris began to bluster and make excuses. "We've had a year of outstanding results. Nothing lasts forever."

"Chris," the Chief Accountant said, "the recent assay report predicted years of high output. What changed?"

"Well . . . err . . . I'm not sure. I'll check and get back to you."

"Send the report to me. I want to compare it to the original."

"I don't have a copy," Chris replied.

"I'll get it from the Department of Mines then."

"Give me a couple of weeks and I'll see if I can dig them out."

"Chris, we don't have a couple of weeks. If the Chairman sees these results without an explanation he'll go mad."

"When is it due?"

"Two days."

"Tell him it's a temporary hiccup," Chris replied. "That'll give us a month to sort things out."

"I'm not telling him an outright lie. Remember Steinkop is a public company."

"So where do we go from here?" Chris asked.

"There'll be an official inquiry if we don't come up with an answer."

Chris tried to end the conversation. "I'll work on it and call you tomorrow."

"Not so fast Chris," The Chief Accountant said. "Have you seen Steinkop's latest stock price?"

Chris didn't answer, but the people on the other end of the line kept firing questions.

"Why did it drop so fast?"

"If the corporation is valued much lower we could be in trouble with our capital ratios."

"Maybe it's a hostile takeover."

"Who's doing all the buying and selling?"

"An overseas outfit. They bought heavily last year when the shares were low and now they're dumping."

"Bit of a coincidence isn't it?"

"That was just before our yield jumped."

"And now heavy selling when the yield has fallen."

Chris threw the phone down and bolted. He called Hugh from another office, completely forgetting not to make overt references to their activities over the phone.

"Hugh, I'm getting a lot of heat from the accounting boys. They noticed the drop in yield and they're asking some awkward questions. What should I do?"

"Ignore it, Chris. Your chairman, Roberts, knows all about it. Plead ignorance to the minions and tell them you're just doing your job. It's somebody else's problem."

"Hugh, they asked about the assay report we rigged last year."

"I'll ask my contact in the government to call your board members. Don't worry, we'll smooth everything over."

"What about my cut of the takings, Hugh?"

"I'll send it next week."

"I heard a rumor you were leaving the country soon."

"Not for a few months. We'll get this business sorted out well before then."

Chris remained worried even after Hugh's phlegmatic and nonchalant attitude. He had several good contacts at Steinkop's head office and a few within some government departments. After pondering for over an hour, he began calling them and edging around the subject of Namibian independence and what impact it would have on the mining industry in South Africa. No one took the bait.

He became even more concerned during a conversation with two members of the management committee at head office. Chris had been working with them on an organizational restructuring project and with the definition of his new position. Hugh had told him they knew about the scheme but not to say anything openly.

"Chris, I don't see what you are driving at. What's the government got to do with our business and what do we care about Namibian independence?"

"Well all I'm saying is that our Board will be briefed very soon, so don't worry about the drop-off in production."

"How can you fucking say that, Chris? We've taken on all sorts of loans and given guarantees based on our increased output. Have you seen what's happened to the share price? There's a special meeting of the Board of Directors tomorrow to discuss it. And you're telling me not to worry?"

At about the same time it finally dawned on Chris what a precarious position he was in, Hugh drove out of his house in Stanton for the last time with just two suitcases of personal effects. He had removed everything else the day before and dumped what he didn't need and put the rest into storage. He paid the servants their wages that morning and told them not to return. A week before, Hugh purchased a used van to get him from Johannesburg to the border with Botswana, because a Rolls Royce in that part of the world would be too conspicuous.

He drove northwest towards the Botswana border, and after four hours of driving arrived at a border crossing in the town of Ramathlabama. At the lightly manned South African border post, a tired looking policeman asked to see his passport. Hugh handed over Jack's passport and confidently waited for the officer to examine it. "How long will you be out of the country, Mr. Barlow?"

"Only a week or so," he replied, "I'm going to Gaborones on business."

The officer stamped his passport and waved Hugh through the checkpoint. Fifty yards along the dirt road Hugh stopped at a barrier across the road marked "Customs and Immigration Post— Botswana".

He looked for signs of life but the whole place appeared to be deserted. Hugh walked to a shabby looking hut alongside the road, but no sign of a customs or immigration official. He stepped outside the hut when he heard the South African policeman shout. "Go to the police station at the airport and get your passport stamped. The kaffirs fucked off a few hours ago. I think they went to a wedding celebration."

Hugh waved his appreciation to the policeman and drove directly to the airport, where, after a four-hour wait, he boarded a plane to Nairobi, Kenya. *No one will trace me on this route, especially using Jack's identity,* he thought. *One overnight stay in Nairobi and I'll be on my way to England—mission accomplished.*

Roger Hamilton left his office and drove to Steinkop Mining Corporation's head office in Johannesburg with his bodyguard, Peter Fourie. The Chairman had called him earlier in the day and offered him what amounted to a blank check to launch an urgent investigation into the events around the stock price collapse and the drastic reduction in the diamond yield.

Roger entered the boardroom to find several members of the management team standing around a conference table exchanging recriminations. Some were plowing through piles of documentation and others were engaged in heated telephone conversations. Roger stood in the doorway amazed at such hectic activity by men of their age. He told Peter Fourie to watch the board members and check if any of them looked nervous or acted out of character.

The Chairman noticed Roger enter the room and banged on the table with his fist. "Gentlemen, please be quiet and sit down. Roger Hamilton has arrived and I want to get this briefing started.

"I discussed the salient issues with Roger earlier today and he's agreed to start work on this investigation immediately. He has complete discretion and authority to interview any employee or director. I expect everyone to cooperate completely and immediately.

"The future of this corporation is at stake. When Roger finishes his investigation we'll meet to discuss his findings and agree an approach. I'll arrange a special meeting of the shareholders to explain all this, but hopefully I can forestall that until Roger finishes his report. Roger, I know it's putting you on the spot, but do you have any immediate thoughts about all this?"

"Well," Roger replied, "It is a bit soon . . . but I came across something similar to this about ten years ago. That turned out to be a one-time theft and things went back to normal. In this case I think the really unusual event occurred a year ago when your yield increased suddenly. Those old assay reports have proven to be remarkably accurate even though they were done thirty or more years ago. That's where I'll start digging. I'll travel to Steinkop and interview your mining staff. Conway is your manager up there isn't he?"

"Yes," the Chairman replied, "do you need him to fly here tomorrow?"

"No. I'll go there with my best people."

"You have it. Use the company's jet."

Although Chris Conway was terrified at the thought of meeting Roger Hamilton, he thought he would be safe as long as the phony assay reports were not examined. The originals were stored in the Records Department at Steinkop, with a copy filed with Department of Mines in Pretoria. Chris deliberately omitted sending a copy to head office, which was the normal procedure. He decided to locate and destroy the original held at Steinkop prior to Roger Hamilton's arrival, which left the Department of Mines' copy to deal with. He tried to telephone Hugh several times to ask if he knew of any contacts there, but Hugh's phone was disconnected. This put even more pressure on Chris's strained nerves.

He went to the Records Department late in the day and told the clerk he would lock up the office after he finished his search. Chris quickly found the file and destroyed every incriminating entry.

Two days later Chris was working in his office when his secretary told him that Roger Hamilton and another gentleman wanted to speak to him. He took several deep breaths and waited for the interview to start.

Chris knew that Roger's investigators had been working furiously, interviewing dozens of workers and collecting statistics from all sections of the mine. He heard about intimidation tactics that were being used by a rather nasty character on Roger's staff, Peter Fourie, who was softening up some of the likely suspects before the actual interviewing started. One look and the interviewees knew he meant business. Peter Fourie stood behind Roger, removed his sunglasses, clenched his fists, and glared at Chris with his cold black eyes.

"How's your investigation going?" Chris asked shakily.

Roger didn't answer, he just stared into Chris's eyes. Chris looked away.

"Chris what's happening here?"

"It's inexplicable."

"Why did you commission a new assay report?"

"I read an article . . . in a mining journal . . . several mines were getting better results mining at certain depths. Just about where we are at Steinkop. So I ordered the tests. A long shot really."

"Which mines?"

"I don't remember now."

"I couldn't find a copy of the assay report, either at head office or here in Steinkop."

"Probably mis-filed," Chris suggested.

"Maybe. What do you make of the high percentage of gem quality stones?"

"That surprised me too."

"Inexplicable again I suppose," Roger added.

Chris remained silent.

"Did you process more earth than usual? Could that be why?"

"No, it's been about the same."

"Let's assume that there are more diamonds per cubic meter of earth at the depth you're currently mining. Why would the number suddenly drop back to last year's level?"

"Roger, you're asking me things that I just cannot answer."

"But you're the Mine Manager, surely you have some ideas?"

"Sorry, I don't."

"Okay, Chris, thanks for your time." Roger walked towards the door, turned and said, "Chris, just one more thing. I met Johnny Getz from the Diamond Surveyors Company yesterday. Wasn't he the fellow that did the sampling and testing for the assay you commissioned?"

Chris gulped but didn't answer. Roger's short and precise interview unnerved him even more than his parting insinuation. He instinctively knew that Roger suspected him and that it would only be a matter of time before Roger found out about the doctored assay report. His only hope, that the South African Government and Hugh stood behind the grand scheme, became even more of a distant dream.

Colonel Van Starden finished reading Virginia's final report on the money laundering case and called her in to his office to discuss the next steps. They had a list of prominent South African citizens and residents that had been contravening the Foreign Exchange Act, and in addition, they had the names of six money market traders and brokers that had also systematically broken that law. He specifically mentioned Harold Budd and referred to him as a prolific thief, one whom the Minister of Justice would definitely prosecute.

Van Starden looked at Virginia when he mentioned Budd's name but she remained poker-faced.

"What'll happen to the individuals we've identified?"

"The liberal leaning ones I'm sure will be contacted by an anonymous source and asked to realign some of their more provocative views, of course in favor of the government. The others will be told to donate some more money to the National Party. All of them will be threatened with a long prison sentence if they continue to act in an antisocial way."

"Basically you're saying they'll get away with it."

"Basically, yes. I'm sure you noticed the two National Party ministers on the list. It would be too embarrassing for the Prime Minister if the names of his loyal supporters were exposed."

"Shall I stop the surveillance?"

"No, leave it in place for a while," Van Starden replied. "We're still getting some interesting information. Have you been keeping up to date with it?"

"Yes."

"Good. If another high priority project starts up we'll shut it down."

"Okay if I take some vacation?" Virginia asked.

"Don't see why not. Take a couple of weeks, but keep in contact."

"Thanks. Anything else in the report you want to discuss?"

"No, excellent job. Well done."

Virginia got up to leave.

"Actually there is one thing."

"You zeroed in on that Budd fellow more so than the others. He was the worst offender I admit, but what made you stick with him so tenaciously?"

"Can I talk off the record?"

"Of course."

"Well, without going into a lot of detail—I'm pretty sure that one of Budd's clients killed a close friend of mine. I found out from one of the bugged conversations and I guess I subconsciously devoted more time and effort to trap him."

"Oh, I see. What's this fellow's name?"

"Barlow. Hugh Barlow."

"I've heard of the family," Van Starden said. "Don't take any action yourself. Wait until you come back from vacation and I'll see what I can do about him."

"Thanks, sir. See you in two weeks."

NINETEEN

When Cap Muller walked into his office early on Monday morning, George Nortier thrust a telex into his hand.

"Give me time to get my coat off, George," Cap said.

He read the telex and without commenting walked over to a wall map of southern Africa. Cap's finger wandered around the map for a while before zeroing in on Botswana. "Where the hell is this place Ramathlabama?"

"It's on the Botswana border about fifty miles south of the capital, Gabarones. It seems Jack Barlow crossed over the border last Wednesday."

Cap read the telex again. Immigration recorded Jack Barlow leaving South Africa at Ramathlabama in a private vehicle. The telex listed Barlow's passport and vehicle license plate numbers. The immigration officer received notice of Barlow's arrest warrant four hours after he crossed into Botswana and sent the telex as soon as he realized what had happened.

Cap knew from experience the difficulties involved in getting the authorities in Botswana to cooperate with the South African police. Politically it was suicide for any member of their government to be seen dealing with the apartheid south. Even if they did agree, their resources were thin on the ground and very poorly trained.

George recommended that they call the local police chief directly, instead of going through official channels, and ask him to detain Barlow on a trumped-up visa violation charge. A few hundred rand in his pocket and everything would go smoothly. Barlow could be deported fairly quickly and without any fuss.

Cap agreed, but he wanted a black officer to arrange things. He told George to find Phillipus Matagwe, the best black officer in the squad.

When they returned Cap knew straight away that Phillipus had something on his mind.

"Phillipus, is there something you want to tell us?" Cap asked.

"Well, sir, it is about the women Barlow murdered. I checked the files Miss Karen worked with . . . "

"How is she by the way, George?" Cap interjected.

"Not too good at first but I think she is getting over it now. Apparently it wasn't just the shock of finding the body parts. She seems to have some sort of nervous disorder – probably working too hard on this case."

"Shame. I'll drop into the hospital at the weekend. Anyway, Phillipus, go on man. We haven't got all day."

"I noticed that four of the five victims all worked for the same company, Aegis Investigations, over two years ago."

"What!" Cap yelled.

"Yes, exactly, sir. Two of the women were administrative assistants. One was an attorney and the other a mining industry analyst. The company disbanded shortly after they left."

"Interesting," Cap said, "and who owned this company?"

"That's the odd thing, sir," George interjected. "There appears to be no record of the owners whatsoever. All the employees were paid, taxes paid, annual returns submitted, but no records could be found to trace the owners."

Phillipus continued, "In addition, sir, the company employed two men. They both seem to have been private detectives in previous jobs."

"Wait for this one, sir!" George said.

"Both men are dead, sir," Phillipus exclaimed. "One man, only thirty-nine, had a heart attack, and the other died in a car accident, sir. His car went off a cliff just outside of East London. No one else involved apparently."

"How did we miss this?"

"Karen must have only checked their current jobs. Her notes say that they didn't know each other. Certainly none of their relatives said anything to connect the victims."

"The odds of six people all being murdered or dying in these circumstances must be astronomical," Cap said.

"About seven billion to one, sir," Phillipus added.

"Okay, don't get too smart," Cap replied. "Why would Jack Barlow murder and butcher four women from the same company? And possibly kill two men also? What about the fifth woman, how does she fit into all this?"

"That's Catherine De Jong, the woman killed at the rowing club," George said. "One other woman worked at this Aegis place by the name of Cushing. We're trying to trace her."

"Look into the deaths of the two men more thoroughly," Cap said. "Get the death certificates and interview the coroner and the doctors who issued them. Speak with the next of kin and see if they know anything about this Aegis Company."

"We'll need more officers on it, sir," George said.

"Okay, leave that to me," Cap replied. "Now back to Mr. Jack Barlow. Why don't you and Phillipus drive to Ramthla . . . what's the name of the place?"

"Ramathlabama, sir," Phillipus replied.

"Go there and find him. We've got the license plate number of his car. It's on the telex. So you should be able to get the make and model quite easily. There're only two large towns in Botswana, Gabarones in the south and Francistown in the north, with one road connecting them.

"Start with Gabarones and then call me before you leave for Francistown. We'll keep your visit unofficial until we find him. Then we'll get some unofficial help from the police in Gabarones."

Two days later George phoned Cap to give him an update. "Sir, he seems to have fled. He caught a flight to Nairobi the day he crossed the border."

"Shit," Cap replied. "I'll contact Interpol and see if we can trace him. In the meantime get back here tomorrow. I've set up a raid on that monastery and I want you to lead it."

"See you tomorrow, sir."

The next morning a convoy of police vehicles screeched to a halt outside the entrance to the monastery. The plan called for a simultaneous assault on the front and back of the building, with George using a walkie-talkie to coordinate the two groups.

The group at the rear, led by George, scrambled over the perimeter wall and rushed towards the huge wooden door of the main monastery building. Two officers whacked the door with sledgehammers until it began to splinter. When the frame collapsed, George called the group at the front of the building and told them to advance.

A monk screamed as the door lurched back and toppled on him. The officers ignored his cries and surged through the entrance trampling over the door and the trapped monk.

One officer stopped and beat the monk over the head with his truncheon. "Take that you fucking pervert," the officer shouted. "Wait 'til we get you in the station."

"Stop that!" George shouted. "Handcuff him and take him away."

George followed the officers into the main prayer hall where they checked each room, but they were all deserted. He ran to the front of the monastery to check on the other group's progress and watched as they rammed through the front gates with a reinforced Land Rover.

By the time they reached the front entrance the officers inside had forced it open. George ordered them to spread out and search the upper level first, and then go down to the basement.

"There's a smell of smoke, sir," someone yelled.

"It's coming from the basement."

George went back outside, dragged the captured monk to his feet, and told one of his men to hold him still.

"Where's the rest of your friends?"

"They've all gone, I swear," the terrified monk replied.

"Stop lying you bastard," George said, as he kneed the monk in the groin. "Come on, where are they? Anymore up-hills from you and I'll finish you off."

"I think they're hiding in the basement . . . but I also saw a stranger running away."

"You think do you?" George screamed. "Where are they? Who was the stranger? What did he look like?"

"A big man in dark clothes. He had sunglasses on. Not one of us and he didn't wear a police uniform. I think he set the fire. Everyone else was asleep."

The monk told him about an underground passageway, a sewage tunnel that led to the outside wall and said that the monks probably went through it. George assumed that it was the same tunnel he used to break-in with Karen.

George continued to interrogate the monk. "About twenty of them you say. And who was that you saw running away? A tall, powerful-looking fellow wearing dark glasses, you say. Well, we've all heard that one before."

George shouted at an officer to check the passageway and then ran back into the monastery, but the dense smoke forced him to turn back.

Flames burst out of the first floor windows, hurling the frames and the stained glass thirty yards across the grounds. The roof creaked, dropped two feet in the middle, and then collapsed into a fiery mass.

"Anyone left in there got themselves a free cremation," George said to his men. "Any sign of the others?"

"No, sir, but officer Esterhausen has found the sewer entrance."

"Let's see if they're in there."

The sound of sirens from two fire trucks distracted George's attention. "They're too late to save anyone, unless they're in the tunnel." When he reached the entrance to the sewer several officers were busy lifting its metal cover. The officers jumped back as smoke belched out of the tunnel.

Firefighters ran across carrying breathing apparatus and one of them clambered into the tunnel. He reappeared a few minutes later. "Must be twenty of them down there. All piled on top of each other."

"All dead?" George asked.

"Every single one. Looks like they were trying to escape through the tunnel and the smoke suffocated them. It was bolted down from the outside."

That's strange, George thought, *we didn't bolt the cover back on when we raided the place.* He looked at the flames towering above the remnants of the monastery and shook his head.

"George, over here."

George turned and saw Cap talking to the Fire Chief.

"It went up too quickly to be an accident," the Fire Chief said. "Someone deliberately set the fire."

"Damn," Cap said. "All our evidence gone up in flames."

"One of the monks survived," George added. "We've taken him back to the station. He said a stranger set the fire but I don't trust him."

"I wanted to interview the leader—Brother fucking John. He had a lot to do with setting up those murders with Jack Barlow. I'm sure of it. Now I suppose Barlow will try to say the monks were to blame for the murders. What a mess."

TWENTY

$\mathcal{R}$oger Hamilton stood in silence for ten minutes as he waited for the briefing to start. He rarely used notes for high-level presentations, so he used the spare time to review the salient points in his head. His concentration broke when the doors swung open and the Chairman of the Steinkop Mining Corporation and several of the directors strode into the boardroom. They looked serious.

Roger signaled to Peter Fourie, his bodyguard, to close the door and wait outside.

Several other senior members of the board were already seated. No one spoke. The Chairman made no introductions, he simply asked Roger to begin.

Roger spoke slowly and deliberately as he referenced handouts set out on the conference table. "Unfortunately I don't have any good news. Let me go over the individual facts first of all, then I'll summarize my findings and suggest what action to take."

For two hours Roger plowed through the facts he had uncovered. Johnny Getz from the Diamond Surveyors Company confirmed that the recent assay report was rigged. His results tallied with the original ones. The results Conway submitted to management differed greatly from Getz's results.

Almost all the additional carats produced were of gem quality, which was not typical at Steinkop. A spectroscopic analysis of the diamonds proved that the additional carats did not originate from Steinkop.

The production utilization statistics over the last year were compared with those submitted in previous years, and apart from the total yield of diamonds, no differences were found.

"It's clear gentlemen that the assay report was fraudulently submitted and the additional diamonds were artificially introduced into the final phase of the production process.

"The next issue to discuss is why. As you are aware, a huge increase in the volume of shares exchanging hands happened just before diamond production increased. A certain offshore company bought many of them last year and disposed of them just before production went back to normal levels. We'd be fools to believe that this was not based on inside information. The company is called General Financial and is incorporated in the Cayman Islands. The directors are not named and I believe it has since been disbanded.

"Finally, I find it hard to believe Chris Conway when he states that he ordered the new assay results based on an article in a mining periodical. Miraculously, according to Mr. Conway, copies of this article are no longer available. However, the results provided by the Diamond Surveyors Company tell the true story.

"Clearly, someone deliberately added the extra diamonds into the production process to inflate the stock price and fraudulently profit from their sale. What we need to discover is who, apart from Conway, is behind this plot and where did the additional diamonds come from? I'm finished now."

The Chairman stood up. Roger could see his face redden and his fists clench. "Thanks very much for that clear and convincing analysis, Roger," he said in a low and controlled voice. "You've earned you fee ten times over." After a long pause he continued. "Get that bastard Conway up here and let's try to get some sense out of him. Where is he now?"

"He's waiting on the first floor, sir," one of the secretaries said.

"Tell him to come up. I'll report all this to the police tomorrow and then inform old Kruger over in the Department of Mines. We're in for a few difficult months, that's for sure."

The secretary returned. "I couldn't find Conway."

"You told him to wait, didn't you?"

"Yes, but he seems to have fled."

"Fire him immediately. Confiscate his Steinkop shares and tell him to get out of the company's house by tomorrow. I suspect the fraud squad will want to interview him quite soon. Roger, could you do a little more digging around and see if any other mines have had this problem? As you all know, a lot of mines don't advertise this sort of thing."

"I'll keep on it," Roger replied.

At the Allied mine in Namibia, Harry Van Rensberg and Ivan Richards completed the day shift. They walked to the car park without exchanging words. Ivan had wanted to say something to Harry for days but found it difficult to work up enough courage to do so. No money had been forthcoming from Gavin and he wanted to get his cut and leave for Cape Town. Gavin's explanation, that Hugh seemed to have disappeared, seemed acceptable because both he and Harry trusted Gavin implicitly.

"Ivan, is something on your mind? You seem distracted these days."

Ivan hesitated for a moment. "Well there is actually."

Harry patted him on the back like a father comforting his son. "Spit it out then. We're in this together."

"I don't know about you but I'm getting nervous. Gavin has started drinking heavily again, and we've had no news from Barlow, no money—nothing."

Harry lit his pipe, took a few puffs, and then casually turned towards Ivan. "What do you suggest we do then?"

Ivan looked at him directly. "I think you and I have the same idea in our minds. Don't we?"

"Well," Harry said, "I think I know what you mean."

They continued walking for a while and then both stopped simultaneously. Ivan spoke softly. "We could just continue stealing for another month. Cut down the amount gradually, and work out a way of getting the diamonds out of the mine."

He waited for a response.

Harry pulled out his pocket calculator and tapped in a few numbers. "That would give us about 20,000 carats. Maybe we could pretend to find them on the mine. It's happened before you know."

"Hand them in to security and get a reward you mean?"

"Ten percent is the normal reward," Harry added. He entered a few more numbers into his calculator. "That would give us 200,000 between us. Mind you, they might not give us all that of course, but it must be at least 50,000 each."

"That's more than enough for me. I'm not greedy."

"Same here," Harry added casually.

"Okay, let's keep it going for another six weeks. Don't mention anything to Gavin. What he doesn't know won't hurt him."

"What happens when he finds out that we've got a reward?"

"Tough for him. We'll tell him to keep our share of Barlow's payoff—if it ever materializes."

They continued removing diamonds for the next few weeks in exactly the same way as before. Harry found a new hiding place for them and both he and Ivan felt confident they would not be caught.

Two days after the calendar month-end, Ivan went to the cafeteria for his lunch break. He sat down at a table on his own and as he picked at his food he felt a tap on the shoulder. Gavin stood over him.

"What the hell do you think you're playing at?" Gavin whispered.

"What do you mean?" Ivan asked, trying to appear innocent.

"You and Harry are still taking the diamonds aren't you?"

"What makes you say that?"

"Because one of the senior accountants called me yesterday and wanted to know why my monthly report doesn't tally with the daily returns. That's why."

"What monthly report?"

"The one I've been doctoring for the past year you idiot. I'm supposed to add up the number of shifts the sorters are paid for each calendar month and divide the result into the total diamond returns. They use it to compare efficiency month by month. I didn't fiddle the report for last month and you pair of goons have continued stealing."

Ivan's head dropped almost onto the dining table. "Oh shit."

"Exactly, oh shit."

Ivan looked around to make sure no one else could hear him. "What can we do then?"

Gavin got up and whispered, "Nothing, just sit tight and hope it blows over." He walked toward the exit and Ivan followed.

As they stepped outside, a Land Rover sped by and stopped next to the entrance of the processing plant. Ivan pointed it out to Gavin without speaking. Shortly afterwards he saw Harry Van Rensberg walking out of the plant, heading towards the car park.

Two security officers came up behind Harry, grabbed him by the arms, and pushed him to the floor. They pulled a small sack from around his waist and handcuffed him. Gavin turned slowly and went back in to the cafeteria, trying not to be conspicuous. Ivan followed.

Several people in the cafeteria were crowded around the windows looking at the scene outside. Gavin pulled Ivan aside and walked with him to the center of the dining room.

"Don't go over to the window," he said to Ivan. "Try to act nonchalant."

"Do you think Security knows about the accounting report?"

"Who knows?" Gavin replied. "I'll see what I can find out. Just go back to work and act normally."

Gavin went back to his office, where his secretary told him that the General Manager, Mike McCarthy, wanted to talk to him right away. Gavin went into his office and pulled a bottle of scotch from behind a cabinet. He took two swigs and put the bottle back. His mind randomly jumped from one subject to another and one excuse to another. He took another gulp of scotch and walked along the corridor towards McCarthy's office.

Gavin felt more relaxed as the effects of the whisky took hold and he began to feel more confident about the meeting. When he reached the end of the corridor he turned sharply to the left to enter the office. His head began to spin and he momentarily lost his balance. He grabbed the edge of the door and steadied himself. "Hello, Mike, I came over as soon as I got your message."

"Have a seat, Gavin. Are you feeling okay? You look flushed."

Gavin put his palm against his forehead and said, "I've got a bit of a temperature. I feel a bit vague but I'll be okay."

Mike McCarthy got straight to the point and told Gavin what he already knew, that Van Rensberg had been arrested earlier in the day. Gavin spluttered a few uncoordinated phrases, partly due to alcohol and partly in an unsuccessful attempt to appear surprised. Mike McCarthy's secretary popped her head around the door and announced that Roger Hamilton had just arrived.

"Send him straight in."

Gavin struggled to get out of his chair. "Shall I go, Mike?"

"No, I want you to stay. Come in Roger."

Roger walked into the office, followed by his shadow, Peter Fourie. Mike McCarthy introduced them and said, "Roger has been on a special project for the Chairman of Steinkop, in the Northern Cape. Apparently they have been having some trouble too. A couple of the board members called me two weeks ago and said that some of our diamonds seemed to have shown up at Steinkop. Roger tracked it down."

"Yes," Roger said, "that's right. We're pretty sure that much of Steinkop's increased yield over the last year came from diamonds mined at Allied. We don't know who the brains are behind the scheme but we've caught some of those involved. This fellow Van

Rensberg is being questioned as we speak and someone high up at Steinkop is under arrest for fraud."

Gavin recovered sufficiently to really appear surprised. "So you're saying that diamonds have been stolen from here and given to Steinkop. Why would Steinkop admit to that? It can't be in their interest even though it's probably illegal."

"Gavin you probably haven't heard that Allied bought out Steinkop last week," Roger interjected. "Lock, stock and barrel. The takeover negotiations have been going on in secret for six months."

This really surprised Gavin. Mike McCarthy told him they would all meet the next day after the security people had interviewed Van Rensberg. "Make sure you get some rest tonight, Gavin. You've gone white."

Gavin walked back along to his own office and slumped in his chair. He told his secretary to leave early for the day and then he called his wife, June.

"June, I'll be home late tonight. There's been a lot of trouble here."

"I've already heard about Van Rensberg. It's all over town. Is it about that? How does it concern you? They don't know about 'you know what' do they?"

"I'll explain tonight." He rang off.

Gavin finished the bottle of scotch while he wrote out the whole story. He started with how Hugh threatened to reveal their original arrangement with Van Rensberg if he didn't cooperate; then the plan to steal huge amounts of diamonds; Hugh murdering a tall, thin man in his house; the minute details involving Ivan's blackmail; and Van Rensberg's complicity in the theft. He finished the letter, put it in an envelope with a postage stamp, addressed it to June, and left the building.

The drive to the security checkpoint took only a few minutes. He passed through the checkpoint unchallenged and slowly walked to his jeep. He drove into town, posted the letter to June, bought a bottle of scotch from the liquor store, and drove out to the beach.

Gavin watched the waves crash onto the beach, each wave reminding him of a phase in his life. He thought about his children. What would they think of him if he were imprisoned? How would June manage without any income? Would he be able to cope with all the embarrassment?

Ten minutes later and with three-quarters of the scotch gone, Gavin pulled himself out of the jeep, staggered across the sand, and collapsed into the cold sea.

TWENTY-ONE

*H*ugh arrived at Heathrow airport in London in the middle of July on a scheduled British Airways flight from Kenya, using Jack's passport. He planned to contact John Marais, a doctor who had immigrated to Britain five years earlier, and impose on him for a few weeks before deciding where to settle permanently. Hugh had dealings with him on two shady financial projects in Johannesburg. Marais had done extremely well from the deals and often invited Hugh to stay with him in London, never expecting him to take up the offer.

Marais' wife, Judith, answered the telephone. Hugh sensed she did not want him to stay but he pushed the point and finally she gave up making excuses and acquiesced. Hugh said it would only be a few nights but once in the door he knew he could safely count on two or three weeks.

When he arrived at Marais' luxury townhouse, located just behind the Dorchester hotel, Judith answered the door and greeted him unenthusiastically.

"Just a few days is it? John's at the surgery. He won't be back before ten tonight."

Hugh ignored the cool reception. "No problem. What's for lunch by the way? I'm famished."

"I'll get the maid to prepare a salmon salad for you. If that's not too boringly plain."

"Sounds good to me. Hope you've got tartar sauce." Hugh threw his two suitcases into the hall. "I'll get settled in. Oh, how are your two beautiful daughters? They must be in their late twenties by now."

"Well, not quite. Wendy is nineteen and in university. Anne is twenty-two. She's has a high-fashion boutique in Carnaby Street."

"Do they both live here?"

"Wendy does, but Anne has her own place in Chelsea."

"How nice. Does my room have a private bathroom?"

"No," Judith replied, "but there's one across the hall from your room. We normally don't use it, so hopefully that will be private enough for you."

Later that evening when Hugh was relaxing in the living room with his feet on the leather-topped coffee table, John poked his head around the door.

"Hugh, I didn't expect you. How have you been?"

"Pretty good. I'm taking an extended vacation. I'll stay in London for a few weeks and then travel around Europe."

John changed his clothes and came back to the living room to speak with Hugh. Judith and Wendy joined them. When the conversation ran out of steam, Wendy turned the television on to listen to the evening news.

Five minutes into the broadcast, the newscaster made an announcement, which jolted everyone to attention.

Earlier today Scotland Yard announced that they were seeking to interview a South African citizen in connection with a serial murder case that has rocked South Africa over the past year. Interpol informed Scotland Yard that Jack Barlow is a major suspect in the case. He is believed to have entered the United Kingdom yesterday on a British Airway's flight

from Nairobi, Kenya. The police spokesman warned the public not to approach him, as he is considered dangerous.

Hugh gulped as he digested the announcement. He noticed Judith's mouth fly open as she grabbed Wendy's arm.

Jesus Christ, Hugh thought. *What the hell's going on?* He froze as a photograph of Jack flashed across the screen.

"Good god, that's your brother," John ejaculated.

Hugh stared at the screen. "Oh no, it can't be." He stopped himself from being too definitive. "But it does look like him." Hugh moved closer to the television while Jack's picture remained on the screen. "Must be a mistake. Mind you, I've never got along with him and I haven't seen him for ages. Who knows what he's been getting up to?"

"He must have arrived in London about the same time as you, Hugh," John said.

"What a coincidence. I'll call South Africa tomorrow and see what's going on. You don't mind if I use your phone do you, John?"

"Not at all. How intriguing."

Hugh realized what had happened, but even though he knew Jack was weird he could not bring himself to believe that he was a serial killer. He worried in case the South African authorities inadvertently found out about his wrongdoings while they investigated Jack.

All night he lay awake piecing together a plan that would cover his tracks and minimize his exposure. At 4:00 AM he went down into the living room and placed an operator assisted call to Chris Conway in Steinkop.

"Who's this?" Hugh heard Chris mutter while the international operator told him that Hugh Barlow was calling from London, England.

"Hugh, where did she say you're calling from?"

Hugh had not planned on revealing his location to Chris. "I'm in East London on business."

"I thought the operator said England."

"Unfortunately not, Chris," Hugh responded, "it's plain old East London in the Cape Province I'm afraid."

Hugh could hear Chris's voice tremble. "Hugh, I'm in big trouble. They've know what we've been up to. I've been fired and I've been charged with falsifying official documents. They can't prove the diamonds were stolen but they know I planted them. Where have you been?"

"How did they find out? Did they catch you doing it?"

"No, but they know I doctored the assay report and they know the diamonds didn't originate from Steinkop."

"Keep calm," Hugh said. "Deny everything, concede nothing, and threaten to sue them for slander. I'll get my attorney on it tomorrow. I'll also have a word in the government circles and tell the police to back off."

"Hugh, no one in the government seems to know anything about the plan to drain the mines in Namibia before independence."

"Who did you contact?"

"Several people—indirectly really."

"No one is going to own up to that. Keep quiet. Don't say a word. Leave it to me. Oh, by the way I'll have your money ready next week. You'll get fifty percent next week and the final fifty in a month. That's guaranteed."

"Hugh, I've lost my job, my home . . . and Cherrie is leaving me."

"Well, that's a blessing," Hugh replied.

"There's no need for that."

"I'm sorry, Chris. It was uncalled for. Look, you'll be sitting pretty for the rest of your life with the money I owe you. If they can only get you on falsifying documents then you'll get off with a fine."

"Well if you're sure."

"Absolutely sure. Where will you be next week, in Steinkop?"

"I doubt it. Best call me at my brother's home in Cape Town."

"Okay."

Hugh immediately booked two more calls, the first to Harold Budd for 6:00 AM London time, 8:00 AM in South Africa, and the second to Roger Hamilton for thirty minutes later.

Hugh told Harold that he'd traveled to England to conclude a confidential financial transaction, and he wanted to use someone else's passport to record the money transfer. Harold dithered a little. Hugh realized that Harold suspected something more, and true to form, he tried to make a profit from Hugh's problem. Hugh became frustrated with the conversation and although he left the issue of obtaining a false passport open, he realized that Harold would not help. *I'll fire off a couple of anonymous letters to the police in South Africa when I get time and drop Budd well and truly in the shit,* Hugh thought.

Hugh decided to cash in all his assets held at Zinnerberg and physically deposit them elsewhere, to completely hide any audit trail associated to Budd that the South African police might stumble upon.

His second call came through ten minutes later. "Roger, it's Hugh. Hugh Barlow."

"Is anything wrong? You seem nervous."

"I'm calling from London."

"What's going on?"

"I'm transporting a lot of cash and I need some personal protection."

"In London?"

"And Zurich."

"Do you need heavyweights?"

"Makes sense."

"I don't have any resources in London, but I have contacts in France."

"Okay, maybe that will come in handy."

"The man I have in mind is a Belgian, Gaston Begas. He lives in Dieppe on the French coast. We had a disagreement over money last year so he won't be pleased to hear from me. I'll go through a third party and get the message to him, so don't mention my name if you meet. Don't try to bargain with him about the fee, just accept what he asks for."

"What's the address?"

"Travel on the ferry from Newhaven in England, to Dieppe. Go to a café called De L'Jette and ask the owner for Gaston Begas. Be careful, Hugh, Begas is a thug with a long criminal record. He goes for the highest bidder—no loyalty whatsoever, so only use him as a last resort."

At breakfast Hugh told John Marais he had called South Africa to ask about Jack.

"I'm absolutely shocked. It is Jack the authorities are looking for. I can't believe it. He's had his problems but never anything like this. I'll go to Scotland Yard and explain who I am. Don't worry I won't give them your address here. I know how embarrassing these things can be."

Wendy's pupils dilated and she moved nearer to Hugh and touched his arm. "Do you think he's the murderer, Mr. Barlow?"

Judith pulled Wendy's hand away when Hugh began speaking.

"I hope not, but I doubt Interpol and Scotland Yard would waste resources on a vague hunch. In any case, best keep this to ourselves. You don't want hundreds of police and newspaper reporters all over the place."

"Absolutely not," John said, "so don't tell all your friends, Wendy."

In Johannesburg the team eavesdropping on Harold Budd picked up several references to the name "Barlow" and immediately contacted Virginia. She told them to bring the transcript to her office that night.

Just after 11:00 PM, Virginia finally listened to a copy of the tape and read the transcript. She took note of the London telephone number that Hugh had passed to Budd and transmitted a telex to the South African embassy in London asking for the name and address of the owner of the number.

Early the next morning the communications clerk gave her a sealed envelope, which she immediately tore open and read. "Mr. John Marais, 376 Auderly Street, Mayfair, London." *What's the bastard doing in London,* she thought.

She made dozens of calls to both her official and unofficial contacts until she had compiled a thorough profile of John Marais and his family. Van Starden hobbled into her office as she attempted to establish a relationship between Marais and Hugh.

He pressed his index finger against his lips and closed the office door. "Virginia, I need a word. We need to contact that Hugh Barlow fellow urgently."

"Funny you should say that." She showed him the transcript of the telephone call. "He's in London. Look at this. The operations team picked it up during their eavesdropping of Harold Budd."

Van Starden flicked through the transcript. "What a coincidence. Well, one of the cabinet ministers needs to speak with him rather urgently. I was told last night."

Virginia felt annoyed that Hugh could command such respect. "Why? What's going on?"

"Not sure. We're to find him and pass the message on—that's all. Apparently the minister in question has been trying to contact him for over two weeks. His house has been emptied and abandoned. No sign of his girlfriend either."

Virginia smiled and said, "I know where he is. I traced a telephone number he passed on to Budd."

"I'll make a few calls," Van Starden said, "and I'll find out how urgent it really is."

Van Starden returned ten minutes later. "Virginia, high priority —get him back to South Africa immediately."

"But we weren't going to take any further action on the illegal money transfers."

"It goes deeper than that. If he doesn't cooperate then we'll go a step further."

Virginia jumped at the opportunity to nail Hugh. "I'll go to London on the next plane."

"Okay, but the fewer that know about it the better. We won't even tell the embassy in London what you're doing – just say you're on a special assignment."

"What'll I tell him if he asks why he's wanted back?"

"Since I don't know myself we had better tell him it's urgent government business," Van Starden replied. "If he doesn't cooperate . . . contact me and I'll find out how far we need to go."

A mental image of Hugh being killed flashed into her mind. "I'd better get going," she said as she scooped up the documents on her desk.

Van Starden chuckled and said, "Good luck."

Virginia flew to London the next day. She followed the normal procedures when she arrived and contacted the embassy officials in Trafalgar Square, who provided a small apartment in South London for the duration of her visit. Nobody would ever associate such a small, dingy place with a clandestine hideaway. She quickly unpacked, showered in tepid water, and dressed in a casual business suit.

It was raining lightly so she put on a raincoat and a hat that covered her face enough to conceal her identity from Hugh, if she inadvertently ran into him. She caught the tube to Hyde Park Corner, walked to Park Lane, and then into Auderly Street. A few minutes observing the street numbers of the distinguished townhouses and newer apartment buildings soon led her to number 376.

A woman had just finished cleaning the outside windows of the townhouse when Virginia walked by. Apart from her, no one else was around. She noticed a small restaurant across the street that would provide a decent view of anyone entering or leaving the house. She went in, ordered a coffee, and sat at a table next the window.

An hour passed and still no sign of Hugh. She couldn't make any more excuses to stay, so she began walking up and down the street, pretending to window shop. The third time she passed the house, on the opposite side of the street, she noticed a man in the doorway. He looked around and up at the clouds before walking out into the street.

It was Hugh. He hurried into Park Lane and headed towards Hyde Park Corner. She followed him, keeping about fifty yards behind until he went into a betting shop at the end of Park Lane. Virginia waited a minute, went inside, and weaved her way discretely through the crowded, smoke-filled room and positioned herself behind one of the many display boards. Hugh stood at the far end of the room reading a newspaper.

Virginia wrote a note on the back of a betting slip and called a cleaning lady over. "Please give this to that man sitting over there. It's a tip for a horse, but don't tell him I gave it to you. Oh, and here's a pound for your trouble."

Virginia slipped out of the door and darted across the street, maneuvered her way in and out of the traffic, and sat on a bench next to an entrance to Hyde Park.

Hugh appeared at the doorway and signaled to the cleaning lady to come out. He pointed to several people walking in the street. She shook her head as Hugh pointed to each one. Virginia kept out of sight until Hugh waved down a taxi and sped off towards Hyde Park Corner.

Virginia returned to the South African embassy and asked for Johannes Kruger, an old friend and colleague. They chatted about old times for a couple of minutes before Virginia got down to business. "It's double hush-hush and I need a bit of assistance."

"Certainly. We were told to help but not to ask questions."

"I need someone to call this number tonight at eight and pass along a message. Here's the text of the message."

"Shouldn't be a problem."

"There's one other thing. Do you have a watcher available for tonight? I want to make sure this guy doesn't bolt after he gets the call."

"I'll sort something out," Kruger said.

Later that evening Kruger made the call to the Marais residence with Virginia listening in.

"Judith Marais speaking."

Kruger asked her to put Hugh Barlow on the line. A minute later a male voice in the background asked Judith to leave the room. Virginia gave Kruger the thumbs-up sign to indicate it was Hugh's voice. They heard the noise of a door slamming in the background.

"Who's this?" Hugh asked.

"Mr. Barlow, I think it would be in your interest to return to South Africa immediately."

"Who's calling? What do you want?"

"Just call me boss."

"What?"

"There's a certain government department that would very much like to interview you. If you return and give them all the information they need, you will probably be left alone. If you don't, however, I predict there will be serious consequences."

Hugh became irate. "How do I know this isn't a prank? Who are you? What's this all about?"

"You know full well what it's all about. You have two days to leave. I'll call the same time tomorrow to confirm that you are booked on a flight to Johannesburg." Kruger put the receiver down.

"He's rattled," Virginia said. "I could hear it in his voice. Is the watcher in place?"

"Yes. Van Starden called earlier and asked me put a few extra resources on. I told him we could do it unofficially for a day or so, but not much longer."

"Appreciate the help."

"By the way Virginia, is this fellow Barlow any relation to Jack Barlow?"

"I don't know. Why?"

"Apparently the police in South Africa have an arrest warrant out for Jack Barlow. They believe he entered Britain a few days ago. The message went around the embassy yesterday."

"What's he done?"

"Possible serial killer—the Johannesburg one."

"Strange," Virginia said, "that's about the same time Hugh Barlow entered Britain."

"Too much of a coincidence?" Kruger asked.

"Certainly is."

The telephone rang in Kruger's office. He answered it and exchanged a few words with the caller.

"Barlow's just left in a taxi, along with two suitcases. They're following the taxi as we speak."

Virginia excused herself and called Van Starden, who told her to personally confront Hugh. The last thing she wanted was for Hugh to find out that she was back with BOSS and actively involved in his pursuit. She returned to Kruger's office and relayed what Van Starden had said.

"We can cover you tonight," Kruger said, "but after that I'll need to get permission from higher up. That means Van Starden will have to make the whole thing official."

"That's the last thing he wants. Anyway, let's see where Barlow goes tonight and take it from there."

The next morning Virginia awoke to the news that Kruger's watcher had lost Hugh. He had changed taxis at Paddington Station and disappeared among the heavy traffic and hundreds of other black taxis. Fortunately Kruger's watcher had noted the license plate of the second taxi. Kruger ordered one of his operatives to locate the taxi driver and find out where he dropped Hugh.

Unbeknown to Hugh, Virginia watched him slip out of his hotel near Waterloo Station. Kruger's man had found the second taxi driver, and for a few pounds he suddenly remembered where he had dropped Hugh.

Since Hugh had no luggage with him, Virginia assumed he hadn't checked out of the hotel.

She followed him as he went into the train station and approached a station worker. After exchanging a few words he went to the first-class ticket window and waited in line. Virginia kept her distance and watched as he purchased the ticket. Hugh walked toward the exit and she followed closely behind. She slowed down to avoid getting too close, but Hugh stopped dead in his tracks, turned, and began to walk back to the ticket window.

Virginia bent over and pretended to adjust her shoe. Her dark red hair fell out from her hat.

"It's you," Virginia heard Hugh say. She ignored the comment for a second and kept fiddling with her shoe until she felt a hand on her shoulder. "I had an idea it was you all along. I suppose you're after your money."

"Something like that. You owe me quite a bit. And don't forget Lordy's share."

"But he's de . . . "

"That solves another puzzle you filthy bastard." Virginia reached into her pocket and clutched her handgun. She felt like killing him there and then but stopped herself. Too many questions to answer and it would put Van Starden and the secret service on the spot.

"Okay," Hugh said, becoming calm again. "What do you want?"

"Let's go somewhere private."

Hugh pointed to a waiting area. Virginia had no intention of revealing her true mission so she played along with Hugh's notion of her motives.

"I want 200,000 in cash and I want it in South Africa. I'm willing to go back to Johannesburg with you and get it."

"Why in South Africa?"

"I don't have any financial gurus like Budd to help me and no fancy overseas bank accounts. I want the money in my hands in the country that I live in."

"How did you know about Budd?"

"That's for you to find out," Virginia snapped, smartly covering her mistake.

Hugh offered her 50,000. Virginia dismissed it with a flick of her hand.

"No way. Pay up or you're a dead man. You know the organization I worked for in the past. Some things are never forgotten." She noticed a look of hatred on Hugh's face as she opened her coat and revealed a handgun.

"Okay, okay, give me a couple of days and I'll go back."

Virginia lost concentration for a moment as she thought of Lordy. "I . . . think we should book a flight now?"

"Let's get a taxi," Hugh suggested. As he stood up he grabbed Virginia's briefcase, pushed her back into her seat, threw the briefcase at her knees, and bolted towards the exit. She recovered her balance and jogged across the station towards Hugh as if she were late for a meeting. Hugh rushed past a police officer. Virginia saw the concerned look on the officer's face, but before he could react she ran past him, lifted her sleeve, and looked at her wristwatch.

"We're late for a flight." He smiled and waved her on.

Hugh made a beeline for the taxi rank. He pushed several people out of the way and jumped into the first available taxi. It could only limp along because of the heavy traffic and the number of traffic lights near the station.

Virginia spurted out of the station and followed the taxi. She kept up until it approached the foot of Waterloo Bridge, where it became impossible for her to maneuver in and out of the hundreds of cars flowing around the traffic circle. She flagged down a taxi and she told the driver to follow Hugh's taxi, saying that she had just missed him leaving the station.

The taxi driver obliged. Hugh's taxi drove around the streets for a while before finally stopping near Tower Hill.

Virginia's taxi was about 200 yards behind when she saw Hugh get out. She told the driver to stop. "Damn, it's not him," she said to the taxi driver. "I'll walk from here."

Virginia saw Hugh look back and catch a glimpse of her. He immediately took off in the opposite direction, so Virginia chased after him. Hugh darted into the crowd at the entrance to the Tower of London and zigzagged his way to a pier where several small riverboats were loading and unloading tourists. Virginia stood on some iron railings and watched his movements through the crowd. Hugh mingled with the tourists until one of the ticket office queues became empty. He bought a ticket and then nudged his way to the front of a line of people who were boarding the Thames Queen riverboat. Virginia rushed over to the ticket office and asked for a ticket.

"Sorry, love, it's full. The next one goes in about five minutes."

She bought a ticket and boarded the second boat. The Thames Queen passed under Tower Bridge just when her boat, called London Pride, pulled out into the river and turned downstream heading for Greenwich. Virginia asked a crewman if all the boats stopped at the same destination.

"Most of them stop at Greenwich, love, at least the ones that go in this direction do. Some of them don't stop there of course;

they just turn around and go back to Tower Hill."

"What about that one ahead of us," Virginia asked, "my friend is on it."

The crewman pulled a tatty schedule from his back pocket, squinted his eyes to read the small print, and replied, "That's the Thames Queen, love. It goes up to Greenwich and does a U-turn, and then goes to Westminster."

"So I won't be able to see him then?"

"No, love, sorry."

Virginia sat on a bench seat overlooking the bow and tried to ignore the stupid commentary being broadcast over the loud-speaker. She had to reach the pier at Westminster before the Thames Queen, otherwise she would lose Hugh altogether.

The Thames Queen approached the landing berth at Greenwich and slowed down to cross to the right side of the river. It made a wide turn and reversed its direction. Virginia focused on the Thames Queen and realized that the two boats would pass very close to each other. In an instant she pictured herself jumping from her boat onto the Thames Queen, just as she had done off the coast of South West Africa.

The London Pride also slowed in preparation to dock at the pier. The skipper clearly intended to let the Thames Queen pass by before steering to starboard into Greenwich. The London Pride's engine started to reverse to counteract the direction of the tide. When it slowed almost to a standstill she put her handgun in her briefcase, walked to the starboard side of the boat, and put one leg over the guardrail. The two boats were only six feet apart. She threw her briefcase across to the other boat and jumped. Her left hand grabbed a rope attached to a rubber tire slung over the side of the Thames Queen. The bottom half of her body went into the murky water but she managed to hold on.

The tourists on both boats let out a yell and then started clapping. *They must have thought I did that for their benefit,* Virginia thought. One of the crew on the Thames Queen grabbed her hand and hauled onto the deck.

"What you do that for, darling?" he asked. "You could have got your lovely self drowned."

"I do things like this from time to time. I'm a stuntwoman in the movies."

The skipper came over and asked what had happened. The crewman said, "She's one of those stuntmen in the films."

"It takes all sorts I suppose," the skipper said. You'd better dry off in my cabin. I hope you've got a ticket."

There were about thirty tourists on the upper deck, but no sign of Hugh. *He must be on the other side of the boat,* she thought. She squeezed the excess water out of her clothes and stood on the upper deck, but didn't see him there, so she went down into the lower deck and stood at the small bar. "There he is," she said under her breath, after scanning the dozens of tourists seated around the windows.

"What d'you say, darling?" the barman said.

"Coke please."

"Unusual stunt you pulled back there."

"Makes life interesting."

"Certainly does. My mates in my local pub would have loved to have seen that. Why don't you drop by tonight? I'll give you the address."

"Thanks, but I'm a bit busy tonight," Virginia replied. She took her drink and moved to a secluded corner of the deck where she could see Hugh.

After a few minutes Hugh left his seat and went into the toilet. She wondered if he had seen her. A little later he reappeared and went to the upper deck using the stairs at the stern of the boat. She crept up the stairwell next to the bar.

"There's smoke coming from the toilet," a tourist shouted.

The tourists left their seats en masse, and those in the lower deck rushed for the stairs.

"Everyone, please keep in your seats," the skipper shouted. The boat's tipping. Keep calm."

Virginia kept Hugh in sight and waited for his next move, while the terrified tourists scrambled to the upper deck. Two crewmen with fire extinguishers tried to get down to the lower deck but the frantic tourists streaming up the stairs prevented them.

The boat listed badly to the starboard side, and the skipper announced over the loudspeaker that he'd decided to dock at Cherry Garden pier.

"Put on life vests and be prepared to get off," he bellowed.

Virginia opened her briefcase, wrapped her handgun and some documents in a plastic bag, put the bag down the front of her pants, and threw the briefcase aside. Hugh had pushed himself to the side of the boat ready to abandon ship.

The boat listed even further to starboard as it turned sideways against the flow of the river. Virginia heard a loud creak followed by the sound of glass breaking. Deckchairs fell into the screaming mass of people as they slid down the sloping deck, desperately trying to remain upright.

The bow struck the pier at 90 degrees and stuck fast in the wooden pier. The boat rolled onto its side, pitching most of the tourists into the river. They were trapped between the boat and the pier as the current pushed the stern in an arc towards the pier.

Virginia held on to a metal rail on the roof and clambered onto the port side of the boat, which still remained above water. She looked into the mass of people bobbing up and down in the water and saw Hugh as he punched and kicked his way to a ladder attached to the pier. An elderly woman began to climb up the first few steps when Hugh grabbed her hair and pulled her aside. He climbed the ladder and made off along a wooden gangway leading from the pier to the riverbank.

Virginia lowered herself into the river and allowed the current to take her twenty yards downstream, where three barges were moored. She grabbed a rope, which was straddling the outermost barge, and pulled herself out of the water. She jumped across to the next barge and then onto the riverbank. Instinctively she scanned the riverbank for Hugh like a cat searching for a mouse.

There were two ways he could have gone. Either along a road leading directly away from the pier or along a walkway running parallel to the river. The screams of the drowning tourists distracted her thoughts. She had never been so torn between two competing courses of action—getting even with Hugh or trying to save innocent people from grisly deaths. The sound of a siren in the distance brought relief on one hand and tension on the other. She shuddered at the thought of having to explain to the British police why a South African agent jumped from one Thames pleasure boat to another in mid-stream. Then of course the inevitable questions about the fire would follow.

Since the police and ambulances would use the road to get to the pier, she decided to look along the walkway. She sprinted for twenty yards but then had to stop because the laces on her casual shoes had stretched and come loose. Several men ran past while she stopped to tighten them, but they all seemed too interested in the commotion at the pier to notice her.

When she looked up she saw a figure move behind a pub about fifty yards ahead. She took the plastic bag from inside her pants and ran towards the pub. Luckily the handgun had stayed dry. She approached the pub, replaced the plastic bag, and checked that her gun was ready to fire.

Virginia noticed a dilapidated warehouse on the other side of the pub, right on the edge of the riverbank. There were several closed loading bays on the warehouse wall facing the river and only a narrow ledge leading from one end of the wall to the other. Virginia found it difficult to estimate the distance between the pub and the warehouse but it seemed to be about thirty yards. She went to the front of the pub to cover the gap between the two buildings.

If Hugh tried to get away he almost certainly would not go back in the direction of the pier. The long, narrow ledge looked like a dangerous choice, so she reasoned that he would probably run between the two buildings. Several dockworkers ran past Virginia towards the pier. They completely ignored her, even though her clothes were still dripping wet and her gun was in full view.

From a professional's viewpoint she knew she should leave the scene immediately. *I'll get him back for Lordy,* she thought. *Fuck the job.*

The pub was closed so she crept past the entrance to the side of the building. A quick peek around the corner revealed no sign of Hugh. She looked behind and across to the warehouse—still nothing. The wail of police sirens intensified and even more people streamed past her, but she refused to become distracted. She wanted to kill Hugh so badly that she could taste it.

A loud metallic clang jolted her. She looked back, but before she could react she felt a thump on the top of her head. Instinctively she held the handgun tight with both hands when she lost her balance. Her legs buckled and she felt sick. She couldn't focus clearly, but she vaguely saw Hugh's face looking down at her and felt the gun being pulled from her grip.

Remember your training, remember your training, she thought. She gripped the gun tighter and took deep breaths. There were more voices in the background. "Leave her alone you wicked bastard. Leave her alone." Hugh's face went away and the force pulling the gun stopped. Her head cleared and she felt a pair of strong hands lifting her from under the armpits. A burly man stood in front of her.

"You okay, love? Who was that bastard? "D'you want me to go after him?"

"No, no . . . err, don't worry. I'll be okay."

"Is that a real gun, love?"

"It's for protection from him—ex-husband and all that. Don't tell the police. I'm not supposed to have it."

"Okay, love."

"He hit you with this dustbin lid."

"That's what he thinks of me," Virginia said, trying to laugh everything off.

After the man left she staggered over to the riverbank. As she spun round she saw Hugh walking along the narrow ledge alongside the warehouse. Instinct told her to follow but logic told her to wait. She steadied herself, carefully checked her gun, and aimed it at Hugh. The first bullet ricocheted off the warehouse wall, nowhere near Hugh, and the second smacked into a barge twenty feet to his right. Hugh reached the end of the ledge and disappeared.

Virginia took several deep breaths and hurried along the ledge, touching the wall with her left hand and holding the gun in her right.

Directly ahead she saw another warehouse but this time with no access to the riverbank. She turned left into a narrow street and saw a chain swinging in front of a doorway of an abandoned building. The door was closed and she saw nothing around that could have moved it. She pushed the door inwards slightly and slipped inside the building.

The only light came from gaps in the boarded windows, so she remained still and listened. A low, periodic thumping sound permeated the whole building and Virginia could not work out what caused it. She moved forward a few steps to avoid a strong smell of excrement, but it seemed to mix with the damp air and cloak the whole place. A scratching sound attracted her attention. *Probably just a rat,* she thought. She felt her way around until she stumbled on a stairway that led down to a lower floor. She trod lightly, feeling each uneven step with the toe of her shoe. The smell subsided when she reached the bottom of the stairs, but the floor started to tremble. The thumping sound increased in intensity and the noise of the river was much more noticeable. A ray of light shone from the direction of the river, enough for her to see another doorway at the end of the room.

She approached the door and heard several thumps coming from behind the doorway. Virginia kicked it open, ran inside, crouched low, and pointed the gun to the center of the room. The light in the room temporarily dazzled her. When she refocused she saw Hugh standing in front of her holding a wooden post over his head, ready to strike.

"So there you are," she shouted. "Did you see how many innocent people you've killed this time?" She gripped the gun tighter.

"That's their problem."

"What sort of monster are you?" Virginia spat out in disgust.

"I ran from the station because I panicked. I'll give you your cut."

Virginia felt her face tighten. The building trembled again, which momentarily distracted her, but she continued to confront Hugh. "And I trust you?"

"Kill me you'll get nothing. What's the point to it?"

"Revenge. Remember Lordy, Karl, Ron and Henny."

"Lordy went for me. I just protected myself. As for the other three well . . . you can't blame me for that—just pure bad luck."

"Get on your knees you heartless bastard. I'm going to enjoy this."

"What about the money for all those relatives? Kill me and they get nothing. You're acting on emotion. Trained agents don't do that. There's no benefit to it."

"On your knees and beg you bastard. Do it. Now!"

"Okay, get on with it then." Hugh looked down. "Wait, wait just a moment," he suddenly ejaculated as he lifted his head. "Tie me up and I'll give you my Swiss bank details so you can draw the money. There's no way I can cheat you then."

She quickly dismissed the idea, tightened her grip on the gun, and stepped forward. The building shook violently again followed by a loud creaking sound. She felt the floorboards move and almost instantaneously heard a booming sound to her left. The brick wall facing the river collapsed and the tip of a river barge punched inside the building like the snout of an attacking shark. Virginia's legs buckled as the floor collapsed and her gun fired harmlessly into the air. Her stomach heaved as she dropped ten feet and landed waist deep in water.

The lower level of the building had flooded and water splashed in and out of a hole in the brick wall that faced the river. Through the hole she saw the side of the barge bouncing up and down in the river and slamming against the damaged wall. *I'm trapped,* she thought.

The huge wooden beams from the upper level had collapsed, completely blocking any hope of escape. They creaked and slipped further, slowly pushing her through the hole in the wall and out onto a small ledge, where she faced the barge, battering the ledge with each swell of the river. She cursed Hugh at the top of her voice. "That bastard has nine lives. Why didn't I just fucking shoot him?"

She pushed against the beams, then against the ceiling, but it was futile. When the water level dropped with the outgoing tide, she knew the overhanging top edge of the barge would descend and almost certainly crush her.

TWENTY-TWO

Colonel Van Starden sat outside the Prime Minister's private office waiting to be called. He finished his third cup of coffee and adjusted his tie for the tenth time. The latest copies of his weekly intelligence reports were neatly filed in his briefcase, in case they were needed. The Prime Minister's personal secretary went in and out of the office several times, passing Van Starden without making a comment. Van Starden checked his notes time and time again to make sure he remembered every detail of every project undertaken in the past year.

The office door opened and a quiet voice said, "Mr. Van Starden, the Prime Minister will see you now."

The Prime Minister never got up nor did he extend his hand. "Have a seat, Colonel." He pressed a button on his intercom and waited until a side door opened and another man walked in.

"Do you know Roger Hamilton?" the Prime Minister asked Van Starden.

"We've met once, sir," Van Starden said, knowing quite well about Roger Hamilton's dealings.

"Let me get to the point, Colonel," the Prime Minister said. "Are you aware of the Turnhalle initiative and the real reason for its existence? You can talk openly."

"Yes, sir. It's to buy time, to delay the independence of South West Africa and set up a puppet government that we can control from the Republic."

"Very bluntly put Colonel . . . but on the whole accurate. The cabinet felt that delaying independence for South West Africa would be advantageous to us. If we could get a puppet government recognized, then all the better.

"We drafted the proposals and went ahead. It became apparent however, that our proposals would never be accepted by the United Nations in any shape or form. We're now of the opinion that South West will probably have to be given up."

"I commissioned Roger to develop a plan that would detail the best way to extract as much wealth from South West as possible. That included legitimate as well as unorthodox methods. If we are going to lose the territory then let's make sure we get all our investments back. We developed the plan in total secrecy. No one else in the cabinet knew about it, save one. The full report was finished over three years ago and filed away for future use.

"Now comes the problem. Only two copies of the report were made . . . and one went missing some time ago. Apart from Roger and I, no one else knew the file's full contents. Several people worked on the project but they were never given the complete picture or told the real reason for the project.

"It was done outside government circles so that no official records needed to be kept. If our enemies get the file our position on South West is doomed and it opens up many problems in South Africa itself. I'll leave you alone with Roger to go over the details. Keep this absolutely secret. Report to me each week with a verbal update."

When the Prime Minister left the room, Van Starden loosened his tie and wiped perspiration from his forehead.

"How did you get involved, Roger?"

"I've been loyal to the National Party and the Prime Minister. He trusts me."

"Even though you're not Afrikaans?"

"Yes."

"Was the file lost or stolen?"

"Definitely stolen."

"Who had access?"

"Before we get into that, Colonel, let me fill you in on the gruesome details. There were nine people involved in the work to produce the plan. I led the effort but a fellow called Victor Barlow had much to do with it. He's dead now. Two other men were on the team, as well as five women."

"Did you interrogate them?" Van Starden asked casually.

Roger paced around the room. "Not quite. They're all dead."

"What?"

"Listen, Colonel, what the Prime Minister said about no one else in the government knowing about the plan isn't exactly true. Several ministers, including the Prime Minister, made a lot of money before we terminated the plan."

"Terminated after the second copy went missing?"

"Correct. The Prime Minister couldn't risk losing half his cabinet and his personal reputation, let alone South West Africa. Everything was wound down, bank accounts closed, and key people moved around. Now we must get the file back and find out if any copies were made."

"Do you have any idea who stole it?"

"I'm pretty sure Victor Barlow stole it. He came to the government offices in Pretoria to update an appendix to the file . . . which he did every three months. The other sections of the file are sealed. He must have switched the real file with a blank one that he brought in his briefcase—an appalling security lapse. I think he bribed one of the guards but since he went missing we'll never know for sure. No one else accessed the file or even went near that part of the storage room after Victor's visit. So I'm pretty sure it was him."

Van Starden shook his head. "Why would he steal it?"

"I believe he planned to copy the file and return the original on his next quarterly visit. With the enormous amount of sensitive information in that file he could have bribed his way out of anything. And that's not counting the financial gains old Victor could have made. He died on the day of his last visit, in the evening. Well I say 'died', but he had a heart attack and died shortly afterwards—all very suspicious."

"How so?"

"The police think his son, Hugh, caused his death, but they couldn't prove anything. Apparently Hugh plied him with drink after an important speech. The doctors said he had an enormous amount of caffeine, sodium and alcohol in his bloodstream . . . unusual for someone with high blood pressure and a history of heart complaints.

"Hugh tried to get Victor's life support system turned off two days after the heart attack, while he was still in a coma. We checked the file after Victor's death and that's when the shit hit the fan."

"So you think Hugh got his hands on the file?" Van Starden asked.

"Almost certainly. Whether Victor was in league with Hugh, or Hugh just stole it, is really academic now. I know the family very well. They're all shady."

"How did all the individuals working on the project die?" Van Starden asked.

"Orders from above. Get rid of everyone involved and make sure none of them left any copies around. There was nothing in the original police report to link Hugh to Victor's death or to the file. However I recently heard some ugly rumors about Hugh, and the detective responsible for investigating Victor's death had a gut feeling that it wasn't just a heart attack. He couldn't put hunches in the report of course. Last week, after the detective and I inadvertently met and spoke about the case, it became pretty clear that events pointed in Hugh's direction. The only reason Hugh is still walking around today is because it took us so long to connect him."

"I see," Van Starden said. He couldn't decide whether to tell Roger about his own ongoing operation involving Hugh and Budd.

Roger continued the briefing. "My biggest problem was getting rid of all these people without getting caught and exposing the whole story. My people were fine about eliminating men but even they drew a line at killing young women with families. The PM told me not to use your boys at BOSS, so I had to devise another plan. I had known for years that Victor's half-brother Jack was a psychopath and I knew that Victor had left his estate to Hugh.

"I made a deal with Jack. I'd change Victor's will if he removed the women. He's part of a weird cult—women haters—that sort of thing. He jumped at the idea. My team broke into Victor's attorney's office and switched the will, and the PM's boys changed the copy filed in the official Registry Office in Pretoria. A word in the ear of Victor's attorney just after his death and everything fell into place.

"But you still haven't got the Turnhalle File back."

"No, and everyone concerned had his or her personal files, homes and safe deposits searched for any inkling of the file . . . nothing. As I said, about a week ago we put two and two together and latched on to our friend Hugh."

"That's why I was told bring him back to South Africa," Van Starden said. "You know that I have Hugh Barlow under investigation for other issues don't you?"

"No, but it doesn't surprise me," Roger said. "What's he done? I'm pretty sure he's in Europe at the moment. I had a call from him asking for help . . . before we linked Hugh with the file."

"Interesting," Van Starden said. Not wanting to divulge any details of his money-laundering probe, he changed the subject. "Why would Hugh call you?"

"Remember I've had dealings with the family for years. You know the business I'm in. He trusts me implicitly, as did his father. I gave him a contact in Dieppe, in France. I'll give you the details later."

"So before we remove Hugh Barlow we must get the file back."

"And make sure there are no copies around," Roger added.

"Why bring my department into all this now? The Prime Minister trusts you."

Roger looked away. "He never said why."

Van Starden thought for a while and said, "What were you planning to do with Jack Barlow? After he did all the dirty work for you."

"My team planned to take care of him," Roger replied. The trouble is he disappeared. I found out later that Jack included some of his perverted friends on the killings. That opened another avenue of exposure, so I had to take steps."

"How so?"

"You heard about that Monastery fire?"

"So that was Jack's sect."

"Exactly. I couldn't let the police start interrogating them just in case Jack had opened his mouth. My best man, Peter Fourie, dealt with them. He set the fire and locked the monks in the sewage tunnel—brilliant piece of work. I thought Jack might have gone up with them but no such luck. I still don't know where he is."

"They're both in Europe," Van Starden said. "You realize that don't you?"

"No."

"The British tracked Jack Barlow entering England at Heathrow airport."

"Seems too much of a coincidence that they're both in London at the same time . . . unless they're in on this together."

Van Starden shook hands with Roger and said, "Exactly."

"Let's work closely together from now on," Roger said, "and set up a joint team. I'll put my best people on it."

TWENTY-THREE

*V*irginia spent an hour trapped between the steel hull of the barge and the heavy wooden beams. The water level subsided almost a foot, and the top of the barge hammered down on the small ledge upon which she was perched. It rammed against the warehouse wall as each swell in the river passed by and missed her by inches. The noise deafened her. She gave up trying to push her way inside the warehouse because the beams were stuck fast. Her only chance of escape was to drop into the water as the barge rebounded from the wall and try to swim underneath it and out into midstream. She couldn't risk swimming alongside the wall to the bow or the stern because the barge struck the wall about every five seconds, which did not allow enough time for her to swim the thirty feet to safety. However she knew if she waited any longer the water level would fall further and the top of the barge would almost certainly crush her against the ledge.

She took several deep breaths and took the plunge into the filthy water. When she reached the riverbed she felt the side of the barge pushing her back against the riverbank. She couldn't see anything so she had to feel her way around. Only about two feet of water separated the bottom of the barge and the riverbed. *Damn. Not enough room to swim under,* she thought. She grasped the slimy riverbank and pulled herself along towards the bow. The sides of the barge sloped slightly inwards from top to bottom, which saved her from being crushed as she maneuvered along the bank. Her heart pounded as she approached the bow. She placed her hand over her mouth and pinched her nose to prevent her lungs from inhaling. It seemed like an eternity before her head finally broke the surface of the water.

She took several short gasps of air and trod water before thrashing towards a rope tied to the bank. She gripped the rope and coughed violently to expel water from her lungs. When she regained her breath she pulled herself onto the bank, laid on her side, and vomited uncontrollably.

The sound of a loud hailer interrupted her. "Are you okay? Do you need help?" Virginia turned her head and saw a police boat, obviously searching the river for survivors. She never answered. Seconds later she found herself on a stretcher on the small deck of the police boat.

"Better go to the hospital, love," the officer said. "You've swallowed a lot of water. They'll have to pump your stomach."

"What? Why?"

"This stuff's polluted—chemicals everywhere. If you dropped your shirt in there it would come out dry-cleaned."

She managed a chuckle and accepted the fact it would be a long time before she could resume the hunt for Hugh.

Several hours later she walked out of Guy's Hospital, feeling shaky and thoroughly depressed, but still determined to catch up with Hugh. She took a taxi to the South African Embassy and went straight to the cable room. Within five minutes a report was on its way to Van Starden in Pretoria.

Van Starden unexpectedly telephoned Virginia and told her he had read her report, and after his long conversation with Roger Hamilton earlier in the day, decided to brief her straight away.

"Who's this Hamilton guy?" she asked.

"Never mind that now. You were only supposed to relay a warning, not chase him clear across London."

She knew he was seething. "I know, sir, but things got a bit out of hand. He recognized me and he took it as a personal vendetta. Not a government thing."

Van Starden calmed down. "Okay, leave it for now, How are you feeling."

"Fine."

"Good. I know where Barlow is heading. I'll send you a coded cable later. There's a whole new dimension to this. I'll meet you in London tomorrow—don't mention anything to the embassy staff."

When Van Starden arrived at Virginia's apartment, she was surprised by his puffed eyes and disheveled clothing.

Van Starden yawned. "I'm too old for all this."

"You look fine, sir."

"Thanks for lying. Did you read the cable?"

"Yes, I need to go to France immediately. It'll take Barlow a while to get his bodyguards lined up and I don't want to miss him."

"Yes, quite. I think we can trust Roger Hamilton's judgment. Remember, get that file back before you eliminate him—and make sure no copies were made."

"That'll be difficult."

"The boys in the technical section can tell if the paper's been photocopied."

"What's the name of the file?"

"The Turnhalle File. Don't repeat the name to anyone else. It has 920 typed pages. When and if you get it back, don't read it. Most of the people who know about it are no longer with us. Just give it to me."

"Hmm ... must be pretty important," Virginia said.

"That's why the operation is unofficial."

"Is that 'Turnhalle' as in the South West African political party our government set up? The quisling government they call it here."

"The very same," Van Starden replied. "You don't want to know any more."

"What about backup?"

"Two men will join you in Paris—Terry White, who you probably know, and Peter Fourie from Hamilton's private outfit. He'll do all the dirty work . . . so nothing'll stick to us."

"Where will I contact you?"

"In the Hotel Bristol, in Paris. I'll keep away from our embassy."

Virginia flew to Paris and briefed the two special section operatives in a quiet part of the lounge at Orly airport. She immediately recognized Peter Fourie from the "Budd" operation, although she didn't know his name.

An hour later they left for Dieppe in a rented car.

PART FOUR

A Bird in the Hand

TWENTY-FOUR

*H*ugh arrived in Dieppe to seek out the contact that Roger Hamilton had given him. Fortunately he carried his passports and other important documents in a large flat belt around his stomach, concealed under his jacket, so he never had to return to his hotel in London before absconding. He used his own passport to enter France because he feared that Jack's name might be noticed by the French immigration officials. However the French were very lax and didn't notice that Hugh's passport had no exit stamp from South Africa and no entry stamp into Britain. Hugh's stomach turned over when he showed the officer his passport and realized just at that moment what a blunder he'd made.

Hugh walked the 200 yards to the Hotel De L'Jette, where he pushed his way into the small, crowded bar and worked his way over to the barman. He greeted Hugh in English and quickly served him a scotch. Hugh exchanged words with a few of the patrons and waited for an opportunity to ask the barmen about the contact Roger Hamilton had given him.

Hugh leaned over the bar and said, "I was told to ask for Gaston Begas."

The barman looked Hugh up and down and said, "Who's

asking?" He didn't wait for an answer; he just went about his business cleaning the counter top.

"Barlow. Tell him it's Barlow."

"Wait and I'll see if he's around." The barman went into a back room and reappeared two minutes later. "He'll be in soon. Have another drink and wait."

Several people came and went but no sign of Begas. The barman saw Hugh's impatience and made another call. "He'll be here in five minutes."

Hugh saw a hard-faced man with short, gray hair walk in to the bar. He was over six feet tall and solidly built. The Barman pointed to Hugh.

"You're Barlow?" Begas bellowed out, as he held out his hand.

Hugh noticed Begas' huge hands, out of proportion to his already large body. "I'm Hugh Barlow. Nice to meet you."

"Maybe," Begas replied. "I'm told you want protection."

"Yes I have some business in Zurich and ... "

"Who's after you?" Begas said, as he stretched out his long fingers and clenched his fists. Without waiting for an answer he caught a bottle of beer the barman threw over to him and flipped off the cap on the edge of the bar.

"Some South Africans," Hugh answered. "They think I owe them money." Hugh felt too embarrassed to say it was a woman on his trail.

Begas gulped the beer down. "Are they dangerous?" He turned towards the barman and barked out, "Franz, give me a liter of Stella."

"They can be," Hugh said. "They're armed."

Begas drank some more beer, belched, and turned towards Hugh. "What happens when you get to Zurich?"

"I'll clear out my safe deposit box at a bank and then disappear."

Begas clenched his fist again. "You want these people hurt? Killed maybe?"

"That would be useful," Hugh responded quickly.

"5,000 a person and 200-a-day expenses for me and two of my friends. American dollars."

Hugh nodded nervously and agreed the price.

Begas continued, "1,000 up front. Any funny business and you'll end up in a canal."

"Definitely no funny business."

"Stay at my place so I can think some more on it."

Hugh paid the barmen and they left. They walked past the ferry port and through the center of the town. Begas didn't speak. He acknowledged a few people with a wave of his hand as they walked to his home. Most of them looked nervous, waved back, and hurried away. They approached an apartment building wedged in by two shops. Begas opened the outer door and vaulted up the stairs to the third floor. Hugh followed as quickly as he could.

A shapely but cheaply dressed woman opened the door and greeted Begas. Hugh thought she looked like a bar tart of some sort. She spoke to Begas in Flemish for quite a while before turning to Hugh.

Hugh could smell alcohol on her breath, although she didn't appear drunk. As Hugh began to see her in the light, he noticed that beneath the coating of makeup she had beautiful facial features. She was only about five feet three inches tall, but well proportioned.

"My girlfriend—Connie," Begas said. He squeezed her behind and roughly kissed the back of her neck.

Hugh felt embarrassed when she kissed him on the cheek and pulled his hand close to her breasts. He looked at Begas to see if he noticed. He did, but his face remained deadpan.

"For fifty francs she's anyone's girlfriend." Begas laughed.

Begas went into the kitchen and Connie motioned for Hugh to sit on the sofa. She sat next to him and smiled. Begas returned with two cans of beer and a glass of wine.

"Barlow, I'll call Dirk and Henry, my two friends. They'll come with us to Zurich."

Connie chirped up, "Zurich is a good place. Can I come with you, Gaston?"

"No. Shut your mouth. This is business." Begas ran his hand through his hair and picked up the telephone. After a few short, sharp words he replaced the receiver. "They'll be here soon."

Connie tried to make conversation, but Hugh was too frightened of Begas to get familiar with her. Begas looked into his glass of beer and said nothing for over thirty minutes until the doorbell rang. Connie jumped up and opened the door, kissed and hugged the two rugged men, and pulled them into the lounge.

"Henry Demol is an Englishman and Dirk Boons is a fellow Belgian," Begas said. Hugh instantly felt more at ease because Connie turned her attention to Demol and Boons.

"You're from England, Henry?" Hugh asked.

"Yes, but my parents are Belgian. They moved to London when I was a boy."

"And he doesn't speak a word of French or Flemish," Begas added.

"Which part of Belgium are you from, Dirk?" Hugh asked. Hugh's head jolted back when he moved towards Boons to shake hands, caused by his repellent body odor. Boons ignored the friendly gesture and lit a cigarette with his yellow, nicotine-stained fingers.

"I don't know . . . some shit house I suspect," Boons finally answered indifferently.

Although Hugh had mixed with some rough types before he had never felt so far out of his element. An hour of strained conversation passed, along with several more drinks, before Begas turned to the Zurich trip. He looked straight at Hugh without blinking. Hugh turned away from Begas' icy blue eyes.

"Barlow, where are these people now?"

Hugh had by now consumed enough alcohol that his inhibitions were diminished. "I saw them in London last week and I'm worried in case they follow me to Zurich. One of them is a woman."

"A woman!" Begas said.

Boons and Demol sniggered.

"Don't underestimate her. She used to work for the South African secret service as a field agent. As good looking as she is dangerous."

"What does underestimate mean?" Connie asked.

Begas sipped his beer, waited a few seconds, and asked, "They don't know you're here then?"

"No, impossible."

"How will we get our weapons over the Swiss border?" Boons asked.

"Hide them in the van," Demol added.

"When are you going?" Connie asked.

"They won't check very much," Boons said. "They'll just look for contraband. They're only interested in making money from foreigners. I hate the Swiss."

"We'll leave on Saturday," Begas said. "Demol, get the van ready. Boons, get the weapons cleaned up." They both nodded.

Hugh noticed Connie's frustration at being ignored. She staggered into the kitchen and returned after a few minutes with another drink. Begas continued to ignore her and asked more questions about Hugh's motives.

Connie stood in front of Hugh and lifted up her short skirt. She thrust her body suggestively towards his face and uttered a few words that Hugh could not understand. He tried to ignore her but she stood directly in front of him.

She dropped her drink, turned around, and pulled down her fishnet pantyhose. Hugh felt his face flush with heat, brought on part by fear and part by Connie's curvaceous behind. She pushed her backside into his face and then flopped down onto his lap.

Begas remained unmoved, but Boons grabbed her between the legs, pulled her onto his lap, and fondled her breasts with his other hand. Hugh couldn't believe his eyes as Demol just laughed, Boons fondled Connie, and Begas sat unemotionally sipping beer. After a few minutes of horseplay, Boons picked Connie up and carried her into the bedroom.

"South African agent you said," Begas muttered. "Why are they after you?"

Hugh turned his head away from the bedroom door and looked at Begas. "She used to be an agent, but she is after me for something else. It's not related to the South African Government in any way."

"Did you stiff her?" Begas asked.

Demol laughed and looked over to the bedroom.

"She says I owe her money."

Boons returned from the bedroom and signaled for Demol to go in. Demol smiled, went into the bedroom, and shut the door.

"How much do you owe her?" Begas asked.

"Nothing, but she says 20,000 dollars."

Begas frowned. "Who's with her?"

"A small team." Hugh felt too embarrassed to admit that it was only Virginia following him.

Demol came back into the room and said to Hugh, "Your turn."

Hugh gulped and looked at Begas, who nodded his acquiescence. He didn't want to have sex but didn't want to appear unmanly in front of the others, so he went into the bedroom.

Connie was lying flat on the bed, completely naked with her legs wide apart. She giggled and beckoned Hugh towards her. Hugh stared at her from head to toe. He had never seen such a seductive looking woman. Without the crude clothes everything matched perfectly. He removed his pants and sat on the edge of the bed. She turned towards him and pulled him down. She played with him for a few minutes before Hugh turned her over and rolled on top of her. He hugged her tightly, pushed his face into her thick hair, and then rolled onto his back, pulling Connie with him.

Hugh got off the bed, dressed, and without speaking went back into the lounge. Begas, unmoved, just sipped beer and watched a soccer match on the television. Boons and Demol had stretched a map across the coffee table and were busy marking a route to Switzerland.

"What's the address in Zurich?" Boons asked.

"The Bahnhofstrasse," Hugh replied.

"It'll cost you 10,000 dollars, Barlow," Begas said, "and 400 each day in expenses."

Hugh felt more confident now. "Why the increase?"

"Take a look outside the window," Begas replied.

Hugh looked out and saw two figures in a shop doorway across the street. "Who are they?"

"No idea," Begas said, "but they're watching this place. One of them is a woman."

"If it's her, how the hell did she find me? I covered my tracks."

"If nobody followed you then you must have told somebody," Demol said.

"Roger," Hugh said. "That two-faced bastard."

Begas' head snapped around towards Hugh as he hammered the table with his huge fist. "Did you say Roger? Is that Roger Hamilton from Johannesburg?"

Hugh didn't try to cover his mistake. "Yes, Roger Hamilton. My father knew him. He deals a lot with . . . "

"Don't tell me what he deals in. He owes me money. I tried to get into South Africa to get him back, but the bastard got the immigration people to cancel my visa."

Hugh jumped in quickly when he saw the hatred on Begas' face. "Look I don't know what he's done to you, but I'll give you 50,000 to go through with the deal, and 10,000 each for Demol and Boots over there."

"It's Boons, and I want fifteen," Boons said.

"And me," Demol added.

"Okay, it's settled," Hugh said.

Begas got out of his chair and walked over to the window. "You sure you've got all that money?"

Hugh felt for his money belt to show Begas one of his bank statements but he couldn't find it. He panicked at first, and then remembered he'd left it on the bed next to Connie. He darted into the bedroom and scrambled around looking for it. It wasn't on the floor so he pulled the clothes away from Connie and rolled her over. The zipper on the belt had been opened but all the documents appeared to be in place. She had taken some hundred-dollar bills but the rest of his cash was still in the belt. Hugh scratched around until he found a bank statement that showed a balance in one of his smaller accounts with Zinnerberg.

He showed Begas the statement. "Look at this. It's a current statement from my bank in Zurich."

Begas snatched the statement and he, Boons, and Demol huddled together to read it.

"Half a fucking million," Demol said.

"So there's plenty to pay you—in cash or by check," Hugh said.

"We'll take cash," Begas said. "Dirk, go to the bar and tell Franz to find out who's watching us and where they're staying."

Begas finished another can of beer and sat motionless awaiting news from Dirk Boons. Hugh felt more comfortable now because he'd satisfied Begas that he had enough money and he hadn't revealed exactly how much he really had in his Zinnerberg accounts.

Connie stumbled out of the bedroom completely naked. She had slept for over two hours and now seemed to be sober. Hugh stared at her as she drank mineral water from a bottle. She spoke in Flemish to Begas and he replied in kind, but in a much softer tone this time.

"Go to bed? I'll be about an hour. If you're a good girl I might let you come to Zurich with us." She kissed him and toddled away to the bedroom, still naked and completely ignoring Hugh's presence. Hugh did not know what to make of it and refrained from making any comments.

Boons returned and gave Begas a quick rundown of what he had found out.

"Three of them, a good-looking redheaded woman and two men. One of the men looks like he can look after himself. He's a big fellow with dark hair—wears sunglasses. They're in the Hotel Deville. Jacques, the manager, tried to pick up the woman. He only tried to fondle her and she back-heeled him in the nuts! Watch out for her."

"Good work," Begas said. "We'll wait two days and see what they do. Then we'll either finish them off or just skip out of Dieppe quietly. Let's get some sleep. Barlow, you sleep on the sofa."

Hugh didn't argue. His mind turned over and over during the night as he lay clutching his money belt. *Why did Roger betray me? Why did Virginia bring two others along? Could anyone else have known my whereabouts? Should I try to cheat Begas or just pay him off? What if Begas takes all the money? Where should I go after Zurich?* He finally fell into a deep sleep.

Hugh woke to the smell of percolating coffee and bread warming in the oven. Connie caught his eye in the kitchen as she sang quietly while setting the breakfast table. Hugh thought about her shapely body from the previous night, completely naked standing in the bedroom doorway.

"Come and have coffee," she said quietly. The boys won't be up for a while. Gaston is a heavy sleeper."

Hugh got up from the sofa and reached over for his pants, trying not to reveal an erection. He caught a glimpse of Connie as she deliberately revealed her buttocks, bending to pick up a napkin. Hugh went into the kitchen and placed his hands on her thighs. She pushed back towards him, so he lifted her nightgown, kissed her neck, and moved his hands between her thighs. Neither of them spoke. Connie lifted her left leg and placed her foot on a chair. Hugh ran his fingers over her thigh with one hand and fondled her breast with the other. He kissed the back of her neck and her ears before penetrating her.

She panted so heavily that Hugh became worried in case Begas heard them. His apprehensions soon passed as he thrust his body into hers. In less than a minute they were both on the kitchen floor recovering from the orgasm. Hugh turned Connie over and pushed his knee between her legs. She climaxed again, almost immediately. They both lay on the cold kitchen floor until the sound of the coffeepot, boiling over onto the countertop, interrupted them.

"Quick, get dressed," Connie said. "Gaston doesn't mind me sleeping with his friends but he'll be mad if I get serious with anyone."

Hugh knew exactly what she meant. They dressed quickly and sat at the kitchen table, ready to eat breakfast. He noticed her green eyes for the first time and found it difficult to look away.

Begas came into the kitchen a little later and poured himself a coffee. "Any sign of Henry or Dirk?"

"No," Hugh replied. "No sign of them."

"Me neither," Connie said.

"Why did you let me drink all that beer last night?" Begas asked, looking at Connie. "I've overslept."

Connie did not answer.

The doorbell rang twice and Boons appeared. He had his own key and he let himself in. "Henry's servicing the van. Everything else is ready."

Begas began munching a breakfast roll and slurping coffee. "We need to decide what to do with our South African friends. You sure they're armed?"

Hugh cleared his throat and replied, "Most definitely."

"If they want money from you, Barlow, then I doubt they'll kill you before they get it. But maybe they'll try to get us."

"I don't know why Hamilton told them," Hugh added.

"He knows I'm after him," Begas said, "so maybe he wants to kill two birds with one rock."

"One stone," Hugh said.

"What do you mean?"

"Kill two birds with one stone, not a rock."

Begas banged the table, knocking a cup of coffee over. "What's the fucking difference? If you're dead you're fucking dead."

"True, true," Hugh said. He realized that Begas did not like contradiction or ambiguity.

When Hugh thought Begas had regained his temper he asked, "How did you get to know Hamilton?"

Begas' icy-blue eyes squinted, which exaggerated the creases in his brow, and he clenched his fists. "I lived in South Africa for years and worked for his outfit for a long time. I did dangerous jobs for him and he fucked me over. He knows that I swore to kill him, so maybe he wants to get me first."

"Let's just slip away unnoticed," Boons said, "get the money from Zurich and then deal with those rock-spiders."

"You've lived in South Africa too then, Boons?" Hugh asked.

Boons glared at Hugh. "What's it got to do with you?"

"Sorry, I only tried to make polite conversation."

"Well don't," Begas said, "just stick to the point and we'll all get along fine."

Begas answered the phone. He spoke for a while in Flemish and replaced the receiver. "That was Henry. Your friends spoke to him on the way here. They want to speak with you Barlow. They say you have some documents of theirs."

"Don't trust them," Hugh said. "It's a setup. I don't know anything about any documents."

"Okay, this is what we do," Begas said. "I'll arrange for them to speak with you on the telephone tonight. Make up a story—any story will do. Tell them you'll hand over the documents on Saturday around midday. We'll leave for Zurich late Friday night."

"But they're watching us." Hugh said.

"Leave that to me. There's more than one way out of these apartments."

Demol returned an hour later. "They want to speak to you privately, Barlow. Why?"

Hugh threw his hands up. "No idea."

Demol had a disbelieving look on his face when he said, "It's government business they said. They don't want anyone else to know about it."

Hugh became defensive and rolled off a dozen reasons why he shouldn't meet them.

"Tonight we'll tell one of them to come to the building entrance," Begas said. "Dirk, you search the bastard and if he's clean, lock the door with the padlock. Then we'll send Barlow down to talk."

Just before 6:00 that evening, Begas and Hugh looked out of the apartment window, watching for the first glimpse of an emissary. Hugh noticed Virginia in the street and told Begas, who ordered Hugh and Boons to the lobby. Hugh walked down the three flights of stairs with Boons directly behind him. He watched as Boons opened the door and went outside. Hugh could see the silhouette of Boons and Virginia through the frosted glass window of the door. Virginia lifted her arms and turned around while Boons searched her thoroughly. The door opened and Virginia came inside.

Hugh saw the hate in Virginia's eyes. "Never give up do you," Hugh said as he shook his head. "What's all this about a document? It's just an excuse to get me, isn't it?"

Virginia smiled. "You know what I mean—Turnhalle."

Hugh felt shock when Virginia said the word "Turnhalle". "How did you know about... you're working for them again aren't you?"

"Let's just say that we'll be tailing you until that document is found. I knew you weren't up to planning all that business with the mines. You took it straight out of the file, didn't you? The ideas, locations, people to bribe, everything."

"That's your interpretation. There's a huge chasm between planning something and actually carrying it out."

"And how does your darling little brother Jack fit into all this?"

"I know you're looking for revenge, but I've got what you want —the file and the money from the operation. So what guarantees can you give me?"

"Carrot and stick, Hugh," Virginia replied. "Hand over the file or we'll kill you. That's a merry message from the South African Government. Do that and give me my cut of the money, and I'll get off your back."

"And I trust you?" Hugh replied sarcastically.

Virginia added cockily, "Do you have a choice?"

Hugh pointed at the ceiling, chuckled, and said, "What about my friends upstairs?"

"I've got all the information on those degenerates. They'll stab you in the back at the first opportunity."

Hugh shook his head. "I don't think so."

"Make up your mind, I haven't got all day."

Hugh thought for a while and said, "Okay, you come back here tomorrow at noon and I'll give you the file. As for the money—I'll write out a statement implicating you in the diamond caper. You sign it in the presence of a notary, put your thumbprint on it, and I'll store it away. Then I'll hand over the money, but if anything happens to me the letter will find its way into the hands of the South African Government. In return, you report me killed to your friends in BOSS . . . and of course, stop trailing me."

"I'll think on it," Virginia said.

"Let's talk tomorrow after I show you the file. When you see my shadow through the door you'll know it's me." Hugh called up the stairs to Begas. "All clear."

Hugh heard Begas shout down to Boons, who opened the front door and let Virginia out.

"I'd like to get my hands on that red-headed cherry," Boons said lustfully.

"You sure you're not a fucking attorney, Barlow?" Begas asked. "I've never heard so much complicated shit."

Hugh felt smug again. "She'll come back and we'll be long gone."

"Do you have a file?"

Hugh denied all knowledge of a file and repeated his belief that they were after him for revenge.

"You're not such a good liar that you can fool me," Begas said, cutting into Hugh's long explanation. "Let's get ready to fuck off tonight."

When they went back to the apartment, Connie was busy packing suitcases. Begas looked at the clothes stuffed inside them and said, "You can't take all those clothes, woman. We'll only be gone for a week."

"It's just a few things I need, Gaston. And I've packed a change of clothes for you."

Begas shook his head and pulled the roadmap from the coffee table. "Henry, do you know the route?"

"No problem. Franz will bring the van at three in the morning."

"Why so late?"

"That's when the bar closes—it won't look suspicious. He'll be at the back entrance of the apartment building, one street over. We'll go over the roof to the next building and down the emergency escape stairs."

"Good," Begas said. "Let's have some beer and get to sleep early. Don't put any lights on, and sleep in your clothes."

Hugh had trouble sleeping again, especially on the lumpy sofa. He fell asleep after midnight, but Connie woke him at 1:00 AM.

"Hugh, did you hear that noise?"

"No," Hugh said, "I was asleep. What sort of noise?"

"A bump and then a scratching noise. I couldn't stir Gaston."

Hugh checked the kitchen and the bathroom but found nothing. "It might have been a cat or maybe the wind blew something over." Hugh looked at her shapely body in the partial light and couldn't resist pulling her towards him. He kissed her mouth and breasts and hugged her tightly. She pushed him off.

"Be careful, Gaston might hear us."

At 2:30 AM, Hugh woke to the sound of Connie attempting to stir Begas. Boons and Demol soon shook themselves awake, after sleeping on the floor next to Begas' bed. Hugh fumbled around and made sure all his belongings were intact before leaving the apartment.

They left in single file and crossed the hall on the third floor, heading for the emergency exit that led out to the roof. The buildings in the street were all linked, which made it easy for them to walk across the roof from building to building.

At exactly 3:00 AM the van entered the back street and stopped directly below them. One by one they dropped down the last section of the escape ladder and got in. Franz drove to the outside of the town, stopped, and bade them bon voyage.

The next day Virginia approached the apartment building at the designated time, while Peter waited across the street in a Citroen, keeping watch as planned. The street wasn't too busy, just a few locals walking to the city center to shop. She crossed to the opposite side of the street from the apartment building and waited.

Ten minutes passed and still no sign of Hugh so she went over to the Citroen and asked Peter if he'd seen anything.

"Nothing. The young couple on the second floor have gone out, and the first floor looks empty. Barlow's gang must still be inside."

"I'll wait ten minutes and then go over." As she said that, an image appeared through the frosted glass window.

"Must be Barlow," Peter said as he lifted his walkie-talkie radio. "BOSS one, come in."

They both heard Terry reply, "BOSS one ready."

"Go ahead BOSS one, go ahead in ten seconds."

Peter and Virginia rushed out of the car and over to the building. Peter lifted a sledgehammer over his shoulder, ready to break the door down. Just as they reached the door, a huge explosion roared out above them. One swing with the sledgehammer and the door lock gave way.

"Grab him," Virginia said.

The door opened and Virginia rushed inside. There, on her knees, was a cleaning lady looking terrified.

"It's not him!" Virginia shouted, unusually ruffled. "It's just an old lady."

"Quick let's go. We must have killed the lot of them."

They sprinted back across the street towards the Citroen. "Get on the radio and tell Terry to meet us at the checkpoint," Virginia shouted, "I'll drive." As Virginia started the car she looked up at Begas' apartment. Plumes of smoke billowed out of the window and flames leapt from holes in the outside wall.

Terry White drove directly to the small village of Pourville after the explosion, where he met Virginia and Peter.

"We really bungled this one," Virginia said after explaining to Terry what had happened.

"How else could three of us grab Barlow from that bunch?" Peter said. "We had to take chances. We're not the KGB with fifty operatives on every street corner to watch one suspect."

"Let's lay low for a while and then find out if Barlow survived. With his luck he probably walked away unharmed."

"I'll disguise myself a little, go back into the town, and find out what happened," Terry said.

"Okay," Virginia said. "We'll stay at that hostel down the road and wait for you."

Later that evening Virginia was in the lounge of the hostel when Terry walked in. "No one killed. They cleared out in the night. The police think Begas did it to collect insurance, but he can't be found. I overheard the locals talking in the bar. They know about us—all pissing themselves laughing. Where's Peter?"

"Hold on, I'll find him," Virginia said. He was using the owner's telephone and when he noticed Virginia, he quickly finished the call.

"Who was that?" Virginia asked.

"Just a personal matter back home."

Virginia was surprised. "Let's go to the lounge. Terry's back."

Terry explained how Begas and the others escaped and then asked what they should do next.

"My guess is that they're heading for Zurich, so let's go. I need to stop in Paris and brief Van Starden."

The next day they arrived in Paris and Virginia went to the Bristol Hotel and told Van Starden what had happened in Dieppe and asked what to do next.

"What about the file?"

"When he escaped in London he didn't have it, but maybe he stashed it there."

"Maybe it's in that bank in Zurich?"

"Probably."

"Go there straight away."

"Can we get more support? This Begas guy knows his stuff and Barlow seems to have nine lives."

"Doubt it. The more people involved the more chance that all this becomes public—just what the Prime Minister wants to avoid."

"It goes that far up the chain?"

"Yes, but I shouldn't have said that."

TWENTY-FIVE

$\mathcal{L}$ate in the evening, after Cap Muller had just finished a review of the latest information on the hunt for Jack Barlow, George Nortier popped his head in Cap's office. Cap threw his eyes up and told George to make it quick. George stood back and to Cap's surprise Karen walked in the room.

"Good god—a female Lazarus!" Cap jumped up and hugged Karen. "Are you sure you're okay?"

"I'm fine," Karen replied. "Once I got over the initial shock I couldn't wait to get back."

"Good," Cap said. "George, what's new in the Barlow case then?"

"A detective in the Hillbrow station called me. Apparently an attorney called Richard Brown spoke to him yesterday."

Cap took his reading glasses off. "So?"

"His cousin, Gavin Brown, committed suicide two weeks ago in South West."

"What's that got to do with the Barlow case?" Cap snapped.

"Some time ago this fellow Gavin Brown left a sealed letter with his cousin-come-attorney, Richard Brown, only to be opened if he died in unusual circumstances. It names Hugh Barlow in a conspiracy to rob the Allied Diamond Corporation of some of their stuff. Barlow apparently blackmailed at least three of them into the caper."

"Is this Jack Barlow's brother, not just more confusion with names?" Karen asked.

"It's Hugh Barlow all right."

"Did we ever find out what happened to him?"

"No," George replied. "If you remember, he emigrated to Australia. That's according to some of his friends."

Cap fired off a few questions without waiting for Karen or George to answer any of them. "Does he know where Jack is and was he involved in the murders? If this letter is bona fide, is there a criminal case for him to answer? Is there a connection between the murders and the diamond theft? What about jurisdiction, South West Africa or here in the republic?"

"No problem on the latter," Karen chipped in. "Prosecute him here or in South West. Pretoria still controls all of that."

"Okay, let's meet this attorney fellow."

"Already arranged for tomorrow at ten. He wants to bring Gavin Brown's widow along as well."

"Why?"

"Don't know. He seemed insistent."

"Okay, I'll interview the attorney—you and Karen take the widow. Karen, contact the Australian consulate and find out when Barlow entered Australia, and then check his departure date from South Africa."

The next day Richard Brown and June arrived at police headquarters. Cap interviewed Richard privately.

"I wanted to discuss June's legal position before giving you the letter that Mr. Brown lodged with me. He also left a suicide note which has value as evidence . . . "

Cap frowned. "What's she done then? It's off the record."

"Some low level thefts at the Allied mine. Gavin instigated it and used her in the plan. It had nothing to do with the large-scale theft mind you—from June's point of view that is. Gavin's note explains that Barlow found out about it and used it to blackmail him. One thing led to another and she's both bankrupted and in a precarious legal position."

"Why even mention the suicide note? It incriminates her."

"Two of Gavin's accomplices are in prison awaiting trial. They know the whole story and might implicate June."

"So she wants immunity from prosecution in exchange for the letter," Cap said.

He left the office, went along to the interview room, and asked Karen to step out. They quickly exchanged notes and agreed that the two stories seemed to tally.

"Mind you, a note describing a murder of an anonymous person, written by someone who later committed suicide," Karen said. "Not exactly a firm basis for a murder investigation."

"True, but finding Hugh Barlow might be more useful to our investigation of Jack Barlow than you think."

"Why?"

"Didn't you read the immigration department's report last night, and the unofficial feedback from the Australians?"

"No, it went directly to you."

"There's no record of Hugh Barlow leaving South Africa recently. The Australians say he's never entered their country, at least legally. The other thing I find odd is that when we looked at Jack Barlow's immigration record it showed that he left the country for a business trip to Zurich the day before the last murder. Here, look at the date of the murder and his immigration records."

"Maybe the monks did that one on their own?"

"Possibly, but check the forensic report. Parts of her body were found in Jack's cellar."

"They could have used his cellar while he was away."

"Again a possibility, but remember Matagwe's report filed after he interviewed the servants at Jack's house? Jack always personally supervised the cleaners, but they cleaned the house on a day Jack was still supposed to be in Zurich. Matagwe looked into it, and apparently it coincided with one of the servant's son's circumcision celebration. He asked Jack Barlow if he could leave early, but

Jack refused to let him go. Matagwe checked with the nurse in the township who performed the circumcision. She had it clearly marked in her records."

"So who used Jack's passport to leave the country, and why?" Karen asked, holding her hands in the air.

"Okay, back to our visitors first," Cap said after a pause. "June Brown and her attorney don't know anything about it. This Gavin Brown guy was just a sucker by the sound of it."

"I'll check with the police in South West and see what they know," Karen said.

"There's no point making June Brown's life any worse. I'll check with the prosecutor's office and try to get her immunity from prosecution."

After June and Richard Brown left, Karen joined Cap and George in Cap's office.

"Cap, I've just had a thought," Karen said. "If someone did use Jack's passport I imagine that the person would need to look very similar to him."

"Unless he changed the photograph, but you'd need a pretty good forger to do that on those new passports."

"Our immigration people check things like that carefully, as do the Swiss."

"So it's someone who looks a lot like Jack Barlow or someone who can disguise himself very well."

"Does Hugh resemble Jack?" George asked. "I can't remember what he looks like."

Cap looked at a photograph of Jack. "Exactly my thoughts. He looks like Hugh for sure, but what about his height and weight?"

"They look very similar," Karen said as she leaned over Cap's desk to look at Jack's photograph. "Does it matter about height and weight?"

"Check it anyway," Cap said.

"I'll ask their uncle, Ralph," George said, "or Hugh's girlfriend, Susan ... "

Karen finished the sentence. "Smith-Peterson."

"Karen, find out today and let me know. If Hugh Barlow has used

Jack's passport he's either a fool or he's completely oblivious to what Jack's been up to.

Karen drove to Hugh's house but as expected it was empty. Next she tried Ralph Barlow's house, where the servants told her that Ralph and his wife were away on vacation. She checked her files and saw that Susan had left an alternative address – her sister's apartment in Hillbrow. She drove to Hillbrow and located the apartment block.

She tried the doorbell several times but no one answered. As she walked away a nosey neighbor from across the hall poked her head out and asked what she wanted.

"I'm Detective Karen Van Der Berg and I need to contact Miss Smith-Peterson rather urgently."

"She left a while ago," the elderly woman said. "All very suspicious if you ask me."

"Why?" Karen asked. "What happened?"

"You'd better come in and have a cup of tea and I'll explain. Do you take milk, Miss Van Der Berg?"

"Yes please, and one sugar. So when did Miss Smith-Peterson leave?"

"June 15th. I know because my son Robert visited me the day after. He has a very important job with a mining company in Rhodesia."

"Why was it suspicious when Miss Smith-Peterson left?"

"I'm just coming to that. Her sister Susan visited her in a terrible state. She couldn't stop crying and she looked as if she'd seen a ghost. It took hours for her to calm down. She's such a nice girl too. Anyway they rushed out of the apartments with four or five suitcases and didn't even close the door behind them. I went over to make sure things were safe, not to be nosey you understand."

"Of course not."

"What a mess—clothes all over the place and paper everywhere. And do you know what I found?"

"No, but please tell me."

She hurried off to the kitchen and poured two more cups of tea. "I found a note scribbled on her notepad. Two or three of them actually. I think it must have been Susan's handwriting because it read like a farewell note to a man called Hugh. There were several spelling mistakes. I suppose because of her hysterical state."

"What did the notes say?"

"I've got them in my drawer here. I didn't want anyone getting hold of them you understand."

"Any idea where Julie and Susan might have gone?"

"Oh certainly. They went to Cape Town to see a friend, Jenny Adams."

"How do you know they've gone there?"

"I overheard Julie talking on the telephone before they left. She asked for the operator to put her through at Jenny's work place. These walls are paper-thin you know. You can hear everything."

When Karen finally escaped from the nosey neighbor she returned to her office, where she briefed Cap and obtained Jenny Adam's address from the Cape Town police. Within two hours she was on a plane for Cape Town.

A detective from the Cape Town police met her when she landed and drove her to Jenny Adams' house in Muizenburg. In the living room were two attractive women sitting on the sofa holding hands.

"Which of you is Susan Smith-Peterson?"

"Me," Susan said. "This is my sister Julie."

Karen did not beat about the bush. She opened her briefcase and threw Susan's hand written notes on the coffee table.

"Miss Smith-Peterson, did you write these notes?"

Susan picked them up and burst into to tears. Julie tried to console her but it took several minutes before she regained her composure.

"Yes I wrote them. When Hugh explained everything in the beginning it all seemed so innocent. More of a lark really. I didn't realize he was so evil."

"We are more interested in the whereabouts of Jack Barlow at the moment. Another team will contact you regarding the diamond theft. Start from the beginning."

Susan rattled off the saga from the time she met Hugh to the day she fled to Cape Town. Karen sat mesmerized as the tale unfolded. When Susan began repeating herself, Karen interrupted and asked specific questions.

"Did Hugh Barlow kill Jack?"

"He planned to kill him in Swaziland but I don't know if he did. I think he murdered someone else in the house because I found blood on the walls of his study. The walls had been washed down, but he missed a few spots. I asked Johnny, the servant, if he knew what happened, but he was too frightened to say anything."

"Do you know where Hugh is, and does he look like Jack?"

"He spoke of moving to Europe. The Australian thing was just a ruse. I think he's in Europe somewhere but I don't know exactly where."

"And the other question?"

"Oh, yes. They're only half-brothers but they look very much alike, facially, height and weight. Hugh's hair is longer and he has a deeper suntan. Why do you ask?"

"We think Hugh Barlow might have used Jack's passport."

"He did steal documents from Jack's house. I forgot to tell you that. He said they were related to his father's will."

"Oh, really. Any idea which part of Europe he might go to?"

"He traveled to Zurich a few times. He had one of those confidential bank accounts over there. I saw some of the documentation once, by mistake."

"Do you remember the name of the bank?"

"It started with a 'Z' I think. Zipperbank or Zillerbank—something like that."

The next day she returned to Johannesburg and briefed Cap on the interview. Cap read the interview notes and agreed with Karen —that Hugh almost certainly used Jack's passport and he didn't know that Jack was a serial murderer.

"Karen, I've received information from the police in South West regarding the diamond robbery. They've handed it over to the people in BOSS, so I couldn't get any details. I've no idea why they did that. Pressure from above I assume."

"Barlow's involved though?"

"Most certainly. The thing is we have two cases of murder now. Hugh Barlow is probably in Europe and he may well have murdered his half-brother Jack. If that's the case we may never be able to prove definitively that Jack is the serial killer. If not, he's roaming around somewhere, probably still in the country. Let's see if Interpol can trace them."

"I'll get that going."

"Put out an arrest warrant for Hugh Barlow to make it official. I'll update David Foster . . . he's holding another one of those review boards soon, but this news should shut him up for a few weeks. I'll get him to approve the Interpol request at the same time."

TWENTY-SIX

It took Hugh and company nine hours to reach the Swiss border. Demol drove and Begas sat expressionlessly in the front passenger seat for the whole journey. Hugh slept soundly in the back of the van for the first two hours, and when he woke he joined Connie and Boons in the boring silence. Boons chain-smoked, and his unrelenting body odor made the journey unbearable for Hugh and Connie, but neither of them dared to say anything. Begas and Demol seemed oblivious to the pungent atmosphere.

As they approached the customs and immigration checkpoint at Basel, Begas uttered his first sentence of the journey. "Connie, flash your tits at the border guards if they start asking questions."

The guard waved them over to the side of the road and asked for their passports. He handed them five forms to complete. Demol collected the passports and handed them to the guard, who carefully checked them and asked who resided in South Africa.

"That's me," Hugh replied. The guard handed him a separate form and asked him to complete it.

"What's the purpose of your journey?"

"Tourism," Demol replied.

"Everyone get out of the van," the guard ordered.

Another guard came over and after exchanging a few words they began to search through the luggage. Hugh watched and smiled as Connie jumped forward and bent down in front of the second guard, pretending to pick something up. She deliberately fell against the guard as she rose and made sure he received an eyeful of her bosom, which distracted him from his task. With one eye on Connie he moved a couple of bags around and signaled to the other guard to let them through. The first guard collected Hugh's form and handed back the passports.

"That was close," Demol said as they drove away. "The guns are stuffed under the back seat."

"Let's get going," Begas snapped. "I want to get to Zurich before dark."

"Where are we going to stay?" Hugh asked.

"My uncle lives just north of the city in an old farmhouse. If he's still alive we'll stay there. It's very quiet. No one will notice us."

"Does he know we're coming?" Connie asked.

"He doesn't have a phone and he can't read. So what's the point? He knows I'll kick his fucking head in if he complains."

They arrived at the farmhouse late in the afternoon. Begas walked up to the front of the house and hammered on the solid wooden door. "Willy, you old bastard, open the door. It's your nephew, Gaston."

The head of an emaciated old man appeared at a window to the right of the door and then quickly disappeared. The door creaked open a few seconds later and Begas waved at the others to come over. Hugh walked in first and stood in the doorway while Begas and his uncle exchanged words in Flemish.

Hugh shivered and buttoned his coat as he looked around the dark room. Several pieces of ancient furniture were positioned around the room and two mangy-looking cats were perched on a heavily stained sofa. The floor was littered with engine parts and other useless metal and wooden articles. He cringed when he noticed several game birds hanging from the ceiling in the far corner of the room. He couldn't decide which was worse, Boons's body odor or the smell of rotting bird flesh. Boons and Demol seemed to accept the squalor, but Connie looked disgusted.

"Not what you're used to is it, Hugh," she said. "I'll clean it up later."

Begas finished speaking with Willy and turned to Hugh. "We'd better go and get the money out."

"It'll be closed by now," Hugh said. "It's Saturday. We'll have to go first thing on Monday morning."

"Lazy Swiss bastards," Boons added. "I hate the Swiss." He flicked his gas cigarette lighter open and tried to burn one of the cats. As the cat bolted Demol let loose with a kick that hurled the cat across the room. They both laughed.

"The quicker we get out of here the better," Demol said.

"What's that bad smell?" Connie asked. "It's making me feel sick."

"Those birds over there I would imagine," Hugh replied.

"Wait 'till the old bastard's asleep and I'll throw them out," Demol said, laughing. "He doesn't speak English does he?"

"No, only Flemish and a little German," Begas replied. "In any case he never remembers things from one day to the next."

Willy wandered off into an adjoining room apparently unperturbed by the invasion of unfamiliar faces in his home, while Connie charged around collecting rubbish from the floor. An hour later just a stale smell replaced the sickening stench that initially greeted them.

"We're going out for beer," Begas said to Connie. "You stay here. Barlow, are you coming?"

"No, I'll wait here."

"Bring some food back," Connie said. "We can't eat the stuff Willy has."

"Okay, make a list," Demol said. "Let's go into Zurich. I doubt there are any bars around here."

"I'm glad they've gone, Connie," Hugh said as he stretched out his arms and legs on the newly cleaned sofa. He yawned and patted the sofa, indicating for Connie to sit down. She sat on the edge of the sofa and looked at Hugh.

"What's it like in South Africa?" she asked.

"Very nice . . . if you're white. Even better if you're rich. But I'm not going back there. The blacks will take over in five or ten years and everything will be spoiled."

Connie asked coyly, "You'll have plenty of money when we've finished here won't you?"

Hugh brushed his hand over the edge of the sofa and nodded.

Connie slid a little closer to Hugh and looked into his eyes. "Where will you go?"

Hugh leaned back on the sofa, moved Connie's long, dark hair aside and rubbed her shoulder. "Monaco, or somewhere just as nice."

"You'll need someone to cook and clean for you, won't you?"

Hugh realized where this was going but he didn't mind. He'd actually built up a strong attraction to Connie. He replied flippantly, "Yes, I suppose so."

Connie pouted a little and shifted along the sofa, away from Hugh. "Will you go there with your wife then?"

"Not married," Hugh replied quickly.

"I bet you have girlfriends everywhere."

"No, my last girlfriend and I broke up a few months ago."

"Oh, good, I mean . . . "

Hugh suppressed laughter and said, "And now I only have one girlfriend left."

Connie angrily slapped Hugh on the thigh. "Who's that then?"

Hugh grabbed her shoulders and pulled her close. "You are, silly."

Connie burst out laughing and hit Hugh on the thigh again. "Don't tease me like that."

They kissed and hugged for a while until Hugh stopped and asked, "Why do you stay with Begas? He treats you like scum."

"It's all I've ever known. He knew my father, and when he died Gaston took me in. I was only seventeen. It was okay at first, but you can see what it's like now. He thinks sharing me with his friends is normal. I don't have any money and nowhere else to go. I got a scholarship to go to university, but Gaston said not to waste my time. He wanted me to work around the house. I started drinking to cover up my embarrassment. I would never act the way I did in the apartment otherwise."

"You're a beautiful woman when you're out of those cheap clothes. I noticed it the night we ... well you know."

She chuckled and moved her body closer to Hugh. "I wish I could get away. I want to get married and have children. Gaston hates children. He won't let me have any."

Neither of them spoke for a few seconds, but when they did they each uttered the other's first name simultaneously.

"Go on," Hugh said.

"No, you go first."

"What do you think of me?" Hugh asked in a serious tone.

Connie hesitated, ran her hands through her hair and said, "I don't like to say really. What do you think of me?"

Hugh held out his hand and pulled her head towards his chest. He held her tightly and kissed her. "I think I've fallen ... "

A noise from the other side of the room startled them. Hugh turned and saw Willy, who was looking at them in a curious way and mumbling. Connie replied to him and Willy staggered over to a window, looked out briefly, and then sat on a wooden chair that faced the center of the room.

"He thinks I'm his daughter," Connie said.

"Is he drunk?" Hugh asked.

"No, I think he's err ... what's the right word in English? When people get very old they get ... dismented is it?"

"Dementia you mean."

"Yes, but what were you about to say to me?" she said. Her eyes were sparkling as she waited for Hugh to reply. Before he could speak, Willy began shouting and sobbing intermittently.

"I'll put him to bed."

Hugh began to think about what he would say to her. He knew that his snobbish friends would never accept her. But who would know? He could never go back to South Africa, so he had no option but to start a new life with a new name. His mind turned over. He had never felt attracted to anyone in this way before. Why was she different? Was she after his money or was it just to get away from Begas? She had a dubious background but she seemed sincere.

Connie came back into the room just as a vehicle pulled up outside. Boons almost fell out of the rear door of the van, and Demol and Begas were singing at the tops of their voices. Connie joined Hugh at the window to see what all the commotion was about.

"They're drunk," she said.

"Paralytic," Hugh added.

She squeezed Hugh's arm and said, "I'm glad, at least they won't touch me tonight."

Hugh looked back at her and nodded. "Go into the other room and pretend you're asleep."

"Yes," Connie replied, "but there's something I need to tell you later."

Hugh opened the door and for the first time he saw Begas laughing. He went over to the van, turned the lights off, and closed the doors. Boons couldn't get up, so Hugh pulled him forward by the arms until he sat upright, grabbed him under his armpits, and pulled him into the house, dumping him unceremoniously on the sofa. The smell on Hugh's hands made him feel sick after touching Boons's armpits, so he went to the bathroom and rinsed them.

When Hugh returned to the living room he saw Begas and Demol attempting to dance together. They fell down laughing several times before finally noticing Hugh.

"Barlow, you stuck up asshole, get the booze out of the van before we die of thirst," Begas screamed.

"Make it quick you fucking idiot," Demol added.

Hugh went to the van and searched until he found a case of beer and several bottles of spirits. By the time he brought the stuff into the house, Begas and Demol had given up trying to dance and were just sprawled across the floor, laughing and cursing. He went back to the van and brought in four boxes of food and stored the packages in the kitchen. By this time both Begas and Demol were asleep. Hugh waited ten minutes and crept into the small bedroom to speak with Connie.

"Are they out?" she asked.

"Totally unconscious," Hugh said. "God knows how much they've had. They won't be in any condition to go into Zurich on Monday if they keep drinking like this."

"Gaston doesn't suffer from hangovers. He'll be up and ready if there's money on the table."

Hugh pulled her closer and asked, "What did you want to tell me?"

"I overheard Gaston talking to the others about taking all the money from you, but they weren't sure whether to go through with it."

This didn't surprise Hugh, but for the first time he felt he'd lost control of events. Roger Hamilton had warned him about Begas, but Hugh had not taken it seriously and he had no contingency plans.

"They're worried in case you go to the police before they get away."

"Keep your ears open and let me know what they decide. We'll think of a way of getting away from them if they try anything."

"Just me and you then?" Connie asked. "Does that mean . . . we?"

"That's exactly what I mean. If you want to that is?"

Connie kissed him and began pulling him on to the bed, but he stopped her. "Let's play it safe. I'll go into the other room in case one of them wakes up." Hugh noticed a sad look come over her face, made worse by the dim light, so he leaned forward and kissed her on the lips. "I love you," he said, and slowly tiptoed back into the main room.

They repeated the same procedure on Sunday. Hugh remained with Connie in the farmhouse while the others went off on another drinking binge.

On Monday morning Hugh woke to the smell of bacon wafting across the room. Connie stood next to the stove and Begas sat holding his stomach and resting his head on the rickety dining table. Boons and Demol were still unconscious; Boons on the floor and Demol perched precariously on the edge of the sofa.

"Have a good night?" Hugh asked Begas in a sarcastic tone.

"Not bad. But these Swiss are miserable bastards. Got thrown out of two bars before we found somewhere decent. Connie, where's my coffee?"

Two hours passed before Demol and Boons were capable of communication. Connie prepared breakfast for them but what they did manage to consume soon came back up.

Hugh egged Connie on to tell Begas that Boons reeked, and she finally whispered to Begas that Boons's body odor made her feel sick.

"Dirk. Have a fucking shower before we leave. Connie says you stink."

"But the water's cold."

"Tough," Begas replied. "We'll leave at nine. Henry, you drive. When we get there I'll go in with Barlow. Dirk, you wait outside in the street. We'll come out of the bank when Dirk gives us the signal that the van is waiting."

"It'll take a while for the bank to get the money ready," Hugh said.

"We'll wait," Begas replied.

The van stopped outside Zinnerberg in the Bahnhofstrasse at 10:00 AM. Hugh and Begas marched through the small entrance into the reception area, where Hugh introduced himself to the guard and asked for an urgent appointment with Herr Kraus. A thin sickly-looking man in a gray suit soon appeared.

"Mr. Barlow, nice to see you again. How have you been?"

"Very well. You are?"

"Obermeier, Hans Obermeier. I don't suppose you recognize me. I had an unfortunate accident some time ago and I've not fully recovered."

Hugh hardly recognized him because he looked much thinner and even more fragile.

"Oh yes, I remember, sorry. It's been such a long time."

"Herr Kraus is not expected back for hours I'm afraid. Can I help you?"

"I want to close my accounts and withdraw the proceeds," Hugh stated.

Obermeier crouched forward with difficulty, adopting his usual deferential pose. "Oh, is there a problem, Mr. Barlow?"

"No, but I'm closing an urgent cash deal."

"Cash," Obermeier gasped. "If I recall you have a high value account with us. In any case, come into my office."

Obermeier interposed himself between Hugh and Begas in a non-verbal attempt to dissuade Begas from entering his office. Hugh just chuckled when Begas ignored the hint.

Begas stood with his arms folded, while a nervous Obermeier fumbled through his files. Hugh saw Obermeier grimace when he noticed Begas' huge hands protrude from the cuffs of his ill-fitting suit.

Obermeier swallowed, adjusted his tie, and said, "Most of your money is in stocks and bonds Mr. Barlow. It will take five days to liquidate everything and I will need Herr Kraus's approval for such a large amount. Will you be transferring the proceeds to another bank?"

"No. I need it in cash."

Begas smiled briefly and nodded, but his face soon changed when Obermeier said, "There's a five percent sales charge for large amounts of cash like this."

"I understand," Hugh replied. "If I sign over the stocks and bonds to the bank now, can you advance the money? I need it urgently."

"We can give you eighty percent up front and the balance after the securities are liquidated. Just sign this form. You can collect the cash tomorrow, first thing."

Before Begas could say anything Hugh put his index finger against his lips indicating to Begas to remain silent. Hugh realized that Begas was totally out of his depth in this type of environment, behaving somewhat like a schoolchild in front of a headmaster. Hugh could see Begas was seething mad because he didn't get his cut straight away, but he managed to calm him down after explaining the rudiments of banking and why banks such as Zinnerberg rarely keep such large amounts of cash on hand. They returned to the farmhouse and waited for Tuesday to crawl around.

Virginia and her team reached Zurich on Monday afternoon. To monitor the entrance to Zinnerberg during banking hours, without being too conspicuous, she had to find a suitably concealed place on the other side of the Bahnhofstrasse. A five-star hotel, the Cosmopolitan Hotel, seemed the only viable solution. After checking in she changed her room a couple of times, giving unusual but plausible excuses, until she found one that provided the best overall view of Zinnerberg. It was on the fifth floor and about thirty yards to the right of Zinnerberg's entrance, on the opposite side of the street.

Virginia waited there, along with Terry White and Peter Fourie, for Tuesday morning and the start of the hunt for Hugh Barlow in Zurich.

In Johannesburg on Saturday, two days before Virginia and her team arrived in Zurich, Cap Muller received an unusual visitor. Cap had almost dozed off in his back garden when the visitor appeared through the gate.

"I hope you're not enjoying that snooze too much?"

Cap turned and gave him a dirty look. He put his glasses on and realized David Foster, his boss, had let himself in. "Oh, it's you, sir! Hello. Is it business or pleasure?"

"Business I'm afraid, Cap. It's about that Interpol request."

"The one for Barlow you mean?"

"It's been turned down."

"Damn!" Cap threw his newspaper down and got up. "What's going on? Why did they turn down a straightforward request? Why in heaven's ... "

"It wasn't Interpol, it was the boys in our secret section."

"What's it got to do with them? This is a straight criminal investigation. There's nothing political in it whatsoever."

"Apparently they screen all requests going overseas and they've taken exception to this one."

Cap regained his composure, sipped his beer, and said, "Any reasons given?"

"None at all. Donkersloot went mad when I told him. He tried to contact the Prime Minister and demand to know why the Justice Minister is being overridden by BOSS."

"He took it as a personal slant then?"

"Seems that way. Might be a power struggle or maybe they really consider this case political. Donkersloot is legalistic to the core. Any funny business and he will bring it directly into the open."

"A real Boer that one," Cap said.

"That's right, but don't underestimate him. He can be as slippery as an eel if he thinks the law is on his side. And it's common knowledge he's after the Prime Minister's job. Between you and me, Cap, old Donkersloot has told me there's a lot of underhand stuff going on behind the scenes."

"How do you mean?"

"Ministers lining their own pockets. Cashing in on the political situation. Everything from arms purchases to aid to the Bantustans. Even in South West apparently."

"Why hasn't he been kicked out of the cabinet then?"

"Too many connections in the National Party and the Broederbond. They can't get rid of him so they exclude him as much as possible."

"I see," Cap said after a long pause. "Back to the subject. What are we going to do with this Barlow fellow? We can't just let it slip."

"I don't want to and neither does Donkersloot. He implied that if you send additional requests on existing Interpol cases, then it doesn't have to go through our approval process again."

"You mean use the 'Jack Barlow' request in some way?"

"Exactly. Tell Interpol that Jack Barlow could be traveling under a false name."

Cap laughed. "Under Hugh Barlow's name you mean."

"I'll leave the interpretation to you, Cap. I'll see to you tomorrow."

Cap immediately called the station and told the duty officer to send an urgent cable directly to Interpol, adding "Hugh" as an alias used by Jack Barlow, plus any South African citizens with "Barlow" as a family name. He sent the cable to the Paris headquarters of

Interpol and asked them to approach the Swiss police as a matter of urgency.

Cap did not have to wait long. On Sunday he received a reply from Interpol. "Male, age forty-two by name of Barlow, Hugh Albert, entered Switzerland at Basel, Passport South African, number 39788351, date of entry at border ..."

Cap called his boss, David Foster, and gave him the news. Foster called back later and told Cap that Donkersloot, the Minister of Justice, wanted to send a couple of detectives over to Switzerland and find out if this person was Hugh Barlow or Jack Barlow. He gave Cap the official contacts with the Swiss police and also promised to make a couple of discreet calls and get some unofficial help. Foster told Cap that Donkersloot's parting words were, "If there's monkey business going on in our cabinet I want to know about it."

Within an hour of the call, Cap and Karen were booked on a flight to Zurich, via London, leaving same day.

When they arrived on Monday morning, they were met by a Swiss police officer, Anton Dietz, who drove them to their hotel. Anton explained his role with the Swiss police force and the procedures they would need to follow.

After Cap and Karen checked in, Anton went through his thoughts on how to locate Barlow. He had already alerted the border posts, so if Barlow tried to leave Switzerland he could be detained. Anton had requested a guest list from all the major hotels, but he would not be able to trace Hugh if he stayed in one of the many small pensions around Zurich.

"We think he'll be in the Zurich area," Cap said, "because his ex-girlfriend told us that he visited Zurich a couple of times recently and apparently he has an account with one of your smaller private banks."

Anton quickly fired back. "Which one?"

"Zinnerberg," Karen piped up.

"Oh yes, I know it," Anton said, looking disgusted.

"Not one of your national treasures then?" Cap asked.

"Not quite," Anton said. "The owner, Herr Kraus, stays about one centimeter on the right side of our banking laws. Kraus is a complete degenerate, no scruples and no manners. The only thing he cares for, apart from money, is his daughter."

"You seem to know a lot about him?" Karen said.

"We've been after him for years after he ripped off one of the police pension schemes some time ago. Nothing could be proved of course but we knew Kraus had his fingers in the pie."

"Can we interview Kraus to see if Barlow has contacted him?" Karen asked.

"We can," Anton said, "but since he's a foreign national, Kraus is not at liberty to tell us anything about Barlow's banking arrangements. If he visits the bank in person, however, then that is another story—he is obliged to answer honestly. Whether he would is another matter."

"Worth trying?" Cap asked.

"Okay, we can go now if you're both up to it."

Anton drove them to the Bahnhofstrasse, stopping on the way to pick up a uniformed officer. He said jokingly, "Makes it more official. Most Swiss defer very easily to people in uniform. At least the staff in the bank will."

Cap and Karen watched and listened as the uniformed officer spoke to the security guard. After a few seconds Obermeier introduced himself, exchanged a few words with Anton and then disappeared into the bank. Moments later he reappeared.

"Herr Kraus is very busy. He can only see you briefly."

They all followed Obermeier into Kraus's office, and one by one introduced themselves. Kraus's huge frame bounced out of his reinforced armchair and back again when the introductions ended. Cap was amazed that anyone of Kraus's size could even move, let alone so quickly.

Kraus rubbed his stomach with his hands, sat back in his chair, and with a broad grin covering his huge red face said, "What can I help you with today, Herr Deitz? A small donation to a police charity maybe?"

"Nothing so painful for you," Anton replied. "We've received a request from Interpol, via our South African friends, to locate the whereabouts of a man called Jack Barlow. He could be traveling using the first name 'Hugh', but we aren't sure."

Kraus released a muffled belch, took a bite from an apple, and said, "I don't see how I can help?"

Cap could see a look of disgust on Anton's face.

Anton composed himself and said, "We believe he visited your bank, possibly in the last few days. You don't mind if I ask your staff do you? I have a photograph here."

Kraus replaced his smile with a look of sincerity. He lifted his eyebrows and hummed as he viewed the photograph. With his mouth full of apple he asked, "What's this man wanted for, Herr Dietz, if I am permitted to ask?"

"Murder," Cap interjected, "possibly a serial murderer."

"Oh dear. Let me see. No, I don't remember seeing anyone who resembles the person in this photograph. Do you Obermeier?"

As Anton took the photograph from Kraus and passed it to Obermeier, Cap noticed Kraus nod slightly at Obermeier.

Obermeier bent forward and took the photograph from Anton. "Yes, I definitely remember this gentleman. I believe he came into the bank this morning."

Cap moved back as Anton moved threateningly towards Obermeier. "Did he leave an address in Zurich?"

Obermeier cowered. "Not that I'm aware of."

"Do you expect him back?" Cap asked.

Obermeier rubbed his forefinger slowly along the side of his nose and briefly averted his eyes. "Not that I'm aware of."

Kraus's grin reappeared. "We'll contact you if this man comes to the bank again." Kraus threw the apple core into a garbage can, but it bounced out and struck Anton on the leg. "Excuse me, Herr Dietz. Obermeier, pick up that apple core and wipe Herr Dietz's shoe."

Cap heard his back click as he crouched down to retrieve it, but Anton moved away before the groveling Obermeier could reach his shoe.

Kraus finished the meeting by lifting the telephone and looking at his watch. "Is there anything else we can help you with?"

When they left the bank, Cap turned towards Anton and said, "That Obermeier fellow is lying bastard."

"You don't say," Anton said. "I'll try to drum up some support to monitor the bank for you."

Karen offered to help with the surveillance but Anton reminded her that only a Swiss officer could make an arrest, Cap and Karen could only observe.

Anton saw Cap's disappointment and offered a little more help. "I'll provide a car for you and make sure you can park in the Bahnhofstrasse without getting a ticket. If you sight him, you must call me straight away and I'll have him arrested."

"Thanks for your help."

"Incidentally," Anton said, "have you prepared the extradition papers? They are very complicated."

"We have an attorney lined up," Cap replied.

"Don't leave it too late," Anton said, as he left the room. "The police can only hold him for a limited time."

"Trouble is, Cap," Karen whispered, "Who do we extradite? Hugh or Jack Barlow!"

"It has to be 'Jack' alias 'Hugh'. We don't have any authority to go after Hugh Barlow."

On Tuesday morning Cap and Karen waited in an unmarked police car on the other side of the street from Zinnerberg, about fifty yards from its entrance, scanning for Hugh Barlow.

TWENTY-SEVEN

$\mathcal{O}$n Tuesday morning Virginia peered out of her hotel window looking for signs of Hugh entering or leaving Zinnerberg. A couple of false alarms earlier made her even more careful. Terry and Peter were in separate cars, cruising the nearby streets, waiting for Virginia to contact them by walkie-talkie radio should Hugh appear.

A few minutes before 11:00 AM, the hand-over time for Virginia and Terry to switch roles, she noticed a Fiat van pull up outside Zinnerberg. Two men got out, waved the van on and went into the bank.

It's him, she thought, and immediately radioed Peter and Terry and told Terry to follow the van.

Karen immediately spotted Hugh at the Bank's entrance and shook Cap out of a sleep.

Cap jumped forward. "Where? I can't see him."

Karen pointed towards Hugh. "The one in the suit, next to that old van."

Cap adjusted his eyeglasses. "Are you sure? I didn't get a good look."

"Almost 100 percent sure."

"Let's wait until he comes out. If it's him we'll call Anton."

Hugh and Begas marched into Zinnerberg. Hugh asked for Herr Kraus while Begas stood behind him with his arms folded. A few minutes passed and Obermeier greeted them.

"Where's Herr Kraus?" Hugh asked.

"He's very busy at the moment. Do you want to wait, Mr. Barlow, or shall I handle the transaction?"

"No, let's just move along, shall we?"

"The money is ready for you," Obermeier said. "I'll have it brought to my office and you can verify the amount and sign a receipt."

A security guard brought a large, solid black case into the room and placed it on the desk in front of Obermeier. He passed a document to Hugh and started to open the case, but Hugh stopped him. Hugh quickly checked the document. It was a statement of all his accounts with Zinnerberg with a section at the bottom for him to sign to formally close the accounts. He signed and gave it back to Obermeier.

Obermeier looked shocked. "You're not going to count it, Mr. Barlow?"

"No, I trust you. I'd like to access my safe deposit box before I leave."

"Of course, follow me."

Hugh picked up the case and said to Begas, "Wait here, I'll only be a few minutes." He saw Begas' face tighten, but he did nothing.

Hugh went through the security procedures and quickly found himself in the vault, sitting in a private booth with the contents of his safe deposit box and the suitcase full of cash. After Connie had told him of Begas' possible treachery he decided to take only a million dollars with him and put the rest back in the safe deposit box. He reasoned that even if he had to wait a couple of years to retrieve the rest of the cash, it beat losing everything.

He opened the government file that he'd left on his last visit. The first page was in Afrikaans with each word printed in bold typeface on a separate line—"WAARSKUWING GEHEIM DOKU-MENT—DER TURNHALLE DOKUMENT." The second page was in English—"WARNING SECRET DOCUMENT. THE TURNHALLE FILE".

He flicked through the file, briefly pausing to look at the section headers until he came to the one he knew well—the section dealing with the diamond mines in South West Africa.

"The trouble this has caused," he soliloquized. "Maybe I should have picked another scheme." He thought about what had happened. *Hastening the death of Father; killing Jack; Susan betraying me; leaving my mansion behind; my position of importance gone for good; the episode in the desert with SWAPO terrorists; nearly being assassinated by Virginia; Begas taking control; Connie; and now what?*

He returned to the present and opened the suitcase. He counted 1,000,000 United States dollars, all in hundred-dollar bills, and set them aside. The rest of the money, almost 8,000,000 dollars, he packed into the safe deposit box and locked it. He put the 1,000,000 dollars into the black suitcase, tucked the Turnhalle file under his arm, and asked the security guard to replace his deposit box.

Begas was waiting in exactly the same spot in exactly the same pose when Hugh and Obermeier returned to the lobby.

"I think we're finished now," he said to Begas. He put the file down and flicked the case open to show Begas the wads of dollar bills. "Let's get going." Hugh saw Begas' face turn red with excitement when he saw the cash. Begas swallowed, wiped his brow, and followed Hugh.

Begas and Hugh brushed past Obermeier as they hurried to the exit.

"Mr. Barlow, wait. Herr Kraus insists you take his limousine. You shouldn't carry so much cash around with you."

"Well I suppose we could," Hugh said looking at Begas.

"You can take him as well," Obermeier said, clearly terrified at offending Begas. "It's parked at the back of the bank, inside the building, so no one will see you leave."

Obermeier gave Hugh his private phone number and implied that if any services were needed outside normal banking practices he would be more than willing to assist. Hugh thanked him and said he would most likely take him up on his offer.

Obermeier led them into the enclosed parking garage where Kraus's Mercedes stretch limousine was parked. Begas told Hugh that he'd never seen anything like it, let alone been inside such a vehicle. The driver opened the trunk and helped Hugh place the black case inside. He slammed the trunk closed and opened the door for Hugh. Begas checked that the trunk was locked before he got into the backseat of the limousine with Hugh. Obermeier, with an expression on his face that looked part grin and part grimace, waved as the limousine pulled away.

"Wait," Begas shouted to the driver. He looked at Hugh and said, "We need to tell Demol to follow us." Begas jumped out and waited for the van to circle round. He told Demol to meet them at an intersection on the outskirts of Zurich and then ordered the limousine driver to get going. "We don't want the driver to know where we're staying," he whispered to Hugh. Hugh just nodded.

Begas helped himself to a large whisky from the cocktail cabinet in the limousine and told the driver where to stop. They approached the intersection and as the limousine slowed down, Hugh could see the van parked on the hard shoulder of the road. The driver opened Hugh's door and walked to the rear of the vehicle. He opened the trunk and handed the black case to Hugh.

"This seems heavier than before," Hugh quipped.

"Let's get going," Begas said. "I'll carry the case." He grabbed the case from Hugh. "You fuck off," he said to the limousine driver, as he charged towards the van.

Virginia answered the phone in her hotel room.

"It's me, Terry. I'm calling from a pay phone. The radio is out of range. Barlow and another guy have just got out of a large Mercedes and transferred to that old van. They have a large, black case with them and a brown parcel. I'll keep following them. Must hurry."

"Where are you?"

"Not sure. It's north of the city somewhere. I must leave otherwise I'll lose them."

"Okay, call when you can with a location."

Begas gripped Demol's shoulder and told him to hurry back to the farmhouse. His face broke into genuine laughter as he shook Demol with his massive hand. The laughter subsided into a permanent smile as he intermittently punched the roof of the van. Hugh played it cool even though he didn't know whether Begas would eventually turn on him and take the money.

Willy was standing on the pathway when they arrived at the farmhouse. Begas jumped from the van with the case and charged along the path. Willy looked at him, mumbled something and smiled. Begas cuffed him with his huge left hand. "Get out of the way you old fool." The blow knocked Willy to the ground. Begas trampled over the old man and ran inside the house.

Demol and Boons rushed behind him, completely ignoring Willy, but Connie ran out of the house to help. Hugh saw her concern and reluctantly helped her to take Willy back into the house. Just as they struggled through the door with Willy, Hugh heard an ear-splitting scream followed by the sound of shattering glass.

"It's paper," he heard Begas scream. "It's just fucking paper."

Everyone stood still momentarily and stared at the open case and its contents. Begas picked up an armchair and smashed it against the wall. Boons trampled on the remnants of the chair and hurled meaningless abuse at the case.

Hugh felt like crying. He felt acid bubbling in his stomach and he fell back against the door and bowed his head. The noise of Begas systematically smashing every piece of furniture in the room brought him back to reality. When he saw the look of fear on Connie's face he ushered her into the bedroom with old Willy and told her to keep out of the way.

"How could this happen, Barlow?" Begas asked. "I saw the money in the case before we left. Are you playing tricks on us?"

Hugh threw his hands in the air. "No, I'm at a loss to explain it."

Begas rammed his fist into the wall and screamed, "If this is a trick, Barlow, you're a dead South African."

Fear of what Begas might do replaced Hugh's feeling of utter gloom and despondency. "If it's a trick Begas, then the trick's on me. I had a million dollars in that case."

Demol grabbed Hugh by the lapels of his coat and shook him. "What happened after you left the bank? What happened?"

"We walked to the Limousine and put the case in the trunk," Hugh shouted. "I saw the driver do it. So did you, Begas."

By this time Begas had seated himself on the floor with his head in his hands, cursing continually. "Yes. Yes. I saw it myself."

Demol released Hugh. "Did you stop?" he asked.

"No, no, no," Begas replied.

Hugh said, "Wait a minute. When I got out of the limousine the driver was just lifting the case out of the trunk. He must have switched it."

"But the trunk was empty before we put the case in," Begas said. "I saw it with my own eyes."

"You're right," Hugh added. "I wonder if it's that wretch Obermeier. He's a slippery bastard. Either that, or Kraus is behind it."

"It must be one of them," Begas shouted. "Who else could it be?"

"The driver has to be involved," Hugh said.

Connie stuck her head around the corner of the bedroom door and said, "Why don't you go to the police and report it stolen? Accuse Kraus."

Hugh saw Begas' face tighten, and his fists clench. He said nothing, just rose slowly and walked towards Connie. Boons and Hugh grabbed his arms and pleaded with him to leave her alone.

"There's no point in taking it out on her, Begas," Hugh pleaded. "She's only trying to help."

Begas relaxed his muscles and unclenched his fists. He reassembled one of the broken chairs and sat down. "Tomorrow we'll wait at the back of that bank until the driver shows up. We'll follow him all day if necessary, until we can grab him."

"What then?" Boons asked.

Begas replied, "We'll cross that river when we come to it."

"Bridge, you mean," Hugh added for no reason. Begas never answered.

Terry White had found a concealed position across the road from the farmhouse from which he could monitor anyone entering or leaving the area. He had followed the van until it turned into the farmhouse and then drove a half-mile further on, where he parked his car. He walked back to the farmhouse through the trees and undergrowth and found a place to hide. He could hear shouts emanating from the house but could not discern what was happening. As daylight began to fade he returned to the car, found a telephone, and called Virginia.

"How many of them?" Virginia asked.

"Barlow, the three thugs from Dieppe, and a young woman. Oh, and an old man."

"Peter will take over from you. Here he is now. Give him the directions. I'll take over in the morning."

"Okay. Tell him to wear something waterproof because it's raining."

In the Bahnhofstrasse Cap and Karen gave up waiting. The bank had closed and several employees had already left, but still no sign of Hugh.

"Maybe there's an exit at the back," Cap said. "Karen, go take a look."

As Karen turned the corner into the small road running parallel to the Bahnhofstrasse she saw Kraus's limousine parked next to Zinnerberg's rear entrance. The driver stood intermittently flexing his arm muscles and peering into the window of an adjacent building. Kraus's huge frame appeared and his driver opened the trunk and passed a large, black case to him. They exchanged a few sentences in German before Kraus squeezed himself into the back of the limousine with the case. Karen continued walking until the limousine disappeared from sight, and then hurried back to Cap.

"What happened?" Cap said.

"Kraus came out as I passed by and spoke to his driver. I didn't catch everything they said, but the driver handed Kraus a case. I think he said, 'all the money's there'. Kraus asked if everything went well and if he'd seen any sign of Barlow and his gang. Then he told the driver to take him home."

"How did Barlow get out without us noticing?"

"Same way as Kraus I suppose."

"What do you suppose he meant by 'Barlow and his gang'?"

"My German isn't perfect but Kraus did sound worried."

"Let's speak with Anton."

TWENTY-EIGHT

*H*ugh lay awake most of the night wondering what to do next. Should he forget the million dollars and just bolt, or should he wait and let Begas and the others recover it? Maybe, he reasoned, Begas might be satisfied with half the money and he and Connie could then find a way of escaping.

He got up at daybreak and looked around the farmhouse to find another way out. From the back window he could see that the land fell away steeply from the farmhouse. It was thick with evergreen trees and bushes for at least 100 yards.

He heard a scratching sound coming from the toilet. It was Willy pulling a piece of wooden paneling from the wall, next to the toilet door. Willy moved the panel aside and went down a flight of stairs into a basement. Hugh followed and noticed light shining through a window on the far wall of the basement. He ignored Willy and looked out of the window. *Now there's a nice way to get out of here without anyone noticing,* he thought, as he fiddled with the window latch to make sure it would open easily.

He returned to the living room to find Begas trying to rouse Boons and Demol from their drunken slumbers. He told them to get into the van and be ready to leave. Hugh wanted to stay behind with Connie, but Begas insisted he come with them. Before leaving Hugh checked that the Turnhalle file was still safely hidden behind a large book cabinet in the bedroom.

When they arrived at Zinnerberg, Demol parked the van in a nearby side street, while Begas and Boons took up positions at the front and rear of the bank. Hugh reluctantly agreed to act as a messenger between them.

Only a few minutes passed before Kraus's Limousine pulled up at the rear of the bank. Begas told Hugh to get Demol and the van and then fetch Boons from the front of the bank. "I'll wait here," Begas said.

When Hugh returned he asked Begas if he had seen Kraus.

"The limo's windows were darkened so I couldn't see the fat bastard, but the rear suspension looked in trouble when it went up the ramp."

"Let's get ready to follow the limo," Hugh said. "If we snatch Kraus from here someone is bound to see us."

Begas agreed and ordered everyone to get inside the van and wait. Nothing happened until lunchtime when the garage door opened and the limousine appeared.

"Follow them," Begas shouted to Demol, "but don't get too close."

They followed the limousine all the way to the Dolder Grande Hotel. It stopped outside the hotel entrance just as the van approached the hotel car park.

"There goes Kraus," Hugh said.

Kraus bounced into the hotel while the driver moved the limousine to the end of the car park, got out, lit a cigarette, and walked to the back of the hotel. Demol drove the van up to the limousine and stopped alongside it.

"He's gone inside," Hugh said.

"Boons, quick," Begas shouted. "Get out and open that trunk. Quick."

Boons fiddled with the lock and popped it open.

"You haven't lost your touch," Demol shouted.

Boons ferreted around in the trunk and held up a black case that looked exactly like the one that Obermeier had given them. He opened the case to show that it was empty and threw it back into the trunk.

"There's a hidden compartment that comes down behind the rear seat into the trunk. One section switches with another. It's powered by a small electric motor. I guess it's operated from the driver's seat. The driver must have switched the cases while you were in the limo. It's a custom job, must have been done by a pretty good engineer."

"Kraus is behind it," Hugh said. "It's not just the driver."

"I wonder how many times he's pulled that one," Begas added. "Okay, this is what we'll do. Let's follow Kraus tonight and pay a little surprise visit to his home."

"Will he keep cash in his house?" Demol asked.

"Who knows?" Begas replied. "We'll get the money back one way or another."

Cap and Karen dropped in to speak with Anton to see if any new information had surfaced and to discuss what Karen had overheard outside the back entrance of Zinnerberg.

"Nothing new on Barlow," Anton said. "No reports, no sightings at all. He must be staying in a private house or he has a good disguise. The Swiss are suspicious of strangers. Someone should have noticed him by now, even in a large city like Zurich."

Cap explained what they had seen earlier.

"Give me a description of the men that were with Barlow," Anton said. "If they are Swiss and have criminal records we might be able to trace them."

"I didn't see them very well," Karen said, "but I got the registration number of the van they were using. It's an old, blue Fiat van with a Belgian plate. Here it is."

"Excellent," Anton shouted. "The border police will have a record of the van entering Switzerland." Anton rushed out of his office.

When Anton returned he beamed as he waved a piece of telex paper above his head. "Got it. The driver's name is Demol, Henry Demol. He is a British citizen—lives in Dieppe, France. The border police checked their records and it seems a group of them crossed the border in the van that's owned by a Belgian citizen by the name of Gaston Begas. Interpol has a long file on this one. He's an ex-foreign legionnaire. Kicked out for crippling an officer. He's got a criminal record a mile long. We're checking the others."

"We just need to trace the van then." Cap said.

"Yes," Anton added. "I'll send the information to all the stations in the Zurich area. If they're using the van it won't take long to find them. Now, back to what you heard Kraus say to his driver. It sounds like Kraus has cheated Barlow—case full of money—client complains about missing money—all Zinnerberg's documents in order. Plays like a broken record."

"How do you know?" Cap asked. "Barlow hasn't complained yet."

"If the money is legal he will. If not then he might take things into his own hands. We have a list of over ten of Zinnerberg's ex-clients who have lodged complaints against Kraus. He's always managed to provide evidence that exonerated himself and his bank. In any case, we'll try to locate the van and take things from there."

That night Begas and Demol hid in the grounds of Kraus's house. Hugh and Boons had dropped them off and parked the van in a secluded area a mile beyond the house. It was set back from Lake Zurich by about 200 feet in a heavily wooded area, six miles from the city center.

They had followed Kraus earlier that afternoon after the driver had dropped Kraus at his back door. A man and a woman, who Demol thought were servants, came out of the house and left in the limousine.

Begas and Demol waited in the woods until a little after 11:00 PM. Begas had pinpointed an easy way to break in—through a sliding French door. The lock looked easy to pick and he didn't see an alarm system.

Begas kept watch while Demol flipped the lock. He carefully

opened the door two inches and slid his fingers into the gap and felt around the edge of the door.

"No alarms," he whispered.

The door opened silently and they stepped inside. The open-plan house made it reasonably easy for them to move around. They checked all the rooms on the ground floor but no sign of Kraus.

"Up that spiral staircase," Begas whispered. "Be careful in case the stairs creak."

They crept up the stairway at an agonizingly slow pace. When they reached the top Begas saw that the stairway intersected a long landing. He could see several closed doors on either side but no indication of which one might be Kraus's bedroom. Begas told Demol to wait in the middle of the landing while he checked each room.

Five minutes passed before Begas finished checking all the doors on the right of the stairway. He walked cautiously to the left side and opened the first door. The room was completely empty and the second door offered the same result. As he moved towards the third door he caught the faint sound of breathing. He turned the door handle slowly and pushed the door forward. The light from the window revealed the silhouette of a huge mass lying on the bed, moving slowly up and down and wheezing like a blacksmith's bellows.

Begas located the light switch and signaled for Demol come in. He clasped Demol's left hand, positioned it over the light switch, and tiptoed across the room to the window. He grasped the curtains with his right hand, took a deep breath, drew his handgun with his left hand, and pointed it at Kraus's body.

With a flick of his right arm he whisked the curtain closed and shouted, "Light."

Kraus's head popped up from the sheets and he instinctively shielded his eyes from the sudden burst of light. "Gisela, is it you?" he mumbled.

"No it's not, you fat Swiss pig," Begas shouted. "Henry, tie his wrists." Begas grabbed Kraus by the ear and jammed the handgun against his temple.

"What's going on?" Kraus said. "What are you doing here? Get out before I call the police."

Demol savagely punched Kraus in the face. "Turn over before I really hurt you."

As Demol lined Kraus's head up for a blow with his revolver, Begas froze when a young woman appeared in the doorway wearing only a flimsy nightgown. Her head almost touched the top of the doorway and her long, blonde hair partially covered her sleepy face. "Leave him and grab her," he said to Demol.

"What are you doing to my father? What do you want here?"

Demol grabbed her by the arm, pushed her onto the bed and said, "Keep quiet or I'll cut your face."

"Turn over you fat bastard," Demol ordered. Kraus rolled onto his side. The weight of his body tipped the bed and he crashed to the floor. The room shook when he hit the hardwood tiles and the metal runner on the underside of the bed jabbed into Begas' shin. He released a muted scream, took three deep breaths, jumped over the bed, and began to beat Kraus methodically in the kidneys with the butt of his handgun.

Kraus's daughter grabbed Begas' arm and attempted to stop the beating, but Begas opened the fingers of his left hand and grabbed her head. His massive hand covered her face completely and after one quick shove she flew back three feet and landed on her back.

"Keep your mouth shut," he threatened. "Kraus! Where's the million dollars you stole from us?"

"I don't know anything about a million dollars. Who are you?"

Begas positioned two fingers in front of Kraus's eyes.

"The million you stole from Barlow the other day," Begas snapped. "Don't try to deny it. We found the false compartment in your limousine. Where is it?"

Kraus shut his eyes. "I don't know anything about it. I swear."

Begas jabbed Kraus's eyes twice.

"Please leave my father alone," Kraus's daughter pleaded.

"Don't worry, Gisela, I'm okay," Kraus said to her.

"Henry, go and see if they have a car in the garage. I'll keep these two covered."

A few minutes passed and Demol returned. "There's an Audi 100 coupe and a Land Rover—one of those army vehicles."

"Let's get them into the Audi," Begas said. "Clean the bedroom up before we leave. You, Gisela, or whatever your name is, where's the keys to the Audi?"

She ignored him.

"Where are the keys you fucking bitch?" Begas demanded. "I'll mess your face up if you don't get them."

"Gisela, do as he says."

She pointed down to the floor. "They are in the hall."

Demol pulled her out of the bedroom.

"Get yourself up from the floor," Begas ordered Kraus.

Kraus struggled from side to side as he attempted to stand up. With his hands tied behind his back and his huge protruding stomach, Begas realized it was near impossible for Kraus to get up. He finally wedged himself against the wall in the corner of the room and managed to right himself with Begas' help. Begas delivered a few kicks in the process to make sure he wasn't faking.

Once on his feet, Kraus became incredibly mobile for his size. Begas stayed behind him as they walked down the staircase and through the adjoining door to the garage. Demol had already pushed Gisela into the back seat and stood waiting for Begas to appear.

"Henry, go and clean up the bedroom. Don't forget her room and bring some of their clothes and personal junk."

Begas told Kraus to get into the back of the Audi. Kraus tried but got stuck, so Begas pushed and punched him until his body squeezed into the car. However, his legs were still protruding, so Begas told Gisela to get out. He went around to the opposite door and pulled Kraus across the back seat, and then told Gisela to sit on top of him.

Demol returned with Gisela's purse and Kraus's jacket and wallet.

"You could make a desert tent out of this jacket," Demol said, "and fit a half-dozen Arabs in it."

"And their fucking camels," an unusually amused Begas added.

They drove out of the garage and into the road with the headlights turned off until they reached the van. Demol flicked the headlights until Boons's head appeared from the driver's side of the van.

"Did you get him?" Boons asked.

"All three tons of the lump of fucking Swiss cheese," Demol replied. "Just follow us."

Virginia and Peter had followed the van from the farmhouse early that morning to the bank in the Bahnhofstrasse and then on to the Dolder hotel. After that they lost contact with them in the heavy city traffic. They had changed their rental car the previous evening for a different make and color, but they still felt the need to be extra cautious and kept quite a distance behind the van.

Virginia decided to return to the farmhouse and ask Terry White if he had seen anything. However, the rental car seemed to lose power just outside the city. They tried to fix it, but eventually had to call the rental company to replace the car. It took almost five hours before they set out for the farmhouse again.

During the drive back Virginia mentioned that when she watched the bank from the hotel she saw a familiar face, but couldn't put a name to it. She was convinced it was a woman she had seen in South Africa. A short time after this she remembered her name. "Peter! Karen Van Der Berg—that's her name! I'm sure of it. She's that detective in the murder squad in Johannesburg. The one that went with us on the monastery raid."

"Are you sure?" Peter asked. "If it's her then what's she doing in Zurich? Maybe she's taking a vacation or something. Maybe she just looks like this Karen woman."

"No, Peter. It's too much of a coincidence. She wasn't dressed like a tourist to start with and for sure she wasn't dressed like a Swiss."

"I'll check with Van Starden, see if he knows anything."

"Okay."

"I've got a feeling something is going to happen very soon."

They arrived at the farmhouse just after midnight and Terry told them that only the girl and the old man were in the house. After they parked the car across the road from the farmhouse Peter went to the back window to make sure that only the old man and Connie were in the house. He gave Virginia the thumbs-up sign, and she signaled to Terry to kick the front door open. Virginia and Terry charged through the door and grabbed Connie.

"What's your name?" Virginia asked Connie.

"Connie," she timidly replied.

"We won't hurt you if you give us Barlow's file. Where is it?"

Connie pointed towards the bedroom. "Behind the book cabinet."

"Okay, go and get it," Virginia ordered.

Connie edged her way into the bedroom without taking her eyes from Virginia's handgun. As she fumbled behind the bookcase Terry shouted to Virginia. "Their van's back with another car. Quick let's go."

Peter took his rifle and ran out the back door and into the woods. Virginia pushed Connie out of the way and scratched around for the file but she couldn't find it. "Where is it you stupid girl? Where is it?"

"I don't know, honestly I don't know. It was there earlier, I swear."

Virginia could see she wasn't lying, so she gave up and rushed out behind Terry. She told Peter to take up a firing position next to the road while she and Terry waited out of sight, ten yards from the road.

Hugh watched Demol jump out of the Audi and draw his handgun while Begas opened the other door and pulled Gisela out. Hugh stared in amazement when he saw Kraus stuffed in the back of the Audi.

"How did you get him in there?" Hugh asked.

"That was the easy part," Demol replied. "Now we have to get the fat, Swiss tub of shit out of there."

Hugh went into the farmhouse and saw Connie sitting on the floor sobbing.

"What's wrong? What happened?"

"That redheaded bitch and two others broke in. They threatened to kill me if I didn't give them that file of yours."

"You didn't give it to them, did you?" Hugh asked.

"No, but it wasn't where you left it."

"Where the hell is it then?"

Begas interrupted the conversation when he walked in holding Gisela by the arm. "Sit over there and keep your mouth shut."

"Begas," Hugh shouted, "the South Africans were here. They've just gone."

Begas ran to the door and shouted to Demol and Boons, "Watch yourselves, those South Africans are around. They might be in the woods. Barlow, turn the lights out."

Hugh helped Boons and Demol drag Kraus from the Audi. They got Kraus to his feet and shoved him into the house, but Boons accidentally tripped him as he stepped through the door. The room shook as Kraus hit the floor like a sack of coal, face first. They rolled him into a corner and took up positions around the house. A minute later Hugh heard the noise of a car engine starting up, and then the screech of tires.

"They must have gone," Hugh said.

"What were they after?" Begas asked Connie.

Hugh jumped in quickly and said, "Me. The redhead wants me dead. They must have thought I was still in the house after you left."

Hugh waited for an opportune moment to speak to Connie. "Where's that file?"

"I don't know. It's been moved."

"It was behind the book cabinet this morning."

Hugh searched the house in the dark looking for the file until Begas turned the lights back on.

"They've gone. Did you see anything outside, Henry?"

"No, nothing around the house or in the woods."

Hugh went into the toilet, the only place in the house that he hadn't checked, and immediately noticed that the toilet bowl wasn't loose. He looked behind it and saw the file, stuffed between the wall and the toilet.

"It must have been old Willy," Connie whispered in Hugh's ear. Hugh was startled because he had not seen Connie follow him into the toilet.

"It's okay, thank god," Hugh said. "The cover's a little wet but that's nothing."

"Willy must have pissed on it."

Hugh felt disgusted.

"What are they going to do with that young girl and the fat man?" Connie asked.

"Don't know, but be ready to run when I say."

Hugh went back into the living room where Begas was giving orders. "Demol, keep watch while we get some sleep. We can work out what to do in the morning. No boozing tonight, we have to keep clear heads."

he sound of shattering glass jolted everyone awake. Hugh's head jack-knifed out from under a blanket, and directly in front of him, almost in slow motion, he saw Demol's body rise slightly and then crumple to the floor. The glass from the window showered Demol and the rest of the room. Even in the dim light Hugh could see that the back part of Demol's head had been blown away. Begas instinctively dived on the floor and covered his head with his hands, while Boons jumped behind the old sofa.

"They're attacking us," Begas said. "Check all the guns and cover the doors. Barlow, get yourself a gun and cover the back door. Boons, are you okay?"

"I'm fine. Demol looks dead."

"Okay, leave him."

"I didn't hear a shot," Hugh said, "but a bullet must have come through the window."

"Keep down everyone," Begas said. "I guess it was a rifle shot. Wait a few minutes and we can work our way into the woods. We only have handguns so we need to get close to them."

Hugh pulled Connie to the floor and covered her head. "Keep down."

Five minutes passed before Begas issued the next set of orders.

"Boons, go out of the side window and work your way around the house to the road. When you hear me scream, run across the road and find a place to hide. I think the rifle shot came from there. Barlow, you go out the back door and find a place to hide. Shoot anyone that tries to get in. I'll get onto the roof and shoot down at anyone coming through the front door."

"What about the window on the other side of the house?" Boons asked.

"Connie, creep over here and take this Beretta. Just close your eyes and pull the trigger if you see anyone trying to get in. It's loaded and ready to fire. Connie, did you hear me?"

"Yes, err . . . I'm coming now."

"Do as he says, Connie," Hugh whispered in her ear.

Begas crawled past Hugh to the bathroom and punched out the slanted window frame on the ceiling. His huge hands grabbed hold of the rim of the window and he pulled himself effortlessly up to the roof.

Hugh reluctantly crawled out the back door and hid behind some bushes. *Might as well make a break for it now,* he thought. He charged back into the house and called Connie. "Connie, come over here. Quick."

She ran over to Hugh and hugged him. "What should I do?"

"Go into the bathroom and get that file. Then get my things from the other room, all my papers and documents, and stuff them in Demol's backpack. We'll make a run for it."

"I'm frightened."

Their conversation ended when Begas screamed at the top of his voice.

"Too late," Hugh said to Connie. "Go back to the window." He ran out of the back door again and dived into the undergrowth. Everything stayed silent for a few seconds until he heard the sound of a vehicle start up, and then drive away.

An instant later Begas shouted, "They've gone."

"How many of them?" Hugh heard Boons shout back.

"Three."

"Okay, back into the house everyone."

Just before daybreak, Begas assembled everyone around Kraus and Gisela.

"Kraus, you've got one chance to get that million dollars back here otherwise little Miss Gisela here gets a bullet in her head."

"But I don't have that sort of money on hand and I didn't take your million dollars."

Begas let lose with several punches to Kraus's head and body. Kraus yelled in pain but refused to agree to hand the money over. Hugh whispered in Begas' ear. "Use the girl to get at him."

Begas chuckled, took Boons aside and exchanged a few words. Boons grabbed Gisela's hair, pulled her head back, and forced his mouth onto hers. She jerked her head away violently, but Boons continued unabashed. He pulled her nightdress down at the front, exposing her breasts, and slowly fondled her. Gisela intermittently sobbed and screamed, and begged her father to give them the money, but Kraus remained silent.

Boons looked at Begas, who nodded, and then ripped her gown completely off, and pushed her to the floor. With a lecherous smile he began to unbutton his pants.

"Okay, okay," Kraus shouted. "I confess. My driver switched the cases in the limousine. I'll get the money for you. Just leave my daughter alone."

"Now that's better isn't it, Mr. Swiss Banker? Here's what you do. Go to your bank and get the money. I'll come along to make sure there's no funny business. If we're not back here by noon your daughter will spend a couple of hours with my friend here. If we're not back by the end of the day then you'll find her in a grave."

"But the bank won't open until nine."

"Open it early. It's your bank isn't it?"

Boons made another move towards Gisela.

"Very well, very well," Kraus replied. "I'll call Obermeier and get him to open up early."

"What excuse will you give?" Hugh asked.

"I'll think of something."

"So you do have that sort of cash in the vault," Boons said, unexpectedly.

"Normally I don't because most people keep their investments in securities, bonds, and gold. But most of your money I took is still there."

Boons grabbed him by the throat. "What do you mean—most of the money? You lying Swiss pig. You told us you never had the money." Boons lifted his fist, ready to hit Kraus, but Begas stepped in and wrestled him away.

"Don't hit him," Begas said. "We don't want him to look too beaten up. His face is already puffed out."

"Why don't we just take all the money and gold in the safe?" Boons asked, as he looked at Begas for support.

Hugh jumped in quickly before Begas could think. "No. We want this Obermeier fellow to think everything is fine and open the bank as normal after you've left. We need a day or so to get away."

"True," Begas said. "Make it look like fatso here is going away for a few days with the million dollars."

"Make a point of counting the money exactly and Obermeier won't think it's a robbery," Hugh added.

Begas thought for a while and said, "We'll drive to your house, Kraus, so that you can call Obermeier and tell those servants of yours that you'll be gone for a few days. Tell that driver as well."

Virginia had kept surveillance all night from the woods, while Peter and Terry slept in the car a few miles down the road. She saw Kraus's Audi pull out of the farmhouse and drive towards Zurich, so she immediately called Terry and Peter on the walkie-talkie. Virginia got worried because they didn't answer straight away. Ten minutes later Peter contacted her and arranged to pick her up.

"Why didn't you respond? We've missed them now. Well, two of them anyway. They drove off in the Audi about thirty minutes ago, but I'm not sure who was in the car."

"One of the walkie-talkies is missing," Peter said. "Terry lost his last night outside the house and I turned mine off to save the battery."

"I know we're all exhausted," Virginia said angrily, "but we can't afford to make mistakes like that."

"Well at least I eliminated one of them," Peter said.

"I'm surprised you hit him in that light," Terry said.

"The idiot lit a cigarette," Peter said, as he kissed his rifle. "I couldn't miss with this beauty."

"What's the plan now?" Terry asked Virginia.

"We'll have to take out another one. Make sure it's not Barlow. I want him for myself."

"Virginia . . . after we get the file back," Terry said.

"Of course," she replied, "that's why we're here. Let's park the car near the farmhouse and keep watch."

Begas and Kraus left the farmhouse at dawn. When they reached Kraus's home, Kraus cleaned himself up and changed his clothes. Begas never diverted his eyes from Kraus for one second. "Don't forget—I speak German," Begas said, before he called Obermeier.

"Obermeier, meet me at the bank at 8:00 AM sharp. I have a big deal in the works. I'll have someone with me so don't get alarmed."

Obermeier opened the garage doors at the rear entrance of Zinnerberg just as Begas and Kraus pulled up in the Audi. They parked the car and walked down four flights of stairs to the underground vault. Kraus never spoke as he struggled to open the highly polished vault door via the combination locks. Begas looked on in amazement when the door opened. It was eight feet high and four feet wide, made of solid steel and six inches thick.

Begas became angry when Obermeier stared at him and asked, "Didn't I see you at the bank the other day, sir?"

"Don't worry, Obermeier," Kraus said, "he's in on the deal."

Begas followed Kraus and Obermeier into the vault, which was a twenty-foot, square room with steel shelves along two of the walls. The shelves contained open metal boxes, many with bundles of bank notes neatly stacked inside. Begas stared intently at a stack of gold bars in the far corner of the room, never having seen so much wealth before.

Kraus flicked his fingers at Obermeier, "We need to count 1,000,000 United States dollars. Get cracking, Obermeier."

Obermeier began the arduous process of counting the hundred-dollar denominations stacked in the metal boxes. His hands gymnastically pulled bank notes from one pile to another like a ferret burrowing out a neat home in the ground.

Begas laughed as Obermeier's face transformed from a bland, yellowish color to a bright red glow as he happily counted the notes. However he soon lost interest and just stared at the gold bullion in the corner of the room.

Begas resisted the urge to shoot Obermeier and take all the cash in the vault because so far no one had been murdered. Also he wasn't sure if Obermeier's friends or family would miss him, and he remembered what Hugh had said, so he stuck to the original plan.

Almost a half-hour passed before Obermeier finished counting and recounting.

"We only have 950,600 dollars," Obermeier said to Kraus.

"Make up the difference in Swiss franks."

Kraus pulled a large metal container from under the steel shelves and began stuffing the money inside. "Let's get moving."

"But, Herr Kraus, we need to update the ledgers," Obermeier said. "It's bank policy."

"You stay behind and do it."

They marched out of the vault and climbed the staircase to street level. Kraus was panting so heavily when he finally reached the top he could hardly move. Begas snatched the metal container from him and darted over to the Audi.

"Get into the front seat, you fat ponce," Begas said. He stuffed Kraus into the passenger's seat and roared out of the garage, narrowly missing the automatic doors as they opened.

Begas pulled into the farmhouse and skidded to a halt. He dragged the metal container out of the car and rushed towards the house, momentarily forgetting Kraus. He opened the front door and shouted to Boons. "Boons, get him inside quickly. I've got the money." Boons did not reply.

Hugh shouted back, "He's in the bedroom with Kraus's daughter. He's done a number on her. I couldn't stop him. He's beaten her senseless."

"Boons," Begas screamed, "get out here and cover Kraus."

Boons appeared from the bedroom, pulling his pants up with one hand and carrying his shirt in the other. "I just gave the girl a good going over. She's a juicy cow. Not very good looking but what a fucking body."

"Don't worry about that now," Begas shouted, "just give me a hand."

He dumped the metal container on the table and forced it open. "Look, Barlow. Here's the money. I got it back. We're rich."

"Don't be too hasty, Mr. Begas," Hugh said, as he raised the Beretta and pointed it out of the window. "Look who's showed up."

Begas rushed to the window to see an empty car parked across the road. "They've surrounded the house. Quick! Get Boons inside with Kraus."

As he spoke a dull smacking sound jolted everyone's attention. Boons fell across the front door with blood pouring from his mouth, and Kraus fell on top of him, unhurt but struggling and crying out for help. Even Kraus's massive weight collapsing on Boons didn't stir his lifeless body.

"Help me, help me, please," Kraus screamed. "I don't want to die."

Begas dragged him into the house and then pulled Boons's body across the doorstep.

"Everyone down," Begas shouted. "Barlow, is the back door locked?"

"Yes, and I've barricaded it," Hugh shouted back.

"Cover the side windows and I'll stay at the front door."

Begas opened the door a few inches and shouted. "Okay, what do you want? Is it Barlow you're after? Is it the money or this damned file? Let's make a deal."

Virginia shouted back, "It's the file. Tie this rope to it and I'll pull it towards me. If it's what we want we'll leave straight away."

"Barlow," Begas whispered across the room, "what's in the dammed file that they want so much?"

"It's government stuff—top secret. I kept it for my protection. I thought as long as they knew I had that file I would be safe, but that redheaded bitch has something personal against me. I told you that before."

"We're outgunned. I'll have to give it to them. Go and get it."

"Okay, it's in the bathroom." Hugh crawled across the floor towards the bathroom.

Begas shouted out of the door. "Okay, wait a few minutes and we'll let you have it."

Hugh passed Connie on his way to the bathroom and whispered, "Follow me and bring that backpack."

Hugh reached the bathroom and lifted the file. Instead of turning back, he pulled the piece of the wall panel away that led to the basement and signaled to Connie to follow. He replaced the panel and clutched Connie's hand as they groped in the darkness.

"Hugh, I'm frightened. Where are we going? It's so dark."

"Don't worry. I saw old Willy go down here a few days ago. It leads into a basement. He stores cheese down here. That's why it stinks. If we're lucky we can get away unnoticed."

Hugh shoved the window frame out, trying not to make too much noise, and then crawled through the gap. Connie passed the file and the backpack through and clambered out. They had covered about twenty yards when Hugh heard the crack of gunshots.

"Ignore it, Connie, just keep going."

Outside the farmhouse Virginia and her team kept well out of range of Begas' handguns. When the firing stopped Virginia told Terry to edge forward and stand to the left of the front door. She signaled to Peter to cover with his rifle.

Everything remained silent as Virginia moved forward. Suddenly she heard a crash and saw Begas jump through a window to the right of the door. He rolled across the ground, firing.

"Terry, shoot the bastard," Virginia shouted, after realizing she'd blocked Peter's firing line. She dived to the ground when she saw Terry fumble and drop his gun. Begas hurled his gun at Terry, hitting him flush in the face, and then dived at Virginia. *He's out of bullets,* she thought.

"My eyes, I can't see," Terry screamed, as he dropped to his knees and covered his face with his hands.

Virginia felt her head jolt to the side as Begas grabbed her hair and lifted her off the ground. She Jabbed at his throat and kicked him in the shin, but Begas just shrugged it off, shook her like a rag doll, and then felled her with a backhand to the side of her head.

Virginia saw stars. She shook her head, rolled over three times to get clear of Begas, and then sprang to her feet. She saw Peter dive at Begas and wrestle him to the ground. He pounded Begas in the head and body, but Begas fought back. He punched Peter hard in the stomach and followed through with a kick to his chest. Peter let out a scream and dropped on one knee, but he quickly recovered and leaped forward at Begas again. Terry picked up his gun and tried to take aim at Begas.

"Don't shoot," Virginia screamed. "You might hit Peter." She picked up Peter's rifle and ran towards them. Terry grabbed Begas around the throat and together with Peter they dragged him to the ground. Virginia saw her opportunity and whacked Begas on the side of the head with the rifle butt. *No effect,* she thought, so she hit him again and again until his body went limp.

"Shall we finish him off?" Terry said.

"No, just tie his hands," Virginia replied. "I'll check the house." She kicked the door open and began searching each room. In the bedroom she found a huge, fat man, flat out on the floor, with a young, blood-soaked, blonde woman holding a towel over his head.

"What happened? Who's he?" Virginia asked the girl.

"My father, Herr Kraus, he's the owner of Zinnerberg. I'm his daughter, Gisela. Those animals kidnapped us."

"Don't worry, we won't hurt you."

"The big one punched Father unconscious and then knocked me senseless. The dead man through there raped and sodomized me." Gisela wiped blood from her stomach. "He made me ... "

"I'll call the police," Virginia said, as she passed a towel to Gisela. She ran to the front door, skipped over Boons's body, and sprinted towards the car. Peter and Terry had finished tying Begas and they were struggling to push him inside the car. Virginia was still determined to get Hugh even though both Terry and Peter were injured and the Swiss police were certainly not far behind.

"Peter, go after Barlow. He must have gone out the back of the house. Take the walkie-talkie and your rifle. I'll go with Terry. Move fast, the police will be here soon. Don't kill him unless you get the file."

Virginia and Terry pushed Begas into the backseat of the car. "Let's get moving," Virginia ordered. "We'll clean ourselves up and wait for Peter to contact us."

"What shall we do with him?" Terry asked, pointing at Begas.

"Gag him and leave him tied to the back seat for now."

At police headquarters in Zurich, news of Kraus's disappearance soon spread. Anton rushed into to his office to tell Cap and Karen.

"We have a break. It looks like Kraus has been kidnapped. He went to his bank earlier this morning with a guy that fits the description of Gaston Begas. They took almost 1,000,000 dollars and some Swiss francs from the vault and then left in a hurry. Our boys checked his home and found it empty, but there were signs of a hasty departure, and his daughter's Audi was missing from the garage. That celebrated lying wretch, Obermeier, reported it to the police. He said Kraus had bruises on his face and looked very nervous."

Before Cap or Karen could comment, another detective entered the room and pulled Anton aside. He exchanged a few sentences in German and left abruptly.

"More interesting news. The police found Obermeier in his apartment, rolling on the floor with thousands of US hundred-dollar bills, about eight million dollars apparently. After a spirited interrogation he revealed that Kraus had swindled a South African businessman by the name of Jack Barlow. Obermeier said he took the money from a safe deposit box at Zinnerberg as a safety precaution, in case Kraus was forced to hand it over to his captors. He's lying of course."

"That must be Hugh Barlow's ill-gotten gains from the diamond theft," Cap said. "Look, Anton, you've been very helpful and open with us, and I don't want to abuse your trust and hospitality. I'm 100 percent convinced that the guy we're chasing is in fact Hugh Barlow, not Jack Barlow. We think Hugh killed his half-brother, Jack, in South Africa and assumed his identity. The problem is that we don't have an arrest warrant for Hugh."

A confused Anton replied, "Why not? Surely you can get your authorities to issue an Interpol request."

"It's not that simple. It's political in nature. We were refused permission to go after Hugh Barlow, so we added an alias to Jack Barlow's request."

"I see," a slightly annoyed Anton replied.

"After murdering Jack, Hugh took his identification and credentials to cover his tracks."

"But why won't your government let you find him legitimately?" Anton asked, shaking his head in disbelief.

"That's where the political issues come in. There's something else going on within the intelligence branch that's being kept from us. Our Minister of Justice has a bee in his bonnet about it. I can't say any more, you understand."

"Well, he'll never see the money again that's for sure," Anton replied. "It was in Jack Barlow's safety deposit box . . . and according to you he's dead."

"I can't wait to see the look on his face when we catch him," Karen said.

"Well let's find him first and . . . " Anton was interrupted mid-sentence by a uniformed officer rushing into the room. The officer barked out a few sentences in German and left.

"Let's go, there's been gunfire reported at an old farmhouse just north of the city. I think it's our friends."

Anton drove them at high speed to the farmhouse. When they arrived several police emergency vehicles were already at the scene. Anton flashed his badge at the officers standing at the door of the farmhouse and went straight in. Cap and Karen followed but the officers stopped them. Anton shouted to them to wait outside.

Cap and Karen walked across the road and waited, praying that Hugh would emerge from the farmhouse.

"What's that crackling noise?" Karen asked Cap.

"What noise? I'm half-deaf."

Karen stepped over the metal barrier alongside the hard shoulder of the road and picked up a radio. She heard more crackles and a few voices.

"Cap, I'm sure I heard the word 'Barlow'. Is this a police radio?"

Cap said, "Let me see." He examined it and pressed it to his ear. "It's a walkie-talkie." He looked at the back of the receiver and read some of the small print. "Karen! This was made in South Africa. Look."

Karen looked at it and said, "You're right. That's odd. Wait . . . listen . . . there's more voices. BOSS one . . . BOSS two. What the hell's all that about?"

Cap took the walkie-talkie back and listened. "I think I know. Put it inside your coat and don't say anything to Anton yet. We'll play follow the leader. It'll lead us to Barlow."

Anton ran over to them and briefly explained what had happened inside the farmhouse and mentioned that they had found the 1,000,000 dollars that Begas had taken from Zinnerberg's vault.

THIRTY

$\mathcal{H}$ugh and Connie collapsed on the wet grass at the bottom of the hill after struggling through 300 yards of thick undergrowth. Hugh clutched the Turnhalle file as if it were his only child, while Connie began soothing the cuts and scratches on her legs and arms with moisture from the grass.

Hugh looked back up the hill, but he couldn't see if anyone had followed them. When he regained his strength he pulled Connie to her feet and began moving further into the woods. The file was difficult to carry, so he threw some of Connie's clothes out of the backpack and stuffed it inside.

They reached a small ravine where a stream wound its way through the woods. After they splashed the cold water on their faces and cleaned their scratches they followed the flow of the water, keeping to the middle of the stream. Walking in six inches of water was easier than struggling through the dense undergrowth, even though the riverbed was rocky and uneven.

They covered two miles before the stream merged with a larger river, and on the opposite bank Hugh could see the outskirts of a town.

"Let's sleep in the woods tonight," Hugh said. "In the morning we'll clean ourselves up and go into that town."

Connie began to cry. "Can't we go in now? Please."

Hugh shook his head. "Too risky. They might be following us."

"Do you think Gaston got away?" Connie asked after drying her eyes.

"Who knows? I heard a lot of gunfire and he was outnumbered three to one. The guy that shot Demol and Boons was an expert marksman. In any case, it looks like I've lost all that money."

"Well, not exactly," Connie said.

"What do you mean?"

Connie pulled the backpack from Hugh's shoulders and dug around for a while. Her hand reappeared with a wad of hundred-dollar bills.

"I took it from the case when Gaston wasn't looking."

Hugh grabbed the wad and flicked the ends of the notes with his index finger and thumb. "Must be 50,000 there at least." He kissed Connie. "Well done. This will get me out of Switzerland and out of harm's way for a while. Let's find a place to sleep."

Fifty yards upstream Peter Fourie, with his marksman's rifle slung over his shoulder, watched their every move through a pair of binoculars. He had caught up with them only minutes before, after following several false trails. He watched as Hugh and Connie clambered out of the stream and into the woods.

He knew Hugh was armed, albeit with only a handgun, so he proceeded cautiously to the spot where they left the stream and picked up their trail. The woods were dense so he stopped and listened for signs of movement, but he could only hear the sound of the wind moving tree branches and the purling of the water in the stream.

He moved further into the undergrowth and a distant sound of a woman's voice caught his attention. Twenty yards further on he saw Hugh and Connie resting against the bole of a tree in a small clearing.

Peter pressed the butt of his rifle into his armpit and adjusted the telescopic sight until Hugh's head came into focus, although at that range he knew the telescopic sight was irrelevant. *Don't see the file,* he thought, *might be in that backpack. Can't be sure. Better to wait.* He moved the rifle down so that it pointed to the middle of Hugh's chest and wrapped his finger around the trigger. He took a short breath and held the air in his lungs, but just before he squeezed the trigger he moved the rifle to the right, away from Hugh.

Pieces of splintered bark flew into the air as the bullet hit the tree. He quickly reloaded and fired another bullet into the tree, then a shot to their left, and watched Hugh and Connie disappear into the woods. Only the ferns, swaying gently back and forth, were left as a reminder of their presence.

Peter tried to contact Virginia on his walkie-talkie, but the range of the transmitter and his position in the ravine made this impossible. He decided to give up the hunt temporarily because he had no food or water and no camping equipment, but he was happy he'd driven them in the direction he wanted.

Before returning to find Virginia, Peter jogged in a large arc around the farmhouse, looking for a village that he'd noticed the previous day, about two miles from the farmhouse. When he reached the village he paused to regain his breath and went inside a small post office. He offered the teller money to make an international call but the suspicious teller declined. Peter upped the amount considerably and after the teller called the international operator to find out the cost of the call, he allowed Peter to use the telephone.

"Only one minute, that's all," The concerned teller warned.

Peter waited ten minutes for the call to go through to South Africa. "Mr. Hamilton, assignment nearing completion. I'm closing in on the file. His friends have been eliminated. Any changes to your plan?"

"No," Roger said. "Get the file and eliminate individuals as ordered."

Hugh and Connie charged uphill through the undergrowth for almost 200 yards until Hugh's legs cramped and he fell against a tree. "Connie, come on. We need to find a safer place for the night."

"I can't, Hugh," she said as she flopped down. "I'm finished."

"There's a rocky outcrop just ahead. Let's see if we can find some shelter there."

Hugh pulled Connie to her feet, took the backpack and threw it over his shoulder. "Come on, one more effort and we'll be safe." He walked behind Connie with his hands under her armpits to support her. Above the rocks the slope of the hill tapered off somewhat, but the landscape was still thick with undergrowth and trees. To his right were more rocks, but the ground seemed relatively even, so Hugh walked in that direction.

A little further on he found a small space covered on three sides by rock, with an overhang that would protect them from rain and keep them completely hidden.

He shook the moisture from some ferns and told Connie to lie on them. To hide the shelter completely he placed some fallen branches across the entrance. He stretched out on the ground next to Connie and placed the backpack under her head. Exhaustion soon took over and Hugh drifted into a deep sleep.

Hugh woke up shivering. He looked out through the branches covering their hiding place, but he couldn't tell if it was sunset or sunrise the next day, so he checked the date and time on his watch. They had only slept for four hours, but Hugh felt as if it had been for a whole night. He shook Connie. "Connie, wake up. Wake up."

"How long did we sleep?"

"Just a few hours. We need to go into that town. It's too cold to stay here tonight."

"What about the sniper?"

"We'll have to take a chance. I don't think he'll bother us in the town. He'll have too many questions to answer if the police get involved."

Hugh thought for a while, *I don't know how that sniper missed us at that range. He killed Demol in the dark. With all those trees around he couldn't have been more than twenty yards away.*

Connie interrupted his thoughts. "How do we get back to the river?"

"We'll keep parallel to the stream."

They set off through the fading light, and to Hugh's surprise they reached the stream in less than ten minutes after clambering down from the rocky outcrop. He saw a wooden bridge less than fifty yards away, and after checking that no one was around, rushed across with Connie.

On the other side Hugh could see the lights of the small town quite clearly.

"Connie, let's tidy ourselves up and find a pension or a hostel. Leave the explanations to me. The town looks larger than I first thought. Maybe we can get a taxi or a car in the morning."

The streets were deserted and everything appeared to be closed but Connie noticed a small sign with a bed and a knife and fork carved on it. They followed the sign and came to the entrance of a small pension.

Hugh brushed himself down and went in. An old man approached him and greeted him in German.

"We're looking for a room for the night," Hugh said. "Do you speak English?"

"A little," the old man said. "We have rooms for you."

"Good," Hugh replied smiling. "We were walking with a larger party and got lost in the woods."

"Yes," the old man said. "That happens much here."

"We'll leave early in the morning and find them," Hugh added.

The old man nodded and took a key from under his desk. "Do you want some food? I have some soup and bread, nothing else."

"That will be fine."

Five minutes after Hugh and Connie settled in their small room, the old man tapped on the door and handed over two large bowls of hot soup and some lumps of bread. The smell of the soup made

Hugh feel even more ravenous. They sat on the edge of the bed and quickly devoured the food.

"This is delicious," Hugh said. "It's only potato soup but it's the best I've ever tasted."

Hugh felt warmth returning to his hands and feet. He threw his wet clothes over the back of a chair and told Connie to run the bath.

"The water's hot."

"I'll jump in when you're finished," Hugh said.

"Get in with me. There's plenty of room."

They squeezed into the bath. Connie lay at one end with her legs resting on either side of the bath and Hugh sat upright at the other end. He felt the warm water radiating through his tired limbs as he watched Connie rub her body with soap and dip her hair into the water. They dried each other, ran back into the chilly bedroom, and jumped straight into bed and cuddled each other to stay warm.

"Hugh," Connie whispered.

"What?"

"You are going to take me with you aren't you?"

"Yes of course, but we need to get out of Switzerland and away from those South Africans first of all."

"I have relations in Marseilles you know. One of them is a forger. I think he is out of jail now. He'll make false documents for us."

"Good. We'll go straight there once we're over the border. With the money you took from Begas we should be able to make a good start somewhere. When all this blows over – if it does – I'll need to come back to Zurich and get to my safe deposit box. I'll need to get in and out of Switzerland under a false name. God knows what Begas has done with that fat oaf, Kraus. If he kills him we'll never get out of the country let alone get back in."

"Boons raped his daughter," Connie said with a look of fear on her face. "Don't forget that."

"I know, but we tried to stop him, so I don't think that will be held against us. In any case it looked like we were being held against our wishes, so the Swiss police might not charge us."

"Will they want us to be witnesses?"

"Probably. Anyway let's just focus on getting away. Wait a few years and then see where we are. The other thing I need to do tomorrow is hide this file somewhere safe."

Connie fell asleep before he finished speaking. Hugh turned the light off and closed his eyes. He tried to think about the best way to escape the following morning, but exhaustion got the better of him and he slipped into a deep sleep.

THIRTY-ONE

*P*eter contacted Virginia and Terry as soon as he finished his call to South Africa. Based on Peter's information, it took Virginia less than five minutes to scan a map of the area and determine how far Hugh and Connie could have gone. They were on foot, at night, in a heavily wooded area. The woods were enclosed on three sides by a river and as far as she could tell only two bridges spanned the river, both of which led into the town. She thought it unlikely Hugh would backtrack and end up at the farmhouse, so she decided that they would cover the two bridges and watch for any signs of his presence in the town.

They bound and gagged Begas for the night and left him tied to a tree, while they slept for a few hours in the car, taking turns to keep watch. No one wanted to kill Begas in cold blood, although Peter openly said he resented the fact that Begas almost beat him in the fight. Virginia thought he might be a useful fall-guy if the police got involved, so for the present he was safe.

At first light Peter and Terry took up positions to cover the bridges, while Virginia went into the town and parked the car in the main square. Terry tied Begas to a tree a few yards behind his position.

Virginia checked that the walkie-talkie was in range and then walked across the square to speak with a man opening a small café. After struggling to make herself understood, she learned that there were only two small pensions in the town. One, just across the square, and the other along a side street on the edge of the town.

The pension in the square seemed deserted so she didn't bother to check it. She headed towards the other pension where an old man was sweeping the pathway.

"Excuse me, I don't suppose you have any rooms available? I would imagine a place like this would be full at this time of the year."

"Oh, no, no. I have three rooms ready. There's only one room taken. A couple that got lost last night hiking through the woods."

"I'll go back and get my friends. We'll have some breakfast and then come back."

"Okay, fine."

Virginia hurried back to the car. The radio turned on when she started the engine and she couldn't help but hear the word "Zinnerberg". She listened intently to the rest of the news report. Her German was good enough to realize that Kraus's kidnap had hit the headlines on the news stations. She called Peter and Terry on the walkie-talkie and told them to meet her in the square.

"We're running out of time," Virginia warned, as she put her head in her hands. "The police know all about Kraus's kidnapping and the firefight at the farmhouse. It's all over the news. There's a massive manhunt underway."

"Who was the second girl? The tall one."

"His daughter," she replied indifferently. "We need to move quickly. There's only an old man in the pension so if we go now we should be able to grab Barlow and the file. Tie the old man up and by the time the police find out we'll be over the border into France."

"Okay, let's go," Peter replied.

"Stuff him in the back seat and throw a blanket over him," she said, pointing to Begas. "We'll get rid of him. He's too much trouble now."

Hugh and Connie woke early that morning and went into the small bathroom and washed. Connie began combing her hair, but the hinge on the bathroom mirror broke loose and she couldn't keep it still. Hugh moved it around to try and fix it in one position, finally setting it on the windowsill. As he moved back to give Connie more room he saw the reflection of a woman working her way along the street at the side of the pension. Hugh poked his head out of the window, looked down, and immediately recognized Virginia. "Shit!"

"What is it?" Connie asked.

"It's that redheaded bitch. She's outside in the alley. Quick! Let's go."

They scrambled into their clothes and Hugh wedged the Turnhalle file inside the backpack along with the rest of their belongings. He loaded his gun and signaled to Connie to open the door.

"Hugh, listen, footsteps coming from the stairs outside."

The footsteps grew louder and louder but then began to fade. "I think they've passed the room," Hugh whispered. "How many of them?"

"Two, I think."

Hugh pointed to the door again. Connie pulled it open slightly, and pushed herself flat against the wall. Hugh pointed the gun into the crack between the door and the frame, and prepared to shoot.

"No one there. They must have gone upstairs." Hugh put the gun inside his belt, grabbed the backpack in one hand, and pulled Connie out the door with the other. They crossed the hall and went down the first flight of stairs.

"Hugh, there's someone down there. Look."

Hugh looked down between the banisters and saw a man standing at the bottom of the stairwell with a gun in his hand. He passed his gun to Connie, moved to the edge of the stairwell, lifted the backpack over his head, and hurled it down at the armed man. He heard him groan and watched him fall backwards.

"Quick," Hugh said to her. "Let's run for it."

They bolted down the last flight of stairs. Hugh picked up the backpack, chopped the stunned man in the neck with the side of his hand, and then raced out of the hotel.

"Hurry up, Connie, follow me."

"Where are we going?"

Hugh grabbed the gun from Connie. "Let's make for the train station. They won't try anything in public."

Virginia charged down the stairs of the pension. "He's not here. Terry where the hell are you?" She ran into the reception and saw Terry struggling to his feet. "What happened?"

"Barlow threw something down the stairwell. It hit me across the shoulder."

"Go and get the car."

Virginia ran to the back of the pension looking for Peter. She found him in the small kitchen trying to placate the elderly owner, who, in broken English, bitterly complained about the intrusion.

"Peter, don't worry about that now. Let's go. Barlow got away."

"I know. I saw them run out the entrance when I checked out the balconies on the top floor. I shouted down to you but you never heard me."

Virginia screamed at him, "Why didn't you shoot him?"

"I was too late taking aim."

Virginia took several deep breaths and resisted the urge to abuse Peter for the oversight. "Come on then, let's get to the car and follow him."

They raced through the pension and out into the small alley. Virginia couldn't believe her eyes when she saw Terry lying unconscious near the car and Begas sitting in the driver's seat. The door slammed and the car's engine turned over a couple of times before revving hard. Virginia dived to the left of the car as Begas accelerated directly at her. She rolled over and cursed as Begas turned into the main road and sped away.

Peter lifted Terry and sat him on a bench at the side of the pension. He slapped him lightly a couple of times until he came round.

"How did he jump you?" Virginia asked.

"The hood was up when I came outside. He must have hot-wired it. He's as strong as a bull that one. One punch and I was out."

"Begas' jaw is broken as well," Peter added unemotionally. "I wouldn't like to have gone up against him in his younger days."

"Peter, search the town and I'll take Terry and try to get some transport. This village is fairly remote. Barlow can't have gone far."

Hugh and Connie were fifty yards from the train station when a car passed them, going in the opposite direction. The car screeched to a halt. Connie and Hugh stopped running, looked round, and saw the car attempting a U-turn. They began running towards the station again, but the car quickly caught up and pulled to a halt in front of them.

"Who's that, Hugh?" Connie cried out, trying to catch her breath.

Hugh quickly slipped the gun into the back of his belt. "It's Muller. He's a South African policeman. Damn it! How the hell did he get here?"

Cap stuck his head out of the window and said casually, "Going somewhere?"

Hugh pulled Connie to the side and tried to catch his breath.

"We need a few words with you, Mr. Barlow," Cap said.

In between deep breaths Hugh gasped, "Why?"

Cap got out of the car. "You know why. I've got a warrant for your arrest in South Africa for the murder of five women."

"You've got the wrong man," Hugh said. "It's my brother Jack you want—Jack Barlow. You know full well my name is Hugh, so don't try that crap on me."

"In that case, Hugh Barlow, I'm arresting you on suspicion of murder. The murder of your brother, Jack Barlow."

"Okay, I'll make a deal with you," Hugh said. "I'll give you each 100,000 to get lost and forget about everything."

"Forget it," Karen replied, smiling. "The police confiscated your money after Obermeier stole it from your safe deposit box."

Hugh cursed.

"And they got the 1,000,000 dollars left at the farmhouse," Cap added. "So you're fucked from two directions."

Hugh pulled his gun and pointed it at Cap and ordered Karen to get out and open the trunk.

"Okay, both of you. Get into the trunk. Get in now." Hugh whacked Cap on the head and shoved him into the trunk. "You next," he said to Karen.

'I'll never fit in there," Karen said.

Hugh pushed the gun under her nose and told her to get in. Karen squeezed herself on top of a groggy-looking Cap and Hugh slammed the trunk closed.

"Where are those damned keys?" Hugh shouted.

"He got in the trunk with them."

Hugh cursed and kicked the car. He fumbled around in the car looking for a catch to open the trunk but couldn't find one. He gave up and pointed to a train waiting in the station. "Let's get on that train, quick." A train with only two cars sat in the station, packed mostly with school-kids. A conductor, with a whistle in his mouth, stood on the platform looking at his watch. Hugh rushed into the ticket office and bought two tickets to Zurich. He grabbed Connie's arm and ran over to the train.

The conductor shouted at Hugh in German.

"What's wrong," Hugh asked.

"Room for one more passenger only," the conductor barked.

"But we're in a hurry. Surely one more passenger won't hurt?"

The conductor held his hands out, pushing his palms almost in Hugh's face.

"Sorry, regulations," he said slowly and forcefully. "There are only two cars on this train and it's already crowded. There's another train ten minutes behind."

Hugh didn't bother to argue. "Connie. I'll get on. Get the next train."

"Where will I meet you?"

"Err . . . the next station down. Wherever that is. I'll wait for you there. Hide in the woods for a while and then meet me."

Hugh didn't wait for an answer. He lifted the backpack, jumped on the second car, and left Connie on the platform with her arms outspread and crying. As he looked around for a seat he saw a man sprinting towards the train. "Oh no, it's Begas," Hugh said under his breath. "Where the hell did that animal come from."

Hugh felt helpless as he watched Begas catch up with the train and grab hold of a bar attached to the emergency door. Hugh willed him to fall, as he felt frantically for his gun. *Damn, it's not there. I must have dropped it,* he thought.

Hugh watched, terrified, as Begas pulled at the emergency door trying to get inside. When Hugh realized Begas couldn't open it, he stood up and faced Begas, confident that the thick glass of the door would protect him. Begas started to shout at Hugh in Flemish but suddenly stopped mid-sentence and held the left side of his jaw.

It's broken, Hugh thought, *and he's covered with bloodstains.* Hugh looked around for a weapon, now convinced that he could over-power Begas. He thought about hitting him with his backpack but worried it would fall on the tracks.

Several passengers came over to see what all the commotion was about, but most of them just shrugged and sat down again. Hugh heard one of them say he was going to complain to the train driver, so he knew he had to act quickly. He released the manual door latch, pushed the handle down hard, and rammed the door into Begas. Hugh slammed the door into him again and again, but Begas still held on. *He's not fucking human. He doesn't feel it,* Hugh thought.

The train went up a sharp incline and slowed to about twenty miles per hour. Hugh worried in case the train stopped completely, giving Begas the chance to board, so he decided to make one final effort to knock Begas onto the tracks. He held the door open about eighteen inches and whacked Begas with his right hand in a hooking motion. Begas let go of the bar, but almost instanta-neously grabbed Hugh's wrist with his massive hand. Hugh felt the grip tighten as Begas clamped onto Hugh's elbow with his other hand. He tried desperately to hold his position but Begas' strength overwhelmed him. The emergency door flew open and Hugh was dragged out of the car.

Hugh fell face down, on top of Begas. He rolled over twice and landed on the tracks, sitting upright, facing away from the train and Begas. His forearms and knees stung like hell, but he wasn't badly hurt. Begas' body absorbed Hugh's initial impact and his backpack softened the blow when he rolled over.

Hugh turned and saw that Begas was flat out. He struggled to his feet, threw off the backpack and walked towards Begas. He kicked him in the head to see if he was conscious and then stepped back, but a pain shot through his body and his knees buckled. Begas mumbled and turned on his side. Hugh froze and waited to see if Begas had the strength to get up. When Begas moved again, Hugh noticed a bone jutting out of his left leg. "Thank god he's finished," Hugh said under his breath.

Hugh rolled him over several times, trying to push his body into the undergrowth, but Begas jackknifed his upper body towards Hugh and grabbed the back of his neck. He pulled Hugh closer and held him in a bear hug. Hugh felt his chest constrict and he gasped for breath. In a desperate attempt to release himself he kicked Begas' broken leg with his heel. Begas screamed and loosened his grip, but as Hugh tried to pull away he felt Begas' teeth sink into his breast. Hugh screamed, kicked violently and gouged Begas' eyes. They rolled over several times, punching and kicking, until Hugh grabbed the ankle of Begas' broken leg and jerked and twisted it. Hugh pushed Begas' limp body away, rolled over twice, and clambered to his feet.

Only a few seconds passed before Begas regained consciousness. "Barlow," he muttered. "You fucking bastard . . . you'd better finish me off because . . . because . . . if you don't I'll . . . "

Hugh had no intentions of going anywhere near Begas again. The bite wound on his chest stung like hell and he almost passed out when he saw that his nipple and about two inches of flesh were dangling on a thin piece of skin. He removed his bloodstained clothes and tore some material from the tail of his shirt. After breathing deeply he snapped off the hanging flesh and pressed the remnant of his shirt over the wound. When the pain eased he tied the sleeves of his shirt around his chest to hold the improvised bandage in place.

He rested for a few minutes and then scratched around in the backpack and pulled out his only spare pair of pants and a thin cotton jerkin. He zipped the jerkin, lifted the backpack, and staggered along the track.

After ten minutes of painful progress, Hugh saw the next train station up ahead. To be extra careful he left the track and moved into the undergrowth, which was difficult going, but he couldn't take the chance of being seen by Virginia or the police.

When he got within fifty yards of the train station he waited in the bushes to rest and to check out the area. Another train pulled into the station and discharged its passengers. When the commotion to died down he went into the ticket office.

"I slipped into a ravine," he told the stationmaster. "Is there a doctor in town?"

"No," the stationmaster replied curtly, "but there is a pharmacy. It's just 100 meters straight ahead."

Hugh left the station and hurried towards the pharmacy. He only walked a short distance before he felt a jab in his back and heard a deep voice tell him to stop.

"What the hell ... "

"Just take it easy, Mr. Barlow."

Hugh turned around and looked up. "Where have I seen you before? You're one of Roger Hamilton's boys. Fourie, Peter Fourie, isn't it?"

When Hugh saw the gun pointing at him his stomach rumbled and his heart began to thump.

"Just move into those woods and keep quiet."

Hugh obliged. He asked what was going on several times but Peter just told him to shut up. Peter pulled a walkie-talkie from his shoulder bag and after a few attempts to make contact with someone, Hugh heard Virginia's voice crackle in the background. Peter gave his precise location and switched off the walkie-talkie.

"How did you find me?" Hugh asked.

"I persuaded your little Belgian tart to reveal your destination. We found her crying outside the train station back in that last village."

"If you've harmed her I'll ..."

"You'll what," Peter said as he raised his gun.

Hugh kept quiet and sat on the ground while Peter rummaged through the backpack. He pulled out the wad of dollar bills that Connie had taken from Begas and waved them in Hugh's face. "Must be 50,000 here. Nice private pension for me."

Hugh sniggered.

"You know who I work for, don't you?"

"I assume it's the South African Government now," Hugh replied. "They must be paying more than Roger Hamilton these days."

"Not really. It's still Roger Hamilton. I'm only on this gig to act as a hit man. They don't like to use their own people when it comes to dirty business abroad. Mr. Hamilton is brilliant at arranging that stuff."

"Yes I know. I know Roger well. I know a lot about his antics—all recorded and nicely filed away."

Peter nodded slowly, "He's well aware of that."

"But in any case what's your point?" Hugh asked, as he lowered his head. *I guess it's all over for me now,* he thought.

"I have a message from Mr. Hamilton. Keep out of South Africa for good. Never return and never mention a word about the Turnhalle file, or of what you are about to witness. Even more important, keep your mouth shut about Mr. Hamilton's dealings. You break that rule and you're a dead man. He'll hunt you down if just one word gets out."

Hugh wiped his brow. "Does that mean I'm off the hook?"

"Maybe. Wait and see what Virginia does."

Virginia and Terry arrived an hour later. Hugh sat in silence as Terry pulled the Turnhalle file from the backpack. Virginia got her gun out and told Peter and Terry to go on ahead and wait for her. "I need this bastard."

"Put it away, Virginia," Peter said. "Your mission was to retrieve the file, not to kill Barlow."

"True, but no one will ever know," Virginia replied.

Peter cut in quickly, "You can forget your personal grudges."

Hugh realized that Virginia was too busy glaring at him to hear or notice Peter. Like a streak of lightning, Peter snatched the gun from her. "Step back both of you."

"What's all this about, Peter?" Terry asked.

Hugh watched, mesmerized, as Virginia gulped and stepped back. He saw that look of inevitability on her face, like a condemned woman as the noose is placed around her neck.

"Sorry, orders," Peter said unemotionally. He fired two shots. The first one slammed into Terry and the second into Virginia. Terry fell down dead instantly and Virginia's body jolted back against a tree. She desperately tried to remain upright as blood poured from her mouth, but she sank inexorably to the ground with her back still pressed against the tree and the fingers of her right hand twitching wildly. She never took her eyes away from Hugh's.

Hugh sniggered when he saw the cold hatred in her eyes fade into stillness and neutrality.

Peter turned to Hugh, put his gun away, and shook his head. With a hint of admiration in his voice he said to Hugh, "Barlow, you're the luckiest bastard I've ever known. Mr. Hamilton will tell the South African authorities that you were killed with the others. Bodies destroyed and so on. You had better make yourself scarce before the Swiss police show up."

Hugh said nothing. He cantered away, the pain from his wounds gone and his body tingling with elation.

Hugh returned to the station and then along the track for about 100 yards. He found a place to rest while he figured out his next move. In the distance he saw someone walking by the side of the tracks. He slipped back behind a tree just in case it was the Swiss police, or even Cap Muller.

The figure got closer. *It's Connie,* he thought. *She's not that bad.*

I'm broke. I need a new identity and I can't go back to South Africa. Her relations in Marseilles can probably help. And I actually think she loves me. That's a first.

He leaned against a tree and pushed his head into the rough bark. *I wish I'd never laid eyes on that Turnhalle file.*

As she came nearer he noticed she was crying. He waited for her to pass him by and called out "What kept you?"

"Hugh, I thought you left me."

"Don't be silly. Come here." He hugged her for several seconds. "Let's get going down to Marseilles and get some new names. We'll call ourselves Mr. X and his wife Connie."

Connie's tears turned from those of disappointment to those of joy. They both laughed until they dropped onto the grass.

DENOUEMENT

$\mathscr{B}$egas was picked up by the police and spent two months recuperating in hospital. He was later tried and convicted of kidnap, rape, theft, and strangely enough the murder of Boons and Demol. During police questioning and during the trial, Kraus denied all knowledge of a man called Barlow and of any involvement with South African agents. He categorically stated that Begas was not only behind the whole thing but he also killed his two accomplices, Boons and Demol, in order to escape with all the money.

However, while Begas was transported from the court to a secure prison, he overpowered three guards and escaped. The police lost all trace of him after the incident. During the trial he constantly blamed Hugh for all the criminal acts and vowed to get even with him and Kraus.

Kraus absolved Obermeier by saying he gave him permission to remove extra money from his vault. Obermeier of course corroborated Kraus's story in exchange for not mentioning anything about Kraus's previous shenanigans. Kraus avoided criminal prosecution but lost his banking license. The Swiss government confiscated the eight million dollars since no one could, or would, prove ownership.

A very embarrassed Cap Muller kicked his way out of the boot of his car at the Swiss railway station. Cap and Karen returned to South Africa without an arrest. The Minister of Justice, Donkersloot, used Cap as a scapegoat for the whole affair and within six months Cap was forced into early retirement. Karen's career in the police went nowhere and she soon left to study for a law degree.

Virginia and Terry were presumed dead, although their bodies were never found. Van Starden was grief stricken over the death of Virginia. His physical and mental state deteriorated so much that he was retired due to health reasons. He died six months later.

Chris Conway was sentenced to ten years in prison and his associates, Van Rensberg and Ivan Richards, were also jailed. Van Rensberg was given a light sentence due to his age, and Ivan was given a suspended sentence after both Chris and Van Rensberg testified that he was blackmailed into playing a minor part in the scheme.

Harold Budd was jailed for twenty years and had most of his assets seized.

The Barlow family's inheritance was the subject of several legal assaults ranging from the combined Allied-Steinkop Mining Corporation to hundreds of avaricious and distant relatives. In the end, the government and dozens of attorneys took possession of the majority of the assets.

Roger Hamilton kept the Turnhalle file and used its contents to feather his own nest for next few years. He told the Prime Minister it was destroyed along with everything and everyone involved in the whole escapade—including Hugh.

South West Africa, now officially called Namibia, cast off the shackles of apartheid and became independent from South Africa some years later, albeit a little poorer because of the Turnhalle file and Hugh's antics.

A true diamond deception.